Bad *Move*

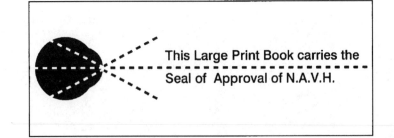

This Large Print Book carries the
Seal of Approval of N.A.V.H.

Bad *Move*

Linwood Barclay

Published in 2004 by arrangement with Bantam Books, an imprint of the Bantam Dell Publishing Group, a division of Random House, Inc.

Wheeler Large Print Hardcover.

The text of this Large Print edition is unabridged. Other aspects of the book may vary from the original edition.

Set in 16 pt. Plantin by Elena Picard.

Printed in the United States on permanent paper.

ISBN 1-58724-842-5 (lg. print : hc : alk. paper)

For my wife, Neetha,
and children, Spencer and Paige

As the Founder/CEO of NAVH, the only national health agency solely devoted to those who, although not totally blind, have an eye disease which could lead to serious visual impairment, I am pleased to recognize Thorndike Press★ as one of the leading publishers in the large print field.

Founded in 1954 in San Francisco to prepare large print textbooks for partially seeing children, NAVH became the pioneer and standard setting agency in the preparation of large type.

Today, those publishers who meet our standards carry the prestigious "Seal of Approval" indicating high quality large print. We are delighted that Thorndike Press is one of the publishers whose titles meet these standards. We are also pleased to recognize the significant contribution Thorndike Press is making in this important and growing field.

Lorraine H. Marchi, L.H.D.
Founder/CEO
NAVH

★ Thorndike Press encompasses the following imprints: Thorndike, Wheeler, Walker and Large Print Press.

1

❖ ❖ ❖

For years, I envied my friend Jeff Conklin, who, at the age of eleven, found a dead guy.

We were in Grade 6, in Mr. Findley's class, and most days we walked home together, Jeff and I, but this particular day my mom picked me up after school not only because it was raining pretty hard, but also because I had a checkup booked with Dr. Murphy, our family dentist. Jeff didn't have the kind of mom who cared about picking him up at school when it was raining, so he struck out for home, no umbrella, no raincoat, stomping through all the puddles in his sneakers.

At one point, the heavens opened up and the rain came down so hard the streets flooded. I remember as we were pulling into the dentist's parking lot you couldn't see past the windshield, even with the wipers going full blast, thwacking back and forth on our 1965 Dodge Polara. It was like we weren't in a car, but in the *Maid of the Mist*, right under Niagara Falls.

Meanwhile, the worst of the rain had let up a

bit as Jeff, now as wet as if he'd done ten laps at the community pool, rounded the corner onto Gilmour Street. Up ahead there was a blue Ford Galaxie pulled up close to the curb, and stretched out on the pavement next to it, on his stomach, was a man.

At first Jeff thought it was a kid, but kids didn't wear nice raincoats or dress pants or fancy shoes. It was a very small man. Jeff approached slowly, then stopped. The man's short legs were stretched out into the street, shoes angled awkwardly, and from where Jeff stood, it looked like his head was cut off at the curb, which really creeped Jeff out.

He took a few more steps, the world engulfed in the sound of rain, and shouted, "Mister?"

The little man said nothing, and didn't move.

"Mister? You okay?"

Now Jeff was standing right over him, and he could see that the man's chest was positioned over a storm drain where water was coursing around him and disappearing. His right arm and head were wedged into the drain. Now Jeff could see why it appeared that the man's head had been cut off.

"Mister?" he shouted one last time. Jeff confided to me that he wet his pants then, but it was okay, because he was already soaked and no one would be able to tell the difference. He ran to the closest house, banged on the door, and told the elderly man who answered that there was a dead man's head in the storm sewer. The old man had a look at the weather and decided to call the police rather than conduct his own investigation.

As best as the police could tell, this was what happened: The man — his name was Archie Roget, and he was an accountant — had left work early and was planning to run a few errands on the way home. He could tell by the approaching clouds that the light rain was about to turn into a deluge, so he pulled over to the curb to get his raincoat out of the trunk. (His wife told police he never went anywhere without a raincoat in the trunk, or a cushion on the front seat to help him see over the steering wheel.) He opened the trunk with his keys from the ignition — this was in the days before remote trunk releases — slipped on the coat, and slammed the trunk shut. Then, somehow or other, he lost his grip on the car keys, which slipped between the iron bars of the storm sewer grate. It was the kind that hugged the curb, where there was a broader vertical opening wide enough to slip an arm in, at least.

Roget got down on his hands and knees, must have been able to see his keys, and reached in. But his arm, like the rest of him, was a few inches too short, so to get a bit more length, he wedged in his head, which was, like the rest of him, tiny.

And his head got stuck.

And then the downpour struck.

Just as the wipers on my mom's car couldn't

stay ahead of the rain, the storm drains couldn't empty the streets fast enough. They backed up, and Archie Roget's lungs filled with rainwater.

The circumstances of the man's death were so bizarre that the story made the papers, even hitting the wires. Jeff was interviewed not only by local reporters, but by newspapers from as far away as Spokane and Miami. He was, at least at Wendell Hills Public School, a celebrity. And if it hadn't been for my dental appointment, I might have been there to share the spotlight. This was my introduction to the cruelties of fate.

I moped around the house for nearly a week. How come I never got to find a dead guy? Why did Jeff get all the breaks? Everyone wanted to be his friend, and I tried to bask in his reflected glory. I'd tell my friends at Scouts, a different group of boys from my school friends, "You know that story, about the guy who drowned with his head in the storm drain? Well, that was my best friend who found him, and I woulda been with him, but I had to go to the dentist." No cavities, by the way. A perfect checkup. I could have skipped the appointment and it wouldn't have mattered. The ironies were enough to make an eleven-year-old's head spin.

My dad felt there was at least one lesson to be learned. "When you grow up, Zack, you remember to join the triple A. It's like insurance. If that man had belonged to the auto club, someone else would have come and got his keys for him and he'd be alive today. Don't you forget." This may have been when I started developing my lifelong obsession with safety, but more about that later.

The reason this whole thing with Jeff was such a big deal, of course, is that finding a dead body's not the sort of thing that happens to you every day. Other than Jeff, I can't think of a single friend or acquaintance who's ever stumbled upon a corpse. Not that I've asked them all. It's hardly necessary. If one of your friends finds a body, chances are good that the next time you see them, they're going to mention it. Right away. It's a great conversation starter. As in: "Oh my God, you won't believe what happened on Friday. I was taking a shortcut, that alley behind the deli? And there's these legs sticking out from behind a garbage can."

There are some body-finding circumstances I don't count. Like if you go to check on your ninety-nine-year-old Aunt Hilda, who lives alone and hasn't answered the phone for three days, and find her rigid in her favorite chair, the TV on, the remote on the floor by her feet, the cat climbing the curtains in hunger. That kind of thing happens. That's natural.

And there are certain lines of work where discovering a dead body's no big thing. Police officers come to mind. A lot of times, they're looking for a body before they actually find it, so you lose the element of surprise. Finding a body when you're already looking for a dead body isn't quite the same as when you're just out for a stroll. "Finally, there it is. Now we can get some lunch."

I'm an unlikely candidate to find a body. First of all, I'm not, unlike a police detective, in a line of work where finding a victim of foul play is a common occurrence, unless you know something about science fiction authors that I don't. And second, when I found a body, I wasn't living in some big city, where, if you believe what you see on TV, people come across dead people about as often as they go out for bagels.

I found my body in the suburbs, where, although I do not have actual statistics to back this up, people are more likely to die of boredom than run into someone nasty. I came across a corpse in as tranquil and beautiful a spot as you could hope to find.

Willow Creek, to be exact. Where my wanderings often take me. Listening to shallow water cascading over small rocks can clear the mind and help one work out plot problems. But when you're engaged in thoughts of interplanetary exploration and whether God can spread himself thin enough to oversee worlds other than our own, there's nothing like finding a guy with his skull bashed in to bring you back to reality.

He was face down, in the creek. And, unlike your typical *Law & Order* extra who comes upon a stranger who's had a date with destiny, I actually knew who this man was, and who might actually want him dead.

A couple of things. Despite how I envied Jeff as a kid, I'd have been happy to go through life without ever finding a dead guy. Because this discovery didn't come with the kind of notoriety Jeff received, but did carry with it the burden of adult responsibility.

And here's the other thing. If this body had been the first and last I'd ever come upon, well, this story would be much shorter. There wouldn't be all that much to tell.

But that's not the way it turned out.

2

❖ ❖ ❖

You won't get very far into this before you start thinking that I am, not to put too fine a point on it, an asshole. At the very least, a jerk. I don't happen to think I'm an asshole, but I'm also willing to acknowledge your typical asshole's not blessed in the self-awareness department. How many assholes know they're assholes? So I guess what I'm saying is that if I know I've behaved like an asshole on certain occasions, then there's no way I could actually be one. But I'd understand if you remain unconvinced. By the time you've heard this story, you might say, "Man, that Zack Walker, he's a major one."

Let's say my motivations haven't always been fully understood or appreciated, although that sounds a bit like boneheaded politicians who lose because they fail to "communicate their message." It's fair to say my methods of instruction, of trying to teach my loved ones how to conduct themselves more responsibly, could have been better thought out. But overall, I'm not a bad guy. I've always loved my family, and all I've ever wanted was the best for them. A good life, happiness, and, above all, security. It's just that my efforts to make sure they live their lives mindful of the risks that exist out there may have occasionally overstepped the bounds, or even backfired. So I won't blame you for coming away with the impression that I've behaved as a know-it-all, a dickhead — an asshole, if you will — who, rather than going around trying to tell everyone else how to run their lives, could have benefitted from minding his own business.

My married history is littered with examples of what an enlightened asshole I am, but the pertinent examples really begin with the day I was walking back to our new home from the corner of Chancery Park and Lilac Lane, where I'd just dropped a check for our latest property tax installment into the mailbox.

The housecoat lady was watering her driveway. She did this almost daily, sometimes more than once in a given twenty-four-hour period, usually decked out in a flowered housecoat. She'd unreel the hose from its wheel beside the garage, grip the nozzle, and squeeze, forcing lawn clippings and other microscopic bits of debris down the asphalt slope toward the street. She and her husband fussed a lot with their yard, weeding, tidying up the line where lawn meets sidewalk. "Thou shalt edge" was one of their commandments, but having a perfectly clean driveway was the ultimate virtue. Free of oil stains, and, usually, of cars, it would have been an excellent place to perform surgery on a sunny day. I waved to her as I walked past and shouted "Looking good!" over the sound of the spray.

Our house is at the corner of Chancery and Greenway Lane, fronting on Greenway, and approaching our driveway I could see something shiny at the front door. Looking more closely, I could see a set of keys hanging there.

My wife Sarah's Toyota Camry had been parked beside my aging Civic while I was gone. She'd evidently gotten home from work, and must have had her hands full with her briefcase or groceries, because her keys were still hanging from the front lock. The house key was fully inserted, and dangling from the ring were the keys to her car (an actual key plus a big plastic remote thingie with buttons for doors and trunk and a red strip that would set off the alarm if you pressed it hard enough), my Civic key, and one that opened her locker at the newspaper's workout room.

This wasn't the first time she'd left the keys in the door. One morning about six weeks ago, when I went down to get the paper that not only provides us with the news, but also pays Sarah's salary, I'd found her keys hanging from the lock. She'd gotten home from work about eight the night before, which meant the keys had been dangling there more than ten hours. Not only could someone have had access to the house,

16

but they could have stolen both cars from the driveway. I'd strolled into the kitchen with *The Metropolitan* and tossed it, along with the keys, onto the table in front of Sarah. She recognized the error of her ways and I got a reluctant confession out of her.

The trouble was, even this wasn't the first time. A couple of months before that, our son Paul, who's fifteen, had found her keys in the door, about five minutes after she'd come home. But that time she claimed she knew, and that she'd come through the door carrying the dry cleaning and was headed back to get them when Paul came in. Nobody bought it, but there remained an element of reasonable doubt. We weren't going to get a conviction.

Maybe that was what had happened this time. It was still possible that at any moment she'd reappear to retrieve her keys, so I decided to give her a chance. I leaned up against the rear fender of her Camry, waiting, and gazed up and down our street.

There's not much to obstruct your view. The town of Oakwood planted maples on the boulevards, between the sidewalk and the curb, to give every homeowner a tree — two, if you had a corner lot as we did — but they'd only put them in a year ago. You could wrap your hand around the trunk, thumb and index finger touching. Someday, long after Sarah and I — and probably our kids, too — are gone from the planet, they may throw a lot of shade, but for now, they're the kind of trees that create little work for neighborhood youngsters looking for raking money. And there are few cars parked on the street, except for the ones in front of Trixie's place, two doors down. She runs an accounting business from home and has clients dropping in. Many of the houses come with double, or even triple, garages, and no one's renting out their basement.

While I waited to see whether Sarah would remember to retrieve her keys, Earl, the guy who lives across from Trixie's, came around the corner in his pickup. He backed into his driveway, got out, opened the garage, and started unloading bags of potting soil from the back of the pickup. When he spotted me leaning against the Camry, I waved, and he nodded back, but not all that invitingly. It had been my intention to stroll over and shoot the breeze, but now I held back. Then Earl looked over his shoulder, I guess to see whether I was still watching him. When he saw that I was, I suddenly felt awkward. So I said, "Hey."

He nodded again, kind of shrugged, and when he didn't turn away, I crossed the street.

"Hey, Zack," he said. Earl wasn't big on conversation. You had to drag it out of him. His head, which he shaved, gleamed with sweat, and his T-shirt was damp. The end of a cigarette was stuck between his lips. Earl was never without a smoke.

I shrugged. "Hey. How's things?"

He waved his hand dismissively. "Keeping busy."

We were both quiet for a moment. I broke the silence with a question of startling brilliance.

"Back from the garden center again?"

Earl smiled. "Oh yeah. Never a day I'm not down there." He paused. "So how goes the writing?"

"Not a bad day." I think Earl had a hard time understanding how I can make a living sitting inside the house all day, not getting my hands dirty. I said, "Walked down to the corner, sent off my property taxes."

Earl looked off in the direction of the mailbox. "How's the house?"

I shook my head. "I've gone through three tubes of caulking on our bedroom window. I don't even bother to put the ladder away. Every time it rains, a little more water gets in."

"You complain?"

"I've phoned the developer. They say they're going to come, nothing happens. I'm gonna drop by the office; maybe appearing in person will make a difference. You hear that thing on the news?"

"What?"

"Guy comes into a variety store, shoots the owner right in the head, right in front of his wife."

"Jesus. Here?" He tossed his butt onto his driveway, reached through the front window of his truck to grab a pack up on the dash.

"No. Downtown. Sarah phoned from work, she'd sent a reporter and a photographer out to cover it, was telling me about it, then I heard it on the radio."

"Jesus," Earl said again. "I'd never live downtown." He stuck a new cigarette into his mouth, lit it, took a long drag, then blew the smoke out through his nose. Earl's history, as he'd explained it to me, involved living out on the East Coast, a bit of time out west. He was divorced, had no children, and seemed an unlikely candidate for the neighborhood, rattling around in a big, new house all by himself. But he'd told me he felt he needed to put some roots down somewhere, and a new subdivision, where a lot of people could use his talents as a landscaper, seemed as good a place as any to make a living. Paul had called on him several times for advice, although "pestered" might be a better word. Earl had been reluctant at first to let my son into his world, but finally, maybe just to get Paul off his back, he'd agreed to give him a few tips, and a couple of times on weekends I'd noticed Earl and Paul shirtless and sweating under a cloudless sky in the far corner of our yard, digging holes and planting small bushes.

"Well, we've been that route," I said. "Living downtown. It was a worry, especially with kids, you know? Teenagers? There's so much they can get into in the city."

"Not that they can't get into trouble out here," Earl said. "You know kids, they'll find

20

trouble wherever they are. Who's that clown?"

Earl had been looking down the opposite side of the street, a couple of houses past Trixie's. It was a guy going door to door. Tall and thin, short gray hair, about fifty I figured, armed with a clipboard. He was too casually dressed, in jeans and hiking boots and a plaid shirt, to be anyone official.

"Beats me," I said. He had drawn a woman to the door, who listened, hanging her head out while she held the door open a foot, while he went through some spiel.

"I'm betting driveway resurfacing," Earl said. "Every other day, some asshole wants to resurface my driveway."

The woman was shaking her head no, and the man took it well, nodding politely. He was moving on to the next house when he saw me and Earl. "Hey," he said, waving.

"Or ducts," Earl said to me. "Maybe he want to clean your ducts."

"I don't have any ducks," I said. "I don't even have chickens."

"You guys got a moment?" the man said, only a couple of yards away now. We shrugged, sure.

"My name's Samuel Spender," he said. "I'm with the Willow Creek Preservation Society."

"Uh-huh," I said. I didn't give my name. Earl didn't give his either.

"I'm trying to collect names for a petition," Spender said. "To protect the creek."

"From what?" I asked.

"From development. Willow Creek is an environmentally sensitive area and one of the last unspoiled areas in Oakwood, but there are plans to build hundreds of homes backing right onto the creek, which will threaten a variety of species, including the Mississauga salamander."

"Who?" It was the first word from Earl.

"Here's a picture," Spender said, releasing a snapshot from under the clip of his clipboard. We looked at a four-legged, pale green creature with oversized eyes resting in a person's hand.

"Looks like a lizard," Earl said.

"It's a salamander," Spender said. "Very rare. And threatened by greedy developers who value profit over the environment." He thrust the clipboard toward us, which held a lined sheet with about twenty signatures on it. There were other pages underneath, but whether they were blank or filled with names I couldn't tell.

I hate signing petitions, even for things I believe in. But when it's an issue where I don't feel fully informed, I have a standard dodge. I said to Spender, "Do you have any literature you could leave me, so I could read up on it?"

"Yeah," said Earl. "Likewise."

Something died in Spender's eyes. He knew he'd lost us. "Just read *The Suburban*. They've been following the story pretty closely. The big-city papers, like *The Metropolitan*, they don't give a shit because they're owned by the same corporations that put up the money for these developments."

This didn't seem like a good time to mention where my wife worked. Spender thanked us for our time and turned back for the sidewalk to resume door-knocking. "That house?" I said, pointing. "That's mine, so you can skip it."

"Salamanders," Earl said to me quietly. "Think you can barbecue them?"

"They'd probably slip through the grills," I said.

We chatted a moment longer. I told Earl, even though he hadn't asked, that Paul intended to pursue his interest in landscaping, maybe go to college someday for landscape design. It was, for me, a surprising development. Most kids his age wanted to design video games.

"He's good," Earl offered. "He doesn't mind getting his hands in the dirt."

"It's not my thing. Writers, you put a shovel in our hands, we start whining about blisters after five minutes."

It was looking very much as though Sarah was not going to come to our front door and retrieve her keys. I felt I'd given her long enough to redeem herself, told Earl I had to go, and headed back to our house. On my way in, I took Sarah's set of keys from the lock and slid them into the front pocket of my jeans. I could hear her in the kitchen, and called out, "Hey!"

"Back here," she said. It was a good-sized kitchen, with a bay window looking out onto the backyard, lots of counter space, and a dark spot in the ceiling above the double sink, where

23

water from our improperly tiled shower stall had dripped down over several months. I tried not to look up at it too often; it made me crazy. I *had* to go over to the home sales office and make a fuss.

My earlier theory that Sarah had come through the front door weighed down with groceries was right. Empty bags littered the top of the kitchen counter. Some carrots and milk still had to be put into the fridge.

I turned to the fridge, which I seemed to recall was white, but was covered with so many magnets and pizza coupons and snapshots that it was hard to be sure. A large part of the door was taken up by a calendar that mapped out our lives a month at a time. It was on here that we recorded dental appointments, Sarah's shifts, lunches with my editor, dinners with friends, all in erasable marker. I noticed, just before I opened the door to put away the carrots and milk, that we were to attend an interview with Paul's science teacher in a little over a week. And a couple of days after that, Sarah's birthday was indicated with stars and exclamation points, drawn by her.

"Hey," she said.

"I heard about the thing, the shooting, on the radio," I said.

Sarah shrugged. "They're gonna take one story for the front, do a color piece for the front of Metro."

"Uh-huh." I had my hand in my pocket, running my fingers over the keys. "You got anything left out in the car that needs to come in?"

"Nope, that's it, I'm done. I shopped, you can cook. I've had it." She'd worked nearly a double shift in the newsroom.

"What am I making?"

"There's chicken, I got some burgers, salad, whatever. I'm beat."

This particular week, Sarah was on a shift where she had to be at the office by six, which meant she was up by half past four in the morning.

"Did you bring in your briefcase?" I thought mentioning the items she typically carries into the house with her might help jog her memory about the keys.

"I got it," she said, sitting down on one of the kitchen chairs and taking off her shoes.

"You wanna beer?" I asked.

"If it comes with a foot massage," Sarah said. I grabbed one from the fridge, twisted off the cap, and handed it to her.

"Massage to follow," I said. "I got something I gotta do. Back in a minute."

Sarah didn't bother to ask what, and took a sip of the beer instead. I slipped out the front door, used her keys to unlock her Camry, and backed out of the drive. I didn't need to go very far. Just down to the end of Chancery, then a right onto Lilac, just down from the mailbox. Far enough around the corner that the car wouldn't be visible from our place, even if you went and stood at the end of the driveway. I

25

pulled it up close to the curb, made sure all the windows were up, locked it, and jogged back to the house, passing Spender, Defender of the Salamander, on the way. Sarah was still at the kitchen table when I came in.

"Where'd you go?"

"I bought some printer paper today and left it in the car," I lied. "And then I saw Earl and got talking to him."

Sarah nodded. She didn't know the neighbors as well as I did, and she'd never taken to Earl.

Her mind was still back at the office. "So this guy, the clerk, his wife's right there when he gets it."

"The variety store thing. Yeah, awful."

"Sometimes you're right."

"Huh?"

"Moving out here. The last thing I wanted to do was move out of the city, but I'll admit I'm not looking over my shoulder out here like we did on Crandall. There's not addicts leaving their needles all over the slides at the playground, girls giving blowjobs in the backs of cars for fifty bucks, no guy waving his dick at you on the corner —"

"I remember him. What was his name?"

"Terry? Something like that? I always just thought of him as Mr. Dickout."

"I ran into him once at the Italian bakery. He was buying some cannolis. Think there's a connection?"

"God, cannolis," Sarah said, taking another

swig from the beer bottle. "I looked, on the way home, at the grocery store, for some. They don't have them out here. No cannolis. It's so hard to find anything like that. Twinkies, those I can get. You want white bread, I can get that for you."

"I know," I said, quietly.

"And there's no place to get decent Chinese," Sarah said. "The kids are always complaining that there's no decent Chinese out here, or Indian. The other night, Paul says he'd kill for a samosa. What happened to my foot massage?"

I was unwrapping some lean ground beef, not thinking about meal preparation so much as the plan I had put into motion. Later that night, maybe, or the next morning, when she got ready to leave for work, there'd be the payoff. At some point Sarah would happen to look out the window, or step out into the night air, and it would dawn on her that her car had gone AWOL. She'd dismiss it at first, figure I or our seventeen-year-old daughter Angie had it, and then she'd realize that I was in my study rereading what I had written that day, and that Angie was up in her room, or fighting with her brother, and she'd take a sudden, cold breath and say quietly, "Oh no."

And right about then she'd picture her car keys in the door, and it would all come together for her.

"I can form burgers, or I can rub your feet," I said. "Or I could do both, but I think I can

27

speak for the rest of the family when I say the burgers should be done first."

There's a set of sliding glass doors that open out from the kitchen to our small backyard deck. I went out there and opened the lid of the barbecue, unscrewed the tap atop the propane tank nestled underneath, and turned the dial for the grill's right side. When I heard the gas seeping in, I pressed the red button on the front panel to ignite the gas.

I clicked it once, then again, then a third time. "This thing doesn't work worth a shit," I said to Sarah through the glass. I tried a fourth time, without success, and now I could smell the unignited gas, wafting up into my face. I turned the dial back to the "off" position and went into the kitchen for a pack of matches. I had done this before — dropped a lit match into the bottom of the barbecue, then turned on the gas. Worked every bit as well as the red ignition button, when the red ignition button was working.

I struck a match and dropped it in, thinking that the gas that had been there a moment earlier would have dissipated by now. But when the air around the grills erupted with a loud "WHOOMPFF!" and took the hair off the back of my right hand, I understood that I'd been mistaken.

I jumped back so abruptly it caught Sarah's attention. She threw open the door. "Are you okay?"

"Yeah," I said, shaking my hand and feeling like an idiot. "Man, that smarts."

The leftover propane was definitely gone now, so I tried a second time, dropping a lit match into the barbecue, then turning the dial. The flame caught with a smaller "whoompf" and I closed the lid.

"You want something for your hand?" Sarah asked.

"No, I think it's okay."

"Let me get something for it." She headed upstairs to our bathroom, where she keeps first-aid supplies. From there she called down, "I've got some aloe here somewhere!"

The front door opened and Paul walked in. "Hey," I said, standing in the front hall, holding my right hand with my left.

"Uhhn," he said, walking past me. Then he noticed that the back of my hand was bright red. "Whadja do?"

"Barbecue," I said.

"That button doesn't work," Paul said.

"I know."

"When's Mom getting home?"

"She's home. She's upstairs."

"Car's not here." He tipped his head in the direction of the driveway.

"I know. But don't say anything."

"About what?"

"That the car's not there. She doesn't know the car's not there."

Paul looked at me. "What happened? Did you

smash it up or something? Because I was gonna ask her to drive me over to Hakim's after dinner."

"I didn't smash it up. I just moved it."

Now he looked at me harder. "You're doing something, aren't you?"

"Maybe."

"Don't do another one of your lame-ass things, Dad. Are you trying to teach her a lesson or something? Because, like, we're all tired of that kind of thing. What'd she do? Leave the keys in the car?"

"Not quite. But sort of. Just go into the kitchen and butter some hamburger buns."

"I'm not hungry."

"I didn't ask if you were hungry. I asked you to butter —"

"I can't find the aloe!" Sarah shouted from the bathroom.

"Don't worry about it," I said, but the truth was, the back of my hand was really stinging. "Maybe we've got something else. Like, I don't know, isn't butter supposed to help?"

"Butter? Where'd you hear that?"

"I don't know. I just thought I had."

"I'm going to go out and get some aloe." She was coming down the stairs now, reaching into the closet for her jacket, grabbing her purse on the bench by the front door.

"Really, it'll be fine."

But Sarah wasn't listening. She was rooting around in her purse, looking for her keys.

"Where the hell are my . . ." she muttered. She threw her purse back on the bench and strode into the kitchen. "I must have left them in here when I brought in the groceries. . . ."

I hadn't planned to make my point about the keys this quickly. Things were ahead of schedule because I'd burned my hand and Sarah was frantic to ease my suffering. It was starting to look as though my timing could have been a bit better.

"I wonder if I left them in the car," Sarah said, more to herself than anyone else. "Except I remember unlocking the door and —"

The bulb went off. You could see it in her eyes. She knew exactly where to find those keys. She strode confidently through the front hall to the front door, opened it, her eyes drawn to the lock.

Things did not turn out as she'd expected.

"Oh shit," she said. "I was sure I'd left them there. Did you leave the door unlocked when you went out?"

"I don't think so," I said.

"Then they have to be in the car." She took one step out of the house and froze. I couldn't see her face at that point, with her back to me and all. But I had a pretty good idea how she must have looked. Dumbfounded. Dumbstruck. Panicked.

"Zack," she said. Not screaming. More tentative. "Zack, Angie's not home yet, is she?"

"No," I said. As far as she knew, I was unaware that her Camry was no longer in the driveway. I came up behind her. "Listen," I said, shaking my hand at my side, trying to make the sting go away. "I should tell you —"

"Shit! Shit! Shit! You were right! Shit! I did it! It's all my fault. Jesus! Oh shit!"

She spun around and pushed by me on her way back into the house. She was headed straight for the kitchen, and I nearly had to run to catch up with her. She had the phone in her hand. "I'm going to have to call the police."

"Sarah." I didn't want her to make the call. The last thing I wanted was the 911 operator getting another false alarm from this address.

"The car's been stolen," she confessed to me. "Shit, I can't believe this. I don't even know what I had in there. What did we have in the car? We had that stuff, from the trip, those Triptiks from the auto club, and a bag of old clothes in the trunk I was going to drop off at the Goodwill, and —"

"Don't call," I said.

"— not that that's very valuable, but Jesus, we were going to give those to people who needed them, not some asshole who steals —"

"Put the phone down," I said. But she wasn't listening. She was about to punch in the number, so I reached down into my pocket, pulled out her set of keys, and set them on the kitchen counter where she could see them.

She stared at them a moment, not comprehending. If her car had been stolen, how could I have the keys?

"It's around the corner," I said, softly.

"I don't understand," Sarah said. "You were using the car?"

"It's around the corner," I repeated, whispering. "I moved it. Everything's fine."

Sarah replaced the receiver, her face red, her breathing rapid and shallow. "Why did you move my car around the corner? And why have you got my keys?"

"Okay, you see, what happened is . . . you know how you thought you'd left your keys in the door?"

Sarah nodded.

"And you know how I've mentioned that to you before?"

Sarah nodded again, a bit more slowly this time.

"Anyway, when I came home, a couple of minutes after you . . ."

"I'd just come in with the groceries," Sarah said slowly. "I stopped for them on my way home, even though I had a totally crappy day at the office, did five extra hours because Kozlowski booked off sick and we had the variety store thing, and picked up some things so we could have dinner."

This was not good. Sarah was developing a tone. That meant she was already ahead of me. She knew where this story was going and how it was going to end. But I decided to tell the rest of it anyway. "So when I came up the driveway, I saw that your keys were hanging from the door, you know, where anyone could find them. This is the thing. You know, it's lucky for you, really, when you think about it, lucky for you that it was me coming up the driveway then, and not some, you know, crazy axe murderer or car thief or something instead, because that's what could have happened. You know I've mentioned this before, about you leaving your keys in the lock, and all I was trying to do was make a point, you see, to help you, so that you wouldn't do this sort of thing again and expose us to any, I guess you could say, unnecessary risk."

Sarah was breathing much more slowly now. And just staring at me.

"So, you see, that's why I did what I did."

"Which was what, exactly?"

"I moved the car, just, you know, just a little ways down the street. Like, around the corner."

"Where I wouldn't be able to see it."

"Yes. That, that was the plan."

"And when I went to look for the keys, I wouldn't be able to find them, and then when I saw that the car was missing, I'd think it was stolen, and would have a *fucking heart attack* so that you could make a point, is that about right?"

"It was never my intention to give you a heart attack or anything. It was merely intended as a, well, as a lesson."

"A lesson."

I swallowed. "Yes."

"I'm finished with school, Zack. I graduated. I have a university degree. I'm an adult now, and the last person I need to take lessons from is you."

"I just felt that this might help you remember in the future."

"You know what else might have helped me remember in the future? You could have taken my keys out of the door, walked up to me, and said something like 'Here, honey, you left your keys in the door.' And I would have been grateful, and said, 'Thank you very much, next time I'll try to be more careful.'"

"Well, in fact, the first time you did it, that's exactly what I —"

"And here's the part that really gets me. I'm running around this house, trying to find my keys, so I can race over to the drugstore, to get you some fucking ointment so you can put it on your stupid hand where you burned it because you dropped a lit match into a gas-filled bar-becue, which, if memory serves me, I have told you before never to do!"

Paul had been standing at the door to the kitchen the whole time, and now that there was a brief pause in the screaming, he decided it was safe to navigate his way between us so he could get to the fridge. "Nice going, Dad," he said. "It's the backpack thing all over again."

Before sending me out to fetch her car, Sarah said to me, "God, you are such an asshole."

You see what I mean. You're not the only one.

35

3

❖ ❖ ❖

Despite the priority I've always put on security, it's not like I always dreamed of making a life for ourselves in the suburbs. We liked living in the city on Crandall. It was a neighborhood rich in history and character. Most of the houses dated back to at least the 1940s, and there were always renovators' vans parked out front of someone's place, bringing a house up to code, tearing out old wiring and replacing it with new, blowing out an attic to make a guest room or den or plant-filled sunroom, gutting a first floor to put in a new kitchen, living and dining room. Narrow lanes separated one house from the other, and garages, often too small to house sport utility vehicles or too full of junk to park even a reasonably sized import, were tucked around back. You could walk to just about everything. The elementary school Paul and Angie attended was five blocks away, and when they moved on to high school they had a ten-block hike that didn't take them any more than fifteen minutes. At the end of our street, which intersected with a main thoroughfare, there was a deli, a used-book store and, a block away, a bookshop that sold nothing but SF (that's "science fiction" to non-regulars), a great Chinese place where Paul always had three of their egg rolls with the paper-thin batter just for starters, a Thai restaurant (nice to have nearby, but too spicy for me), and an Italian bakery where Sarah would often pick up those cannolis on the way home plus a loaf of the best bread I've ever eaten. There was also a diner that didn't appear to have changed in fifty years, with narrow booths, counter stools that spun, and cracked black-and-white-square linoleum. You could get a breakfast of three eggs, sausage, home fries, and toast for $4.99. There was a secondhand dress shop, a tattoo joint, a head shop, an independent pizza place, and a video store that was sure to have the latest titles directed by Woody Allen or John Sayles or John Waters or Edward Burns. There was Angelo's Fruit Market, where you probably paid a little more for seedless grapes or a head of romaine than you did at one of those massive chain grocery stores where the produce section has its own area code, but you'd never get to meet Angelo's daughter Marissa at a place like that, who at age four could ring up your order, make change, and say something like "Be sure to say hello to your lovely wife Sarah." I'd have paid ten dollars a bunch for bananas for the pleasure of her conversation.

The neighborhood didn't empty out through

the day, not like the suburbs everyone left behind to work in the city. It wasn't a place people used only for sleeping. There were young families, old retirees, and everything in between. Every morning, Mrs. Hayden, whose husband died back in the sixties in a Pennsylvania mine cave-in, would walk past our front porch on her way to the corner, where she would buy her morning paper. We thought it was sweet when Mrs. Hayden said she started buying *The Metropolitan* in honor of Sarah, but it was a mixed blessing, because Mrs. Hayden would invariably stop when she saw Sarah out on the porch to point out grammatical, factual, and spelling errors she'd encountered in that week's various editions. And sometimes the crossword was all screwed up.

But Sarah was used to this sort of thing. She would explain patiently to Mrs. Hayden that newspapers must gather, interpret, and present thousands of facts in a very limited time, and what was amazing, to quote one of the paper's esteemed and now deceased editors, was not how much newspapers got wrong, but how much they managed to get right. And Mrs. Hayden would listen politely and say, "But why doesn't your political cartoonist know the difference between 'its' and 'it's'?" Sarah would then ask Mrs. Hayden if she would like a cup of tea or a glass of cold lemonade, and Mrs. Hayden would invariably say yes.

One of our neighbors was an actor who did a

lot of TV series work and shared stories about Oliver Stone after getting a minor role in one of his movies, and the man who lived behind us was an artist with an attic studio illuminated by skylights. One block over was the extremely famous woman who'd won that incredibly prestigious literary prize for that book everyone raved about even though I'd never met anyone who'd gotten to the end of it. You'd see her occasionally down at Angelo's, or carrying home some Chinese takeout. One day, Sarah saw her in the secondhand dress store. "What did the paper say she got for an advance on her last book? One point two mil? And she's looking through five-year-old DKNY stuff?"

We only had one car when we lived on Crandall, which could sit for several days behind the house, depending on which shift Sarah was working. When she was on days, she'd walk down to the end of the street, hang a left, and catch the subway two blocks away. It dropped her off within three blocks of the paper. She'd take the car if she had to work evenings. She's a lot less paranoid about personal safety than I, but even she recognizes the risks associated with hanging out at bus stops and on subway platforms late at night.

It was a great place to live in so many ways. Culturally and artistically rich. Architecturally diverse. A place where you knew your neighbors. Convenient to schools and transportation.

Then the needles started showing up.

Discarded plastic syringes on the edge of the curb. You'd hear noises under the streetlamps after you'd gone to bed. You'd look out the window and see half a dozen young people huddled around a lamppost, not sure what they were doing exactly, but you suspected it wasn't anything good. The next morning you'd go out, and maybe there'd be a scratch down the side of your car, or a back window smashed. I went outside once, around one in the morning, when they were gathered at the end of our driveway, and from about twenty feet away asked them to move on. One of them turned slowly and looked at me with eyes that were at once sleepy and menacing, and invited me to come over, drop to my knees, and perform an intimate service on him.

I turned to go back in, but as I did, I could sense a stirring within the group, a heightened level of conversation, as though they were formulating a course of action, and there was every reason to believe it involved me. I didn't want to break into a run, figuring that would attract them, the way sudden movements will provoke a pack of dogs to attack. I tried to walk faster without appearing to do so. I was climbing the three steps to the porch when I glanced over my shoulder and saw them moving, as a group, in my direction, so I bolted the last couple of steps to the door, flung it open, and yanked it shut behind me, the slam loud enough to wake everyone in the house and probably everybody on the street. And my pursuers stopped and began to laugh, high-fiving triumphantly, congratulating themselves at how easily they'd intimidated me. My heart was pounding, my face hot with shame.

And there were the hookers. There was an area they worked fairly regularly, three streets to the east, and after that neighborhood's residents' association appeared before the city council and embarrassed the mayor into doing something about it, the police swept the area for several nights in a row. The residents proclaimed victory. They had driven the prostitutes from their streets. What they didn't know was that they'd driven them three blocks west over to ours.

A woman who lived down near the corner who was a lot more politically active than I'd ever been got the ball rolling, drawing up a petition and getting nearly everyone on Crandall to sign it, but not before the street was littered with used condoms, and several Grade 2 students on their way home from school got an education in oral sex when they spotted a man getting his money's worth in the back of a Jetta. So the police did a sweep of our street, and the action no doubt moved westward again. At this rate, in about four months, the hookers would be working out of the Glen River and have to trade in their spike heels for hip waders.

The principal at our kids' high school, using a massive set of bolt cutters, snapped the combination lock off the locker next to Paul's and found two handguns that had been used in a home invasion. The kid whose locker it was gets his daily instruction in a different institution now.

One day, Angie said she was followed home by a guy in a long raincoat. We drove her to school for three weeks until the cops arrested some old guy for flashing.

Another time, a sixteen-year-old broke into Mrs. Hayden's place, punched her in the face, and made off with her purse containing eleven dollars.

I guess that's when I began hounding Sarah and Paul and Angie to make sure the front door was always locked. Not just when we were out. All the time. I demonstrated how, when anything of value was left near the front door, like a purse, anyone could step in, grab the item, turn around and be gone, and no one would hear a thing. Certainly not if we were upstairs, or in the basement. But even in the first-floor kitchen, you didn't always hear someone come in. We could be on one side of the wall while some stranger ripped us off on the other.

And don't leave packages visible in the car, I said. Angie had a backpack she would leave on the front seat until she needed something from inside it later. "Someone'll smash the window to grab that," I'd tell her.

"There's nothing *in* it," she'd say, convinced I was a total moron. "It's not like I get some huge allowance. There's no *money* in it."

At which point I would explain that most thieves did not have X-ray vision, and wouldn't realize the backpack was worthless until *after* they'd smashed in the car window and run off with it. And Angie would roll her eyes and say something like "You are becoming totally paranoid, Dad. Isn't there, you know, some medication you could take or something?"

And then there was Jesse.

None of these signs of the neighborhood's deterioration prepared us for the murder of Jesse Shuttleworth.

When I saw her picture on *The Metropolitan*'s front page, I recognized her instantly. I had seen her, often, shopping at Angelo's with her mother. Five years old, curly red hair, a fondness for bananas. Loved to be read Robert Munsch stories, hated Barney the dinosaur.

Last seen alive on a Wednesday afternoon, around four-fifteen, at the mini-park one block over from ours. Mother had looked out the window, seen Jesse on the swing, looked out again two minutes later, the swing empty but still swaying.

After looking for her for half an hour, the mother called the police, and they swarmed the neighborhood. There was a command center set up within a couple of hours, dozens of cops going door to door, looking behind hedges, checking garages. Volunteer teams of searchers were set up who walked through the nearby ravines. Sarah, who oversaw the team of reporters covering the disappearance, was uncharacteristically quiet about work when she came home. She sat in front of the TV and watched *Seinfeld* reruns and went to bed early, but woke around three, unable to get back to sleep.

Four days later they found her body in a refrigerator in a second-floor apartment rented by a man, supposedly from out west, who had been going by the name Devlin Smythe. There was a composite sketch. Shaggy headed, moustache, strong chin. Stocky build, they said. A man he'd done some electrical work for recalled seeing a Salvador Dali-inspired melted watch on Smythe's shoulder ("body art," the man called it) when he'd rolled up the short sleeves of his T-shirt on a hot day. "He rewired my house," the man said of Smythe. "He did good work."

His landlady called the police to say she hadn't seen him, not since that little girl disappeared, and that he was overdue with the rent. A string of minor break-ins in the neighborhood came to an end about the same time. The police figured she hadn't lived much more than an hour after her disappearance from the playground. She'd been suffocated.

I followed the case closely, clipping every story, with the idea that I might write about it someday. Maybe take a break from science fiction and write a true-crime story, or a novel based on the incident. But this was a story without an ending, without an arrest, and so my clipping file got buried in the bottom drawer of my desk.

It was also the story that pushed me over the edge, that convinced me it was time to make a life for ourselves someplace else, someplace safer, someplace where we didn't have to be looking over our shoulder twenty-four hours a day. But as unnerved as Sarah was by Jesse's murder, it never occurred to her that we should pull up stakes. These things happened. You moved on.

I found myself looking at the ads in the Sunday paper's real estate section.

"Did you know," I'd tell Sarah, who was reading through the news pages, criticizing headlines, "that if we moved, like, twenty minutes out of the city, we could get a place twice this size?"

Sarah said, "I can't believe this. How hard can it be to include a location? This guy gets mugged, we couldn't give the closest cross streets? People want to know if these things happen in their neighborhoods." I think, sometimes, working at a newspaper takes all the fun out of reading one.

Instead of responding, I said, "Like this place, out in Oakwood?" I had been drawn to the ads about Oakwood because I had driven out there several times. There was a hobby shop out that way, Kenny's, that carried a full line of SF-type model kits. "It's got a master bedroom with an en suite, three other bedrooms, one of which could be turned into a study, and a full basement. I bet we could carve off part of that for a darkroom for Angie. She keeps up this interest in photography, she'll want that. I might even get back into it. And there's a two-car garage. Can you imagine if we had a two-car garage? And a driveway? No more sharing an alley with the Murchisons?"

We could get more for our money. The kids could have larger bedrooms. A rec room where they could entertain their friends. I didn't have to mention anything about how crackheads, hookers, and child murderers weren't common fixtures at the corners of streets with names like Green Valley Drive and Rustling Pines Lane.

Sarah agreed, one Sunday, to drive out and have a look. We got on the expressway, drove twenty miles, and took the exit that delivered us to Valley Forest Estates in the town of Oakwood. Despite what its name suggested, the development was well above sea level, and there wasn't a tree in sight. The subdivision was in its early stages, giving it a kind of post-nuclear-attack look. Mounds of dirt, foundation holes, stacks of lumber, cement trucks rumbling by. As I turned into the parking lot for the model homes, Sarah surveyed the landscape and said, "Do you think we need moon suits? Will there be a breathable atmosphere?"

At the sales office, a woman in a pale yellow linen suit, standing at the most high-tech photocopying machine I'd ever seen, ran us off spec sheets and artists' conceptions and floor plans of all the different models, with details on square footage, custom detailing, broadloom choices, warranties, proximity to commuter rail lines.

"We have many features that can be roughed in, like intercom systems, central vac."

"Central vac," I said, in case Sarah hadn't heard. I did most of the vacuuming in our house, but I figured she'd still be impressed.

"It's very convenient," the woman said. "You just empty the canister whenever it's full. It's mounted in the garage, just by the door into the laundry room."

Something clicked for Sarah. "Laundry room?"

"Well, of course."

"But it's off the garage?"

"Yes. You can use it like a mudroom, of course, have the kids come in that way. They can slip off their boots and snowpants and enter the house from the laundry room area." Even when they were little, we'd been unable to get our children to wear snowpants or boots. It was a mix of seasonal denial and a resistance to any-thing geeklike.

"So let me understand this," said Sarah. "There's a laundry room, on the ground floor?"

"Yes, just around the corner from the kitchen."

"Do you have a model we could look through?" she asked.

I was going to great lengths to mask my real

motives in getting us to move out of the city, convincing her that it had nothing to do with paranoia and everything to do with having more space for us and the kids. Meanwhile, Sarah was blatant in her willingness to turn her back on everything the city offered to get a ground-floor laundry room. No more trudging down a narrow flight of stairs to a damp basement.

"You have no idea how great that would be," she whispered to me as the saleslady walked us through the model homes next to the sales office. I couldn't tell for sure, but she seemed to be getting turned on.

It didn't matter which model home we strolled through, they all had ground-floor laundry rooms. And once Sarah became sold on that idea, she was more open to other features, like more cupboard space in the kitchen, two sinks in the en suite bathroom, a walk-in closet ("Oh my God"), and a skylight over where our bed would be. "Great when there are full moons," the saleswoman pointed out when she noticed Sarah looking skyward.

"Is there a high school nearby?" Sarah asked.

"Well," the saleswoman said, hesitantly, "not *yet*. But I'm sure once the neighborhood grows, and demand for educational facilities becomes great, the school board will have no choice but to build one. But there is a bus that goes by and gets them where they have to go."

We brought the kids out the next week to show them around.

"Kill me now," Paul said.

"What's the name of this development again?" Angie asked. "Loserville Acres?"

Now that I had Sarah onboard ("No more traipsing up and down stairs with laundry baskets," she said on the drive home from our first tour, sliding her hand up the inside of my thigh), we worked on the kids as a team. Bigger bedrooms, huge basement rec room, extra space in the driveway for when the kids got their own cars —

"We're going to get cars?"

Overselling can get you into trouble. There was some slight backtracking. "If you get jobs, and make enough money, and want to buy yourselves cars, there will be a place to park them."

Now that it was clear that a new house would not come with a pair of Mazda Miatas for them, the kids remained opposed, especially Angie, who had a tight circle of friends. But I knew, in my heart, that getting out of the city was the best thing for them, and for us. I didn't want my son's locker to be next to a home invader's. I didn't want my daughter hopscotching her way around used condoms and syringes on her way home. I wanted Sarah to be able to head out the door to work in the morning without running into some punk who'd run off with her purse.

We met with a Mr. Don Greenway, who closed the deals. If you'd been taken into his office blindfolded, you'd have thought it was in some elegant downtown complex. Plush carpeting, track lighting, a massive map along one wall showing the various phases of the housing development. You'd never have known you were in a complex of mobile homes bolted together as a temporary sales office.

"You're making an excellent life decision," said Greenway. I wondered whether it was his real name. It sounded like one of the streets in Phase Two. And then I remembered, it was the name of the street where we'd looked at an available lot.

I pointed to the map. The areas where construction was under way were shaded green. But several networks of streets, which surrounded a small creek that meandered through the area, remained in white.

"Are you not going to build there?" I asked.

"Eventually," said Greenway. "Those are subject to zoning approval by the town council. Some of the council members seem concerned by its proximity to an environmentally sensitive area, that some little salamander is at risk, but they don't understand that Valley Forest Estates will complement the natural attributes of this area, not detract from them. Now, will you be wanting a bidet? We find many customers, particularly those who've come from Europe, like to have at least one." I was unfamiliar with the sensation of having my ass hosed down from below, and said we would be fine with conventional American fixtures.

We put our house on Crandall up on the

market, and sold it in two days. There was a brief bidding war. There were, evidently, people who wanted into our neighborhood as much as we wanted out. We got $20,000 more than our asking price, moved to the new house once the builders had completed it, with no mortgage, and a bit of money left over in the bank. In the basement, we created a walk-in-closet-sized darkroom for Angie, and then finished off the rest of it so the kids would have someplace to hang out with their friends.

"If we make any," said Angie, struggling to show her gratitude about the darkroom. "I bet everyone who lives out here is a loser."

I should have felt liberated once we settled in, free of my downtown paranoia. But I still took precautions, still locked the car when I parked at the nearby plaza on a milk run, still insisted on driving Angie to her friends' houses once it was dark. Sarah, on the other hand, thought she could let her guard down now that we lived in the suburbs. A key left in the front door was no big deal. Hey, there's no crime out here. No one's stuffing little girls into refrigerators. "What's the point in living in this godforsaken sterile Wonder Bread and Miracle Whip world if we have to be looking over our shoulders as much as when we lived on Crandall?" she asked.

I guess with me, old habits die hard.

So here we are. It's been nearly two years now, and the reviews are mixed. There's no decent Chinese takeout nearby, no SF bookshops, no

Mrs. Hayden, no walking to work, no walking to school. A pound of butter means a five-minute drive to the closest convenience store. We live in a house that is indistinguishable from any other on the street, prompting Paul to rename the subdivision Clone Valley. It was this struggle to distinguish our home from the others that spawned his sudden interest in gardening. The massive garage jutting toward the sidewalk like a whale's mouth trying to swallow passersby is the predominant architectural feature of our home. There isn't a tree within a fifteen-block radius that could cast a shadow. And the closest video store has one hundred copies of the car crash movie *The Fast and the Furious*, but if you asked the kid behind the counter for that Irish flick where the townsfolk conspire to trick the lottery officials that the local winner is still alive, he'd say, "Is that the one by Tarantino?"

I wouldn't deny that there were tradeoffs, that we had given up eclectic for sterile for the sake of a ground-floor laundry room. But I had something now that I couldn't count on when we lived on Crandall.

I had peace of mind. We had minimized our risks.

4

❖ ❖ ❖

I didn't sleep well that night, after the incident with the car keys and hiding Sarah's car down around the corner. This might have had something to do with the fact that I slept on the couch in the family room, which is leather, which meant the covers kept slipping off, and every hour or so I would wake up, freezing from neck to toenail.

I shifted into a sitting position around 4:30 a.m., turned on a light, and thought about going for a walk. Almost every day, I'd take one through Valley Forest Estates, passing houses in various stages of completion. Many were done and landscaped, like ours; others looked nearly finished but lacked lawns and exterior details like light fixtures. Sheets of drywall lay stacked out in front of several others. There were the skeletal homes, nothing but wood frames that allowed you to see through the entire structure, and finally, at the furthest reaches of the development, there were huge holes in the ground, some with concrete basement floors poured.

Beyond that, fields, and a pathway that led down to the banks of Willow Creek, home, evidently, of the soon-to-be-extinct Mississauga salamander.

It was, I decided, too dark for a walk. And besides, it was better to save it for when I most needed it: that time of the day when I'd be staring at the computer screen, unable to write another line of dialogue or describe the workings of an alien monster's digestive system. Walks were the best way to work out plot points.

These walks, to some degree, had gotten me interested in the community, at least to the point of reading what was going on in it. There's a tendency among us suburbanites, especially those of us who have moved from downtown but still have strong ties there, like Sarah with her job, to not give a rat's ass about what's going on in our own backyard. The suburbs are just the place where you live, but the city is where everything happens. So you read about what the downtown mayor is up to, even though he's no longer your mayor, or the police chief, even though he's no longer your police chief, because city politics and city crime are always going to be more interesting than suburban politics and suburban crime. First of all, there's more of it. And it tends to be a lot sexier. No matter where you live, you probably know the name of the mayor of New York City. But who's the mayor of White Plains? Who presides over the council of Darien, Connecticut? And who cares?

Three times a week, a local paper — called, appropriately, *The Suburban* — would land at our doorstep, free of charge. It was nearly as heavy as the sport utility vehicle that shared its name, thick like a weekend paper. But there was no magazine, no book section, no Week in Review. *The Suburban* rarely got above twenty pages, but it was stuffed with enough flyers to wrap an entire English village's fish-and-chips orders for a month. The news stories most likely to get in were also those most likely to attract ads, so the opening of a new restaurant or hardware store always rated a few inches of copy. *The Suburban*'s editorials were of the "on the one hand this, on the other hand that" variety, and went to great pains to offend no one.

The only thing consistently worth reading was the letters page. There'd be someone ranting about high taxes, maybe a letter from a local politician defending himself against a taxpayer rant in the last issue, someone else complaining that the whole world was going to hell and someone ought to do something about it.

So, having decided against an early morning walk in the dark, I grabbed some unread *Suburbans* that had been stashed on the lower shelf of the coffee table, and leafed through them. I spotted a familiar name on the letters page. There was a submission from one Samuel Spender, who identified himself as president of the Willow Creek Preservation Society.

When will this council, and in particular the members of the Land Use Committee, recognize the importance of the Willow Creek Marshlands, and prevent the destabilization of this environmentally sensitive ecosystem? Development has already been allowed to encroach too closely upon this area, but there is still a chance for the council to do the right thing and stop the approval of the final phase of the Valley Forest Estates development. This phase, if allowed to proceed, will put another hundred homes within a pop can's throw of the marshlands, threatening the homes, and the very survival, of a wide variety of species, both land-based and aquatic.

Standing at the banks of Willow Creek, surrounded by some of the only trees within a five-mile radius, I had worked out several characters' motivations over the last few months. (Does the alien slime monster eat the Earthling's brain out of hunger, or did a troubled upbringing make him do it?) When you stood next to Willow Creek, held your breath, and listened to the sounds of the shallow waters flowing by, you could almost imagine that you weren't a few hundred yards from a soulless subdivision. I could remember, when we went in to sign the deal to buy our house, seeing this area on an oversized map on the wall behind Greenway. I had to agree with Spender's letter, that it would be a shame to see the land near the creek developed, but felt like a hypocrite at the same time. What had this entire area looked like before the developers took over? What had the land where our house now stood been before the surveyors marked out where the streets would go, and the bulldozers came in and leveled everything? Had it been woodlands? Had it been farmland? Did corn used to come out of the ground where we now parked the cars? How many birds and groundhogs and squirrels had to relocate once the builders broke ground on Valley Forest Estates?

But at least our house didn't back up onto a marshland. It's not like we were tossing our trash into the creek. I've never been what you'd call a rabble-rouser, a guy who stands up at meetings and demands change. I'm not the type of taxpayer who gets on the phone to his representative and demands a stop sign at the corner. I've always been content to let others be activists, and maybe that comes from a background of reporting. You felt you were doing enough just by keeping a record of what the champions for change were up to. I gave you a voice, I got your story into the paper, but don't ask me to get involved personally. I've got articles to write.

I didn't know that the developers of Valley Forest Estates were a bunch of environmental rapists, but I did know that they were unable to properly caulk a window or keep a leaking shower from staining the kitchen ceiling below.

Maybe they should be stopped from building more homes anywhere, not just on the banks of Willow Creek.

When I was finished reading the *Suburbans* and some sections of the *Metropolitans* from the previous weekend, the sun was up. I heard Sarah go into the kitchen, and she said nothing when I wandered in.

The remainder of the day before had not gone well. I expected to make amends with Sarah shortly after I returned with her car. But she took the car out again as soon as I was back with it. She went, it turned out, to the drugstore, and bought a tube of ointment for my burned hand. She pulled into the driveway half an hour after she'd left and found me sitting at the kitchen table, where I had been wondering whether Sarah had left me for good and what that meant in terms of how many burgers I should throw onto the barbecue. She pulled the tube out of her purse and threw it at me, nailing me right in the eye.

She didn't speak to me for the rest of the evening. We started out in the same bed, but there was a gulf between us under the covers. I reached over tentatively once, to touch her back lightly, a lame gesture at trying to open communications, but Sarah shifted away, and matted the covers down around her as a defense against any more entreaties. So I slipped out from under the covers, tucked a pillow under my arm and grabbed a blanket from the closet, and went downstairs.

Paul and Angie, taking their mother's side, had given me the cold shoulder the rest of the day. Paul had filled Angie in, when she got home, on my car-hiding stunt. I tried to explain to them, while their mother was upstairs, that it hadn't been my intention to be mean. What I'd done was for their mother's own good. Sure, she was angry with me now, but did anyone think she'd ever leave her key in the lock again? Huh? Did they?

They walked out of the room on me. And the next morning, at breakfast, they said nothing as they poured themselves juice and spooned down some strawberry yogurt. Actually, Paul used a spoon only to finish off the residue of yogurt he was unable to consume by tipping the small plastic container up to his mouth and hurtling it down like an extremely thick milkshake. And then they left together, walking a half block to the corner to meet the high school bus.

I offered to make Sarah some tea and toast, but she indicated she was fine, she'd take care of it, although what she actually said was "Move."

I went to reach for the kettle to fill it from the tap, but she nudged me out of the way and grabbed it herself.

"I'm really sorry," I said.

Sarah said nothing.

"And thanks for the stuff, that ointment. I was surprised you still went out and got it for me. I wouldn't have blamed you if you hadn't. I put it on my hand and it was right back to normal this morning. It stung a bit in the night, you know, but then it went away, so, thanks."

Sarah got out a teabag and a slice of bread for the toaster. When couples aren't speaking to each other, all the other sounds in a room become heightened. The ticking of the electric kettle warming up, the scraping of the butter knife across hot toast, the clinking of a spoon against the inside of a china cup. As much to break the silence as to find out what was going on in the world, Sarah turned on the small under-the-cupboard TV. In addition to reading a couple of papers every morning, she watches a lot of CNN and local news so that she has a good handle on what's happening before she gets to the paper.

"— the third house in the region police have raided this year," said the morning man with the very nice hair. "Police are alarmed by the growing number of people who have turned their homes into massive marijuana-growing operations. Not only is it against the law, but it's a major fire hazard, considering that these illicit growers bypass the electric meters, sometimes inexpertly, and all that extra power can overheat circuits with disastrous results.

"A woman in Bentley says the thief who stole her purse from her shopping cart also made off with a winning lottery ticket for $100,000. Lottery officials say they are paying special attention to people coming in to claim prizes.

"Finally, more about a story that still haunts

this city, nearly two years later. Police say they may have some leads in their hunt for Devlin Smythe, wanted in the death of little Jesse Shuttleworth, who —"

Sarah scrambled for the remote on the kitchen table and turned up the volume.

"— was found dead in a refrigerator in Smythe's apartment. Police believe Smythe also went by several other names, including Devin Smythe, Daniel Smithers, and Danny Simpson. There have been reports of suspects matching Smythe's description in the Vancouver and Seattle areas."

"Jesus. Two years," Sarah said. "They always call her 'little.' Of course she was little. She was five years old, for Christ's sake." It was the most she'd said in my presence since the day before.

"Authorities in those areas are assisting local police in their inquiries. Coming up: Take a close look at those bills you've got in your wallet. They may just be counter—"

Sarah turned off the TV, dropped off her plate and cup in the sink, and went upstairs to brush her teeth before heading into the city. I refilled the kettle and plugged it in to make some coffee for myself. While the water heated I went into my study around the corner from that ground-floor laundry room, which was no longer the aphrodisiac it once was, booted up my computer, and opened the file folder next to the keyboard where I kept the pages of my manuscript. The word "Position" was scribbled across the

61

otherwise blank title page, but that was just an inside joke. The real title, the one that would appear in the publisher's spring catalogue, was *TechnoGod*. There were 357 more pages under that title one, and only a last chapter to write and some proofreading to do before bundling it off to my editor.

I write science fiction, mostly, and you could probably figure this out by stepping into my study. Or else you'd conclude that I'm a thirteen-year-old boy trapped in the body of a forty-one-year-old man. Maybe you'd be right on both counts. The room is littered with SF kitsch. *Star Wars* figures, *Terminator* statuettes, plastic *Jurassic Park* dinosaurs from Toys "R" Us, a rubbery shark from *Jaws*, small diecast models of the various flying machines from the *Thunderbirds* puppet show, an assortment of *Enterprise*s from all the *Star Trek* series and movies. My writing center constitutes the short end of a large L-shaped desk, while the long end is my modeling center. On this particular day there were two model kits on the go — a foot-long *Seaview* submarine from the 1960s television series *Voyage to the Bottom of the Sea*, and a resin model of Ripley, the Sigourney Weaver character from the *Alien* movies. I like building models of things — spaceships, submarines, futuristic cars — more than assembling models of people, but I've always been partial to anything related to the *Alien* flicks.

I'm aware that it may not be normal for men

in their forties to collect such toys, but then again I don't make my living in a normal way. Being an author of more conventional fiction would be unusual enough, but writing SF puts you in a different category altogether. Science fiction writers don't find their books reviewed in *Time* or *Newsweek* or *The New York Times*, although the latter has its token science fiction column in the book section every couple of weeks. I've never understood the ghettoization. Science fiction offers cutting-edge social commentary, inventive allegory, a grand vision of where our current social and political trends are taking us, an exploration of the human condition told through high-tech metaphor. And, of course, little monsters with razor-sharp teeth bursting out of people's chests.

I'd been putting the finishing touches on my fourth book, and had hopes, as all authors do, that *this* would be the one that would once again earn me some critical attention, even if only in the cozy SF community, but in the pit of my stomach knew it wouldn't be. The novel would be published to little fanfare. There would be virtually no publicity. The author tour would consist of two magazine interviews by phone. It would be ordered by the major book chains in such disappointing numbers as to make it impossible to create an impressive display of copies near the front of the store. Instead, it would be put back in the regular stacks, spine out, on a shelf reachable only by NBA stars, thereby guaranteeing that no one would ever find it. The publisher would arrange one book signing, not at one of the big chain bookstores, but at a mall store, where I would be seated behind a table in view of passing shoppers weighed down with Gap and Banana Republic bags and carrying containers of vinegar-soaked New York Fries, who would wonder who I was but not care enough to stop and ask, and I would smile and nod as they passed, and then, miracle of miracles, a middle-aged couple would slow as they walked by, pause and look at the display of my books, turn, and approach, and my heart would begin to swell, that someone was actually going to talk to me, and maybe even buy a book, which I would be delighted to sign, to make out personally, even. And the woman would say to me, "Do you know where the washrooms are?"

I actually thought this new book might have a chance. It was a sequel to my first novel, *Missionary*, a title my publisher really liked because it would make people think that, at some level, it was about fucking, but which was actually about missionaries of the future. Or more precisely, reverse missionaries. The time is several hundred years from now, and religion has been outlawed on Earth. Faith has been overtaken by technology. Computers are God. The missionaries decide to take their message to other worlds, to persuade civilizations deemed more primitive than ours to abandon their beliefs in supernatural beings and embrace the computer chip.

64

Things go badly when our know-it-all Earthlings, in the act of setting ablaze a house of worship on the planet Endar, have the life crushed out of them by a huge hand reaching down from the clouds.

I'm not a particularly religious person, but this book found its way into Christian bookstores as well as the mainstream ones, did reasonably well, and it was that book's success that has kept me going since. It seemed odd to see *Missionary* in the window of a religious bookshop, displayed alongside *God Is My Anchorman*, by a noted network news executive, and the collected scripts of *Touched by an Angel*. The book probably never would have made it there if the shop owners knew my editor thought its title would make people think about fucking. He's not a particularly religious person either, but it was his irreverence that prompted me to tentatively call my new book *Position*. My second and third books tanked (number two, *Slime*, was about nasty sewer creatures that pass among us by disguising themselves as cable company executives; and number three, *Blown Through Time*, about a guy who goes back in time to keep the inventor of the hot-air hand dryer from being born, had real potential, I thought, but went absolutely nowhere), so my decision to revisit my missionaries was an easy one. They seemed my best hope of coming up with another modest hit.

I was in the newspaper business when *Mis-*

sionary came out. I'd started out as a two-way, a reporter-photographer, which meant that most out-of-town assignments went to me. No need to buy two airline tickets for a reporter and a photographer — one seat would do. Although I liked shooting pictures, I grew weary of being on the road so much, and when a position became available at the city hall bureau, I applied. This, as it turned out, was a mistake. I became an expert in everything municipal. I knew all there was to know about planning acts and planning boards and official plans and amendments and amendments to amendments and zoning restrictions and parking enforcement and snow removal and zero-based budgeting, and there were times when I thought I'd like to take a copy of the city's collected bylaws, tie it around my neck, and throw myself off the pier at the foot of Majesty Street. I began to wonder if maybe journalism just wasn't my thing, and I plotted an exit strategy. My first book, written late at night and on weekends, became my way out.

The money from *Missionary* didn't go as far as I'd hoped, which meant taking the odd freelance assignment. I'd written articles for *The Metropolitan* (some futurist stuff, where the city would be in fifty years, that kind of thing), some magazine pieces. But with a nonexistent mortgage on the new house, we figured we could manage fairly well on Sarah's income until my next ship came in.

So I worked from home, was there when the

kids left for school and when they got home, and could be counted on most days to give Sarah a kiss goodbye before she left for the paper. It didn't look as though that particular service would be required this day. All Sarah said as she headed out the door to the car was a simple "See ya." Enough to let me know, officially, that she was out of the house, and that she wasn't interested in any precommute snuggling. I watched from behind the curtain as she got out her keys, opened up the Camry, backed down the drive, and disappeared down the street.

Writer's block arrived before noon, so around eleven, on the way back from my walk along Willow Creek, I swung by the sales office for Valley Forest Estates. Phone calls hadn't worked. Maybe a face-to-face encounter would be more effective where honoring a new-home warranty was involved.

The office was just as you drove into the neighborhood, a couple of mobile homes stitched together with an elegant front built around it as a disguise. I had a feeling that once the development was complete, they would pack up their fancy desks and high-tech photocopying machines and architectural models of the subdivision, rip out the trailers, and build one last shoddy house on the lot where it stood.

Okay, maybe that's unfair. We'd had some problems with the house, but surely they could be fixed. I would turn on the charm with these dickheads.

As I entered the sales office, I glanced at the wood-paneled wall, where pictures of the various sales staff and company executives hung. I was looking for the guy who sold us the house. There he was. Don Greenway. The man our street was named for. Every day we basked in his celebrity. It was like living on Tom Cruise Boulevard and meeting Tom Cruise.

I approached the reception desk.

"Hello," said a perky blonde woman in a white blouse, her hair falling down around her shoulders. "Welcome to Valley Forest Estates."

"Hi," I said. "I wonder, is Mr. Greenway in?"

"Do you have an appointment?"

"No. I was just hoping I might be able to catch him. I was passing by."

"Were you thinking of purchasing a Valley Forest home? Did you want to see some of our brochures or take a look at our model homes?" She smiled the whole time she was talking, like an *Entertainment Tonight* reporter.

"No, we already own a home here," I said. And the receptionist's smile instantly vanished.

"Oh, I see. And what did you want?"

"Well, we've had a couple of problems and I wanted to see about getting them fixed."

"Oh." I had the sense that I was not the first person to come in here with a complaint. "Well, Mr. Greenway is very busy today, but if you'd like to leave your phone number with me, I'll make sure that he gets back to you at his earliest possible convenience."

"Well, that sounds great, but we had some trouble before, when we first moved in, with water seeping into the basement? And I had to drop by here several times before anyone came to take a look at it. And I've been in here before about our upstairs window, how I have to caulk it outside all the time, but the wind and the rain still manage to come through, and now our leaky shower has caused part of our kitchen ceiling to discolor, so there's this big stain, you know? If it's all right with you, I'll just wait around awhile until Mr. Greenway becomes available."

"Well, Mr. — What is your name, sir?"

"Walker. Zack Walker."

"Mr. Walker, I assure you, Valley Forest Estates takes any problems you might have very seriously, and I will convey to Mr. Greenway your concerns and —"

The door to the office where Sarah and I had signed the deal to buy our house opened and out stepped Don Greenway, all five-foot-six of him, about forty-five, a bit of a paunch held back nicely by keeping the jacket of his expensive suit buttoned.

"Stef," he said to the receptionist, "I wonder if you could get me the papers for —"

"Mr. Greenway," I said cordially, extending my hand. "I'm so glad I was able to catch you."

Stef said, "Yes, this gentleman, Mr. Walker,

was waiting to see you. I explained to him that you were quite busy today but that we could set something up."

"It'll only take a minute," I said.

"You look familiar to me," Greenway said. "You're on my street, at the corner of Chancery Park."

"That's right," I said. "My wife Sarah and I."

"You went for the upgraded carpet under-padding."

Whoa. He was good. "That was us," I said. "I wonder if you have two seconds."

"I'm really on my way to a showing, but sure, go ahead."

I told him about our most recent problem, the stained ceiling in the kitchen, caused by, I believed, water leaking from an improperly tiled and caulked shower stall on the floor above. "I think someone needs to come in and redo the shower, and once that's done, fix the hole in the drywall in the kitchen. I understand these things are still covered for two years, if I remember the contract we signed and all."

Greenway considered what I'd said. "You sure you've been using the shower properly?" he asked. "Because if you're not, that could be your problem."

"Using it improperly? We turn it on, stand in there, and shower. If there's a wrong way to do that, we haven't figured it out yet."

Greenway shook his head, suggesting I didn't understand. "Pretty long showers?" he asked. "I seem to recall you saying you have teenagers? You know how they can be, letting the water run and run and run."

"Look," I said, starting to bristle, "I don't see what that has to do with anything. Water's leaking out and wrecking the ceiling in the kitchen. And I think you guys should do something about it. This isn't the first time we've had a problem, you know, and I don't exactly think we're the only ones in the neighborhood who've been having problems." I thought of Earl, whose windows were often fogged up with condensation. I'd been meaning to ask whether he'd launched a complaint of his own. "My neighbor across the street, for example, all his windows, they've got moisture or something trapped between the panes, you can't see through them, and —"

"I don't have to listen to this. By your own admission, you've acknowledged that your teenagers are running that shower virtually twenty-four hours a day, so it's no wonder some water may have spilled over the sill and that's why you're having the problem you've described."

"By my own admission? I never said that. *You* just said that. What's the deal here?"

Greenway's cheeks were starting to get red, and a vein in his forehead was swelling. He was raising a finger to me, about to say something else, when he saw someone over my shoulder coming through the front doors. Now the finger was moving away from me and pointing to the newcomer.

"You get the hell out of here!" Greenway said.

I whirled around to see who he was talking to. I recognized him instantly as Samuel Spender, still dressed in his jeans and hiking boots, but this time wearing a white cotton shirt. He glared angrily at Greenway.

"I know what you're up to, you son of a bitch," Spender said. "You think you can buy them off but you can't."

"Get out! Get the hell out!"

Stef, the receptionist, was on her feet. "Mr. Spender, I'm going to have to ask you to leave or we'll have to call the police."

"Go ahead and call them," Spender said. "I got lots to tell them."

"You have nothing but rumor and lies," Greenway spat at him. The vein on his forehead was a garden hose now, ready to blow. "You're out to ruin people's jobs, to end their livelihoods, to save a few fucking tadpoles, you fucking moron."

"It's salamanders, not tadpoles, you jackass, but you wouldn't give a shit either way, would you?"

Greenway started to lunge for Spender, and instinctively I stepped in to hold him back. He broke free of my grasp, which really didn't amount to much, but my brief interference seemed to have been enough to make him reconsider any sort of physical attack.

Spender hadn't stepped back when Greenway appeared ready to attack. He looked ready to fight if he had to, and if those hiking boots were any clue, he got a lot more exercise than Greenway and could probably clean his clock.

"You can't buy me," Spender said. "I'm not for sale." And then he left, kicking the trailer door wide open on his way out. Greenway stuck an index finger down between his neck and shirt collar, moved it around in a futile attempt to let in some air. He reached inside his jacket for a handkerchief and blotted his cheeks and forehead.

"You should sit down," Stef told him.

"Get me Carpington, and then Mr. Benedetto," he said, went back into his office, and closed his door. Stef got back in position behind her desk and picked up the receiver, then noticed I was still standing there.

"What about my shower?" I asked.

She looked at me for only a second, then started making calls for Greenway.

Back home, I plunked myself down in the computer chair, and sat, staring at the screen, for a full ten minutes, working up my nerve. Then I called Sarah.

"City. Sarah here."

"Hi. It's me."

It was like I'd placed a long-distance call to the North Pole. You could feel the chill coming through the line.

"What," Sarah said.

"I just wanted to say again that I'm sorry."

Nothing.

"Did I tell you about that guy who was going around the neighborhood with a petition?"

"What guy?"

"Okay, then I didn't. Some guy, his name's Spender, he's trying to keep Valley Forest from building homes near Willow Creek."

"Oh."

"Anyway, I ran into him when I was over at the sales office today."

"You told them about the mark on the kitchen ceiling?" Now, she was talking.

"Well, I brought it to their attention, anyway. They might need to be reminded again. They seem to have a lot on their minds over there. It's not that big a job. I might be able to do it myself."

"You're joking."

"I could take a shot at it. I've got the caulking gun. I could put some stuff in the corners of the shower, see if that took care of the problem."

"I've seen what you can do with a caulking gun. There should be a three-day waiting period before people like you are allowed to own one."

"Anyway, what I wanted to ask you was, do the names Benedetto and Carpington mean anything to you?"

"What?" Annoyed again.

"Benedetto and Carpington. They came up when I was over at the Valley Forest office. Greenway, you know, the guy we bought from? He got in a bit of a discussion with this Spender guy, and those names came up."

"Well, Carpington, I think, is the councilman for our area," Sarah said. "In the city, I always used to know the name of my alderman and the school board members, but since we moved I don't keep track as well. But I think that's the guy."

"And Benedetto?"

"That sounds familiar. Hang on —" big sigh "— let me do a library search." I heard her hitting several more keystrokes, muttering "Come on, come on" under her breath. "Okay, it's Tony Bennett's real name, but that's probably not the guy you're looking for. There's two other hits for this year, four for last, then, like thirty, the year before. Just a sec." More waiting. "Yeah, here's why I remembered the name. He's some developer-wheeler-dealer guy, government department that was unloading tracts of land had a guy who allegedly, hang on, I'm trying to get another screenload here, okay, allegedly took kickbacks from this Benedetto guy so that his bid for the lands would be accepted. Of course, the bids were ridiculously low, then Benedetto resold the land in parcels and made ten times the money back."

"So what happened?"

"I'm just looking ahead here. Looks like not much. There was some sort of government investigation launched, but you know how those things can go. People forget about it, it never gets wrapped up, who knows. That's it."

"Thanks," I said, paused. "What time you

think you'll be home tonight?"

"Gosh," Sarah said, "it could be late. I misplaced my keys, so the car's probably stolen, so I could be late." And she hung up.

5

The next morning, the morning of the day that I found my first dead guy, Trixie asked me, "So what, exactly, was The Backpack Incident?" She was sitting in our kitchen, taking a sip of her coffee.

Trixie lived two doors down and, like me, didn't head into an office every day. I try hard to be interested in what other people do for a living, but when Trixie first told me about running a home-based accounting firm, I kind of glazed over. Any occupation in which the majority of your time is spent filling in lots of forms and adding up columns of numbers is one I want to stay as far away from as possible.

We had regular curbside chats, like the ones I had with Earl, and we were dragging our garbage to the end of the drive two days after I'd decided to teach Sarah a lesson about leaving her keys in the door.

"Hey," I said.

"How's things?" she said, dropping a recycling box full of newspapers by the edge of the street. She looked smart, even in a pair of ratty jeans and sweatshirt. Trixie's a good-looking woman, late thirties, petite, with dark hair and green eyes, and the first time we introduced ourselves I commented that I couldn't recall hearing the name Trixie since *The Honeymooners*. It conveyed to me a kind of wholesomeness from another era.

We got talking one day about what we each did for a living, and she asked whether I was taking advantage of all the possible tax deductions for a person who works from home. She gave me a couple of useful, and free, tips. As someone who ran a business from home herself, she seemed to know all the angles.

This day, when she asked me how things were, I guess I didn't respond positively enough. I merely shrugged, so she strolled over. "What's up?"

"I'm sort of in the doghouse," I said. "Sarah's barely talking to me. It's been a day and a half now."

"What did you do?" she asked.

"You feel like a coffee?" I asked. "I was just getting ready to work and put on a pot. Unless you're busy."

Trixie glanced at her watch. "My first client isn't coming by till after lunch, which still gives me time to get into my workin' clothes, so sure, why not."

While I got out cups for the coffee I told her about hiding Sarah's car, and how things had

78

unraveled from there. Trixie didn't express any real shock. She wasn't a judgmental person. She was open-minded on social issues and tolerant of human frailties. Over earlier cups of coffee, she'd advocated same-sex marriages, defended Bill Clinton's personal behavior, refused to demonize welfare recipients. And she called things as she saw them.

"God, Zack," she said, shaking her head and reaching for one of the Peek Freans cookies I'd set out on a plate. Sarah'd taught me never to serve right out of the bag. "You're a piece of work. And a control freak. Where do you get off, trying to control everyone else's behavior?"

"Sarah called me an asshole."

Trixie nodded. "Big surprise there." She had a bite of a jelly cream. "What do the kids think when you pull a stunt like that?"

That's when I told her about how both of them had suggested that this was a sequel to The Backpack Incident. That was when Trixie asked her question.

"It's kind of embarrassing," I said. "It's like a sickness with me or something, that I have to take desperate measures to make my point. Usually matters related to personal safety and security. That's the whole reason why I hid Sarah's car. Not to make a fool of her, but to teach —"

"Yeah yeah, I heard all that. So what's up with the backpack thing?"

"When the kids come home from school," I

79

began, "they walk in the door and drop their stuff wherever they happen to be standing. Jackets, shoes, whatever. They haven't opened the front-hall closet door once since we moved in here. I don't even know if they know it's there. The concept of slipping a coat onto a hanger has eluded them right into their teens."

"Uh-huh."

"And their backpacks just get dumped wherever. You come in the front door after the kids come home and there's a good chance, if you're not watching where you're going, you're going to fall over them."

"No one knows the hell that is your life."

I smiled. "Gee, is Sarah home? That could be her talking. Anyway, I was yelling at them to take their backpacks upstairs, and for a while there it's like they were actually listening to me, but that just created another problem, because they'd lug their backpacks up to the top of the stairs — and I don't know whether you've ever lifted a high school kid's backpack these days but you'll throw your back out if you try — and they'd leave them there."

"Where?"

"At the top of the stairs."

"But that's where you wanted them, right? Upstairs?"

I nodded furiously. "Yes, yes, but not right at the top of the stairs. Okay, picture this. You're carrying a laundry basket or you've got something in your hand you're looking at, and you get to the top of the stairs and generally assume that the way is clear."

"But it's not."

"They've left their backpacks right there, in the way, so if you're not paying attention you'll trip on them and break your neck."

"Okay, so you talked to them about this?"

"Oh yeah. Many times. And they'd always say the same thing. 'Okay, Dad, we hear you.' In that really tired way kids have of talking. I know you probably told me this but I don't remember — you don't have any kids, right?"

Trixie shook her head.

"So anyway, the next day they'd come home and leave them in the same place again. Sarah nearly killed herself, grabbed onto the railing at the last second to keep from going headlong down the stairs."

"She got mad."

"She blew her stack. Took the backpacks and literally threw them down the stairs. I thought that would do it, better than anything I'd ever done. But a couple of weeks later, they both came in after school, ran upstairs, and dropped their backpacks in the same place."

Trixie nodded slowly. "The last straw."

"Yeah. I decided it was time to take action."

Trixie smiled, rolled her eyes. I continued: "They'd both gone into Paul's room. They're not like a lot of brothers and sisters. They fight, but not all that much. They talk to each other, find out what's going on. There's things they talk about, Sarah and I have no idea. So Angie was in Paul's room, and they'd turned on some music in case I decided to put my ear up to the door and listen in."

"Which you would never do."

"So I take the two backpacks, and arrange them along the stairs on the way down, as though they'd been knocked by someone who hadn't seen them." I paused. "And then I went down to the bottom of the stairs, and arranged myself across them."

"What do you mean, arranged yourself?"

"Like, you know, I'd fallen. I worked my legs up the first four steps or so, lying on my stomach, then put my head down on the carpet at the bottom of the stairs, with my arms stretched out."

Trixie didn't say anything for a moment. Finally: "You're kidding."

"No."

"You didn't spread some ketchup around? Like from the corner of your mouth, or out of your nose?"

"The broadloom is really new," I said.

"You pretended to be dead." Trixie wasn't asking a question, just making a statement.

"Well, wounded, anyway. I could have been knocked out. Not necessarily dead. A concussion or something. It's not like I wanted them to assume the worst thing right off the bat."

"So they came out and found you?"

"Not right away. After about five minutes of

lying there, I was getting a bad crick in my neck. I decided I needed to make a sound, a falling sound, so I slapped my hands on the floor as hard as I could. But when we were picking our upgrades for the house, we got the expensive underpad, so it hardly made any noise at all. So I got up, and jumped as hard as I could on the floor, then got back into position as fast as I could."

I took a breath. "I guess Angie heard it, because she showed up at the top of the stairs first, and I guess she took the scene in pretty fast, because she screamed, and then Paul showed up behind her, and Angie came down the stairs, and I was doing a pretty good job of not moving, and holding my breath —"

"So you were trying to look dead."

"And Angie was calling out my name and asking if I was okay, and I guess I had my eyes open just a slit, to see what was going on, and I notice that Paul isn't there, and the first thing I think is, Doesn't he care? His father's broken his neck and he doesn't want to offer me an aspirin or something?"

"Let me guess. He'd gone to make a phone call."

I nodded. "Two, actually."

I told Trixie that when Paul reappeared at the top of the stairs, I opened my eyes all the way. Angie nearly screamed, and when she did, Paul almost slipped down the stairs himself. I pulled myself into a sitting position. Angie asked me what had happened, was I okay, and Paul was telling me not to move, an ambulance was on the way.

"An ambulance?" I said. "What the hell did you call an ambulance for?"

"I thought you were dead! Aren't you hurt?"

I shook my head violently. "No no no! I'm fine. Can't you see that I'm fine? I was just trying to teach you guys a lesson about leaving your goddamn backpacks at the top of the stairs. How many times have I told you not to do that?"

"I don't know, Dad," said Paul. "How many times have we told you not to pretend you've killed yourself?"

"I can't believe you," said Angie, who was pulling away from me. "You're totally whacked."

Paul was shaking his head slowly, then stopped suddenly. "Oh, shit."

"What?" I said.

"I guess I better call back Mom."

"You called your mother?"

"When I saw you lying there dead, yeah, I thought she might want to know."

"Jesus Christ," I said. Who knew that my son was going to act so responsibly, calling 911, getting in touch with Sarah. Kids can let you down in the strangest of ways. "You have to call her back," I said. "Tell her I'm okay." And then it hit me. "The ambulance! Call back the ambulance! Tell them not to come."

Paul started to move, then stopped. He

looked very pissed. "I'm not calling the ambulance."

"What?"

"You call them. You explain it. I've had enough of this bullshit." He came down the stairs, grabbed his backpack as he went by, stepped over my outstretched legs, and went downstairs to play video games.

"Way to go, Dad," Angie said, getting up to go into the kitchen.

In the distance I could hear a siren. I jumped up, ran into the kitchen, and dialed Sarah's number. I got one of the other editors on the desk.

"She just flew out of here," he said. "Her husband was in an accident or something."

"This is her husband."

"It's Zack, right? It's Dan. We sat together at the Christmas party? Jeez, how are you? Are you okay? You at the hospital or something?"

"I'm fine. Do you think you could find Sarah, catch her in the parking lot before she heads home?"

"I don't know, she left here a couple of minutes ago and she was really moving, you know?"

I wondered whether Sarah had her cell phone with her. Of course, even if she did, there was no guarantee she had it turned on. I'd talked to her about this in the past. What good is having a cell phone with you if you don't have it on, I told her. If we need to reach you in an emergency, and your phone is down at the bottom of your purse, where you can't hear it even if it is on, well —

There was loud banging at the door. "Hang on, Dan," I said. "I think that's the ambulance."

"So somebody else got hurt? One of the kids?"

"Just hang on." I set down the receiver and ran to the front door, where I saw two uniformed attendants, a man and a woman. They were carrying leather bags and had radios that crackled clipped to their chests. I put on my friendliest smile.

"Hey," I said. Like maybe they'd dropped by to ask for a donation to Mothers Against Drunk Driving. Where was my checkbook?

The woman said, "Hello, sir. We have a report that someone's fallen? Down the stairs?"

I laughed. "That was me. But I'm okay, really."

The man said, "We should still have a look at you, just the same, make sure that you didn't suffer any injuries."

What I didn't know until later was that Sarah did, in fact, have her cell phone with her, and was frantically trying to call the house from her car. She'd tried once in the parking lot at the paper, then again on Lakeshore as she headed for the ramp to the expressway. Trying to keep one eye on the road, one eye on the phone, pushing the "send" button, repeatedly getting busy signals, trying again. I'd left the phone off the hook, of course, expecting to get back on the line with Dan.

"No, no, really," I protested to the ambulance attendants. "I'm okay. I wasn't hurt."

"The dispatcher said a young man, your son, called to say his father had fallen down the stairs."

"Not fallen, exactly. More like *arranged*, I guess you'd say."

The attendants glanced at each other. The man said, "Perhaps we could have a word with your son."

"He's downstairs playing video games," I offered. They exchanged glances again. As if playing video games was not typical behavior from a boy who supposedly had just found his father dead at the bottom of the stairs. Maybe they didn't have kids, couldn't understand.

"You see, I was just goofing around," I said. "It's about their backpacks. They leave them at the top of the stairs —"

"You tripped on a backpack?" the woman attendant asked.

"No, but I *could* have. That was the point I was trying to make."

Angie was watching from the door to the kitchen, smiling while she ate a small bowl of ice cream. The ambulance attendants were finally persuaded that I had not been injured, nor had anyone else at this address. They returned to their vehicle, but not before warning me that if something like this ever happened again, they'd report it to the police and have me charged with mischief or making a fake call to 911 or something along those lines.

I went back to the kitchen and picked up the receiver. "Dan?"

"Yeah?"

"I guess it's too late to catch her. Listen, sorry, really, it's just a big mix-up." The receiver was back in its cradle only a second before the phone rang. I snatched it up.

"Yeah?"

"Zack! Oh my God! Zack! I've called a hundred times. What's happened?"

"Sarah, everything's okay. Just calm down. Absolutely everything is okay. I'm fine, the kids are fine, everybody's fine."

"But Paul called, said you'd fallen down the stairs, that you weren't moving —"

"I know, I know, but it was really just a misunderstanding. I was just lying there, that's all."

"Just lying there?"

"Basically."

Sarah was quiet at the other end of the line for a moment. "You're telling me there's no emergency whatsoever."

"That's right!" I tried to be cheerful.

"So I'm getting written up right now for running a red light for no good reason."

Angie, who wasn't able to hear everything her mother was saying to me but knew from my expression that it wasn't good, whispered, "You want me to ask the ambulance guys to come back in half an hour? You might need them after Mom gets home."

I told Trixie that was the end of my story. She had another cookie and looked at her watch. "I really should get going. I've got to get changed."

"You look great," I told her. I waved my hands in front of me, drawing attention to my own jeans and six-year-old souvenir T-shirt from a trip to Walt Disney World when the kids were much younger. "That's the bonus of working from home. It doesn't matter how you look."

"But you don't have clients coming to the house," Trixie said. "I do."

"Hey, thanks for those tax tips. I write off some of the kitchen now, too, in addition to my study, since I make my meals here. And my model kits. If I'm writing sci-fi, I should be able to deduct a model of the *Jupiter 2* from *Lost in Space*, right?"

"Absolutely." She was on her feet now.

"So what should I do?" I asked her. "To make it right with Sarah?"

"You could start by not acting like such a jerk," Trixie said. "It's a wonder Sarah didn't give you a spanking."

I chuckled. "She'd probably be afraid it wouldn't be an appropriate punishment, that I'd like it too much."

And there was the tiniest twinkle in Trixie's eye.

There was one small part of the story I didn't tell Trixie. After The Backpack Incident, when Sarah got home and showed me her ticket (a fine plus points), we had to go to Mindy's, a grocery store about five minutes from our place, to pick up some things for dinner. She was going to go alone — I think she actually wanted to go alone — but I thought it would be better if I tagged along and attempted to be helpful. Try to smooth things over a little bit. Maybe explain why I did what I did. That my motives were honorable, even if things didn't quite work out the way I'd planned.

Sarah dropped some bananas in the cart's child seat, next to her purse. "You do this kind of thing all the time," she said. "You're always telling us what to do. Don't leave the stove on, check the batteries on the smoke alarm, don't drink the milk after the expiration date, don't leave the front door unlocked, make sure the car's locked, make sure you put the steak knives in the dishwasher with the points down so no one slits their wrists when they reach in —"

"That's a good rule," I pointed out. "Remember that time you got cut?"

"Don't overload the circuits, make sure —"

"Okay, okay, but that's all good advice. It's just commonsense safety stuff. I mean, I *could* have fallen down the stairs, and I *could* have broken my neck. The fact that I didn't, that's a *good* thing. It's really the happy ending to this whole mess, if you want to know the truth. Remember how mad you got one day, throwing their backpacks down the stairs? I think the kids learned a valuable lesson today without there having to be an actual tragedy."

"I think the kids are thinking the real tragedy is that you survived."

I didn't know what else to say, so I wandered over to look at the pastries. I felt like a chocolate cake. An entire one, just for me. I looked back over at Sarah, who had moved away from our cart to grab some pizzas in the frozen food aisle.

And she had left her purse sitting in the cart, unguarded, where anyone could walk off with it. Maybe she was only going to be a second. But then she looked at the frozen juice, and some frozen vegetables, the whole time with her back turned to her purse.

I returned to the cart and guarded her purse until she was done with the frozen foods.

"What?" she said. "Why are you looking at me like that?"

"Your purse," I said. "Anyone could have walked off with it. You shouldn't leave the cart unattended like that. You'd lose your cash, credit cards, everything. Wasn't there something on the radio, some woman had her purse stolen in the grocery store, lost all the pictures she'd just had developed of her sister's wedding?"

"We carried the story on the Metro page."

"There you go," I said. "So you already know, and still you leave your purse unguarded."

Sarah looked at me long and hard. "You need to learn to pick your moments better," she said. "And another thing."

"Yes?"

"Go fuck yourself."

6

Once I'd thrown the cups into the dishwasher after Trixie'd gone back to her place, I put on my walking shoes. I was going to try something new today. Walk *before* I got stuck at the computer. Maybe a little exercise first thing, filling my lungs with fresh air, would set me straight for the entire day.

I set a brisk pace for myself through the areas of the development where construction was in full swing. Some days, I was a six-year-old boy again, transfixed by oversized trucks unloading lumber, workers swinging prebuilt roof trusses into place, the rhythmic hammers as roofers put down shingles. I could stand and watch for an hour or more, until someone started wondering whether I was a building inspector.

But this day I longed for the restfulness that the creek offered. I wanted to meander along its bank, hear the sound of water trickling by as twigs cracked under my feet. Maybe think of a way to get back into Sarah's good books. Maybe there was something I could get for her, like a gift certificate from a spa, or I could take her someplace nice for dinner, maybe back into the city to one of our favorite spots around the corner from our house on Crandall. No, maybe not. That would just lead to comments along the lines of "If only we had places like this where we live now." I'd find something good in our new neighborhood. I'd ask around. Surely people in Oakwood appreciated fine dining, they could recommend something to me other than DQ or Red Lobster. Maybe if —

I spotted the hiking boots first.

The heels pointed skyward, the toes dug into the dirt. The soles, mud caked between the treads, faced me as I approached the bank of Willow Creek. It was an odd sight at first, given the angle from which I was strolling. The boots seemed planted into the ground there on their own, and it was only as I got close that I was able to see that they were laced onto an individual, who'd been hard to spot before, what with most of his body being underwater and all.

I said something out loud, like "Jesus Christ" or "Holy shit." I'm not sure. When you find your first dead guy, it's like that cliché about when you're in a car accident, and everything seems to move in slow motion. Of course, the dead guy wasn't moving at all. The only things moving were me and Willow Creek as it flowed around the body.

It was a man, in boots and jeans and a plaid shirt, and even though he was facedown in the shallow water, the crown of his head just barely above the surface, I had an inkling of who he was.

Part of me thought that maybe, just maybe, he might still be alive, even though he had a very visible gash in the back of his head that offered a view of what I could only assume was brain. So I stepped into the water, grabbed hold of him by his arms, up close to his shoulders, and rolled him over. It wasn't that hard, the water giving him a bit of a weightless quality, and once I could see his face I knew that the Mississauga salamander had lost its greatest ally.

I pulled Samuel Spender up onto the bank, resting his body on its back. Lifeless eyes stared skyward. It was clear to me now that he was long gone. There would be no need, I thought, for any heroic mouth-to-mouth efforts at resuscitation.

I thought of my friend Jeff Conklin, where he might be three decades later. I finally caught up to you, Jeff.

I reached into my jacket pocket for the cell phone I carry around most everywhere. It wasn't until then that I realized how upset I was by this discovery; my fingers were shaking too much to punch in the numbers. You might think that punching in 911 wouldn't be that hard, but when your background is in journalism, and your wife still earns her living at a newspaper, you know that the first thing you do in an emergency is call the city desk. And that's more than three numbers.

I took a couple of deep breaths and dialed.

"City."

"Hi. I need to talk to Sarah. It's an emergency."

"Hey, is this Zack?"

"Yeah. Who's this?"

"It's Dan. Remember we talked that time, when you pretended to hurt yourself on the stairs, and your kids called the ambulance? Sarah told us all about it. That was really something."

"Listen, Dan, I need to talk to Sarah. Like I said, it's an emergency."

"She's just coming out of the M.E.'s office. What is it this time? The house on fire or something? Fire trucks on the way?"

"Put her on the fucking phone, Dan."

"Yeah, sure, fuck you, too. Hang on."

Sarah took the phone. "Hello?"

"It's me."

"What is it? What did you say to Dan, to make him tell you to fuck off? He hardly knows you. If he did, I could understand."

"Look, something's happened. You know that environmentalist guy? The one who wants to save the creek?"

"No."

"Spender. Samuel Spender. Didn't I tell you about running into him when I went over to the sales office the other day?"

"Oh yeah, I remember. That's when you

96

asked me about those other names. Benny something, and Carpington. So?"

She still had a tone. I said, "That's right." I took a breath. At my feet, Spender's battered head slowly listed to the left. "The thing is, I'm down by the creek, I was doing my walk —"

"Must be nice."

"And I found him here. In the creek. He's dead."

Sarah paused. "What?"

"He's dead. I just dragged him out of the water. He's dead, Sarah."

"Is this another one of your tricks? Because if it is, I swear to God, I don't know what the hell you're trying to prove this time."

"It's not a trick. I'm standing here, right over him. He's dead like I'm a jerk."

I heard Sarah breathe out. "Whoa. Have you called the cops?"

"No. I called you first."

Sarah didn't question that.

"Okay," she said. "I'll send someone out, and a shooter." Photographer. "Call the cops as soon as you hang up, but you should write us something, freelance, about six hundred words, what it's like, finding a body, how you discovered it, how —"

"I know the drill, Sarah."

"Okay." A pause. "You're okay, right?"

"Yeah."

"Okay. Call me back when you can."

I hit the "end" button and then punched in

911. I told the operator what I'd found, where I was, and promised to stay put until police arrived. Moments later I heard a siren, then car doors opening and closing beyond a ridge of trees. "In here!" I called.

There were two officers who responded at first. A male-and-female team. The woman, decked out in full uniform and belt and gun, with dark hair tucked up under her official-looking hat, took me aside.

"I'm Officer Greslow," she said. "You found the body like that?"

"No," I said, and explained.

"So you moved the body." I nodded. Officer Greslow didn't look very happy with me.

"His face was in the water, I was afraid maybe it had just happened, so I pulled him out. But once I had him out, I could see that Mr. Spender was, you know, dead."

"Mr. Spender? You knew this man?"

"Well, I knew who he was. It's Samuel Spender. He's some environmental guy? He had this association, to protect the creek? You know, fighting the developers?" God. I had fallen into Valley Girl up-speak, ending all my sentences with question marks. Somehow, it made me sound guilty of something.

"And you're a member of this association?"

"No. He was going around the neighborhood — I live just up there, over the hill, in one of the finished sections of the development — collecting names on a petition to stop houses

98

from being built down around the creek here."

"Did you sign it?"

"Uh, no, no I didn't."

"So you didn't like what Mr. Spender was doing?"

"No no, it wasn't that at all. I just, I don't know, I didn't really care, I guess. Not at the time. Listen, what do you think happened to him?"

She glanced back at the scene. There were more cops now, a couple of them putting up yellow police tape. "It's a bit early."

"He might have tripped," I said. "On a rock or something, maybe he tripped, hit the back of his head, then rolled over into the water."

"Maybe."

"You think someone killed him?" I asked. "Because, you know, I mean, the whole reason we moved out here, well, it was to get away from this kind of thing. I'm sure it was just an accident, because, well —"

Something had caught Officer Greslow's eye. Two people coming through the woods, one holding a camera.

"Fucking press," she said. "How'd they find out about this so fast?"

I said nothing.

After Officer Greslow finished with her questions, she turned me over to a detective who asked me the same things all over again, plus what I did, how long I'd lived in the neighborhood, why I was down by the creek, what I'd had for breakfast. Really. He let me go after about ninety minutes, but not before reaming me out for walking all around the crime scene and possibly obscuring important footprints around where Samuel Spender had gone into the drink. The reporter and photographer from *The Metropolitan* left the scene before I did, and I suspected they'd be waiting for me out by the road when I came out, but they weren't.

I called Sarah on my cell. "They're finally done with me."

"You okay?"

"Yeah."

"So what happened? How'd the guy die?"

"I don't know. He had this big gash in the back of his head, and he was face down in the water, so I don't know, I get the idea the cops think somebody killed him, but it could have been an accident, easily. It's very slippery down there, he could have slipped on a rock or something, then fallen in the water and drowned. Did I ever tell you about, when I was a kid, this guy I almost found dead, but instead my friend found him? It was almost like this. Guy falls down, then drowns."

"Yeah, you told me."

"Anyway, I'm gonna walk home now, start writing something for you. What did you say, about six hundred words or something?"

"Listen," Sarah said, softly. "About that. They don't want it."

"Whaddya mean? I thought it was a great angle. Former reporter, goes on to write science fiction, finds a body. It's a perfect first-person thing. It would be what I believe you call an exclusive."

"I know, and I thought it was a great idea. But we've already heard back from Scott and Folks." The reporter and photog I saw. "And they've phoned in, say it's just some guy, might be murder, might not."

"Yeah, so?"

"Well, it happened in Oakwood. The main desk doesn't care about the suburbs. Nothing ever happens there."

"But something did just happen here."

"Yeah, but the way they see it is, even when something does happen in the suburbs, it's not worth running, because nothing ever happens there."

I stood there at the edge of the woods, where there were seven police cars lined up along the shoulder of the road, and said nothing.

"You there?" Sarah asked.

"Yeah. I'll talk to you when you get home."

While I would have been up for writing an account of my early afternoon adventure, I wasn't much in the mood for getting back to work on my book. But I sat down at the computer anyway, and there was an e-mail from my editor, Tom Darling. It was, for Tom, a fairly long message. It read, "Whr is it?" Tom was the kind of guy who could edit *Moby Dick* down to a news brief.

I wasn't overdue with the manuscript. My contract gave me nearly another month, but Tom was used to me handing things in ahead of schedule, so for me to be taking the time I was allowed was probably throwing him into a panic. The sequel to *Missionary* was already in the fall catalogue, so not to deliver it on time would be something of an embarrassment to Tom and those to whom he answered. I clicked on "Reply" and wrote, "Had computer virus, lost manuscript with only one chapter to go. Will have to start again. Hope this isn't a problem." And then I clicked on "Send."

Tom must have been sitting on his computer when my note arrived, because less than two minutes later I was notified of a new message. It read, "Dnt fck wth me." How a guy with these kinds of typing and people skills ended up as an editor with a name like Darling was beyond me.

I called up a chapter I'd been working on, but couldn't concentrate. I brought up a *Star Wars* computer game and tried to destroy the Death Star, but even the images of intergalactic explosions couldn't erase Samuel Spender, as I'd last seen him, from my mind.

So I turned away from the computer, looked at a shoebox full of receipts and tax statements, and tried to occupy my mind with financial matters. Soon I'd have to gather all my tax stuff together and try to figure out my annual return.

Rather than hire an accountant to figure out all the possible deductions, I usually tried to do it myself, relying on bits and pieces of information gleaned from talking to others who worked from home, like Trixie.

She was a better person to talk to than most. She'd sat at the kitchen table and told me about her business as an accountant. She suggested that maybe it was time to stop getting free advice, much of it unreliable, and go to an expert. I could turn everything in the shoebox over to her, and she would find more deductions than I ever could. I decided right then and there to bring my shoebox over to Trixie. The truth was, I wanted to tell someone about what had happened, about finding my first body. I was, to put it mildly, a bit wired.

I decided to call her first.

I got out the phone book, then couldn't remember her last name. I wasn't sure I'd ever known her last name. For that matter, what was Earl's last name? I'm not good with names, first or last. You send me into a party, introduce me to a dozen people, and I won't retain so much as an initial.

I thought maybe if I looked up accountants in the yellow pages, when I came across Trixie's last name it would jump out at me. There were three full pages of them, and I ran my finger down one column after another, scanning, looking for a name that would make me go "Yes!"

Nothing.

I repeated the exercise, this time looking for an accountant whose office was on our street. No luck there, either.

So maybe Trixie didn't list herself in the yellow pages. Maybe it was a word-of-mouth thing. Or maybe clients were referred to her. The bottom line was, I wasn't going to be able to phone her at the moment.

I stepped out the front door and far enough into the yard to see Trixie's place. Her Acura was in the driveway, plus a new, small Lexus, in black. So she had a client. I didn't want to bother her when she was in the middle of doing somebody else's books. I could wait until they left.

Down the other way, the housecoat lady was out watering her driveway again. I hadn't forgotten her first or last name, because we'd never been formally introduced. I would nod hello as I walked by, and that was good enough for me. I'm not sure what kind of conversation you can expect to have with someone whose only goal in life is owning a driveway clear of microscopic debris.

Nothing doing across the street at Earl's house, although even from here I could see that he was probably adding his name to the list of those who were unhappy with the work done by Valley Forest Estates. His windows remained cloudy, no doubt condensation trapped within the center of the glass. In our old house, we had windows that had been put in about twenty years ago, and peering outside was akin to looking through a pair of dirty eyeglasses. You might expect that sort of thing with an older place, but it was a real surprise to see it in a house as new as Earl's. I looked back at our own home, scanning my eye across the first- and second-story windows, wondering when I could expect the same thing might happen to them.

I couldn't get a very good view, standing as close to the house as I was, so I went out to the curb to take in the whole picture, and while I couldn't see anything wrong with the windows, I noticed for the first time that the framing around the front bay window was slightly crooked, and that the house numbers over the double garage were not centered properly. Honestly.

The front door of Trixie's house opened and a well-dressed man, mid-fifties I'd guess, came out. He was a bit tentative about it, glancing out to the street as he did so. He reached into his pocket for his keys, unlocked the Lexus with his remote, then strode quickly from the front door to the car. As he did so, his eyes happened to lock on mine.

"Hi!" I said. I may have my faults, but I'll always say hello to people.

He looked as though I'd just shot him with a dart. He quickly got into the car, where he was obscured by heavily tinted windows, backed out onto Greenway, then headed down the street, the Lexus making a deep, throaty roar the whole way.

The guy looked rattled, no doubt about it. Maybe Trixie'd told him he was going to have to pay a lot more in taxes than he'd budgeted for. Maybe he'd have to turn in the Lexus.

If he was rattled, maybe Trixie was, too. Maybe this was a bad time. I went back into the house.

I was actually working when Sarah got home. Not building a kit. Not flying a model of the starship *Enterprise* around my study, humming the theme from *Star Trek*. Not playing *Star Wars* computer games. I was working on the last chapter when I heard Sarah unlock the front door and come in.

I didn't call out. I didn't know whether she was still angry with me about the keys thing. But I started hitting the computer keyboard with more intensity, so she'd know I was home, hear where I was, and possibly think I didn't hear her come in because I was consumed with work. Soon, there was some racket coming from the kitchen, where it sounded as though she was putting away some food, and then it was very quiet, save for the sound of my typing. Although shortly before her arrival I'd actually been writing, I wasn't, at that moment, being overly creative. What I'd typed since I'd heard Sarah's key in the door was "Sarah's home so I better sound busy and it sounds like she's inside the house now and she's going into the kitchen and she must have bought something for dinner and

I hope it's something good because it's just occurred to me that I've eaten nothing this afternoon what with finding a dead guy which can have something of a negative effect on your appetite and"

And then I could sense her presence behind me. I work with my back to the door, which means the screen is visible to anyone walking in, but fortunately, Sarah doesn't have telescopic vision like the Superman statuette up on my shelf.

"Hey," she said, standing in the doorway.

I whirled around in my computer chair. "Hi."

"Sounds like it's going really well," Sarah said. "I didn't know, after what happened to you today, whether you'd feel like working."

I shrugged, clicked the mouse in the upper right corner and made the text vanish from the screen. "I only got back to it in the last hour or so. Got an e-mail from Tom that kind of encouraged me to get going."

I turned back to the computer and heard Sarah come up behind me. She rested her hands on my shoulders.

"I was wondering if we could be friends," she said.

I didn't say anything.

"I picked up some fettuccine and some chicken, thought I'd make us something nice for dinner."

I hesitated. "Sounds nice," I said.

"And just so you know, not only did I take the

keys out of the door, I set them on the table, and locked the door behind me."

I definitely said nothing.

"You know what that means?" she asked. She slid her hands down more so that they were rubbing across my chest.

"What does that mean?"

"It means we're locked in the house, and I think we're all alone."

"The kids will be home any time now, I think."

"Why don't we give them twenty bucks for pizza, tell them to get out of the house, and after I've made you some dinner, maybe we could mess around."

I spun around slowly, nuzzling my head between Sarah's breasts. They were very nice breasts. "That might be nice," I said. "That might be very nice."

Sarah slipped her arms around my head, drawing me in even closer, if that was possible. "I don't know how much work you've got left here, but I'll have dinner ready in about twenty minutes. Okay? And then you can tell me more about finding that man's body. That must have been awful."

I came up for air and looked into her face. "I'm sorry for being such a jerk. With the keys, and the car, and everything."

Sarah smiled. "You can't help yourself."

"Possibly."

And she bent down and kissed me, a quick

peck at first, then a longer, more exploratory kiss, with her long dark hair spilling across my face, that hinted of much better things to come. She untangled herself from me, smiled, and left for the kitchen while I swiveled back around, made an adjustment in my jeans, and brought my chapter back onto the screen. I deleted the parts I'd written since Sarah's arrival, then re-read the last few paragraphs before that to reacquaint myself with where I was in the story.

A few moments later, from the kitchen, Sarah said, "Shit!"

I jumped up and ran in to see what was wrong. A chunk of drywall, about the size of a paperback, had fallen from between the pot lights, in that spot where the shower water leaked down. It had landed on the just-opened package of fresh pasta.

7

❖ ❖ ❖

My first instinct, in the hours following the discovery of Spender's body, even without knowing exactly how he'd died, was to give everyone a security lecture. Don't talk to strangers or pick up hitchhikers, make sure you haven't left the keys in the door, make sure you throw the deadbolt, obey your "walk" and "don't walk" signals, don't use the electric hair dryer while you're sitting in the bathtub, wait an hour after eating before swimming, never run with scissors.

But I sensed this was the wrong way to go. It had only been a couple days since the hidden car incident, and now that Sarah and I were speaking to each other again, I didn't want to set things back. My goal was tolerance. I would not let things get to me. I would let things go. Like water off a duck's back. I'd stop telling everyone how to behave. I'd mellow out.

I'd learn to chill.

When Paul and Angie got home, I told them what had happened down by the creek. Angie said, "Are you sure the guy was dead? Maybe he was just pretending to be dead to teach you a lesson about safe hiking." Then she ran for her camera and persuaded her brother to come with her so she could take her first pictures of a crime scene. On their way out, Sarah shoved a twenty into her hand and told her to buy her brother and herself some pizza for dinner, and to eat it at the restaurant, not bring it home.

"Oh God," Paul said under his breath to his sister. "They're going to go at it."

After Sarah and I had picked the drywall out of our fettuccine, and had dinner, Paul's worst fears were realized. There's nothing like brushing up against death to reinvigorate the love-making process. My disposition was definitely improving.

My resolve to be less of a know-it-all jerk was tested early the next morning, when I found the front door unlocked. Once Angie and Paul had returned from dinner, Paul had gone back out with his friend Hakim, sneaking from one movie to another at the multiplex, buying tickets for a PG show and then slipping into the theater showing an R-rated slasher pic where women with heaving bosoms kept falling down while trying to run away, so he wasn't in until after midnight. When I went down in the morning to get *The Metropolitan*, the bolt on the door hadn't been turned. And there, sitting within an arm's reach of it, was Sarah's purse. I nearly mentioned it to him at breakfast, but didn't. Next time, I'd just wait until Paul was home and go down and check the door myself.

Paul left for school at the regular time, but Angie hung in, going downstairs to put the finishing touches to a photography assignment. I noticed a hot smell as I walked past her bedroom. She'd left her curling iron on, which was resting atop her dresser, the cord still plugged into the wall. So I unplugged it. Made no mental note to rent a smoke machine to send dark billowing clouds out of her bedroom window, or arrange to have a fire truck parked at the curb for when she came home.

"Let it go," I said aloud as I emerged from her bedroom on my way downstairs to the study to get to work.

From the basement, she called to me. Her voice, coming from behind a door, was muffled. "Dad! Come down for a sec!"

In the brochure, Valley Forest Estates had called it a "wine cellar" or "cold room," a place to keep fresh vegetables or store fine bottles of white and red. The room was no more than five by seven feet in size, and we had turned it into a darkroom.

"Hang on," she said, making sure her film was safe from any invading light, then opened the door to admit me into the blackness. My eyes adjusted to the soft red light, the smell of developing fluid swirling up my nostrils. I was brought in occasionally as a technical adviser, having spent a lot of time in a darkroom when I worked in newspapers, but this time Angie just wanted me to see what she was doing.

"What's the assignment?" I asked.

"Just wait," she said, moving the white paper back and forth in the solution. Gradually, images began to take shape. "I love this part," Angie said. "It's like watching something being born. A lot of the kids, they've got these digital cameras, they do everything on the screen. It's kind of cool, but there's no suspense, you know? This way, half the fun is in the anticipation."

A street sign came into view. "Chancery Park." Then houses.

"It's our neighborhood," I said. "You took some pictures of the street. Isn't that nice."

But as each shot materialized, it became clear that Angie was up to much more than that. The pictures, all black-and-white, had a starkness about them.

"There are no people," I said. "The streets are empty."

"Yeah," said Angie. "I captured them just the way they are. And see how the trees look like twigs, and in this shot, I've lined up the houses so you can see how they're all exactly the same."

"Very effective," I said.

"I'm calling it 'Dying in Suburbia: A Study in Redundancy.'"

"It's good," I said quietly. "It's very good."

Angie was still on the same theme as I drove her to school later, since she'd missed the bus.

She said, "How much longer are we going to live out here?"

"Excuse me?"

"How much longer? We've been out here, like, almost two years and when are we going to move back into the city? Would we be able to buy back the house on Crandall? It wouldn't have to be that house, although it would be nice, unless the new owners are, like, a bunch of psycho goths who've ripped out the walls and painted the ceilings black or something."

"Where did you get the idea we were moving back into the city?"

"I just figured, sooner or later, you'd see what a terrible mistake it was to move out here and we'd go back."

"What are you talking about?" I said, glancing over at Angie as I pulled away from a stop sign. "Who said this was a terrible mistake?"

"Well, first of all, the house is falling apart and —"

"The house is not falling apart."

"Mom said last night the ceiling fell right into the pasta."

"The ceiling did not fall. A small chunk of it fell because it was wet because there's a leak in the upstairs shower, which can be fixed, which does not mean the house is falling apart. And the builder has some two-year warranty or something, so don't worry about it."

Angie looked out her window and said nothing.

"I go to school with a bunch of losers," she said, finally.

I let that one hang out there for a while. "What do you mean, losers?"

She shrugged, a kind of like-this-needs-an-explanation? shrug. "I know you and Mom thought moving out here would mean you'd never have to worry again about schools, about drugs and all that shit. But you have no idea. We've got the Crips, and crackheads, and — I mean, look at Columbine. That was, like, the middle of nowhere. That wasn't some inner-city school or something. And look what happened there."

"What are you saying? That there are guys in long black coats waiting to shoot up the school?" I had shifted into parental overdrive.

"No, no, jeez, no, God, don't go all hyper on me. All I'm saying is just because we moved out of the city doesn't mean that there aren't still weird people in my school. There's weird people wherever you go. Just 'cause we've moved doesn't mean we're never going to run into crazy people again. It's really no different out here than anyplace else, at least from that point of view. But you don't have people willing to be eccentric."

"Okay, you've lost me. We've got weird, but we don't have eccentric."

"I mean, like, remember my friend Jan? The one with the boots, and the tears in her stockings, and the orange skirts?"

"And the thing in her tongue?"

"Yeah. Like, she barely rated a second glance at my old school, but if you moved her out here, where everyone's wearing their Abercrombie & Fitch, they'd think she was totally strange."

"She *was* totally strange."

"Yeah, but that's the point. She kind of was, but no one noticed? You could do that downtown, and no one really thought about it. Out here, there's this suburban thing, where you have to be borderline normal all the time."

In some inexplicable way, I knew what she was talking about.

"That's why, for example, Paul wants to get a tattoo," Angie said. "So he can be just a little edgy out here."

"Paul wants a tattoo?"

Angie glanced at me, realizing she'd broken a confidence. "He didn't tell you?"

"No. Not yet."

"You didn't hear it from me, but he's thinking about it. There's a place, in the plaza, that'll do them."

"He can't get a tattoo. He's not even sixteen yet. They wouldn't do it."

Angie rolled her eyes. We were almost to the school. "Is there more?" I asked.

Angie was quiet.

"Haven't you made any friends here?"

Angie shifted her chin around, a nod in disguise. "Not really. I had friends at Bannerman, like Krista, and Molly, and Denny, but I had to

116

leave them because it wasn't *safe* there, we had to move to a neighborhood where everything would be *okay*." There was a mocking tone. "Well, so what if there was a flasher and a few hookers or some needles on the sidewalk? At least it was interesting."

"You know you're welcome to have your friends out here any time you want," I offered. "Invite them on Friday or Saturday, do a sleepover thing in the basement."

Angie looked at me as though I'd just stepped out of an episode of *Ozzie and Harriet*. "God, Dad, I'm not five. And, like, they just can't wait to come out *here*."

I stopped the car out front of the school. "I hate this place," Angie said, slipping out the door and closing it behind her.

I swung by Kenny's hobby shop to see whether a model I'd ordered, of the dropship the Marines use to fly from the mother ship to the planet's surface in the movie *Aliens*, had come in. I could have phoned, but going in person to check gave me an excuse to wander the shop and see whether any other new things had arrived. Kenny catered to a variety of hobbyists — model railroaders, slot car fans, fliers of radio-control airplanes — but his selection of SF-related kits was fairly extensive for a full-range hobby store.

My model hadn't shown up. "Maybe next week," said Kenny, who was leaning over the counter, mini-screwdriver in hand, trying to re-attach a wheel to a metal reproduction of an old Ford Thunderbird. "You ever wonder," Kenny asked, not taking his eyes from his work, "why men have nipples?"

I thought about that for a moment. Not about the question itself, but at the sorts of things that preoccupied Kenny. "Not really."

Kenny bit his lip and held his breath, not wanting the tiny screw to slip from its hole. "It just doesn't make any sense at all. They don't do anything, they serve no purpose." Then: "How's the house?"

"Shower's still leaking into the ceiling in the kitchen, drywall's falling into the kitchen. The tub taps drip, the wind whistles sometimes around the sliding glass doors. The caulking around our bedroom window is useless. I don't even bother to take down the ladder. I'm squeezing caulking in every couple of weeks."

"There's another guy, lives in your neighborhood, says he's had trouble with his windows, and wiring problems, you know? Breakers popping, that kind of thing."

"We haven't had that. Yet."

I asked Kenny if he had the latest issue of *Sci-Fi & Fantasy Models*, which he didn't, so I said I'd see him later and got back in the car.

Driving home, my thoughts turned to Angie. Our problems with shoddy house construction were minor compared to hers. Her world was falling apart. Paul had adapted to our move out here much better. He made friends more easily, didn't place a lot of demands on them. As long as they were interested in playing video games and didn't have any moral qualms about sneaking into movies that they weren't supposed to see, that was good enough for him. He'd even struck up that semi-friendship with Earl, developed an interest in gardening and landscaping. Not that things were perfect with Paul. His marks were lousy. School bored him. There was that upcoming appointment with his science teacher. And now, there was this new development about Paul wanting to get a tattoo.

He and I would have to talk.

Maybe, I thought as I drove through the streets of Valley Forest Estates, I'd made a terrible mistake. I'd dragged us out here out of fear and delivered us into mediocrity. And then I shook my head and decided that my initial instincts had been right — the recent corner store robbery downtown reinforced my decision. Just because the suburban architecture was bland didn't mean our lives had to be. We still had our interests and our passions no matter where we lived. We didn't have to give those up just because we no longer lived downtown.

The evidence that we were safer here than downtown was still overwhelming, and I had that thought in mind when our house came into view and I spotted the unmarked police car parked at the curb out front.

"Did you see anyone else near the creek before you found Mr. Spender's body?"

His name was Flint. Detective Flint. Short, squat, in an ill-fitting suit, wearing a hat like you'd expect to see on Lee Marvin back in the 1960s. He was sitting across from me at the kitchen table, and he'd turned down my offer of coffee. His hands were busy making notes in a small reporter's pad.

"Uh, no, I didn't see anyone," I said.

"Not coming out of the woods as you were going in, headed for the creek?"

"No, I didn't see anyone at all. You think he was down there with someone?"

"Well, there was someone else down there with him at some point," Detective Flint said, pushing his hat back further on his head. "Mr. Spender didn't bash his own head in."

I stared at him for a moment. "So you're thinking now that it wasn't an accident?"

"Mr. Walker, we've never thought it was an accident. Mr. Spender was a victim of homicide."

"I'd been thinking it was an accident," I said. Okay, maybe I'd been *hoping* it was an accident. I'd been telling myself it was *probably* an accident. That he'd tripped, bashed his head on a rock, then rolled over into the water. "You're sure?" I said.

Detective Flint poked the inside of his cheek with his tongue. His cheek bubbled out like he was Kojak eating a Tootsie Pop. "We have some experience with this kind of thing," he said.

"No, I wasn't suggesting you didn't, it's just, this isn't exactly downtown, you know? You don't expect this sort of thing around here."

"Yeah, well, sometimes we're a bit behind, but we do our best to catch up," Detective Flint said with sarcasm. "Mr. Spender was struck on the back of his skull with a blunt object with considerable force. There wasn't even any water in his lungs. He was dead before he fell into the water."

"I see."

"So you didn't see anyone at all."

"No."

"I understand from Officer Greslow that you knew the deceased."

"Not personally. But I knew who he was. That he was a naturalist, environmentalist-type person."

"You know anyone who might want to do Mr. Spender any harm?"

I half-laughed. "Of course not. Like I say, I hardly knew him, and . . ." And I thought back to that day when our paths had crossed at the Valley Forest Estates offices, and I'd had to hold Don Greenway back from lunging at him.

"What?"

"It's nothing. I'm sure it's nothing."

"Why don't you let me be the judge of that?"

"Well, I don't want to go around accusing people of murder, I mean, that's pretty serious."

"Yes. It is."

121

"Well, you must know that he didn't have a very good relationship with the people at Valley Forest Estates. It was in the paper, letters and articles."

"Yes, we were aware of that. Do you know anything about that beyond what's been in the papers?"

I hesitated. Sure, Don Greenway was angry that day. But it's one thing to get a little hot under the collar, and another thing altogether to whack a guy in the head so hard his brains leak out. And not only that, if I sent homicide cops after Greenway, would I ever get my leaky shower fixed?

"One day," I said slowly, waving my hand in the air like it wasn't that big a deal, "when I was over at the Valley Forest Estates offices, I saw Spender and Don Greenway get into quite an argument."

"Greenway."

"He's the head of the company, I think. We bought this house from him. Our street's even named after him."

"What was this argument about?"

I told him. Flint made some notes in his book, flipped the cover over, and slipped it into his jacket.

"Do you think," I said, hesitantly, "that you could not mention that I told you this, if you're talking to Mr. Greenway? He's, uh, supposed to fix some things around the house here, and he might not be so inclined to do it if he knew I

122

was, you know, ratting him out."

Flint's eyebrows went up a fraction of an inch. "Ratting him out," he repeated.

"Yeah. Isn't that what you call it? Or squealed? Is it squealed?"

"Ratting him out is good," said Flint, who showed himself out.

I might not have my police terminology down pat, but I knew the words to describe how I felt: freaked out.

My friend Jeff might have found a dead guy, but I'd found a dead guy who'd been murdered. Surely this beat a guy who just got his head stuck in a storm drain and drowned. And yet I didn't feel even the slightest bit full of myself. What I felt was scared.

By how long had I missed encountering Samuel Spender's killer? Just because I'd seen him have an argument with Greenway didn't mean that had anything to do with his death. What if Spender had been the victim of some nutbar who would have been just as happy to kill me if I'd come along a little earlier? And what if that nutbar was still roaming around the neighborhood, which, up to now, had always been a crime-free paradise?

I needed someone to talk to about this. I tried Sarah at work.

"Dan. City."

I hung up. I was not talking to that asshole again. I walked to the front window, where Detective Flint was still sitting in the front seat of his cruiser, making some more notes before pulling away from the curb. Across the street, Earl's truck caught my eye. He was home.

He'd want to know about this.

The pickup was backed up to the garage, which was open, and the door from the garage to the laundry room was propped open. Earl was either loading up the truck or taking things into the house. It made no sense to ring the front doorbell, so I entered the garage, mounted the two steps to the laundry room door, and called in, "Earl?"

No answer. Maybe he was lugging plants or something through the kitchen and out the sliding glass doors to the backyard. Most of the houses in this neighborhood had the same basic floor plan; you could go blindfolded into one you'd never been in before and find your way around.

I took half a step into the laundry room, called his name again, and noticed that in the space where I would have expected to find a washer and dryer, there was nothing. How long had Earl lived here? I guessed he was the kind of guy who liked to hang out in laundromats.

A gust of warm air went past me into the garage. The house was hot. Humid, really. "Earl?"

I heard some banging about in the basement. He was making enough noise that he couldn't hear me. I took a few more tentative steps into the house and could see moisture dripping down the insides of the windows. The basement door was only a couple of steps away, and I stood in its frame, feeling the warm humidity drifting up from there.

"Earl?" I shouted over the banging.

And then it stopped, abruptly. There was a moment's silence, then Earl's voice: "Who is it?" There was an edge to his voice.

I walked halfway down, to the landing where the stairs turned. "Earl, it's okay, it's Zack. I just had this detective over to my place, asking about that guy —"

"Don't come down here!"

But by then I'd reached the bottom step and could see that Earl's windows were not fogged as a result of some manufacturing defect.

He was on a short ladder, stripped to the waist, working on a string of lights suspended across the room, dangling a few inches below the unfinished ceiling. There was a network of temporary ductwork that looked like dryer hose, but ten times as thick. I could hear ventilation fans, and the glare from the dozens of light fixtures was nearly blinding. It took my eyes a few seconds to adjust, but when they did I was able to focus on what appeared to be hundreds of long-leafed plants that took up nearly every square inch of floor space. I've never been much of a horticulturalist, but I knew enough to know these were not prize-winning orchids.

I don't know much about guns either, but I recognized what Earl had in his right hand, pointed straight at me.

"Jesus, Zack," Earl said. "You ever heard of fucking knocking? And what's this about a detective?"

8

As I looked about the room, dumbstruck, Earl hurriedly pulled on a shirt and then ushered me up the stairs to the kitchen. He got two beers out of the fridge and motioned — actually, more like directed — me to take a seat at the table. He set his handgun on the table where I could have reached it if I'd wanted to. I didn't.

"What's this about a detective, Zack?" Earl asked. He did not look amused.

I was having a bit of trouble collecting my thoughts. "A police detective, he just left my place."

"What was he asking?" Earl took a nervous swig of his beer. "Was he asking about me?"

"No. He was asking about that guy they found down by the creek."

"Are you sure? You're sure he wasn't asking about me?"

"No," I said, more emphatically this time. "I'm telling you the truth. It was about the guy in the creek."

Earl nodded, slowly, but he was still eyeing

me warily. "I heard about that. On the radio."

"Yeah, well, it did kind of make the news. It was that guy with the petition, who talked to us the other day."

Earl downed some more beer. "Okay. I remember him. You found him?"

I nodded. "The cops say he was murdered. So they had a lot more questions for me, since I came across him when I was out for my walk."

Earl was shaking his head, like he wasn't listening to me. "Shit. Thank God it was about that and not me. I'm running a business over here and can't afford to have the cops finding out about it. So, why are you over here then, if it wasn't about me?"

"I just came over here to tell you about it. Thought you'd be interested. Looks like maybe I caught you at a bad time."

Earl took a deep breath, let it out slowly. He ran his hand lightly over the gun. "So, Zack. You gonna turn me in?"

"Jesus, Earl." I finally twisted off the cap of my own beer and had a swallow. "It's so fucking hot in here."

"There's a lot of humidity in a greenhouse kind of operation," he said matter-of-factly. "That's why I keep a lot of beer in the fridge. And bottled water, soft drinks, that kind of thing." He got out his cigarettes, some Winstons, tucked one between his lips and lit up. "I notice you didn't answer my question."

"What question?"

"About whether you're going to turn me in."

"Look, Earl, it's not like I'm worried about the pot, exactly. I mean, everyone's doing it, I gather, not that my own kids are."

"Of course," Earl said.

I ignored that. "What worries me is you're in a line of work that requires you to keep a gun around. That's not a good thing, Earl. Most people, unless they're cops, don't need to pack heat."

Earl said quietly, "Lots of people, not just cops, need guns."

"The thing is, are we going to be having midnight shootouts on the street here? Is everyone else in the neighborhood at risk of getting caught in the crossfire?"

He pursed his lips and tapped the barrel of the gun with his index finger. "It's just a bit of insurance," he said. "That's all. You don't have to be worried."

"I just don't like guns, is all."

"So if I tell you that you don't have anything to worry about because I've got a gun over here, are you going to turn me in?"

I breathed in deep through my nose, felt a trickle of sweat run down my forehead. "No," I said. "I'm not going to turn you in." And instantly wondered whether this was a promise I could keep. I decided to lighten things up. "I guess there's a lot of chips in the cupboard, in case you get the munchies, too."

Earl snorted. He waved his pack of Winstons.

"This is the only thing I smoke," he said. "I'm trying to look after my health."

"I can see that," I said.

"Look at us. You're having a beer. I'm having a beer. I'm having a cigarette. The beer gives us pleasure, mellows us out, might even kill us if we abuse it. And this cigarette" — he waved it around with dramatic flourish — "will very likely mean the death of me someday."

"I feel you're making your way toward a point."

"All I'm doing downstairs is meeting a need. I'm providing a service. Just like," and he gestured toward me, "writing pornography, say."

"Earl, I don't write pornography. I write science fiction."

"But if you did write porn, it would be the same thing."

"But I don't, and it wouldn't be."

"Okay, but you're missing my point. People have needs, and no matter how many rules you pass, how many laws you make, they're going to have them met, one way or another. People are stressed out more now than ever before in the history of the human race. Pressures from work, pressures from home, we're trying to raise kids the same time as we're looking after elderly parents, we wake up every morning with something new that hurts that didn't hurt yesterday, like you're bleeding from the ass or you can't feel your toes, or maybe you're getting cancer." He waved his cigarette around, took another drag.

"We don't know whether there's a hijacked jet out there with our name on it. Maybe the whole fucking world is going to blow up tomorrow. Some guy with a dirty bomb is gonna walk into the stock exchange. Who the fuck knows? People need some relief, and that's all I'm in the business of doing."

"Earl, your entire basement is a pot crop. If the cops find out, you're finished."

Earl grimaced, running a hand over his shaved scalp. "Life's a risk, right, Zack? Surely you understand that."

I said nothing. Most of my efforts of late had been directed toward minimizing risk. "How's it going so far?" I could imagine Sarah asking.

"Do you even live here?" I asked. "Do you own this house?"

Earl blew out some smoke, nodded. "I got a bed upstairs, and a TV. And I keep the fridge stocked. I even manage to do a little bit of entertaining." He gave me a sly grin, and a nod of his head toward an empty wine bottle and two dirty wineglasses over on the counter by the sink. "But I've kept the decorating to a minimum. Someone else owns the place, some Asian businessmen, I do the gardening, no one's the wiser."

I guess, without realizing it, I had been staring at the gun while Earl talked. He said, "You can't be too careful, this line of work. Sometimes your Asian businessmen get in a disagreement with your Russian businessmen, you don't want to

131

get caught in the middle without a little rein-forcement. But you have to understand, that would be a very rare occurrence."

I nodded toward the gun. "Is that thing regis-tered?"

Earl sighed. "Zack, were you a hall monitor in school? Were you the kid the teacher got to keep an eye on the classroom when he had to go down to the office?"

I didn't say anything.

"I knew it," Earl said, draining his beer bottle. "You mind grabbing me another beer out of the fridge?"

I obliged. A powerful rotting smell hit me as I opened it. "Shit, Earl, I think you might want to clean this out." I looked in the vegetable hamper, where some celery was liquefying.

"I got no sense of smell," Earl said, tapping his nose. "I can't even smell these smokes, but I'm hooked on them just the same."

I handed him his beer and he twisted off the cap. "All those lights downstairs," I said. "Your electric bill must be through the roof."

"I bypass the meter," Earl said. "I'm handy."

I took another swig from my bottle. It was covered with moisture, the label was starting to peel. For a long time I said nothing, then finally, "I keep thinking about Paul and Angie."

Earl said nothing, but he watched me closely.

"You talk about pressures. I think of the pres-sure my kids are under. More than you or I were under back when we were in school. And it's a lot easier to succumb when the thing they're giving in to is so readily available, when it's being processed right across the street from where they live."

Earl nodded thoughtfully. "I appreciate what you're saying. I would never give anything, I swear to God, to your kids."

"But the people you do give it to may end up giving it to my kids."

Earl ground out his butt in a metal ashtray and lit up another smoke. "I don't know what to say. I'm not expecting the Nobel Prize or anything."

"Does Paul know what you're doing here?"

Earl shook his head. "No, he's never been down there. I've made sure of that. Of course, he knocks first." Ouch. "I just help him with his questions about plants and flowers, what needs shade, that's all. He's a good kid."

I had a sip of my beer. "So how'd you get into this line of work?"

"Pays good. No taxes. I need the money. I can make a lot, and I can make it fast. What can I say? I'm not the sort of guy who'd do well at an insurance company or a bank."

I put my head in my hand, rubbed my forehead. Sweat collected in my palm. I could feel a major headache coming on. Maybe it was the humidity. "I don't remember this kind of thing happening when we lived on Crandall."

"You were on Crandall?" Earl asked. "Nice street, nice houses. There was that little fruit

133

place at the bottom of the street."

I put down my hand, took one last drink, and looked Earl in the eye. "I won't do anything. Not right away, anyway. And if I do, I'll give you some warning. But in the meantime, maybe you should think about some other way to make a living. And please, don't come around our place carrying that." I pointed to the gun.

Earl put up his hands, cigarette smoke trailing from his right one, like he was under arrest. "Never." Slowly, he lowered his hands.

"Let me tell you a story," he said. "A guy used to be a cigarette smuggler, took cartons by boat from the U.S., across Lake Ontario, when Ottawa was taxing the shit out of tobacco. He'd bring them to the Indian reserve, up near the Thousand Islands. I'd pick up a carton from him now and then, what he didn't turn over to the Indians. Anyway, he made a lot of money this way, and it was illegal, no question about it, the customs people wanted him, the cops wanted him. So one night, he's going across with a couple of other guys, and suddenly there's this other boat, you know? With the searchlight, and someone on a megaphone telling them to stop? The other guys, they throttle up, figure if they can get back past the midpoint of the lake, they can't touch them, right? And the customs boat comes up alongside, and this guy's buddies, they ram the boat, and one of the feds, he goes right off the bow, into the drink, but he's not splashing around, like maybe he hit his head or something? And my friend, he sees this guy, looking like maybe he's going to go under, and he dives in. His buddies on the boat, they think he's fucking lost his mind, this is their chance to get away, while the other customs guys try to find him, but my friend, he can't do that. He figures there's no time to waste, and he gets this guy, grabs hold of him, screams for the feds so they'll get a light on him and pull them both in."

I didn't say anything.

"So, anyway, my friend got charged, of course. But he saved that asshole's life. All I'm saying is, there's good in everybody."

I stood up to leave. "I hear you, Earl. Thanks for the beer."

I went back across the street, passing Trixie's driveway, where a low-slung blue BMW was parked next to her Acura. I unlocked my front door and went inside, flipping the deadbolt behind me. I went into the kitchen and reached into the fridge for another beer.

The phone rang. I nearly jumped out of my skin.

"What's new?" Sarah asked. I could hear her typing in the background, sending memos or editing stories while she chatted.

"Oh," I said, "not too much."

Except that the police dropped by, confirmed that the man I found in the creek definitely was murdered, so there's a killer roaming around the neighborhood, and Earl, our neighbor across the street, has a gun in case his Asian employers start shooting it up with the Russian mob in a turf war over the massive pot-growing operation he has in his basement. Other than that, things were pretty quiet.

"Okay," said Sarah. "I just thought I'd say hi. That was fun, what we did last night."

"Huh?"

"Oh great. You've forgotten. I got the kids out of the house? With pizza money? Remember?"

"Oh, yeah, of course. Yeah, that was good."

"I'm so glad I made an impression."

"No, sorry. You did. Really. We should do that again soon."

"You sure you're okay? You sound kind of funny."

"No, really, I'm fine. Just working."

"Whoa," said Sarah. "Meeting time. Gotta go. See ya tonight." And she hung up.

Even though I was out of Earl's humid house, I was still sweating. I should have told Sarah about him. I hadn't promised Earl I wouldn't tell her. But what if Sarah wanted to call the police? What then? I'd only promised Earl *I* wouldn't call the police. I didn't promise that I'd keep *Sarah* from calling the police.

Maybe that was my out. Tell her, let her do the dirty work, get me off the hook.

Right. Earl would understand. Earl, our neighbor who packs heat, would understand.

And then again, was it really that big a deal?

Weren't the pot laws twenty years behind the times? The place wasn't a crackhouse, for cryin' out loud. So a guy has a few plants in his basement. Okay, so maybe it wasn't a few. So maybe Earl had a fucking farm where most people have a pool table. But was it any of my business?

And there were risks in telling Sarah, or the kids, what I knew. Risks to my reputation and integrity. The first thing they'd do is remind me whose idea it was to move out here in the first place: "Way to go, Dad. Thanks for rescuing us from the evils of the city."

I went into my study and tried to work, but couldn't focus. I kept getting up, going to the living room window, looking through the blinds to Earl's place. At any moment, I expected to see a fleet of Ladas with Russian mobsters pull into the driveway, guns a-blazin'. Or maybe the cops, driving up on the lawn, pouring out of their cars in riot gear, guns drawn, surrounding the house. Tear gas is lobbed in. Men in gas masks break down the door, and moments later, Earl is dragged out by an officer on either side of him, thrown facedown onto the driveway, his hands cuffed together behind his back. Men in spacesuits start hauling out hundreds of plants and packing them into the back of a specially sealed van.

But nothing like that happened. The housecoat lady watered her driveway. The BMW, driven by a man in khakis and a sports jacket, his eyes shielded by sunglasses, backed out of

Trixie's driveway. A kid, a rare sight in the day in this neighborhood, actually rode by on a bicycle. Earl came out, got in his pickup, and drove off.

And I stood in the window, peering through the blinds, spying on the neighbors, and wondered what kind of a person I was turning into.

9

Sarah's paper never did run much more than a digest item on the death of Samuel Spender. As she'd predicted, her editors didn't much care about a death, even a murder, in the suburbs. To get attention out here, you had to be an actress or a former model. You could be eighty years old with a walker, die in a brutal purse snatching, and if, some six decades earlier, you'd posed before the cameras, the papers would run headlines along the lines of "Ex-Model Slain in Purse Grab!" And they would find a glamour shot from sixty years ago, and run it with a caption that said, "In happier times."

The Suburban, to its credit, ran a respectable news-story-slash-obit on Spender in the edition that came out two days after his death. Under the headline "Outspoken Naturalist Found Slain in Creek," the story read:

Samuel Spender, a naturalist and conservationist noted for his relentless defense of wilderness areas, as well as his spirited tangles with the Oakwood Town Council, died violently Wednesday in Willow Creek.

Police said Spender, 54, an Oakwood resident since 1965, was hiking through one of his favorite spots when he was confronted by his assailant.

His head was struck with a blunt object, and his body left in the shallow waters of the creek. A nearby resident who was out for a stroll found the body and phoned police from a cell phone.

Oakwood Police Detective Edward Flint said police are pursuing a variety of leads in the investigation, but would not say whether they were expecting to make an arrest shortly.

Ironically, Spender, president and founder of the Willow Creek Preservation Society, died in the very area he had fought for several years to protect. When Valley Forest Estates unveiled plans to build a subdivision in the former government lands near Willow Creek, Spender sought the help of environmental experts who found that houses encroaching on the creek could adversely affect the creek, a natural habitat for several species.

Experts working on behalf of the development were able to persuade the council, however, that a subdivision would have a negligible effect, and the subdivision's initial phases were approved. Spender, who worked for an Oakwood engineering firm, was still fighting, however, to halt the development's final stage, which would see houses erected right up to the edge of the creek.

Don Greenway, president of Valley Forest Estates, expressed shock and horror at Spender's death.

"While we did have our tangles and disagreements, I think we both believed in the same thing, and that's the preservation of the environment. I knew that could be done, and still allow for homes where people could raise their families, as they do here in Valley Forest Estates. Mr. Spender felt otherwise, but there's no denying his commitment to making this a better planet. This is a terrible tragedy, and the police have our complete support in bringing his killer to justice."

Greenway's words were echoed by Ward 7 Councilman Roger Carpington, who told The Suburban: "Sam Spender was an inspiration to all of us who care about this community. His input on Willow Creek's preservation was invaluable in helping the council formulate its land use policies."

Spender, who was predeceased by his wife Linda in 1993, leaves two sons: Mark, 28, of Seattle, and Matthew, 25, of Calgary. Funeral arrangements were not available at press time.

And that was it, except for a picture of Spender, a file photo taken by a *Suburban* photographer that had run with a feature on the man when he was still alive, and a headshot of Councilman Roger Carpington, a balding, round-cheeked individual with thick glasses. Spender was shown standing at the edge of the creek where I'd found him.

Clearly, the police hadn't disclosed to the local reporter the name of the person who'd found Samuel Spender's body. Surely I would have gotten a phone call if they had. I found it interesting that Don Greenway had been sought out for a comment. You'd never know, from the way he'd been quoted, that he and Spender were on such bad terms.

Did Greenway have something to do with it? And what about this other guy quoted in the story, Roger Carpington? He'd been one of two people Greenway had wanted to talk to after his fight with Spender. What was that about? Was Carpington supposed to do something about Spender? Did my local councilman moonlight as a hired killer? And what about —

"Okay," I said, sitting at my desk. "Enough. Write your fucking science fiction book."

When I wasn't thinking about Spender, I was thinking about Earl. I didn't want Paul getting any more gardening advice from across the street. The day the drug cops did finally swoop down on him, I didn't want Paul in his company. Not that Paul couldn't learn a lot from

Earl. Judging by the fact that those basement plants of his were thriving, he did have the magic touch. And the thing was, it was hard to believe Earl was all bad. He had, after all, helped focus Paul's interest in gardening and landscaping.

I was hoping things would work themselves out without my doing anything, that if Earl was going to get caught, it would be someone else who turned him in, someone else who spotted something suspicious, like his fogged-up windows and the constant hum of ventilation fans.

Someone like Trixie, maybe. How would she feel, knowing something like this was going on across the street? I wondered if she already knew, had any inkling. Her house, after all, was directly across from Earl's. Every time she looked out her window, she saw his place. Maybe she'd seen something, noticed him backing into the garage late at night, loading up his truck, heading off for a delivery. This couldn't be good if you were in the accounting business, meeting with clients all the time, having an illegal pot operation going on a stone's throw away.

It wasn't just the nature of Earl's business that had me worried, or that he had a gun and might use it if necessary. I'd seen stories in *The Metropolitan* about basement marijuana operations and the massive amounts of electricity they consumed. Earl had mentioned he'd had to do some rewiring, so as not to arouse the suspicions of the utilities people. Which meant that his place was probably a fire waiting to happen.

It was a safety hazard.

It was one thing to wave the red flag of guns and illegal drugs before me, but safety hazards, well, that was very difficult for me to overlook.

All Earl needed was one overheated wire to set the entire house ablaze. And once his house was engulfed, would flames spread to the houses on either side of him, or jump across the street to ours, or Trixie's?

It was enough to keep one from finishing a chapter about busybody atheist missionaries trying to bring technological enlightenment to the rest of the galaxy. So I walked out the front door, noticed there was no car in Trixie's driveway other than her own, and decided this would be a good time to drop by. Get her take on what was going on in the neighborhood, see if she had any inkling of what was going on across the street without tipping my hand, even get some tax advice.

And I'd be very clear. I wasn't looking for free advice. I wasn't one of those people who walk up to a doctor at a dinner party and say, "I've got this thing in my shoulder when I move my arm like this, you got any idea what that could be?" She could treat me like anyone else, charge me her regular rates, that was fine. The good thing was, I didn't have to get out the yellow pages and start cold-calling accountants whose reputations I did not know.

I rang the bell. I always feel a bit stupid, standing outside a door waiting for someone to answer, so I slipped my hands into my pockets and tried my best to look nonchalant for anyone who might drive by, which no one did, since almost every other person in this neighborhood was earning a salary in the city through the day.

I rang again, then pressed my ear to the door to see whether I could hear any activity inside.

And then I heard Trixie's voice, tinny, coming from a small speaker box mounted on the wall to the right of the door.

"Can I help you?"

"Hey, it's Zack and —"

"Please press the button to talk."

I placed my thumb over the small, square black button and pushed. "Trixie? Zack. I catch you at a bad time?"

"Oh, Zack, hi. What's up?"

"Sorry, I would have called, but I didn't have your number, and I couldn't find it in the book."

"Is there anything wrong?"

"No, listen, I can come back."

"Look, I thought you were my next appointment. I can't really come to the door right this second. Why don't you put the coffee on, and I'll be by in about an hour?"

"Sure. Sounds good."

As I was turning to walk down the driveway, a beige Impala pulled in. A casually dressed man got out and, as we passed each other, he gave me a wink.

I plugged in the kettle, measured some coffee into the coffeemaker, and while I waited for the water to boil, sat at the kitchen table and, pencil and paper in hand, started making a list of things to do.

1. Finish last chapter.
2. Fix barbecue.
3. Write letter to Valley Forest Estates demanding action.
4. Bomb offices of Valley Forest Estates.
5. Shove stick of dynamite up ass of Don Greenway.
6. Prepare materials for tax return, get advice from Trixie.
7. Finish caulking around bedroom window.

I glanced out the sliding glass doors and noticed the extension ladder still leaned up against the brick wall of the house, the caulking gun hooked over one of the lower rungs.

8. Buy new tube of caulking.

I put down the pencil and poured boiling hot water into the coffeemaker. If Trixie was true to her word, she'd be over in about twenty minutes. Since that didn't give me enough time to tackle any of the items on my list, I went into my study and started working on my model of the *Seaview* submarine from *Voyage to the Bottom of the Sea*. I was having trouble getting the rear fins to stay on properly, and was applying some liquid cement to the underside of the left one when the doorbell rang.

"Hang on!" I shouted. This was probably Trixie, but I was still in the habit of locking the door behind me every time I came in, so I couldn't invite her to walk in on her own. I tried to set the fin in place, but I was going to need to hold it for several seconds, so I abandoned the project and ran to the door.

I was surprised to see that my visitor was not Trixie, but a rugged-looking man in his late twenties, early thirties, wearing a jean jacket and pants flecked with paint and drywall compound and other building materials. In one hand he held an oversized toolbox, and the other was shoved into the front pocket of his pants, only the thumb sticking out. His face was long, lean, and unshaven, at least for a day or so, and his short brown hair was slightly spiked with gel. He was chewing on a toothpick.

"Yes?" I said.

"This is 1481 Greenway?" he said.

"Yes," I said hesitantly.

"I'm here about the shower. Mr. Greenway sent me over. I'm Rick."

Thank you, Detective Flint, for not ratting me out!

"Oh!" I said. "Yes! Come in!"

His boots, I noticed, were dappled with dried mud. He made no effort to remove them as he stepped inside and advanced across the broadloom.

"Up there?" he said, standing at the foot of the stairs, looking up, his back to me.

"Yes," I said. I followed him up and into the bathroom. It was a bit warm up there, and he slipped off his jean jacket and tossed it casually on the vanity, knocking down a little display of small round soaps carved to look like roses, which Sarah likes to put out for guests but which no one has ever dared use to wash their hands. I put them back in their dish and slid them into the corner, next to a single brass antique candlestick holding a single white candle. Rick set down his toolbox and opened it, revealing an assortment of tools and rolls of tape and tubes of caulking. He opened the glass door to the shower, looked down, sat on the bottom of the shower door opening, and ran his hand along the seams where the floor met the wall.

"You see where the grouting is cracked and coming apart?" I said, trying to be helpful. Rick said nothing.

"The water got in there," I said, "and must have been dripping down to one place in the kitchen, and that's where the drywall fell away."

Rick picked away at some of the loose grouting and threw it out onto the bathroom floor, some of it landing on my shoe. He reached not into his toolbox but his back pocket and pulled out what appeared to be a Swiss Army knife, but when he pressed a button I couldn't see and the blade swung out in a fraction of a second, I gathered this was an implement without a corkscrew, bottle opener, nail file, or screwdriver.

He picked away at more of the loose grout with the knife. I felt a responsibility to make conversation.

"So you work for Valley Forest?" I said.

Rick slowly turned so he could look at me over his shoulder. "You figured that out, huh?"

I went downstairs. I saw Trixie approaching the front door and opened it before she had a chance to knock.

"Hey," she said.

"I've got one of Valley Forest's finest upstairs looking at the shower. I'm hoping he won't run off with Sarah's flowered soap collection."

We went into the kitchen and I got out two cups.

"Sorry I dropped by unexpectedly," I said. "I would have called, but I didn't have your number, and I'm embarrassed to admit this, but I don't even know your last name."

Trixie smiled. "Snelling."

I tried to recall all the names I'd scanned under accountants in the phone book. I couldn't recall seeing Snelling. So I mentioned it.

"I'm not in the book yet," Trixie said. "Should be in the next one."

I put Trixie's coffee in front of her, then some more of those Peek Freans. "I guess your next appointment showed up just as I was leaving."

"Yeah, he was a bit early."

"I was trying to think whether I knew him from anywhere," I said. "Or whether he knew me."

"Oh yeah?"

"Because he looked at me and winked."

Trixie blew on her coffee, grabbed a cookie. "Really."

"It just struck me as odd."

Trixie seemed not to care. She chewed on her cookie. "So what were you coming over for? Unless it was to invite me over for coffee, which is a good enough reason."

"First of all, I was going to ask you, officially, if you'd do my tax stuff. Figure out my deductions, file my return, you know."

"Sure. No problem."

"But not for free. I don't want to take advantage. Just charge me whatever your going rate is." I paused. "What is the going rate?"

And there was that twinkle in Trixie's eye again. "Don't worry about that," she said. "I can probably do it in no time, I've got the program on my computer."

"If you're not going to charge me, I'll find someone else."

She took a sip of her coffee. "Fine. I'll bill you. Will that make you happy?"

I sat down across from her and grabbed a

cookie. "The neighborhood's been kind of funny lately, don't you think?" I said.

Trixie cocked her head slightly. "What do you mean?"

"Odd things going on. Like what happened down at the creek. That guy, who wanted to preserve Willow Creek, who got killed?"

"I heard about that. A real shame."

I told her my role.

"God," she said. "I never found a dead person."

"I saw him a few days earlier, at the sales office. He got in this big argument with Greenway, you know, the hot shit who's in charge of the development."

Trixie nodded knowingly, like maybe she knew this Greenway character. I didn't ask.

"I had been over there, asking about getting someone to fix that hole." I pointed up by the pot lights. "And fix the shower, where the water was leaking from, and this Spender comes in and they start yelling at each other." I gave Trixie a few more details, how Spender said he couldn't be bought, about Greenway ordering him out.

"And then there's Earl," I said. I waited to see whether Trixie would pick up on my opening.

"What about Earl?" she asked.

"Have you noticed anything, I don't know, out of the ordinary at Earl's place?"

Trixie studied me, bit softly into her lower lip. She seemed to be sizing me up, deciding what I might or might not know, and what she might be willing to let on that she knew. Finally, she said, "You mean the fact that Earl has a huge pot business in his basement? Is that what you're referring to?"

"Yeah," I said. "That would be it."

"Look," Trixie said. "You know me. I don't judge. Live and let live. Take what I do." She paused. "People tell me their secrets, their financial secrets, and it takes a lot for people to open up enough, to trust you enough, to tell you what's going on with their lives. So you learn to be accepting. Earl's never caused me any trouble. Take you, for example. When you moved in here, and I found out you were a writer, I thought, I'm okay with that."

I was taken aback. "Why wouldn't you be?"

"Well, writers can be kind of weird, but like I said, I try not to judge."

Trixie finished her coffee. "You said you wanted my phone number."

I handed her my list, said she could write it on there. But first she read what I had written.

"If you get around to sticking that dynamite up Greenway's ass, give me a call before you light the fuse. That would be something to see."

I blushed. "I guess I better throw that out. Write your number at the bottom and I'll tear it off."

When Trixie left, I slipped the sheet of paper with the phone number on it into the front cover of my address book. Then I heard Rick coming down the stairs.

"All fixed?" I said cheerily.

"I dug out the grouting," he said, buttoning up his jacket.

"And regrouted?"

"Nope. I'll have to come back to do that."

"You don't have that stuff with you?"

"Like I said, I'll be back."

"Like, later today?"

"No. Sometime."

"Tomorrow? Because, you know, we can't take a shower there the way it is now."

"You got other bathrooms, right? Use a bathtub."

And he left without saying anything else.

I went up to the bathroom to see what he'd accomplished. Crumbs of grouting were littered across the floor of the shower and the bathroom, mixed in with small chunks of mud that had come off Rick's boots. I shook my head, was about to go look for the vacuum, and something caught my eye.

Actually, it was the absence of something that caught my eye. The brass candlestick that should have been on the vanity was gone.

The theft left me rattled. At first I thought maybe I'd been mistaken, that I hadn't seen the candlestick only moments before in the bathroom. But I knew it had been there. It wasn't as though someone had broken in and made off with all our appliances. The candlestick was a small thing, something Sarah had picked up at a flea market for under twenty bucks, but that didn't make me feel any less angry. It was the gall, the nerve, that shook me. That Rick the Grout Flinger, that useless son of a bitch, would think he could just pick up something of ours and walk out of the house with it, it seemed unthinkable.

I wanted to get on the phone, get Don Greenway on the line, and tell him he better send Rick right back here, not just to fix our fucking shower, but to return our fucking candlestick. But I knew how that would go. The last part, anyway. Assuming Greenway even bothered to ask Rick about it, Rick would deny it. And then where would I be? Would Detective Flint put aside his murder investigation to find the notorious Walker residence candlestick thief?

So this was life in the middle of the boring burbs. Our developer was sending thieves to deal with our leaky shower, there was a basement marijuana farm across the street, and I'd found a murdered environmentalist in the creek.

Maybe that lovely house on Driftwood Drive with the fountain out front was the new headquarters for the Mob? Were the Hells Angels opening their latest chapter on Lilac Lane? Were Al Qaeda terrorists planning their next attack from that new house on Coventry Garden Circle where sod was being laid yesterday?

When Paul came home from school, and later Angie, I told them I wanted to talk to them, with their mother, that evening. When Sarah arrived, I told her there was something I'd been waiting to discuss with the entire family. I gathered everyone in the kitchen. Sarah took a seat, Paul leaned up against the fridge, Angie stood in the doorway so she could make a fast getaway. I took up a position by the dishwasher.

"Okay," I said. "I've tried to ease up a bit lately on the safety stuff. Not hound people about keys and locking doors and all that kind of thing, but I'm just a bit worried that people are going to become complacent without some friendly reminders."

No one said anything.

"There are bad things going on in this neighborhood. Just because this isn't the city doesn't mean people out here can't be up to no good. I mean, it was good, moving out here, and while there've been the odd rough spots, that you" — I spoke to Angie — "don't care much for your school, and I know there's a bit of a commute for your mom" — Sarah just stared at me — "and if anyone seems to be adjusting out here, it's Paul, but the point I'm trying to make is, we have to be on guard, we have to be watching over our shoulder, we have to keep our eyes peeled for anything unusual."

Still no one said anything, although I noticed the three of them exchanging glances.

"So we're agreed? We remain on alert, we

watch ourselves, we don't do anything foolish? No purses left on the front seat of the car, no keys in the front door, no leaving the door unlocked when we go to bed at night. Just general commonsense rules is all I'm asking for here."

Angie cleared her throat. It appeared that she was going to be the first to weigh in with some useful suggestions as to how we could live our lives more safely.

"Is anyone else concerned about the fact that Dad has turned into this paranoid freakout crazy person?"

10

This might be a good time to revisit what I would call the Asshole Issue.

Maybe you've already reached a conclusion. Let's say you've voted in the yes column. Zack Walker is an asshole. No doubt about it. Made up your mind during The Backpack Incident, haven't looked back. If that's how you feel now, I don't see you changing your mind anytime soon.

But maybe you've been less quick to judge. Maybe you're on the fence. You understand how a man's concern for his family could lead him to behave a bit irrationally at times. You've been there. Well, we're coming to the part that will reinforce your convictions, one way or the other.

A day or so after my safety lecture, Sarah and I had gone over to Mindy's Market to pick up a few items. Despite my rant, I was trying to be less fanatical in my approach to family safety, and part of that included being more relaxed generally about things. So when Sarah arrived home and said she wanted to go and pick up some groceries, I offered to come along. I'd been in my office, making pencil notations on some pages I'd just printed out, and met her at the front door after she changed into a pair of jeans and a sweater. We each grabbed light jackets because, even though we were well into spring, there was a cool wind blowing in from the north.

There was lots to talk about. At least lots for Sarah to talk about. It had been a busy day at *The Metropolitan*.

"So I tell Leanne, you know Leanne?"

I said yes.

"I want her to go down to the waterfront, where there's a press conference being called by Alderman Winsted, about all this garbage that's piling up by the yacht club, but it's raining out, and she says she can't go because the ground's going to be soft and mushy, and she's wearing this new Donna Karan thing, and these nice shoes, because she thought she was going up to cover the Wang trial —"

"The which?"

"Wang. The guy who cut up his girlfriend and dropped her body parts all over five counties."

"Okay."

I was struggling to release a cart, which was jammed into the next one.

"Except the Wang thing has been put off a day, and Walters called in sick —"

"Again?"

"I know, this is like the fourth time in two months, and it's always his first day back after a couple off, and he always calls from Ottawa, where he's boffing this chick from the *Citizen*, and the way I figure it, he just wants a long weekend, right? And then the M.E. wants to know why some fucking moron copy editor rewrote Owen's story about the guy who was charged with possessing all this kiddie porn, and his defense is artistic freedom, and I say, maybe it's because Owen wouldn't know an interesting opening sentence if it came along and bit him on his nose, and he says that may be true, but maybe next time, the copy editor could rewrite it in such a way that she doesn't switch the names of the accused and the defense lawyer. Anyway, what happened with you today?"

"Nothing." I had the cart free now and we were trolling past a display of fresh fruit.

"Did you hear from the kids today?" Sarah asked.

Paul had phoned on his cell around noon to ask whether I could check in his room and see whether he'd left a science assignment on top of his dresser. I was on the cordless. "Okay, I'm in your room now, looking at the top of your dresser, and I see no science assignment," I said.

He paused at the other end of the line. "Pull back my covers and see if it's in my bed."

I tried that. "No luck," I said. "But I have found a *Penthouse*."

"Never mind."

I hadn't heard anything from Angie, although before leaving in the morning she informed me that I owed her $127. Had I *borrowed* $127 from her, I asked, because if I had, my memory had been wiped clean of the incident. She sighed and reminded me that we had agreed to reimburse her for half of the cost of her new pants and top, an arrangement about which I knew nothing.

"I told her that," Sarah said.

"Well then, *you* owe her $127."

Sarah said we needed romaine, maybe a couple of steaks, and we were totally out of fabric softener. I expressed concern about how often we were using the barbecue, which, by the way, I still had to get fixed.

"There was a story, in your paper, about how when meat cooks over hot coals, it turns into pure cancer."

"Don't believe everything you read in the paper," she said. As we passed the newsstand, the cover of *Time*, which was about a new blockbuster science fiction movie, caught my eye.

"I'll just be a sec," I said, and Sarah rolled on ahead without me.

I flipped through the *Time*, glanced at the covers of several other magazines (Oprah had managed to make the cover of her own magazine again, which I thought warranted some sort of inquiry), and quickly scanned my eye over the newly released paperback novels. By the time I decided to rejoin Sarah, she was long gone.

I walked along the front of the store, between the checkouts and the ends of the aisles, peering down each one, looking for a glimpse of her.

I spotted her down the aisle where they kept all the pastas and tomato sauces and twenty-three different kinds of Kraft Dinner. She was about three-quarters of the way down, and about halfway stood a nearly empty shopping cart, purse tucked into the spot where you can place small children. As is usually the case, Sarah had her eyes on the shelves, and not on the cart, or the purse. Fortunately, there was no one else anywhere near the cart, so she wasn't immediately at risk of having it snatched.

I passed by the only other person in the aisle, a young blonde woman in an off-white suit looking at garbage bags, and as I approached Sarah I waited to see when she might take her eyes off the various spaghetti sauces to check that her purse was still where she'd left it in the cart.

I was doing a slow burn.

It was clear that I was completely wasting my time trying to get anyone in my household to exercise even the most basic level of common sense. I had, I knew, become something of a nag where Sarah and her purse were concerned. There had been stories on the news. That woman with the lottery ticket. That other woman, who'd lost the pictures of her sister's wedding. There were some things you just didn't do, and leaving your purse unattended in a busy grocery store was one of them.

It appeared, from where I was standing, that the purse wasn't even snapped shut at the top. Wasn't that thoughtful. A thief didn't even have to go to the trouble of running off with her purse, he could just peek inside and help himself to what he wanted.

What was she thinking? You need your hands free when you're shopping, she'd tell me.

You might think that a woman who spends her day sending journalists to court to write about men who've cut their girlfriends up into bits and distributed them like Wal-Mart flyers would be aware that there are a lot of not-nice people out there. People who might walk off with a woman's purse while she is debating the merits of onion-and-garlic versus three-cheese pasta sauce.

It was only a matter of time before someone walked off with that purse. So I had a choice to make. Would it be a stranger, or would it be me?

Don't do it, my conscience said. Don't do it.

The incident over the keys, and my hiding her car, seemed largely forgotten. We were talking to each other, Sarah and I. Things had been fairly remarkable between the sheets the last week or so, and I had performed, if I may say so, spectacularly. There was peace in our time.

And yet.

I could stand by the cart, guard the purse while Sarah perused sauce. But what about next time, when I wasn't with her? While she had her back turned for only a minute, someone would quietly loop his hand around the strap and tuck that purse inside his jacket.

I had the power to do something instructive. Something helpful.

I sidled past the cart, empty but for a package of low-fat cookies. Was Sarah about to make us all start watching our calories? I came up alongside her and said, "You almost done?"

"I thought it wouldn't hurt to pick up a couple of extra things. You know how you walk around, you see things you need that you forgot you needed."

"Uh-huh," I said, sneaking a look back at the cart. "Look," I said. "If you don't mind, since it looks like you're going to be in here longer than you originally planned, I'm going to go wait for you in the car."

"Yeah, sure, whatever," she said, grabbing a bottle of extra-spicy sauce. "Do we like this?"

"The kids hate it," I said. I turned and walked away. As I went past the cart, I grabbed hold of the purse in one smooth motion, clutching it with my left hand, sweeping it under my jacket, and holding it there with my right arm. I sailed up the rest of the aisle, trying not to look too suspicious. I suspect that most purse snatchers look the part, their eyes darting back and forth, the whole furtive-glance thing. My expression was different. I looked smug. I had on one of those smiles, not where your teeth show, but where your lips are pressed together and your cheeks puff out. A self-satisfied smirk. A real son-of-a-bitch grin.

I exited past the newsstand, the automatic doors parting before me, still holding the purse tight against my body under my jacket. I didn't want anyone to see me walking with it, not because someone might think I was stealing a purse, but because no guy wants to be seen holding a purse for any reason, even a legitimate one.

With my left hand I reached into my jacket pocket and withdrew my car keys. I pushed the button on the remote key that pops the trunk, and as I approached our Toyota, the rear lid gently yawned. I lifted it open wider, leaned over the cavity, and let the purse slip out.

It was heavy. This was the other thing about Sarah's purse. The odd time when she does hand it to me, I can't believe how much it weighs. Half of this, she tells me, is change. Whenever she gets change, rather than take the time to put it into the zippered pouch of her wallet, she just throws it into the bottom of her purse. It's like the bottom of a fountain in there, only not as wet.

I wasn't too worried about hiding her purse in the trunk. I knew that when she came out from the store, she wouldn't have any groceries to put in there, because by then she'd have found out she had no way to pay for them. This, I told myself, was going to be absolutely beautiful.

I got in behind the wheel, slipped the key into the ignition, and turned on the radio, not really listening to what was playing. I was overwhelmed by a tingly, anticipatory feeling, not unlike the sensation I had as a child when I would hide in my sister Cindy's bedroom closet after school, waiting for her to come upstairs. I'd crouch in there, trying not to move or breathe for fear of rattling the hangers, waiting for the door to open, so I could spring out, scream "Ahhhhh!" and relish Cindy's look of horror and amazement. That was how I felt, sitting out there in the car, in the parking lot of Mindy's Market, waiting for Sarah to come out, to get in the car with her own look of horror and amazement, to tell me that when she went to put her sauce in the cart, she discovered that her purse was gone.

I wasn't sure how long to let this go on. Not very, I figured. Just long enough to make the point. She'd be angry, no doubt, but later, I had a hunch she'd thank me. She'd realize that when you've got a choice between having your purse snatched by your husband and someone you don't know, there are fewer credit cards to cancel when it's the former.

The car was parked in such a way that I could see the store in my rear-view mirror, and I kept watching for Sarah. "Come on," I whispered.

And then suddenly there she was, striding toward the car.

"Showtime!" I said to myself.

There was no purse slung over her shoulder and, consequently, no groceries. Not looking very happy, but yet, not as unhappy as I'd expected her to look. Not running, no look of panic about her, exactly. Maybe she was on to me. Maybe she'd spotted me running off with her purse but hadn't let on. Maybe she was looking to turn the tables on me again.

She came up the passenger side, opened the door, and got in.

"God," she said.

I was hesitant. "What?"

"We have to go to General Mart. I couldn't believe their price on romaine. I don't care if we can afford it, I'm just not going to pay that kind of price. It's an outrage."

"But what about the other stuff?"

"They didn't have the fabric softener I like, and by then I didn't even check the steaks. I knew we'd have to go someplace else, so I just put back the sauce and decided to hell with it. So let's go."

Okay, I thought. So she hadn't even needed her wallet, which meant she didn't have to go into her purse, which meant she hadn't even noticed that it was missing. It's really terrible when you've got a surprise all worked out and the victim won't cooperate.

As I backed out of the spot and turned left out of the lot, heading for General Mart, I pondered how long I wanted to let this play out. When she got to the checkout line at General? I didn't know that I could wait that long for the payoff. I wanted Sarah to learn her lesson now. The point would get made, I'd get my sense of satisfaction, and Sarah could start getting indignant right away, instead of later.

We were coming up on a light when I said, ever so casually, "Uh, where's your purse?"

And Sarah's whole body stiffened for a second, the way mine used to when I'd be on the subway and, for a moment, think I'd misplaced my wallet, and my stomach would do cartwheels. But I could reach around at those moments and feel my back pocket and be reassured that my wallet was in its proper place. Sarah was going to have no such option.

But then she laughed. A short chortle.

"I almost forgot," she said. "I didn't bring it."

The light turned yellow and I slowed. As it turned red, I said, "What do you mean, you didn't bring it?"

"Well, it's so heavy, I've started using this." She leaned back in the seat, opened up her jacket, and pointed to the black leather pouch she had strapped to her waist.

"What the hell is that?"

"You won't believe this, but I finally decided to listen to you. I think it was that story about the woman who lost her winning lottery ticket in her purse that did it for me. Not that I've got a winning ticket. But this forced me to pare down all that useless crap I always carry around, and my shoulder even feels better not carrying all that weight, plus I don't have to keep my eye out for my purse all the time. Sometimes you're not the big stupid idiot everyone says you are."

11

❖ ❖ ❖

"What's wrong, Zack?" Sarah asked. "You don't look so good."

"I'm fine," I said.

"You sure? You seem a bit off."

I wasn't sure at all. In fact, I thought there was an excellent chance that I would be sick all over the dashboard at any moment. "No, I'm just fine."

"I don't know where they get off, charging that much for romaine. Do they think that people don't shop around, that we don't know that if we go down the street a ways we can get it for less? Maybe it's a convenience thing. They figure people don't mind paying more for something if it means they don't have to bother to go someplace else. But if you're getting several things, and you can save money on all of them, it just makes sense to go someplace else. Anyway, General has a pretty good butcher's counter, so we can get steaks there every bit as good as Mindy's." There was a long pause. "Are you not talking to me, or what?"

"Yeah, I'm talking to you."

"Tell me again what you got done on your book today."

"Oh, some last-minute editing stuff. Finishing the last chapter. I'll probably send it to Tom by the end of next week."

"Are you happy with it?" Sarah asked.

"Yeah, sure, I guess. I don't know. Probably not." I glanced over at Sarah in time to see her shake her head and smile.

"You're always like this when you finish a book," she said. "You read through it and think it's the worst thing anybody's ever written."

"Even I didn't think it was that bad."

"You know what I mean. You're your own worst critic. Is that what's got you? Letdown?"

"I never said I was down."

"You just seem a bit off, that's all I'm saying."

I didn't say anything. I had a lot on my mind. Jail, for example. As we drove to General Mart, I found myself looking in the rear-view mirror more than I usually do. I figured someone would be after me. Someone *should* be after me.

I had, after all, stolen something. But I was not, I told myself, a purse snatcher. Not technically. A purse snatcher was someone who ripped handbags from the clutches of their owners, usually little old ladies who didn't have the strength to hang on to them and who got knocked down in the process, suffering a broken hip. I had broken no little old hips.

I drove for a while without saying anything,

then: "You're sure you didn't bring your purse?"

"Huh?"

"Your purse. You're sure you didn't bring it along, out of habit, even though you're wearing that thing on your waist?"

"A fanny pack."

"Pardon?"

"It's called a fanny pack."

I glanced down at her lap. "That doesn't make any sense at all. It doesn't hang over your fanny. It hangs over your, well, it hangs over your front. Maybe they thought 'crotch pack' didn't have as nice a ring to it."

"They also call them waist bags, but that sounds like something somebody with a colostomy wears," Sarah said. "Do you not like my fanny pack?"

"It's fine. I like it. I just don't understand why you decided to stop carrying a purse. You have a lot of stuff. You can't get everything you need into a little bag like that. You *need* a purse." I seemed to be running out of breath. "You should really be carrying a purse."

"Let me ask you a serious question," Sarah said.

"Yeah?"

"Have you lost your mind?"

"No, all I'm saying is, this is a bit of a shock. You live with someone for almost twenty years, you see her carrying a purse every day, which is, like, a hundred thousand days or something, and then, one day, without warning, she decides to go around with a fanny pack. I just, I don't know, I would have liked a little warning is all."

Sarah looked at me and said nothing. There was a long pause, and then she said, "You know you just drove past General Mart."

I glanced around, saw the market over my shoulder, and said, "Shit." There was one of those concrete medians down the center of the street, which meant I had to go up a full block and make a left before I could turn around.

"I still say there's something wrong with you," Sarah said. And then, like a bulb going off: "That reminds me. All this talk about purses."

"What."

"In the store, after you left, there was this woman, she started going absolutely nuts."

"What woman?" But I had a feeling I already knew. A blonde lady, looking at garbage bags, who liked low-fat cookies.

"She was just up the aisle from me."

"What did she look like?"

If Sarah thought this question was unusual, she didn't let on. "I don't know, mid-twenties, thin, blonde hair. Wearing a white suit. She looked kind of familiar to me, actually."

"You know her?" This was hopeful. With a name, I could get this purse returned right away.

"No, I just felt I'd seen her someplace before. So she goes, 'Where's my purse?' You know, screaming that her purse is missing, and she looks totally frantic, which I guess I would be too if someone grabbed my purse."

"What do you mean, grabbed it? Did she *see* someone take her purse?"

"I don't know. You just assume, I guess. She called down to me, standing by her cart, asks if I've seen her purse, like I'm keeping track of her stuff, and I guess I shrugged no, and then she ran to the front of the store, and that was the last I saw of her." Sarah took a breath, made a funny expression with her mouth, like she wanted to say something but didn't know how.

"So it's like I said," she said.

I was making a left at the light and heading back toward General. "Whaddya mean?"

"Well, you're the one who's always telling me not to leave my purse in the cart, and that's probably what that woman had done, and someone happened along and just took it. You only have to be looking away for a second and it's gone. And the hassle! You have to cancel all your credit cards, get a new driver's license and God knows what all. And then there's your keys. You figure, a guy takes your purse, he looks at your license and knows where you live, and he's got your keys. I mean, most guys probably take the cash and ditch the purse, but there's always that chance, right?"

"I suppose," I said, pulling into a parking spot.

"So what I'm saying is, you were right. I guess it was just lucky that today I happened to be wearing this fanny pack, or it might have been my purse that got swiped instead of that lady's."

"Yeah," I said. "Lucky."

"Are you coming in or waiting out here?" Sarah asked, her hand on the door handle.

Come in or stay out? Come in or stay out? I had this small matter of a strange woman's purse in the trunk of the car. If I went in with Sarah, there'd be no opportunity for me to get rid of the purse before we came back out to the car, popped the trunk, and Sarah asked, "Whose is that?"

"Let me tell you about my new hobby, honey," I could say. "I collect handbags now. From strangers. Sometimes they contain valuable prizes."

But if I stayed with the car, what exactly was I going to do with the purse? I could hide it under the trunk floor, jam it in next to the spare tire. Or maybe I —

"I have an idea," I said. "How long do you think you're going to be?"

Sarah shrugged. "I don't know. Fifteen, twenty minutes maybe."

"Maybe I'll whip over to Kenny's. You know I ordered that model of the dropship from *Aliens*? The one the Marines ride to get to the planet's surface?"

Sarah shrugged again. The mere mention of SF trivia was enough to shut down any further questions. She said, "Sure. Just pick me up at the door here."

And she was gone. I backed the car out of the

spot and pointed it back in the direction of Mindy's. While I was not yet prepared to come clean with Sarah, I figured if I could find the woman in the white suit, an honest approach was the best one. If she was still at Mindy's, I'd tell her my wife had asked me to take her purse to the car, and that I'd gone to the wrong cart and grabbed the wrong one. Not the truth, exactly, except for the part about making a mistake.

And it was an honest mistake. There had been no intent to steal anything. When you grab your own wife's purse, even if, technically speaking, she is not aware of it, surely that's not stealing. This was like, I told myself, going out to the parking lot, seeing a car that was the same make and model and year of your own. Suppose, just suppose, your key happened to work in this other car, and you got in, and started it up, and drove away, well, that wouldn't be stealing, would it? Anyone with an ounce of common sense could understand that. And this thing with the purse wasn't any different, so long as no one noticed that when I left the store I hid the purse under my jacket, and that I had looked about me suspiciously as I dumped it into my trunk, like I was dropping a dead baby in there.

I parked and hit the lock button on the remote key. I didn't want anyone else making off with my stolen purse. I passed by a kid who was rounding up shopping carts and went into the store, hoping that the woman might still be there. Talking to the manager, perhaps. What I dreaded was that she might have already called the police, but I saw no patrol cars in the lot, and a quick scan of the line of checkouts showed no officers. I did the same routine as when I was looking for Sarah, walking past the end of each aisle, looking from the front of the store to the back. I slowed as I went past the aisle where Sarah had been looking at pasta sauces and the woman with the blonde hair had been checking out garbage bags. There, still halfway down the aisle, was the shopping cart with nothing but a box of cookies in it.

For a moment I thought, Just put the purse back. Drop it back in the cart, let someone else find it. Maybe the woman would come back later, check with store management, and they'd tell her, "Lady, it was right there where you'd left it. If it had been a dog it woulda bit ya."

All I had to do was nip back to the car, smuggle the purse back in, place it in the cart and —

And then the kid I'd seen rounding up shopping carts out in the parking lot appeared at the end of the aisle, reached for the box of cookies to put it back on the shelf, and hauled the cart back to the front of the store.

Out of desperation, I made one more round of Mindy's, but the woman was clearly gone. Although I'd hoped to resolve this situation by talking to no one other than the woman herself, which would have been awkward enough, I could see now I was going to have to make some inquiries.

I approached the woman at the express checkout. "Excuse me," I said, "but is the manager around?"

She pointed. "Checkout 10. Wendy."

There, I found a heavyset woman in a "Shop at Mindy's!" apron ringing through an elderly couple's groceries. Her name tag read "Wendy."

"Pardon me," I said, coming around from the bagging side. Wendy grabbed one item after another, passing them over the scanner. The couple both looked at me, wondering who the hell I thought I was, interrupting their business this way.

"Hmm?" said Wendy.

"Was there a woman here, about ten minutes ago, who'd lost her purse?"

"At this checkout?"

"No no. Not right here. But in the store. I understand there was a woman all upset about losing her purse."

Wendy kept advancing the conveyor belt, scanning items, not looking at me. "I heard something, but she didn't ask me about it."

"Maybe she talked to someone else? Or called the police?"

"If she talked to anyone else, they would have let me know about it, and if anyone called the police, you can be damn sure I'd hear about it."

"You're sure?"

Wendy took her eyes off what she was doing long enough to give me a look that seemed to suggest that this was the sort of thing a person might remember, especially if it happened in the last five minutes. "Okay," I said. "Thanks." And I turned in a hurry, thinking that I better get back to the other grocery store, where Sarah might already be waiting out front for me. I got back in the car and started the engine, but before putting it in drive took a moment to assess the situation.

Why hadn't the woman gone to the store management to report her purse missing? She'd had a fit in the aisle. Sarah had seen that much. But what had she done after that? Maybe she'd gone out to her car, thinking she'd left the purse there. But she wouldn't have been able to get into her car, of course, because the keys were most likely in the purse. Unless she didn't have a car, and walked to do her grocery shopping. There were hundreds of houses within walking distance of Mindy's. It was about a fifteen-minute walk from our neighborhood. So maybe she walked back home, thinking that her purse hadn't been swiped, but that she'd forgotten it. But if she got home and found her door locked, she'd know she had her keys with her when she left, which would mean that she'd left home with her purse. And if she'd had her purse when she left, and didn't have it now, that meant that yes, someone had swiped it.

And furthermore: Who's on first?

Was there a point to this line of thinking?

There was an easy way to solve this, I told myself. Get the purse out of the trunk, check the wallet for a name and an address, go to her house, return the purse, offer a million apologies, hope to Christ she had a sense of humor.

An excellent plan. But first, I had to pick up Sarah. She had said she'd be fifteen or twenty minutes, and I was pushing half an hour now. As I feared, Sarah was already standing out front, weighed down with four white plastic shopping bags.

"Pop the trunk," she mouthed from the other side of the passenger-door window.

Shit shit shit shit shit. Wasn't this what went through my mind only half an hour earlier? That Sarah would come out and want to put the groceries in the trunk? Of course, my plan back then (it seemed like hours ago) was that by now the purse would be back with its rightful owner.

I shouted, "Just throw them in the back!"

"What?"

I fumbled with the power window switches on the armrest under my left hand. First I put down the left rear window, then the right rear, then the window where Sarah was standing. She had that tired, why-did-I-marry-him look on her face. "You figured it out, huh?"

"Just throw the stuff in the back seat," I said. She sighed, opened the rear door, and set the bags on the floor. She slammed it shut and got in the front.

"Sorry I'm late," I said.

Sarah nodded. "Did you get anything?"

"Hmm?"

"At Kenny's. Did you get anything? Did the drop-thingy come in?"

"No," I said. "It hadn't come in. But it's hard to get, they stopped making it years ago, and Kenny doesn't even know for sure whether he can get one. I'll just have to keep looking around, you know? Like, maybe next time we go to New York, I can check that shop down in Greenwich Village, the comic store that had all the really obscure model kits?"

"Whatever," Sarah said. "I got the steaks, and some romaine, which was, if you can believe this, the same price as it was at Mindy's, there must be, like, a frost or something in California, I don't know, and the other stuff I needed, plus I got some more frozen pizzas. I bought five of them on the weekend, and I looked in the fridge last night and there wasn't a single one left."

"Don't look at me."

"The kids must be making them after we go to bed. I make them dinner, they say they're not hungry, that they went out for lunch, or had a snack at someone's house after school, and then at ten o'clock they're in the kitchen heating up pizzas. It makes me crazy."

I said nothing the rest of the way home. I knew Sarah was still thinking there was something wrong with me, but she wasn't going to bring it up again. She grabbed the bags from the back seat while I went to open the front door, but it was already unlocked. There were several pairs of shoes in the front hall, kicked about haphazardly, which meant Paul and Angie had brought some friends home with them. As Sarah went past me into the kitchen, I said, "Hang on, I think I left something in the car. I'll be back in a second."

I pressed the trunk button on the remote and watched it swing open. I reached inside and grabbed the purse in my right hand. This was the first time I'd had my hand on it since learning it wasn't Sarah's, and it was like touching ice. A chill swept over me.

"Stupid stupid stupid stupid stupid," I whispered to myself.

Of course, now that I knew it didn't belong to Sarah, I realized that the purse did not look familiar to me. It was a dark brown leather bag, and Sarah's tastes ran to black and deep blue. To Sarah, this would be one of the more moronic aspects of this crime. I could almost hear her now: "If you'd been asked to kidnap *me,* instead of steal a purse, would you have been able to pick me out of a crowd? Or would you have come home with the housecoat lady?"

Again, I tried tucking it under my jacket, which looked almost as ridiculous as if I'd simply carried it out in the open. But I was able to get through the front door and into my study without Sarah seeing me, although she heard me and called out, "You want to start up the barbecue so we can do these steaks and then help me rinse this lettuce?"

"Yeah, in a minute," I said, slipping the purse out from under my jacket.

About then, Paul and three of his friends — Andy, Hakim, and Darryl — came bounding down the stairs from his bedroom, rounding the corner and heading for the door to the basement. Darryl had several video-game cartridge boxes in his hand, indicating to me that they were planning to park themselves in front of the downstairs television for the next several hours. Andy caught a glimpse of me as he passed the study door and shouted, "Hey, Mr. Walker!"

"Hi, guys," I said.

"Nice purse, Mr. Walker," Andy said. "Suits you."

My heart skipped a beat. "Thanks," I said, closing the door. I flicked on the desk lamp next to the keyboard, sat down in my writing chair, and set the purse on the table.

Sitting there, in the quiet of my study, the video game noises in the basement and the soft sounds of water running in the kitchen both muted by the closed door, with the handbag of a woman I did not know on the desk in front of me, I began to sweat. I took a couple of deep breaths, letting them both out slowly, in a bid to get my heart rate down a bit.

"Relax," I said. Okay, I had done a stupid thing, a really stupid thing. But this was a problem that could be solved. In short order.

Before Sarah got wind of it and had something she could lord over me the rest of our marriage.

I unzipped the top of the purse and peered inside. I didn't want to look very closely. I had a sense of the invasion I was perpetrating. All I wanted was a wallet. For a name and an address. The purse had some heft to it, there was a lot of stuff in there, but my interests were very specific. I just wanted to track down the owner.

There were some tissues, a couple of white tubes down in the bottom I realized were tampons (oh man), a film canister, a couple of letter-size white envelopes stuffed with papers, a small makeup bag, a set of car keys with a "VW" emblem on the side, and a red leather wallet. Gingerly, I reached into the bag and took it out.

I unsnapped and opened it. There was the usual assortment of credit cards. I took one out, a Visa, and read the name: Stefanie Knight. Okay, Stefanie, now we just have to find out where you live. I rooted around in the wallet. There was a twenty and a five, a mini-pocket for coins that was heavy with pennies, and there, tucked in with the cash, was a hard plastic card that looked like a driver's license.

I took it between my thumb and forefinger and held it under the lamp. Her photo wasn't terribly flattering; driver's license pictures never are. Her hair wasn't quite as blonde when it was taken, and there were dark lines under her eyes, like the picture was taken during a police lineup rather than at the DMV. But there was a passing resemblance to the woman in the off-white suit that I'd walked past in the grocery store.

And I had the same feeling, looking at the photo, that Sarah said she'd had upon seeing the woman, that she knew her from someplace. I studied the photo for several seconds, tried to place her. I felt as though I'd seen her someplace recently, but exactly when and where wouldn't come to me. It's like when you see your mailman at the mall; you know you know him, but seeing him out of context throws you, hinders recognition.

Next to the photo was her actual license number, a long jumble of numbers and letters, and below that, her name — KNIGHT, STEFANIE J. — and an Oakwood address on a street I didn't know: 2223 Deer Prance Drive. If not our own neighborhood, it sounded like a street in a new development someplace.

So, I had a name and an address. All that was left was for me to do my civic duty and return the purse to her. In an hour, this would all be over, and there'd be nothing else to do but laugh about it.

12

❖ ❖ ❖

I wrote Stefanie Knight's address on a piece of paper and tucked it into my pocket. Then I put the wallet back into the purse. I was going to have to take the purse back out to the car again, and needed something to put it in so I wouldn't have to keep hiding it under my jacket. I opened the closet in my office and found, tucked way in the back, a Nike gym bag that was stuffed with some old track pants, sweat socks, and a couple of T-shirts. It brought back memories of a time when I believed in physical fitness.

I yanked the clothes out to make room for the purse, felt myself getting a bit queasy, and then wondered whether it wasn't bad enough that I had stolen Stefanie Knight's purse. Did I have to return it smelling like moldy cheese?

So I threw my clothes back into the gym bag and looked for something else. I found a heavy-weight plastic shopping bag with a drawstring top that had come from a shoe store, and stuffed the handbag into that.

I had a map book in the car to help me find

Deer Prance Drive. Hanging on to the bag from the drawstring, I slipped out the study door, careful not to be glimpsed from the kitchen, and made my way out to the front step. I'd toss the bag into the car and —

"Hey," said Sarah. She was standing at the end of the driveway. How did she get out there? Did she have a transporter in the kitchen? And she was talking to Trixie, dressed in a pair of jeans and a sweatshirt.

"Oh, you're out here," I said. Trixie gave me a knowing smile.

"Zack," Trixie said.

"Trixie was telling me you guys had coffee the other day."

I nodded. Things seemed to be spinning.

"You people who work from home," Sarah said, pretending to scowl. "No bosses to answer to, coffee breaks whenever you want them. No commute into the city. I should be so lucky. What I don't get is, and this is something I've talked about with Zack, when you work from home, don't you start feeling isolated, with no coworkers to talk to?"

"Well," Trixie said, "that's not always the case."

"Sure," I said. "I'm on the phone a lot through the day. You're still talking to people, even if it's not face-to-face."

"Of course, you have people coming to your house," Sarah said to Trixie.

"That's right. And it can get pretty busy, they

185

start stacking up like planes."

Sarah chuckled. "You know, I wouldn't miss commuting in to *The Metropolitan*. Maybe you could use an assistant."

Trixie nodded with mock enthusiasm. "Sounds great. I'd be happy to show you the ropes."

"I really should get going," I said.

"Where would that be, exactly?" Sarah asked. "I thought you were going to start the barbecue for the steaks. And what's in the bag? You taking back some shoes?"

"No, it's an old bag. I've got something in here to take back to Kenny's."

"You were just there."

"I know. I was telling him that that Batman kit I bought a while ago came without some of the parts it was supposed to have, and he said trying to order individual parts would be impossible, so he said just return the whole kit and he'll try to get a replacement."

"And you need to do this now."

"He closes pretty soon, and I was thinking I might work on it tonight, after dinner."

"I always liked Batman," Trixie said. "Although I guess my favorite was Catwoman. Something about the outfit."

Sarah sighed. "If you can, be fast, 'cause I'm getting hungry."

I tossed the bag into the back seat, then worried Sarah would look in it. But so long as she believed it had something to do with Batman, I was safe. "I'll just get the barbecue going," I said, and ran back into the house, through the kitchen, and out through the glass doors to the deck. I opened the lid on the barbecue, turned on the gas, and, forever the optimist, pressed the red ignition button.

Nothing.

I clicked it a second time, then a third. "Goddamn thing." Why did I think it would suddenly start working now, just because I had an urgent errand to run? This'll work forever, the salesman said when we bought it. How long ago had that been? Three months, four?

By now, there was enough propane circulating in the atmosphere that if the red button beat the odds and actually worked on the fourth try, they'd be picking up pieces of me in Trixie's backyard. I turned the valve off hard, waved my hand around to disperse the gas, and went into the house for some matches. Confident there was no leftover propane hanging around in the atmosphere, I turned the gas back on and immediately dropped a lit match into the bottom of the barbecue. There was a soft "poof" as the flame ignited.

I got the burners on both sides going, then lowered the lid to let the heat build up.

Paul and his buddies were coming into the kitchen as I came through the glass doors. "What's to eat?" Paul asked.

"I'm just heating up the barby," I said. "If your friends want hot dogs or something, I think we've got some in the fridge. I've got to go out for a few minutes."

"Don't forget your purse," said Andy, who was already into our fridge like it was his own. "You got any Coke?"

"Dad," Paul said. "You got a sec?"

I didn't, but I stopped anyway. "Yeah?"

"Angie told me she told you what I wanted to do."

I was trying to remember. "Maybe you could refresh my memory."

"About a tattoo."

"No."

"No, she didn't tell you?"

"Yes, she told me, and no, you can't get one."

Paul was crestfallen. "Can we, like, talk about this?"

"We are talking about this. And I'm saying no."

"I don't believe this. You haven't even heard me out. You don't even know what I'm asking for."

"Are you asking whether you can get a tattoo?"

"Maybe, yeah, but —"

"You're too young. You need my permission, I think, at any reputable tattoo parlor, to get a tattoo at your age, and I'm not signing."

"Everyone has them, Dad. It's not a big deal."

"I'd love to discuss this with you, but I have an errand to run."

"Sure. Walk away."

I grabbed my cell phone off the table by the front door and slid it into my jacket pocket on the way out, didn't stop to chat with Sarah and Trixie, who were still at the end of the drive, and squealed out.

Once I was down around the corner on Lilac, where I couldn't be seen, I pulled over and got out the map book. Deer Prance Drive was on the other side of Oakwood. I got across town in about fifteen minutes and found that Stefanie Knight's house was in a new development that was every bit as architecturally fascinating as our own, except this one was completely finished, no uncovered foundations, no houses waiting for sod.

Deer Prance was off Autumn Leaves Lane (God almighty, where would it end?), and as I turned onto it, I leaned back in the seat enough that I could reach into the front pocket of my jeans and fish out the piece of paper with the street number on it. There was still another hour of sunlight, and the house numbers were easy to read.

Deer Prance was a street of relatively new townhouses, and I found 2223 on the left side, about two-thirds of the way down. The driveway already had an old Ford Escort in it, and there was no room either behind or next to it for my car, so I found a spot at the curb.

As I got out of the car, the drawstring of the bag looped around my hand, I noticed that for a new development, this stretch already had a slightly run-down look. The paint was peeling on some of the garage doors, one car up the street was on blocks, and tucked out of the way between 2223 and 2225 were a rusted-out stove and an abandoned tricycle.

As I mounted the steps, I noticed two cases of empty beer bottles, just outside the door, waiting to be taken back to the store. There was an aluminum screen door between me and the wooden front door, but I didn't have to pull it open to knock. There was no glass or screen in it, so I rapped directly on the wood.

I could hear some talking inside, and a radio going, but no sound of approaching footsteps. After about ten seconds, I knocked again.

Inside, a woman's voice: *"Jimmy!"*

A pause, a young man's voice, from somewhere deeper in the house, perhaps upstairs: "What?"

"Door!"

"Get it yourself! I still can't find Quincy!"

"Jesus, why the fuck did you let him out anyway?"

"Get the frickin' door yourself, your legs broken?"

"You better find him lickety-split!"

I heard some padding toward the door, and then it opened only a crack.

"Yeah?" I saw a sliver of a woman's face. One eye, a cheek, half a mouth.

"Uh, hi. I was looking for Stefanie?"

"Stef? You're looking for Stef?"

Stef. Now that rang a bell.

"Yes," I said. "Would she be in?"

"I'm gonna invite you in," the woman said. "But when I open the door, you have to come in real fast. Y'understand?"

Hesitantly, I said, "Sure."

And then the door swung open wide, the woman grabbed me by the wrist and dragged me inside, then closed the door forcefully. I was going to have to be fitted with a whiplash collar.

"I don't want Quincy to get out," she said. I glanced around the floor, looking for a little dog or cat, but saw nothing.

This woman might have been fifty, but it had been a hard fifty. Her hair was gray and pinned back, and she wore a white short-sleeved blouse with enough grease stains to qualify it as a Jackson Pollock. Her short sleeves revealed meaty shoulders and upper arms.

"So you want Stef?" The woman cocked her head just a little, looked me up and down, and her eyes danced darkly.

From upstairs: "Is it for me, Mom?"

"No!" Not taking her eyes off me. "Just keep looking!" She sighed. "She don't live here," she said coolly, glancing down at the plastic bag that hung from my wrist.

"Oh. Okay. See, I had this address for her, but if I've got the wrong house . . ."

"You got the right house. But she don't live here no more. She hant lived here for a couple years at least. What's your business with her?"

I wasn't sure whether to say. So instead I

asked, "Would you happen to be Stefanie's mother?"

"Yeah."

"I had something I had to return to her, and was going to drop it off here, but if she doesn't live here, maybe you could tell me where I might find her."

"Is it whatever you got in the bag there?"

"Maybe if you had an address?"

The woman jerked her head to motion me further inside. I followed her into a narrow kitchen where the sink was stacked with dishes and a cigarette sat burning in an ashtray on a table that was part of an aging aluminum and formica set that couldn't have been original to this house. The table surface, what you could see of it, given the number of empty beer and wine bottles, was pockmarked with cigarette burns. "Just follow me," she said.

There were more burns on the cracked linoleum floor and several places where it had been gouged, revealing plywood underneath. The counter next to the overloaded sink was littered with more dishes and more empty beer bottles and crumpled Big Mac cartons flecked with shreds of lettuce and smears of Special Sauce.

"Like I said, she hasn't lived here for, I don't know, a couple years now."

She'd never notified the DMV of a change of address, I figured. It occurred to me that maybe she didn't come from a home where a high priority was placed on attending to such details.

"Whaddya say your name was?"

"Walker," I said. "Zack Walker."

"You look a bit old for Stef."

Well, I thought, not necessarily. Just how old did she think I looked? I mean, surely it was not un-heard-of for some men in their early forties to at-tract a woman who appeared to be in her mid- to late twenties. Maybe I didn't work out a lot, and perhaps I could stand to lose a few pounds, but —

Shut up, I told myself.

"We're not, you know, going out or anything," I said. "I just needed to give her something. Maybe I could leave it with you."

"I dunno. Like I said, she don't live here, and she does drop by occasionally but I don't know when. She's so busy, you know, buying her fancy clothes and working for her fancy boss. Hasn't got time to come by here, unless she needs some money, of course. And I'm betting she's making enough that she could pay me back some, be-cause I've got my own expenses, raising her little brother here on my own after Victor left us high and dry, don't you know."

That's when I decided I couldn't leave the purse here. I didn't know the history between this woman and her daughter, but it was a safe bet that as soon as I handed that purse over, this woman was going to take whatever cash was in it, and I didn't want that to be my fault.

I said, "You know, I'll probably be running into her again soon, so I won't bother you with this."

"You work with Stef? You one of those realtor people?"

"Realtor? No. Where does Stef work?"

"Over at one of them new developments. In the office. Forest Estates it's called."

"Valley Forest Estates?"

"I think."

And then I remembered. The receptionist who didn't want me to see Greenway. Small frickin' world.

"Well then, I'll just pop into the sales office," I said. "It's not far from where I live. You see, we were in the checkout line at Mindy's, and she was going through her wallet and I didn't notice until she was gone that she had dropped her driver's license, so I grabbed it, and this was the address that was on it, which was why I just dropped by here, you know, to give it back to her."

Stefanie Knight's mother looked at me, then at the shoe bag I was carrying. Was it big enough to carry an entire driver's license?

"Or, you know, if you could let me know where I could find her, I could drop this off even before I run into her next time, because, you know, if she gets pulled over or something and has to show her license to the cops, well, I'd hate to see that happen."

"You think the cops want to talk to her again?"

"Oh no, heck, I wasn't suggesting that. Just for a ticket, they set up these radar traps all over the neighborhood, you know, getting their quota, whatever."

"That's what you got in that big bag there? Stef's driver's license?"

"No, no." I paused. "I just bought some new shoes."

"And you brung them with you to the door?" She cracked a smile, called out, "Hey, Jimmy, man's got a new pair of shoes he wants to show ya."

"Listen, how about if you tell me where I can find her, and just in case she calls here before I find her, I'll leave you my name and —"

I would have said more, but I felt something large and heavy drag across the back of my legs, exerting a kind of pressure, and then, while the pressure was being maintained on the back of my legs, felt something press against the front of them down by my ankles. And I looked down, and it appeared, at a glance, that a tree trunk was wrapping itself around my legs. And I said:

"God! What the — shit!"

I didn't just stand in one place while I said this. I started jumping up and down, threw myself up against the refrigerator, knocked a box of Froot Loops off the top and to the floor, where the contents scattered across the cracked linoleum, crunching under my feet as I continued dancing about, trying to disentangle myself from what was clearly the biggest fucking snake that ever found its way to North America.

"*Jimmy!*" the woman screamed. "We found Quincy!"

The snake moved away from my legs and slithered its way silently through the table and chair legs, heading for the dining room.

"That's Quincy," Stefanie's mother said. "I think you scared him."

"Jesus!" I said. My heart was pounding so hard I felt it would explode through my jacket like that little critter in the *Alien* movie. "What is that?"

"Quincy's a python," she said. "We were going to name him Monty but that seemed so obvious. He was a gift from one of Stef's old boyfriends, but I gotta tell you, there are days I'm not so sure we wouldn't have been better off with a dog."

Jimmy was barreling down the stairs, running through the kitchen and into the dining room. "Come here, you son of a bitch!"

"He's harmless," she said.

"You're allowed to keep a python?" I said.

The woman frowned. "You're just like everyone else. It's a kind of prejudice, you know? There's a lot of misconceptions about pythons, but the fact is, they can make very nice house pets. I mean, what do you really know about pythons?"

"I've seen enough jungle movies and documentaries on the Discovery Channel to know they like to wrap themselves around you until you can't breathe anymore. And later your friends can't find you but your snake has gained two hundred fucking pounds and looks like he swallowed a Pinto."

"Well, I wouldn't sleep in the same bed with him, if that's what you mean. But Quincy's not really like that. He's a nice python, and he loves us." To her son: "But you know, Jimmy" — wherever he was in the house now — "I think maybe we could use a break from Quincy for a while. Maybe he'd like a little vacation. Give Richard a call, see if he'd like to take him off our hands for a day or so, I can go visit my sister."

I tried to get my breath, my eyes darting about the room. "Maybe you could give me that address."

She shrugged, grabbed a pen and a piece of scratch paper, and scribbled something down. "I don't know the number, but it's on Rambling Rose Circle. She's got a little blue Volkswagen, one of those Beetles, the new kind?"

"Yes," I said. But I wasn't expecting to see a car in the driveway. The VW keys were still in Stefanie Knight's purse, and odds were that the Beetle was still in Mindy's parking lot.

"I think it's the third or fourth house in, on the right," she said.

"Let me borrow your pen," I said. On another piece of paper I wrote down my name, and was about to put down my phone number, when I thought better of it. So far, I'd managed to shield Sarah from the knowledge that she was married to the biggest idiot on the planet. Clarification: It was possible Sarah already understood she was married to the biggest idiot on the planet, but she was still unaware of his most recent stunt. I'd confessed to stupid things in the past, but nothing approaching this. My attempt to teach Sarah a lesson had backfired on such a grand scale that I could see no good in letting her, or the kids, find out about it. The last thing I needed was Stefanie Knight phoning the house, getting Sarah, and asking for me so that she could get her driver's license — if she accepted my story as I'd related it to her mother — or her entire purse back.

So instead of a phone number, I put down my e-mail address. "Just have her contact me there and tell her I have something of hers." I left the piece of paper on the counter by the sink.

"Her driver's license."

"Sure. And a couple of other things. I think she'll know."

"Like I said, I don't think I'll be seeing her. She don't choose to drop by here."

"Maybe if you got a dog," I offered.

She scowled. I turned and went for the front door, stepping gingerly, scanning the floor from side to side, occasionally glancing overhead. There was no sign of Quincy. As I squeezed out the front door, I heard Jimmy shout from the back of the house: *Mom, get the darts!* I ran back to the car as quickly as I could.

Once behind the wheel, I looked at the slip of paper Stefanie's mother had given me. Rambling Rose Circle. When this was all over, and I'd pulled myself together, I was going to call that Carpington guy, our local councilman, and demand that a new bylaw be drafted requiring all future streets to be named "Main" or "South" or "Hill."

I opted to try her house, rather than the Valley Forest Estates sales office. It was, I suspected, long past closing time, and I didn't want this to be hanging over me until the next day. I looked in my map book again and found Rambling Rose, a cul-de-sac on the north side of Oakwood in another newly developed part of town that was even closer to the grocery store than our house. This, I was discovering, was what Oakwood was: one Valley Forest Estates after another. Thousands and thousands of acres stripped of trees and bulldozed flat so a seemingly infinite number of cookie-cutter homes could be built and moved into by families who had fled the city for the good life.

On the way, I stopped at a phone booth and looked for any Knights in the phone book on Rambling Rose, found an S. Knight at number 17, made a note of the phone number on the scrap of paper Stefanie's mother had given me, and got back into the car.

It was getting to be dusk, around 7 p.m., when I pulled up out front. It was everything you'd expect a new home in a new subdivision to be. An all-brick house devoid of any distinctive architectural touches, dropped on a thirty-foot lot. Accommodating the two-car garage and driveway meant that from the street, the house was one huge rectangular door with a couple of windows above it on the second floor. Cement patio stones ran down the left of the garage, leading to a front door.

Slim panels of opaque glass flanked the door, and the one on the left was smashed in halfway down. Someone had kicked it in, presumably, to reach inside and unlock the door. This wasn't, I told myself, as alarming as it might seem. Stefanie must have walked home, or gotten a lift, and without her keys couldn't get into her own house.

I would pay for the glass, I told myself. And any other damages, or cab rides. Whatever. Any expenses Stefanie Knight incurred as a result of my stupidity, I would make them up to her. In addition to offering blanket apologies.

I rang the bell. With the glass broken, I could hear the inside chime clearly.

When no one showed up after about ten seconds, I rang it again. Waited another ten seconds, and knocked on the door. Hard.

I crouched down and put my head in front of the broken glass. "Hello?" I shouted. "Ms. Knight? Anyone home?"

Nothing.

If I had learned anything in the last few days, it was to not go into people's homes unannounced. Even though the front door might be unlocked — even though I had a key that would open it if it wasn't — I was not setting foot in this house without an invitation.

I pulled out my cell phone and the scrap of paper with Stefanie Knight's phone number on it, and punched it in. I held it to my ear, and when I heard it ring, with my other ear I could hear a phone ringing within the house. It was like stereo.

After four rings, the machine kicked in. "Hi, this is Stef. I can't get the phone right now, so please leave a message." I opted not to.

I could have left the purse in the house, tossed it through the broken window, but anyone could break into her place now, so that didn't seem like a plan. Should I drive back to Mindy's and see if she was there, trying to get into her car? Maybe she had a spare set of keys, came home and got them after breaking the window, and had gone back for her Beetle. Or maybe she'd gone to the Valley Forest Estates office to get some help from someone there.

I could drive around trying to find her, but all roads led back here. Maybe it made the most sense to camp out front in the car.

Or, I thought suddenly, instead of a phone message, I could leave a note in her mailbox.

There wasn't enough space left on the scrap of paper, so I went back to the car, grabbed my checkbook from the glove compartment, and tore off the print-free cardboard strip at the back. I wrote, "Dear Ms. Knight: Found your purse, will drop it off at Valley Forest offices tomorrow morning. Zack Walker." And added, again, my e-mail address.

And I walked back up the driveway, around the side of the garage, and slipped it into the metal mailbox, leaving a half-inch of the note exposed beyond the flap so she'd be sure to spot it.

Okay, my work here was done. Already, I felt a weight beginning to lift.

Coming back around the corner of the garage, I happened to look down and spotted something dark and shiny. I stopped, and saw that oil was leaking out from under the double-wide garage door. There was a puddle forming, about the size of a shoe print. Whatever kind of car was in there, it was leaking badly.

But something about it didn't look quite right, so I kneeled down and touched the end of my pinkie into it, and held it in the direction of the streetlight, which had just come on.

It was red.

With my other hand, I reached into my pocket for a tissue and wiped, somewhat furiously, the blood off my finger. I must have done it five times, moving the tissue to a clean spot each time.

I paced back and forth for half a minute, wondering what to do. Down the other side of the garage was a regular door, with a window, and I held my hand up to the glass and looked in. It was dark in there, of course, with very little light getting in, but there was something on the garage floor, down by the big door, and it looked an awful lot like a person.

I ran around to the other side, to the front door, tried it. It was locked, so I reached in through the broken glass, found the deadbolt above the door and turned it, opened the door and charged in.

The route to the inside garage door, which was in the laundry room, took me through the kitchen, and I was there long enough to notice that the sliding glass door to the small backyard was smashed next to the lock. What sense did that make? Why did Stefanie need to break two different windows to get into her house?

Once I reached the laundry room, I opened the door to the garage and ran my hand up the inside wall, looking for a light switch, found it, and flicked it up.

A bare bulb over the center of the garage cast a cold and eerie glow across the room. It was cool. There wasn't much in there. No cars, not even any oil stains on the floor, a few moving boxes stacked along the back wall. There was a weed trimmer, and a lawn mower to deal with that small backyard. Hanging on hooks screwed into the wall were a garden rake, a hoe, and one of those claw things you see advertised on TV that stir up topsoil while you're still standing. Paul had made me buy him one. One hook was empty, but it was probably where Stefanie normally hung the shovel that had been used to smash in the side of her head.

She was stretched out pointing toward the driveway, the side of her face laying in the blood that was slowly finding its way under the garage door. There were gashes on the sides of her hands, perhaps where she'd deflected earlier blows from the blood-splattered shovel left on the floor next to her.

"Stefanie?" I said.

Then my cell phone started ringing from inside my jacket.

13

❖ ❖ ❖

"I believe," said Sarah, "that the barbecue is now ready for the steaks. I believe it's possible that the barbecue has been ready for the steaks for the better part of an hour. I would hazard a guess that we have used enough propane since you left to keep a family of four in Iceland warm for the better part of a December. The salad leaves are washed and dried and sitting in a bowl. Your children have decided that they've waited long enough to eat, and left five minutes ago with Paul's friends for McDonald's. I, however, thought it would be rude to leave and find dinner elsewhere, or cook up a steak on my own, and leave you to eat all by yourself when you came home, if you were ever to decide to do such a thing." She paused. "Are you there?"

"Yeah," I said. The splotches of blood on Stefanie Knight's off-white suit looked black as night.

"So are you coming home or what? Or should I go ahead and eat without you?"

"I think you should probably go ahead and eat without me."

I could hear Sarah breathe in, startled. "What's wrong? Oh God, have you had an accident or something?"

"No, I'm okay. I just kind of got into a thing, and I'm going to be a little bit delayed, that's all."

"What sort of a thing?" Sarah was over being sarcastic. Now she was worried.

"Uh, it's Kenny," I said.

"What about Kenny?"

"His wife. She's been sick, and we got talking, and I couldn't just walk out on the guy, you know. He needed someone to talk to."

"Oh, that's terrible," Sarah said. "What's wrong with her?"

"It's, uh, you know, a thing. One of those female things."

"Is she in the hospital?"

"Yeah, she's in the hospital. He was going to go see her as soon as he closed up the shop."

"Is she having an operation? A hysterectomy? Is it cancer?"

For a writer, I was having a hard time making this up as I went along. The black puddle on the concrete garage floor was getting larger, ever so slowly.

"I think it's some sort of an injury," I said. "She might have fallen."

Sarah was thinking. "So it's a female thing, but it might be an injury. What did she do,

Zack? Fall on her uterus?"

"I could have some of the details wrong. Kenny doesn't seem to know. Or at least he didn't tell me."

I could picture Sarah shaking her head on the other end of the line. Even though she'd never met Kenny's wife (I had never met Kenny's wife; I wasn't even sure that Kenny *had* a wife), that didn't make her any less sympathetic.

"You're a good friend of his," Sarah said. "I mean, God knows, you're in his store all the time. You tell him that if there's anything we can do, just ask."

"I'll do that. He'll appreciate that."

"Just take whatever time you need. We'll do up the steaks when you get home."

"No, you go ahead and eat. I'm not, honestly, I'm not even that hungry anymore."

"Okay. I'll see you when I see you."

I pressed the "end" button on the phone, but I didn't slip it back into my jacket. I held it in my hand for a moment, thinking that it was time to press 911. This was no crank call. I wasn't pretending to be dead at the bottom of the stairs. There was no car hidden around the corner. What we had, ladies and gentlemen, was a legitimate emergency on our hands here.

I pressed the "9" on my phone. Then I pressed the "1." I was about to press the "1" a second time, but my index finger hung over it, half an inch away.

Just hold it a minute there, pardner. Think

about this. Think about this really hard.

What would Detective Flint's first question be? How was it, exactly, that I came to be at this address, and to have found Stefanie Knight's body?

Was I a friend of Stefanie Knight's? No.

But I knew Stefanie Knight? Not really.

Then how was it I happened to be in her garage and found her body?

Well, that was an easy one. I was here to return the purse I'd stolen from her.

And slowly I pulled my finger away before I punched in the last digit of 911. I slipped the phone back into my jacket.

This was, I told myself, a very bad situation. A very bad situation that could get a whole lot worse by calling the police and hanging around to answer their questions.

And yet, didn't this go against everything I believed in, everything I'd ever told my children? How many clichés had I uttered over the years? Here's a sampling: Don't be afraid to get involved. Treat others as you would have them treat you. Don't walk away from trouble. Own up to your mistakes.

And of course, my personal favorite: The policeman is your friend.

I was not sure, in this particular instance, that that was the case. I suspected that the policeman would not be my friend, and that by calling one, I might end up with a new roommate named Moose, who'd sleep on the lower bunk and want me to be his dance partner.

It's probably worth pointing out at this juncture that I do not have what you'd call a long history with the law. I am not the kind of person, as you've probably gathered by now, who's "known to police." I've always played by the rules, paid my taxes on time, pled guilty to parking offenses and mailed in my check within a day of finding a ticket under my windshield.

So it's safe to say that if the police were to find a woman dead in her garage, I would not be on the list of usual suspects. However, I could probably jump to the front of that list in no time by placing a call to the authorities to report the murder of a woman whose purse I had stolen only a couple of hours earlier.

As bad a day as I seemed to be having, I had to concede that it was a picnic next to the one Stefanie Knight had put in.

First, her purse is stolen, and when she finally finds a way home, some nutbar smashes her head in. What were the odds that two things that bad (the second one being considerably worse than the first) could happen to one person on the same day?

Unless, of course, the two events were related.

I was feeling pretty sick, and scared, already, but at that point a new chill swept through me.

Surely, there was no connection. It simply wasn't possible that my taking this woman's purse could have had, in any way whatsoever, anything to do with her death. The police might think so, but that would be an opinion formed through only a cursory inspection of the facts. I knew better. Just because two things appeared to be connected didn't mean they were.

Then again, they might be.

I pictured the leather purse back in my car, and thought about what might be inside it. As much as I had regretted invading Stefanie Knight's privacy by taking something that belonged to her, that ship, as they say, had sailed. The time had come to be a bit more intrusive.

But not here. I had to get out of here. It hadn't occurred to me until that moment that the person who had killed Stefanie Knight might still be in the house, or returning to it shortly. It was time to get the hell out.

I unlocked the regular door that led from the garage to the outside, the one I'd peeked through earlier, and quietly walked down the driveway to my car parked at the curb. I unlocked it, got behind the wheel, and slipped my keys into the ignition. And stopped.

Fingerprints.

What had I touched?

A deadbolt, for starters.

And the front doorknob.

And the door to the laundry room, and the door from the laundry room to the garage, and the light switch, and the door from the garage to the outside . . .

I thought that was it.

I reached around into the back seat, where we

keep a box of tissues on the floor, and grabbed a huge wad of them. There was no one on the street, so I got out of the car, walked back up the drive. I'd never relocked the front door, so as I turned the knob I wiped it down, then the inside doorknob, and the deadbolt. From there I went to the laundry room door, wiped down both knobs, then the door to the garage. It had a safety hinge, so the door would swing closed on its own to keep residents safe from a car spewing exhaust, and I didn't think I had touched the inside knob, but wiped it down just the same. Then the light switch, and the knobs on the door leading out of the garage.

My head was pounding. I was sure I'd touched nothing else, left no other clues behind. I didn't feel that I was keeping the police from finding the real killer. I hadn't wiped down the shovel handle, for example. Surely that would be the first thing the cops would dust for prints.

I'd been careful not to step in any of the blood, but looked at the soles of my shoes anyway. I rubbed my shoes on the grass once I'd stepped back outside, then got back into the car. Slipped the key back into the ignition, turned over the engine, put the car into gear, foot off the brake and onto the accelerator and —

Mailbox.

I hit the brake, glanced back up at the house, and backed up far enough that I could see the front door and the mailbox. There, peeking out from under the flap, was my signed note for Stefanie Knight.

Once I had it in my pocket and was driving home, I kept wondering if there was anything I'd missed. I swung into a fast-food joint, headed straight for the men's room, and flushed all the tissues, including the one I'd used to wipe the blood from my finger, down the toilet. I tore the note written on the back of my checkbook into a dozen pieces and flushed it as well. Then, as an afterthought, I ripped up the scrap of paper from Stefanie's mother and flushed a third time. As I exited the stall, a man washing his hands glanced at me, no doubt wondering just how severe my bowel disorder was.

I got back in the car and felt I'd thought of everything. I'd covered my tracks well.

Oh fuck.

My name and e-mail address were on a piece of paper in that woman's house. When the police came to tell her about her daughter's murder, she'd tell them about the man who'd been by earlier that evening, looking for her, supposedly to return a driver's license.

Think. Think.

My fingerprints weren't anywhere at Stefanie's house. As far as anyone could tell, I had not been inside. I could stick with the story that I'd found her driver's license. Ditch the purse behind Mindy's, if I had to. Police could think some kid stole the purse, driver's license fell out, I found it, attempted to return it. Went to the address on the license, met her mother, got a further address, went there, found no one at home, window smashed in, thought that looked funny, called 911.

That way, I'd look less suspicious. Being the guy to make the call.

I'd crack in an instant. Five minutes under the hot lights and I'd spill my guts.

No, no, I wouldn't. I could pull this off.

But first, I wanted to get home and look inside Stefanie Knight's purse. What I wanted to find in there was nothing. Nothing that would lead someone to want her dead if she'd lost it, been unable to produce it, to give it back.

When I got home I went straight to my study and was taking the purse out of the bag when I heard Sarah call to me from upstairs. "Zack? That you?"

I tossed the purse behind a box of old papers I kept under the desk and went upstairs, finding her in our bedroom, emptying a basket of clean laundry and slipping it into drawers.

"How's Kenny?" she asked.

Kenny? I thought. Was there something wrong with Kenny?

"Huh?" I said.

"Kenny's wife. How's she doing?"

It came back to me. "Aww, she's okay. She'll be fine. Should be out in a day or two."

"That's good," Sarah said. "He didn't say what's wrong with her?"

"No, not in detail, and I didn't want to ask

unless he offered, you know."

"How long's Kenny been married?"

"I don't know exactly. He's about my age. Probably as long as we have, I'd guess."

"Have you ever met his wife?" Sarah asked. She seemed to have a lot of questions.

"No, she's never come into the shop when I was there, or if she did, I didn't know it was her."

"Do you know her name? In case you wanted to send a card?"

"What did he say? Mary? Marian? Something like that?"

"Could it have been Gary?"

I looked at Sarah, who had stopped putting away clothes and was staring right at me.

"Gary?"

"That's right."

"What is that short for? Gariella or something?"

"No, just Gary."

"Why on earth would you think Kenny's wife would be named Gary?"

Sarah paused a moment, like she was working up to something. "Kenny phoned here tonight, while you were out."

Houston, we have a problem.

"He did."

"Yes. He called to tell you that that thing you wanted had come in, and he'd hang on to it whenever you had a chance to drop by."

"Okay."

214

"And then I told him how sorry I was that his wife was not well. And you know what he did then?"

"No. What did he do then?"

"He started laughing. So hard that he started choking. He thought that was a very funny thing for me to say."

"So his wife's not sick after all?"

"Kenny doesn't have a wife," Sarah said. "But he does have a companion."

"A who?"

"Kenny said he couldn't believe you didn't know that he wasn't exactly the marrying kind. He said he lives with a man named Gary, and that Gary is very well, thank you very much."

This was enough to make me forget all the events that had transpired in the last couple of hours. "Kenny's gay?"

"Evidently."

"No shit. Kenny's gay?"

"I don't really think that's the issue here," Sarah said.

"How long I been going to that store? Eight, ten years, maybe? Way before we moved out here. You'd think maybe in all that time I'd have learned to read the signals."

"You've missed plenty of others before."

"I'd never have guessed. But now that you mention it, he never has talked about a wife or kids or —"

I knew instantly I'd made a blunder. "So," Sarah said, "he's never mentioned a wife. Yet if

I'm to believe anything you say, not only does he have one, but she's under the weather."

"Sarah, listen, I know I may have seemed a bit odd tonight."

"Gee, I hadn't noticed."

"It's kind of hard for me to explain right now. I just have a few things I have to attend to, but, listen, it's not like I'm having an affair or anything."

In some households, mentioning the word "affair" might be enough to raise suspicions, start an argument, make someone burst into tears. Sarah reacted differently to the suggestion that I might be seeing someone else.

She began to laugh.

"Why is that so funny?" I asked.

She smiled. "You having an affair. Of all the people I'd suspect of having an affair, you'd be the last. You know why?"

"Why?"

"Because you'd have too guilty a conscience. When you've done something wrong, you can't hide it. It shows in your face. You get kind of flushed, you perspire. I can spot these things."

I shot a sideways glance into our dresser mirror. I looked warm. Sweaty, even.

"No," Sarah said, regaining her composure. "I think I've got it figured out. I know what's going on."

"You do."

"Yep."

"What is it you think is going on?"

She approached me and smiled. "I think maybe, just this once, for the first time since we've been married, you've actually remembered my birthday and decided to do something special about it."

I tried to smile as Sarah slipped her arms around my waist. "That *is* what's going on, isn't it?"

I locked my arms around her and she pressed herself into me. "It's never very easy to pull one over on you," I said.

"You've been running all over the place. When I was at the market, after we got home. What are you up to?" She turned her head up toward mine and breathed on my neck. Her hands were moving from behind my waist and settling on my butt.

"I really can't tell you now," I said, my mouth on her ear. "I want it to be a surprise."

She grinned, and moved her mouth onto mine. She darted her tongue in a couple of times, then pulled away. "Go close the door," she said.

"Aren't there kids in the house?" I said. I needed an excuse not to go through with this. I was a bit concerned, what with all the things currently occupying my thoughts, that I might not quite be up to what Sarah had in mind.

"They still haven't come back from McDonald's," she said. "We'll hear them come in."

"I don't know," I said. "Maybe we should wait till later."

"I don't think so," she said, unbuttoning the top of her jeans and slipping onto the bed next to a pile of rolled socks and clean towels. "Close the door."

I went around the bed and pushed the door closed. Then Sarah reached up for me, pulled me down onto the bed, undid my belt buckle and the top of my jeans.

"Really, hon, I think they might come home any moment."

"What do you think of Trixie?" Sarah asked.

"Trixie? What about Trixie?"

"There's something about her. She's very sexy, don't you think?"

"I don't know. I never really noticed, I suppose. We've just had coffee a couple of times." I had nothing to feel guilty about where Trixie was concerned, but under pressure I might confess to anything right about now.

Sarah pulled back and looked at me. "What's with you? This isn't an interrogation. All I'm saying is, there's something about her, more than meets the eye. Did you catch that thing she said, about Catwoman? How she liked her outfit?"

"I don't know. I don't think I remember."

Sarah smiled at me, slipped her hand down into my jeans. "How would you like it if I got a Catwoman outfit?"

"Well," I said, aware that I was not responding to Sarah's touch the way I normally did, "it would probably be very hot. There'd be chafing. A lot of chafing."

Now Sarah had noticed that her touch was not producing the desired effect. "Is somebody sleepy?" she asked.

"Maybe," I said. "I think he's got a lot on his mind."

Sarah pulled out her hand, rested it on my shoulder. "Is everything okay?"

"Sure, yeah. Everything's fine."

Sarah suddenly became very positive, like she was putting the best spin on a bad lab result. "It's perfectly normal, you know. It happens. I wouldn't worry at all. Like you say, you've had a lot on your mind, finishing up your book, and, you know, at your age, sometimes something like this is going to happen."

"I don't think this is an age thing."

"I didn't mean that. I'm just saying, that when you're in your forties, and you're tired, you know, this can happen." But now her face was changing. Instead of worrying about me, she was thinking about herself. "Unless it's me. Unless I don't, I don't know, please you the way I used to."

"Believe me," I said, "that is not the case. It's what you said. I'm tired, and stressed out, and old. Very old."

Sarah sat up on the edge of the bed. "I guess I was trying to sneak in a quickie because, well, there was another phone call."

"What?" Oh God. Was this how it felt to jump out of a plane and then realize you'd forgotten your chute? Who could have called? Homicide

219

investigators? The Mounties? The FBI? Agent Mulder?

"Work. I have to go in tonight."

"You're kidding."

"The overnight assignment guy's off sick. I'm going to have to cover it. I can't believe it. If I'd known, I'd have had a nap as soon as I got home. I don't know how the hell I'm going to stay awake."

"What about tomorrow morning? You have to stay and do a double?"

"No, they'll get someone else to do that. I'll probably get home about 8 a.m., unless they can get someone to relieve me sooner, which I doubt. Don't bother making me any coffee in the morning. I won't want to stay awake then, I'll just crash, sleep till noon or one, and I won't have to go in the rest of the day." She chuckled. "In a way, it's like getting tomorrow off."

"It's a hard way to get it."

She shrugged. Sarah had, some time ago, worked midnight shifts for five years on the city desk. This was after we'd had children, otherwise they might never have happened. But she had gotten used to it, so the odd night here and there wasn't such a big deal to her.

She gave me a quick kiss. "I've gotta freshen up before I go in. But we're going to talk more about this tomorrow. Maybe we need a dirty weekend. Get away for a couple of days. I think we owe that to ourselves." Sarah disappeared into the bathroom. I zipped up, went downstairs and met Angie coming into the house. Just as I'd feared, I'd never heard her or Paul come back.

"Hey," I said. "Two questions."

"Shoot."

"When's Mom's birthday?"

Angie rolled her eyes. "Day after tomorrow."

I breathed a sigh of relief. There was still time, if I hadn't been gunned down by then trying to evade arrest. "Okay. Number two. Did you know Kenny was gay?"

She'd been in his hobby shop a number of times, usually under protest if we happened to be running errands together, or if she was in there to pick up the obligatory birthday, Father's Day, or Christmas gift. "Duh," she said. "Only a retard couldn't see that." She was going to head for the kitchen, then reconsidered. "Mom said I should ask you for the money you guys owe me."

"Later," I said, and slipped into my study and closed the door.

I turned on my desk lamp, got the purse out from behind the box of papers, and set it down. I took out the wallet first. This was the only thing I'd really looked at, but not very carefully. Stefanie Knight carried three different Visa cards, a Master-Card, a bonus points card for a major drugstore chain, and, of course, the driver's license I'd examined earlier. I withdrew other things from the purse, an item at a time. A brush with several blonde hairs caught in it.

Half a dozen lipsticks and lip liners and various other lip things I didn't know much about. Those tampons still in the paper wrapper. Some handfuls of coins that she'd obviously just thrown into her bag rather than slip into her change purse. VW and house keys, film canister, receipts from grocery stores, drugstores, self-serve gas stations, some dating back more than two years. Three ballpoint pens, one of which looked dried up, three nail files, half a dozen eyeliners. Two white letter-size envelopes, thick with papers. Real estate papers, I guessed. The flaps were tucked in, not sealed, so I decided to take a peek into one of them.

I felt as though someone had suddenly stomped on my chest.

Money. Lots and lots of money.

All fifties. Dozens and dozens of them in the first envelope. Dozens and dozens of them in the second envelope. Thousands of dollars. I couldn't begin to guess how much.

I felt that what had quickly developed into a very bad situation was now a hell of a lot worse.

14

❖ ❖ ❖

They were crisp, new fifties, and I emptied both envelopes and spread the money out on the desk next to my computer. I counted out the bills in stacks of twenty, for $1,000 each. It took about five minutes, and when I was done I had twenty piles, for a total of $20,000.

That would buy a lot of low-fat cookies.

I'd never seen this much cash in one place before. I wasn't even sure I'd ever seen so much as a thousand dollars in cold, hard cash before. When I went to the grocery store, I was lucky to find six bucks in my wallet. Evidently, when Stefanie Knight went to pick up some bread and milk, it was a major event. She didn't want to take any chances on running short.

In her wallet she'd had only $25 in bills. No fifties. But these two envelopes of cash were something else again. What was she doing with this kind of money? What would *anyone* be doing with this kind of cash? Normal, upstanding, regular law-abiding people did not walk around with $20,000 on them. Even people for whom $20,000 was lunch money. I doubted even Bill Gates walked around with $20,000 in his wallet. (You'd throw your back out, for one thing, when you sat on it.)

When you walked around with $20,000 in your purse, the chances were pretty good that you had done something bad. Even if the money had come from a legitimate source, a down payment in a real estate deal, for example, why wouldn't Stefanie have deposited it someplace? Was she like Janet Leigh in *Psycho*, walking out of the office at the end of the day, deciding to start a new life with money from some eccentric home buyer who only dealt in cash?

It seemed time for a review.

I was a thief, possessed information about a murder that I had not passed on to the police, and now had $20,000 in possibly stolen money on my desk. And if that weren't enough, my wife was under the impression that (a) two days from now, she was going to get the best birthday present ever, and (b) her husband was impotent.

But I could not bring myself to call the police. Now, a lawyer, that might be a good idea. I could tell him everything, let him advise me on the best course of action. The only problem was, the only lawyer I knew was the one who handled our house deal. A specialist in land-transfer taxes was not what I needed right now.

As I considered my options, I gathered up the stacks of bills and started stuffing them back into the two envelopes.

"Dad?"

I whirled around in my chair, and as I did, three of the fifties were swept off the desk and onto the carpet. Angie poked her head into my study.

"I'm going to the mall and I need some mo—"

Her eyes landed on the fifties as they fluttered to the floor. "Money," she said. "It looks like my timing couldn't have been better."

I would have scooped up the three bills, but it seemed more important to cover up the hundreds of bills, and purse, and the rest of its contents that were spread across my desk. There was an instruction sheet for the *Seaview* submarine kit on the workbench end of my desk, big, like an unfolded highway map. I grabbed it with one hand, trying not to be so fast as to be obvious, and casually dragged it over the stuff I didn't want Angie to see.

She was into the room and diving for the money like an owl on a mouse. She grabbed the three fifties and smiled.

"This is just what you owe me," she said triumphantly.

"You can't have that," I said. "And besides, you already said we only owe you, what, $127?"

"Okay, so, like, this is a little more, but I also paid for my lunch all this week, and you usually help out with that, so you probably owe me more than $150, so you give me this and we'll call it even. These are nice. You just print these up?"

"I need that money," I said. "You can't have that."

"I'm going to the mall, Mom's already leaving to go back to work and she doesn't have any money, so why can't I have this? You always do this to me. You owe me money and then you find all these excuses not to give it to me and that's not fair." She was already folding the bills and sliding them into the front pocket of her jeans.

"You don't understand," I said. "I got that from the money machine today and need it tomorrow and —"

"What's that on your desk?" She had her head cocked at an angle, trying to peek under the instruction sheet.

"Nothing, just some stuff for my book," I said.

"Is that a purse? Did you get Mom a purse for her birthday?"

This was not good. "Fine," I said. "Take the money."

She spun on her heel. "See ya." She was out the door and I could hear her thick-soled shoes stomping toward the front door.

"Goodbye!" someone shouted. I thought it was Angie at first, then realized it was Sarah.

"Yeah!" I shouted. "Try to stay awake!"

"I'll drop Angie off at the mall!" Sarah shouted. "I'll take the Camry!"

"Okay!" I shouted back. If Sarah took the Toyota, I'd still be left with the Civic if I needed to take Paul someplace, pick Angie up at the mall later if she didn't have a ride back with one of her friends, or meander over to another crime scene.

What I really wanted to do was go nowhere, to hide out in this bunker of a study, even though I knew I wasn't safe here. I wasn't safe anywhere as long as this purse and its contents were in my possession. I should just get rid of it. Put it in a garbage bag, drive to the far side of town, and toss it in a Dumpster behind an industrial complex. Money and all. Get rid of everything.

Take the credit cards and license and anything else that had Stefanie Knight's name on it and chop them up, run them through the food processor, dump them in the sink and grind them up again in the garbage disposal. Take her house and car keys and drive downtown to the harbor district and throw them off the longest dock. I'd made a mistake, I'd done a stupid thing, but I hadn't killed anyone. I'd never intended to hurt anyone, and I didn't know, with any certainty, that I was in any way responsible for Stefanie Knight's death. Maybe whoever killed her did so for reasons totally unrelated to her losing a purse filled with $20,000.

Sure. And the bombing of Pearl Harbor had nothing to do with America going to war with Japan.

I weighed the risks of coming forward, of

calling the police, of turning this purse over to them. I had a wife, two children, a house, a so-so writing career. Wouldn't doing the right thing — if it even was the right thing — put everything I'd worked for, our lives as we'd come to know them, in jeopardy? I couldn't do anything now to save Stefanie Knight, but I could pull myself together, start thinking rationally, and at least save myself and my family from untold horrors and embarrassment.

Get a grip.

I had a book to finish. It was time to focus, to put these last couple of hours aside. Isn't that what Clinton used to do? Hadn't I read about how the former President compartmentalized his problems? How he could meet with the lawyers about the Monica Lewinsky problem, discuss testimony he'd have to give before the Starr inquiry that could potentially see him removed from office, then get up and walk down the hall and give his full attention to a discussion of the Mideast situation?

Sure. That was me. Clintonesque.

I took another deep breath. I shoveled everything of Stefanie Knight's back into the purse, zipped it up, and put it back in the shoe bag. Maybe, with Angie gone to the mall, and Paul no doubt down in the basement with his friends playing video games, I would have a moment to start destroying evidence.

And maybe once I'd finished doing that, I could turn my attention to work.

Out of habit, I fired up the computer. Before I brought up the word-processing program where I stored the chapters of my novel, I thought I'd check and see whether I had any mail.

I clicked on the mailbox icon.

I had two messages. The first was from Tom Darling.

"Nd 2 tlk abt cvr art. Cll me tmrrw so we cn set up mtng wth art dpt."

The business of books and editing and cover designs seemed awfully distant right about now. Like news from a past life. How long would it take to stop being haunted by what I'd seen tonight? Days? Weeks? Would I ever be able to forget the sight of Stefanie Knight's head smashed in, a bloody shovel at her side?

I didn't recognize the name of the sender of the second e-mail. It would have been pretty hard to. It was a string of numbers, followed by @hotmail.com. Every once in a while I got fan mail. Readers could find my address by doing an Internet search and linking up with the writers' union website.

I opened it. It was a short note, with no name at the end, and it didn't appear to be a fan letter. It read:

"Dear Mr. Walker: I'm looking for something I think you got. Don't do something stupid and give it to some body else."

15

❖ ❖ ❖

I probably read the message a dozen times. It didn't become any less scary the more I became familiar with it.

There's a funny thing about e-mail. Even though it and the rest of the Internet exist somewhere out there in the ether, when something ominous appears on your screen, addressed to you, it feels as though the writer's there in the room with you. You've suffered a home invasion without the duct tape. You want to lock the door, but it's too late. There's no place to go.

So someone had been to visit Stefanie's mother and learned my e-mail address. Someone who was clearly not with the police. And that was no cause for celebration.

It was time to stop kidding myself about whether Stefanie Knight's death and the $20,000 in her purse were related. Here's how I figured it played out: Someone had gone to her house expecting to get that money, and when she didn't have it, she was murdered. Then her killer started looking elsewhere, and showed up on her mother's doorstep. But she didn't have it, either. But hey, she said, there was a guy here earlier, said he had her driver's license, was acting kind of funny. Here's his name and e-mail address.

I read the note one more time: "Dear Mr. Walker: I'm looking for something I think you got. Don't do something stupid and give it to some body else."

Hadn't I done enough stupid things already tonight? I certainly had no interest in doing any more.

It was the absence of any specific threat that made the note all the more chilling. It was implied. I already knew what this guy would do to someone who didn't hand over something he wanted. I'd been in that garage. But then again, he didn't know that I knew Stefanie Knight was dead. Maybe he intended his note to be more matter-of-fact. Maybe I was reading too much into it.

Earth to Zack. Wake the fuck up.

I clicked on "Reply" and wrote: "To Whom It May Concern: Regarding your e-mail about my possessing something you're looking for, I'm afraid I simply have no idea what you're talking about."

I read it over twice, thought it sounded about right. Didn't protest too much, just stated plainly that he had made some sort of a mistake. An incorrect assumption. A case of mistaken identity, perhaps.

I hit "Send."

My study door opened. God, did Angie want more money? How much do you need, honey? Ten thou, fifteen?

Paul said, "Are you ready?"

I looked at him blankly. "Ready for what?"

"Jesus, you forgot? We have to be there in ten minutes."

"What are you talking about?"

"The interview. The parent-teacher thing. It's been written on the fridge for weeks. At eight. I have to get my ass reamed out by the science teacher, and you're supposed to be there for it. You and Mom said you were gonna go? And now she's been called in to work and you have to do it solo."

The air seemed to be thinning. "I can't do it," I said.

Paul did a combination rolling-of-the-eyes, sigh, and shoulder-rolling-head-slumping thing which, if it were an Olympic gymnastic move, would have earned him a 9.9. "You *have* to go. If you don't show up for this, I'm dead. Ms. Wilton will kill me. She wants me dead already. She *hates* me. Maybe if she gets a chance to talk to you, she'll let up on me a bit. You could tell her to stop giving me a hard time."

"Maybe you need people giving you a hard time."

Another eye-roll. "We have to be there in less than ten minutes."

"Where are your friends?"

"They took off. We're going to get together

later at Andy's house."

"You don't have any homework?"

"Nothing."

"No science homework?"

"Look, are we going to go or what?"

I swallowed. "I'll meet you at the front door in two minutes." Paul vanished and I turned back to the computer. I was about to close the mail program, when the computer beeped.

"You have mail," it said.

Shit. Was this guy sitting by his computer? The number guy from Hotmail was back. I opened the message. It read:

"Don't jerk me around, asshole. There can't be that many Z. Walkers in the phone book."

And that was it.

"I'm ready!" Paul shouted from the front door. "Let's roll!" I closed the letter, exited the mail program, and turned off the computer before grabbing my jacket and my cell. I flew past Paul on the way to the car, and he pulled the front door shut.

On the short drive over to the school, Paul said, "What's with you tonight, anyway?"

"I'm okay. I just have some things on my mind."

"You just seem, I don't know, weird."

"Really, I'm fine. Let's worry about you and Ms. Winslow."

"Wilton."

"Hmm?"

"It's Ms. Wilton. Not Ms. Winslow. That'll

233

make a really good impression, Dad, going in and calling her by the wrong name. Like I'm not in enough shit already."

We said nothing else to each other. The school parking lot was nearly full, and many other parents were walking into the building, some accompanied by their teenage children, some not. But they all assumed a kind of condemned-prisoner gait.

Paul led me down a series of hallways and up a flight of stairs to Room 212, where a small nameplate reading "Ms. J. Wilton" was affixed to the door. "There's still someone in there," Paul said, peeking around the corner. "That's Sheila Metzger's mom. She'll kill her when she gets home."

I was growing weary of Paul's tales of mothers who wanted to kill their daughters, of teachers who wanted their students dead. "What are we supposed to do?" I whispered so our voices wouldn't drift from the hall into the classroom. "Just wait around out here?"

"I guess, until Sheila's mom comes out. Then it'll be our turn."

"What kind of trouble are you having with science anyway?"

Paul shrugged. "It's really stupid. Like I'm really going to need science when I grow up."

"What do you want to be when you grow up?"

"I dunno."

"Then how do you know you won't need science?"

"Because I won't."

"Look how interested you've become in gardening. That's science."

"No, that's planting and digging. Most of the guys I know getting landscaping jobs for the summer don't exactly have to wear white lab coats."

"So why does she hate you, this Ms. Wilton?"

"She just does."

"Could you be more specific?"

"I think she may have an attitude problem."

As I leaned up against the brick wall, I thought about the second e-mail. I'd never stopped thinking about it while I tried to go through the motions with Paul and this parent-teacher interview thing. If I'd thought the first note was ominous, the second one was off the scale. This guy was planning to come look for me to get what he wanted. There couldn't be too many Z. Walkers in the phone book, he'd said. How many Z. Walkers were there, exactly, in the phone book? Suddenly, I had to know.

"Is there a phone book around here?" I asked Paul.

"A phone book? I don't know. Probably in the office. What do you need a phone book for?"

"I just need to look something up. It'll only take a minute."

"You can't go now. She's going to call us in any second."

I peeked around the corner as Paul had done a moment earlier. Ms. Wilton was huddled over one of four student desks pulled together into a

235

single grouping, Sheila's mother sitting across from her. They were reviewing papers, talking in hushed tones. It looked to me like they weren't even close to finishing.

"I'll only be a minute," I said, and darted off down the hallway to the stairs. I ran back toward the main entrance, past parents waiting outside classroom doors for their appointments. I expected, at any moment, to be told to stop running in the halls. I assumed the office would be near the front of the school, and I was right. Since this was an open-house kind of evening, the door to the office was unlocked and the lights were on. I stood at the counter and called out, "Anyone here?"

A short, middle-aged man in a dark suit who I assumed was the principal poked his head out of an adjoining office. "Yes?"

"Sorry, but would you have a phone book I could borrow for a sec?"

He looked puzzled, but nodded, went over to a desk, found one, and brought it over to the counter. I flipped it open to the back, found "W," flipped through the pages for the Walker listings. I ran my finger down the dozens and dozens of Walkers, down through the alphabet. For every letter, there were several Walkers. I scanned right to the end, found a slew of "Walker W's," not one "Walker X," a couple of "Walker Y's," and then I found my own listing. "Walker Z," followed by our address and phone number.

There was only one "Walker Z."

"Shit," I said.

"Pardon?" said the principal. I didn't bother to close the book before turning around and running back down the hall, up the stairs, and down the corridor where I'd left Paul, expecting to see him waiting his turn to see Ms. Wilton. But he was gone.

I looked into the classroom and there he was, sitting across from his teacher. I swept into the room, breathless.

"Sorry," I said. "Really sorry. Sorry I'm late." I extended a hand to Ms. Wilton, who took it reluctantly and smiled grimly. I grabbed a chair. "So, listen, really, sorry, but thank you for making time for this meeting."

"Of course."

"So, what's the problem with Paul here?"

"Well, first of all," said Ms. Wilton, opening a binder and examining a chart with all sorts of numbers and checkmarks and notes on it, "Paul seems to have a problem getting to class on time. He's rushing in at the last minute, which causes a real disruption to the class, especially when everyone else is settled in."

It was pretty hot in there, especially after all the running I'd done. I pushed my chair back, causing it to squeak against the floor, to allow myself room to work my jacket off. "Just hang on a second," I said, struggling to free myself from one sleeve while in a sitting position. Once I had the jacket off, I slipped it over the back of the chair. "You were saying?"

"When Paul comes to class late, it can cause a disruption to the class."

"I can understand that." I turned to Paul. "Is this true?"

He shrugged. "Sometimes I'm coming from gym, and we have to get changed, or have a shower, so I don't always get here on time."

Time, I thought. How much time did I have? How long before this stranger found his way to our house? And what did he plan to do when he got there? He could have the purse, the $20,000, it didn't matter to me. Just take it and get out of our lives. As long as I handed it over, there was no reason for him to hurt me or any member of my family. He didn't know that I knew he was a killer, so it wasn't like he had to eliminate me as a witness. I'd tell him pretty much the truth. I found the purse at the grocery store, just wanted to return it, you must be her husband, nice to meet you, here it is, have a nice day, don't slam the door on your way out.

"Paul also has some difficulties in staying focused," Ms. Wilton said. "The material we're covering is fairly complicated, so if you're not paying attention, you're going to have a lot of trouble when it comes to tests and assignments. Mr. Walker?"

"Yes?"

"You follow what I'm saying?"

"Of course. He has to be on time. I'm in total agreement there."

"No, I was talking about how Paul needs to pay more attention."

"To what?"

Ms. Wilton seemed to be the kind of person who got irritated very easily. There was a tone in her voice when she said, "To what goes on in class. To what I'm saying."

"Oh, again, I agree." To Paul, I said, "Aren't you paying attention in class?"

He shrugged. "I try. But I'm just not very interested in science. I mean, what's the point? What am I going to do with this stuff?"

I looked back at Ms. Wilton. "Over to you."

Ms. Wilton's eyes narrowed. "Mr. Walker, you're an author of science fiction novels, are you not?"

Again, this tone. This was not the way a fan usually brought up my work. "That's true, yes. I've done a few novels."

"Wouldn't you agree that even if you don't intend to become a rocket scientist, or an epidemiologist with the Atlanta Centers for Disease Control, that a general background in science is valuable? Even though your focus is fiction and good storytelling, haven't you benefitted from a general understanding of scientific principles in your line of work?"

Slowly, I nodded. "That's an excellent point." I turned to Paul. "That's a good point."

"That's all I'm trying to do here with Paul. To give him a good grounding in science. He doesn't have to find a cure for cancer, but he should at least know, for example, what keeps an airplane aloft, the aerodynamic principles involved that keep it from crashing to the ground."

I've never really understood why airplanes don't crash into the ground, but this didn't seem like a good time to ask for an explanation.

"Paul's got a 55 for this semester, and there's only a few weeks left of school, and a major exam coming up, and he's going to have to work hard to make his mark a passing one," the teacher said. "And it would help a lot if Paul spent less time listening to his little gadgets and more time listening to me when I'm speaking."

"Gadgets?" I asked.

"Pagers and phones and those, what do you call them, MP5 players?"

"MP3," Paul corrected her. "That's all I've got. I don't bring a phone or pager to class."

"As you can imagine," Ms. Wilton said, addressing me, "it's very difficult to compete for attention against all the technological toys that are out there these days."

I nodded. "Sure, I can —"

And the cell phone in my jacket pocket started to chirp. "I'm sorry," I said. "Could you excuse me for just a second?"

I turned around in the chair, reached into my pocket, and withdrew the phone. "Hello?" I said, smiling sheepishly over my shoulder at Ms. Wilton.

"Zack?"

Sarah.

"I totally forgot. I tried to get you at home and there was no answer. The interview with Ms. Winslow."

"Wilton," I said, smiling at the teacher.

"Yeah. You're supposed to be there."

"It's under control," I said. "We're doing it right now."

"Oh, God, sorry. I better go."

"No, that's okay."

"What's the teacher say?"

"Well, he needs to be paying more attention, you know, that kind of thing. How 'bout with you? How's it going there?"

"Oh, pretty quiet. A fire downtown. But this is interesting. They've called out the homicide guys in Oakwood. Not too far from our place. Some woman bought it."

"Really?"

"Some kid, going to the door trying to sell chocolate bars, finds the driveway covered in blood, it's leaking out from the garage, cops come and find this woman with her head bashed in. I got two people out there, trying to get something for the morning edition."

Ms. Wilton was starting to look, if this was possible, even more annoyed.

"Listen," I said. "I'll give you a call later, okay?"

"Okay. See ya."

I slipped the phone back into my jacket. "Sorry."

"I have other people waiting," Ms. Wilton

said, "so why don't I sum up. Paul needs to get to class on time, start paying attention, and leave his electronic toys in his locker when he comes to class."

I nodded enthusiastically, then shrugged as we headed for the door. "I don't know where he gets it from," I said.

On the way out to the car, Paul refused to look at me, but said, "Thanks a whole lot, Dad. It's hard to imagine how that could have gone any better."

16

"You wanna slow down a bit, Dad?" Paul said. "I've never seen you drive this way."

I'd ignored the stop sign coming out of the high school parking lot, and floored it when the light at the intersection ahead of us turned yellow. It turned red well before I was through.

"Excuse me, Mr. Safety?" Paul said again, trying to get my attention.

"I want to get home," I said.

"Okay, but remember, I said I had to get dropped off at Andy's?"

I wasn't sure, after the interview with his teacher, that Paul deserved to go out with his friends. Any other time, I would have taken him home and sent him to his room with orders to study until his eyes started to bleed, but at the moment I had too much else on my mind. And it might be prudent — given that a man I knew only as an e-mail address who was likely a killer had made it plain to me that he was going to figure out how to find me — to have as many members of my family as possible out of the house.

243

So I made a detour on the way home that would take us by Andy's house, and despite traveling well over the limit, there was still time for Paul to push his most recent agenda.

"I'm not talking about a big tattoo. Just a small one, where you'd never even see it. Like on my back, or shoulder, or my butt."

"You want to get a tattoo on your butt."

"It's not like it's going to bother you or Mom. You won't even see it."

"If no one's going to see it, then why bother to get it done?"

Paul measured his words carefully. "Well, someone might see it. Eventually. Just not you guys. There's all sorts of neat designs. I can show you, on the Web, just so you don't think they're all gross. They're really a form of art."

"A form of art that can never be removed. You get a tattoo, you've got it for life."

"They have ways of getting rid of them."

"I'm not so sure they're effective. And I think they're pretty painful." I was feeling so tired, and developing a headache. Although I'd not been all that hungry, given what I'd seen this evening, the lack of anything in my stomach was taking its toll.

"I'd just like you to think about it, that's all. Lots of people have them, and it doesn't make them criminals or anything. Lots of my friends do, and I know grown-ups who've got them, too. You know Mr. Drennan, the math teacher? He's got this little butterfly on his arm, and there's this guy in Grade 9, his parents let him get this guitar tattoo on —"

We were pulling to a stop out front of Andy's. I said, "What does your sister think of this? You don't see her pestering me for permission to do this." Paul often turned to Angie for the guidance and wisdom her many years afforded her.

"Jeez, Dad, she's already got one on her —" And he saw the dawn of surprise in my eyes and stopped. He opened the door, said, "See ya," and bolted for Andy's place.

I didn't have time to think about where Angie might have a tattoo. I sped home, killing the lights of the Civic as I pulled into the drive. When I turned the key in the front-door lock, the bolt didn't slide home the way it usually does. Paul had been the last one out when we'd gone over to the school, and I couldn't recall seeing him lock it. But then again, Angie might be back from the mall and just hadn't locked the door when she stepped into the house.

No one listens to me.

"Angie?" I called as I stepped in. I turned off my cell and left it and my keys on the table by the door, and walked into the kitchen. "You home?"

There was no answer. I called again, louder this time: "Angie!"

No one called back. But I could hear noises coming from the kitchen. The opening of the fridge, the clinking of bottles.

"Sarah?" Maybe she'd come home early. No,

that wasn't possible. Her car wasn't in the drive, and she'd called me from the office only moments ago, when I was in Ms. Wilton's class. "Who's there?"

I walked past the door to the study, where the purse stuffed with cash was still stowed, and into the kitchen.

It was Rick, leaning up against the dishwasher, drinking an Amstel from our fridge. He was in his jeans and jean jacket, which he wore over a black T-shirt. Heavy black boots stuck out from the bottom of his worn jeans. He was smiling enough for me to see that one of his front teeth was chipped.

"What the hell are you doing here?" I asked. "And where's my candlestick, you son of a bitch?"

Rick lost his smile. "That's not a very nice way to talk to a guy you want to fix your shower."

"I don't want you to fix anything. I'm going to speak to Mr. Greenway about you, about the fact that you're a thief, that when you walk into someone's house to fix something, there's no telling what you'll walk out with. Just get out. We'll find someone else to fix our shower."

"I didn't even realize when I came here the other day," Rick said, "that your name was Walker. All they gave me was an address."

"Well, that's me. Walker. And I'm asking you to leave."

"Zack Walker. With a 'Z.' "

That's when it hit me that Rick wasn't here to work on the shower.

He reached into the front pocket of his jeans and pulled out the sheet of paper I had left behind at Stefanie Knight's mother's place, the one with my name and e-mail address.

"When I looked your name up in the book for an address, I thought, Shit, I know that house. I been in that house."

I said nothing.

"When I got here, I found the door was open. You really should lock up when you leave. You never know who's going to barge right in. But I had a look around the whole house this time. Haven't seen it since it was under construction. Nice place. Looks like you got a son, and a daughter. That right?"

I nodded very slowly.

"So I was trying to find Stef tonight, she had something of Mr. Greenway's I had to pick up, and went by her place, and when I couldn't find her there, I decided to drop in on her mom. You met her, right?"

"Her mother, yes. And her brother."

Rick nodded. "You meet Quincy?"

"We met."

"I gave them Quincy. It was a gift, like. I love snakes. I think they're really beautiful. Merle, that's Stef's mother? She's a nice lady. We got to be friends when Stef and I were a thing, you know?"

"Yeah."

247

"But Quincy's been giving them a lot of trouble lately. He's a bit of a handful, I admit, but he's a good snake. So they asked me to take him off their hands for a while. You want to come out to the car and see him?"

I felt a chill. "No, like I said, we met."

"I got him out in the trunk. Gonna take him back to my place. You're sure you don't want to come out, pet him?"

I shook my head.

"Because, if I don't leave here with what I want, then I might insist that you come out and pet him."

"I'm sure we can work something out."

"Merle and Stef, they don't talk that much, but Stef drops by once in a while, you know, so I thought, maybe she was over there. But she wasn't, but Merle started talking about this man who came by, saying he had something that belonged to Stef, but he was acting kind of funny, and I got a bit suspicious, you know. And he left this e-mail address. So they let me use their computer so I could send you a little message."

"Yes."

He smiled. "So if you've got something of Stef's, why don't you just hand it over to me, and I'll be on my way."

"Okay," I said. "That's fine. Follow me."

I led him out of the kitchen and down the hall to my study. He stepped into the room, looked around, his eyes landing on the various items of SF kitsch, and said, "Whoa, I missed this room when I took my tour. This is quite the setup you've got here."

He leaned in close to the shelves to admire the models and trinkets and action figures, stepped back to check out the posters on the walls. "This here, I know this is a Batmobile, but which one?"

"From the animated series."

"I always liked the one from the old TV show, you know, from the sixties, where they had the words 'pow' and 'bam' and everything, when they took punches at each other. It had the red pinstripes, and little bat symbols on the wheels? I always thought that one was cool. I had a little Dinky Toy of that one."

"It was a Corgi, actually," I said.

"Huh?"

"A Corgi toy, not a Dinky Toy. It's right there, on the shelf above."

He looked up. "Oh wow. Shit. That's it. That's the one I had as a kid." He took it off the shelf and admired it. "Fuck me. That's really cool." He felt the heft of the metal model in the palm of his hand. I wanted to tell him to be careful with it but held my breath instead. "It's a beauty, looks like it came right out of the box, still got the little antenna on it and everything."

"Yeah, it's mint."

"Where did you get this? My stuff, from when I was a kid, my mom just threw it all out, I guess. Fuckin' bitch."

"That's mine. I mean, it was mine when I was

a boy. I've kept it all these years."

The man nodded, impressed. "You keep your stuff nice."

I shrugged. "Well, I try. I've saved a lot of toys and things from my childhood, some better than others."

"Well, it looks like it really paid off." And then he slid the Batmobile model into the pocket of his jean jacket and smiled at me. Just like that, daring me to ask him to put it back on the shelf.

"Wait a minute," Rick said, looking at the books on the shelves, including several duplicate copies of the ones I'd written. "Zack Walker. Is that like Zachary Walker?"

"That's right."

"I know that name." His eyebrows went together, like he was trying to remember something from a very long time ago. He pulled a copy of *Missionary* off the shelf. "Did you write this?"

I nodded. "That was my first book, yes."

"Is this the one where those guys go to another planet and try to get the people to stop believing in God?"

"Yes, that's the one."

"Shit, I loved this book! I read it while I was inside."

Inside? Inside what? Most people did their reading inside, unless they were taking their books with them to the beach in the summertime.

"Yeah, this was good," Rick said. "I found it

kind of spiritual, if you know what I mean. Man, I can hardly believe I'm meeting some hot-shit writer."

"Well, not that hot shit, actually. My other books have done only so-so. But that one, it did the best, and I'm finishing up a sequel to it now."

Rick's eyes widened. "Are you kidding me? When I finished that book, I thought, Hey, what would happen next? Would the Earth guys suddenly get religion, or would they just be killed, you know, for not believing, or maybe back on Earth they'd send some more guys to see what happened to them, like in *Planet of the Apes*, you know, where they sent another astronaut after Charlton Heston found the Statue of Liberty on the beach there? Oh shit, I didn't spoil the ending for you, did I?"

"I've seen it."

"Check this out," he said, reaching into his back pocket and digging out a silver cigarette lighter featuring the *Star Trek* insignia, the rounded upside-down "V" that was the symbol for the Federation of Planets, on the side. "Like it?" he said, turning it so I could see the emblem more clearly. "Got it from a guy inside. I looked after him, and he knew I liked *Star Trek*, so he gave it to me."

There was the word again. I was starting to get an idea of what it meant to be "inside."

"Sort of like you giving me this Batmobile," he said, patting his jacket pocket. "Now I'll do

251

my best to look after your interests, too."

I tried to smile.

"Now," he said, getting back to the purpose of his visit, "how do you know Stefanie?" He put emphasis on the word "know." " 'Cause you don't really strike me as her type, though I could be wrong."

"No no," I said. "I don't know Stefanie at all."

"Because I know she's been seeing somebody else lately. Maybe even a couple people, you know."

"Not me."

"Uh-huh."

"No, you see, her mother's address? That was the only one I had for her. I did find something of hers, and I was just trying to return it, that's all."

"And what would that be?"

"Her purse."

"And why do you have her fucking purse?"

"I found it," I said. "She'd dropped it at a store."

Rick nodded knowingly. "Did you have a good look at what's inside that purse, Mr. Walker?"

"I looked at her license, so I could find a way to get in touch with her."

Rick eyed me suspiciously. "I think you're giving me a load of bullshit, you know that?"

"No, really, I have it." I was about to dig it out for him when the phone on my desk rang. We looked at each other, neither of us knowing whether I should answer it, and then it rang again. I leaned over and looked at the call-display feature. "It's my wife," I said. "I better answer it."

"I'm not here. Understand? Unless you'd like that phone cord wrapped around your neck."

"Sure," I said, unconsciously raising one hand to touch my neck while I reached for the receiver with the other. "Hello?"

"Me again," said Sarah. "I tried the cell and when I didn't get you I figured you must be back home."

"Yeah."

"How'd the interview go? With Ms. Wilton?"

"Oh, you know. Okay. More or less. Not so good."

"What do you mean?"

"Well, he's not, he's, well, he could be working a little harder. That's pretty much the gist of it." Rick was taking a model of the *Millennium Falcon* off my top shelf, examining it.

"There was nothing more?"

"Well, some, but I can tell you all about it when you get home. How's it going there?"

"Pretty quiet."

"What about that story you mentioned to me earlier?"

"The body out our way? Still waiting for more details. Cops don't have a name or anything yet, but she was banged up pretty bad."

"Hurry up," Rick whispered.

"I'm worried about you," Sarah said. "I think

you need to take some time off. I've never seen you stressed out quite the way you were tonight."

"I'm okay."

"I was talking to Deb, you know, on Foreign? Her husband, he had the same problem, and he got that prescription? The little blue pill?"

"You were telling Deb about this?" I asked.

"No, not specifically. Just generally, you know?"

"Sort of like, I know this guy, but it's not necessarily my husband, who's got erectile dysfunction?"

Rick grinned, made a drooping finger.

"No, don't worry about it. You seem really touchy."

"I'm sorry. Maybe I'm just a bit hungry."

"You must be starving. Throw on the other steak, have something to eat."

"Maybe so. Listen, I gotta go, I think I've got to do a pickup at the mall."

"Oh yeah, did Angie get some money from you?"

"Yeah, she did."

"Okay, look, I gotta go too, things are starting to heat up around here. Love ya." And she hung up.

I replaced the receiver.

"Chatty broad," Rick said. "What did she want?"

"Just to check in and say hi. She's at work."

Rick nodded. "Let's have it."

I swept away the instructions for the *Seaview* model, revealing the purse. "Here it is," I said. "Just take it and get the hell out of my house and don't come back."

Rick grabbed it from me, turned it upside down, and dumped the contents on the floor. "Where is it?" he asked. "It better fuckin' be here."

"Here," I said, bending down and grabbing the two thick white envelopes. I opened the flap of one of them and fanned my thumb across the fifties. "There's $150 missing. I'll give that to you."

Rick stared at the cash, dumbfounded. "Jesus," he said. "That's a shitload of money. Where the fuck did that come from?"

And I thought, not for the first time that night, that it was possible I did not have a firm grasp of what was really going on.

I heard the front door open. "Dad!" someone screamed.

Angie. Home from the mall.

17

It was unlike Angie to call out my name upon
arriving home.

It was unlike Angie, upon returning from an
outing of any kind, to call out for me or her
mother. It was rare for her to shout out so much
as "Home!" When Angie came through the
door, she tended to head into the kitchen for a
snack or straight up to her room to phone somebody. More often than not, coming into the
house was something both the kids conducted
with the utmost stealth. They did not always
want to advertise what time they returned
home, and would open the front door like bomb
deactivators, making sure the knob made no
sudden latching sounds, moving through the
hall without turning on the lights, creeping up
the stairs and slipping into their rooms unde-
tected. When Sarah or I awoke at midnight,
wondering why we hadn't heard one of them
come in, we'd get up and find them in bed,
feigning sleep, in all likelihood fully dressed
under the covers, pretending to have been there

for at least an hour when they'd only been home ninety seconds.

So for Angie to shout out my name, that could not mean anything good.

My mind raced. Did Rick have an accomplice? And weren't things already going downhill fast enough with one bad guy in the house? How might things proceed with two?

I don't know quite how to explain what happened next. I think it was a primal thing. A father's instinct kicking in, I don't know. I just knew at that moment that I had to do whatever I could to protect my daughter. When Angie screamed, it caught Rick by surprise as it had me, and he turned away from me, looking to the study door, and at that moment — don't ask me the brain processes that went into this — I grabbed my *Lost in Space* Robot statue off the shelf and swung. Hard.

I'd picked it up two years ago, in that store in New York, in the Village. A comic shop that had every SF model and souvenir you could think of. I hadn't much liked the sixties series, but as with a lot of crappy fantasy shows, I still loved the hardware. This was a solid resin model of Robot, the one who was always shouting "Danger, Will Robinson! Danger!" and it stood a good foot high on its stand. It had a bit of weight to it, and it felt formidable in my hand as I grabbed it.

It crumbled into several pieces as it connected with the back of Rick's head, and I guess I was expecting him to whirl around and kill me right there, but darned if he didn't drop right to the floor. I stood over him, ready to club him a second time with the remnant of Robot that was still attached to the base, but he wasn't moving. "Jesus," I said, under my breath, "I've killed him."

"Daaad!"

I put the busted model back on my desk, threw the two envelopes and everything else Rick had dumped onto the floor back into the purse, came out of the study door and rounded the corner into the laundry room, where I stuffed the purse into the empty washing machine.

I arrived in the front hall sweat-soaked, my heart pounding, wondering who I'd have to hit in the head next.

Evidently, it was going to be Officer Greslow.

She was decked out once again in her deep blue uniform, hat, and broad black holster from which hung, among other things, what appeared to be a very large gun. A radio clipped to a strap across her chest crackled. How did they get here so fast? I wondered. How did they know I had a suspected killer in the house? Who cared? It was time to talk. Time to tell everything.

"God, Dad, thanks a lot," Angie said upon seeing me. Her eyes were red; she'd been crying.

"Why, Mr. Walker," Officer Greslow said. "Imagine running into you again."

"Yes, hello," I said, feeling a mixture of relief and anxiety. "Well, I can't believe you're here. Were you watching the house, was that it?"

"Uh, no, Mr. Walker, we weren't. Why would you think we'd be watching the house?"

"Uh, well . . ." Something was wrong here.

"Mr. Walker, is this your daughter, Angela Walker?"

"Yes. Yes, she's my daughter." Come on, I thought, let's get past introductions so I can tell you about this guy in the study who I just killed, but it was totally self-defense. I understand that, in addition to investigating the murder of Samuel Spender, you may already be investigating another murder this evening, and this is the guy, you can wrap the whole thing up, no thanks necessary. Just want to do my part as a good citizen.

"Maybe we could sit down," the officer said. I motioned her into the living room, as far away as possible from my study, and gestured toward the couch. We all sat down. I said, "I'm a bit confused."

"It's the money you gave me!" Angie said.

"What are you talking about?"

The officer leaned forward, her leather belt creaking as she moved. "Mr. Walker, your daughter used three fifty-dollar bills this evening to make a purchase at the Groverdale Mall."

"It was for pants," Angie said.

"What was the problem?" I asked.

259

"Sir, the saleslady ran the fifties under their scanning machine and determined the bills were counterfeit."

"Counterfeit?"

"So you still owe me $150," Angie said.

"They called security, who in turn called us, sir. Had it just been the one counterfeit bill, they might not have held your daughter and called us, but having three did raise some suspicions. A closer examination showed that the bills all carried the same serial numbers."

"Counterfeit?" I said again.

The officer ignored me. She continued: "Your daughter says that she obtained these bills from you. Is that correct, sir?"

"Uh, yes, that's true. I gave them to her tonight, before she left for the mall."

"I can't believe you did this to me," Angie said. "Like, about a hundred of my friends were in the mall and they all saw me being led out and put in a police car. I'm gonna have to change schools."

"Mr. Walker, where did you get these fifties?"

Oh, let's see. From a purse I stole, which belonged to a murdered woman. Probably murdered by this guy in the study, who I just hit in the head, and who could probably use an ambulance, if it isn't already too late?

I said, "I guess from a bank machine."

"A bank machine."

"I suppose. I go to them all the time. Some of them, you know, if you're taking out as much as

260

two hundred dollars, they dispense fifties. Instead of twenties."

"Yes, sir. Which bank machine would that have been?"

Think think think think think. "I'm all over town. It could be any one of a dozen, I suppose. I, I really have no idea."

"Could I see your bank card please, sir?"

"My bank card?"

"Yes, sir. I can take down the number, take it to the bank, track where you've been getting your money, and that will help us narrow down which branch these fifties might have come from."

"Oh, sure." I reached around into my back pocket and took out my wallet. "This is the one I use," I said, sliding it out and handing it over to the officer. She wrote down the number in her notepad and handed it back.

"Is my daughter going to be charged?" I asked.

"No, sir. It looks to me like just one of those things, but we will be keeping the counterfeit bills."

"You see?" Angie said. "You owe me that money. And I don't want it in fifties this time."

"Sir, do you have any more fifties? From the same ATM?" the officer asked.

You might want to check the washing machine, I thought. You might find $19,850 worth.

"I don't think so," I said.

"You mind my checking your wallet, Mr.

261

Walker?" Officer Greslow asked. It wasn't really a request. She already had her hand out, waiting for me to hand it over. I did so. She looked where I keep my cash, and there was nothing there but a couple of small bills, and then she handed the wallet back to me.

For a moment, she didn't have any more questions. She was jotting down a few further notes. This was my last chance, I realized, to tell her everything. About the purse. About finding Stefanie Knight. About her probable killer coming to see me. About his body in the study.

"Okay then, Mr. Walker, we'll check this out, and in the meantime, you might want to give any fifties you come into possession of in the future a close look. Check for the lettering, it should feel a tiny bit raised. A lot of counterfeiters, what they're doing now is, they're using really top-notch photocopying machines. They're not actually forging and doing their own printing anymore, which is why this is becoming such a problem."

"Uh-huh."

"And let me give you my card, it has my name and badge number and where I can be reached in case you think of anything else, you can give me a call."

"Thank you."

"Nice to see you again," she said, touched her fingers to the brim of her hat, and withdrew. As she left, my last chance of coming clean went with her.

Angie and I stood in silence for a moment. It wasn't every day the police brought your daughter home in a marked car for passing bogus bills. That you'd given her.

"Where's Mom? I need to talk to Mom."

"She's at work, honey. Remember?"

"I'm going to call her."

"No, don't do that. She called me earlier, and it's pretty wild there tonight. This would be a very, very bad time to call her."

Angie started heading toward the kitchen, which would take her past my study. I blocked her way. "Just stay here for a minute," I said, touching both her shoulders lightly.

"What? Can't I go to the kitchen?"

"Just stay here for a minute!"

My tone gave Angie a jolt. She stood still while I turned and ran to my study. I eased the door open. Maybe he wasn't dead, I thought. Maybe I'd just knocked him cold. It used to happen to Mannix every week on TV. Somebody hit him in the head with a gun butt, he was back on his feet after the commercial, no harm done. Even if this guy was Stefanie's killer, I hadn't signed on to be his executioner.

"Oh man," I said.

Rick was gone. I came back out of the study, bolted into the kitchen. The patio door was wide open. Evidently, I'd not killed him. And when he realized the police were in the house, he'd made a break for it. I slid the door shut, and when I returned to the study, I found Angie there, looking at the pieces of the Robot model all over the carpet, as well as a couple of makeup items from Stefanie's purse that I'd failed to scoop up.

"What happened here, Dad?" Angie asked. "Your robot thingy. It's all smashed."

"I just had a little accident, that's all."

"And what's Mom's makeup doing here?" She picked up an eyeliner, sneered. "Oooh. She doesn't even use this kind."

"Angie, do you have any place you could go tonight?"

"Go?"

"A friend's, to sleep over."

"You never let me go to sleepovers on a school night."

"I know, but you know, it's your mom's birthday in a couple of days, and I think she's going to be able to get off shift soon, and I thought I'd surprise her when she gets home. Order in some food, put on some music, maybe —"

"Oh God, don't tell me any more. That's so gross. Yeah, I could probably go to Francine's. Her parents are in Europe, she'd like the company."

"Why don't you go throw some things together and I'll drive you over."

Angie shrugged, turned to go upstairs. "You still owe me $150," she said.

"I'm sorry about what happened," I said. "I didn't know that money was counterfeit."

She shrugged. "It was kind of cool, actually. I never got to ride in the back of a cop car before."

18

While Angie packed an overnight bag, I called Paul's cell phone.

"Yeah?"

"It's me. You still at Andy's?" I could hear other young males goofing around in the background.

"Quiet, it's my dad!" he shouted. Then, more quietly, "Yeah, I'm here. I gotta come home already? You only dropped me off here like half an hour ago."

"No, you don't have to come home. I was wondering how late you could stay there."

"You *want* me to stay here?"

"Long as you want. Any chance you could sleep over?"

"On a *school* night?"

Since when did my children become so concerned about staying up late on a school night?

"Yeah, sure, it's okay. Angie's going to stay with somebody, and it only seemed fair to offer you the same opportunity."

"Who is this, really?"

"It's your father, Paul."

"So I get reamed out by my science teacher, and for punishment, I get to stay out all night? If I told you I'm failing math, too, would there be money for me and Andy to get hookers?"

"I was just telling Angie, it's your mother's birthday in a couple of days, and I think she's going to be home from work soon." A lie. A total lie. "And I wanted to make her arrival extra special."

There was silence for a moment on the other end of the line. Then, echoing his sister: "Oh gross." Just how did teenagers think their parents brought them into the world, anyway?

"So do you think you can stay there?" I asked.

"Hang on, I'll check." He covered the mouthpiece, and I could hear a muffled exchange in the background. Paul came back on the line: "Yeah, it's cool. But I didn't bring over any stuff."

"What do you need?"

"Like, a toothbrush? And another shirt, but not something you'd like, but a T-shirt, just grab something that's on my floor. And could you grab my pillows? You know how I can't sleep on strange pillows. And my comforter. I'll probably be sleeping on the basement couch, and I don't know how many blankets they've got."

I grabbed a pen by the phone and started to make a list.

"And my hairbrush? I don't want to use somebody else's hairbrush. Oh, and some toothpaste? I don't think Andy's family has mint toothpaste. And I guess some underwear. I don't need pajamas, though. I'll just sleep in my clothes."

"Anything else?" I asked, trying to hold back the sarcasm.

"I don't think so. It's just the one night."

"I'll drop this off in a while," I said. "I have some other things I have to do first."

"Okay. See ya later."

Angie came into the kitchen and I handed her Paul's list. "Can you gather those things up for your brother?"

She scanned it. "His comforter? What about his teddy bear? Should I pack that, too?"

"Just do it, okay?"

I wanted her out of the house as quickly as possible. I didn't know where Rick had gone, or whether he planned to come back. Given that he'd left empty-handed, and with a nasty bump on the head, it seemed logical to assume that he might return to get what he'd come for, and exact a bit of revenge. When I glanced outside I saw that the police car was still sitting there, Officer Greslow making some notes with the inside dome light on. As long as she was there, I figured we were safe from another visit.

I made sure the patio door was locked, as well as the side and garage doors. And while I waited for Angie to pack her things and Paul's, I slid the bolt on the front door.

Nothing was making any sense. When I'd

handed Rick those two envelopes of what I now knew to be counterfeit money, he was dumb-struck. The cash, it was obvious now, was not what he had come for.

There had to be something else in the purse.

"Okay," said Angie. "I'm ready." She had her own backpack slung over her shoulder packed with her things, and jammed under her arms were Paul's pillows and comforter, and a plastic bag filled with his toiletry items.

"Where's his backpack?" I asked, wondering why she hadn't used that instead of a plastic bag.

"It's already jammed with his crap. I wasn't reaching into it and taking anything out. He'll probably come by in the morning before he goes to school anyway to get his school stuff. It's on the way."

Before I unlocked the front door, I looked out the window to make sure no one was lurking there. "What are you doing, Dad?" Angie asked. The police car's brake lights came on as the car was shifted into drive, and then it pulled away slowly from the curb.

I opened the door. "Come on, quickly," I said, locking the door after Angie and hustling her to my old Civic. We tossed everything into the back seat, not wanting to soil Paul's linens with any potentially oily messes in the trunk.

Once the car doors were closed, I locked mine and ordered Angie to do the same. "What's with you tonight?" she asked. "You're more paranoid than usual."

I decided to tell her something that, while not addressing the issue directly, was still true. "I guess I'm on edge. Your mom phoned from work tonight, said there was a murder not too far from here."

"Really? Another murder? That's like, what, two in a week? In the *suburbs*, Dad? You told us these things never happened in the suburbs."

I ignored that. "Some woman was found dead in a garage. Beaten to death."

Angie decided that was not joke material, and said nothing. As we sped away down Chancery Park, I had to ask her for directions. "I don't know where this friend of yours lives."

"Turn right at Lilac," she said.

We drove on in silence, Angie speaking only to give directions. About five minutes later, we stopped out front of a two-story house with a couple of expensive cars in the driveway. Angie had her hand on the door handle when I reached out and touched her arm.

"I'm sorry, honey," I said.

She shrugged, avoiding my eyes. "I guess there's no way you could know the money was fake."

"No, not about that. I'm sorry about moving us out here. I know you haven't liked it out here, that you miss your friends downtown. I was only trying to do what I thought was best at the time."

Angie looked at me now, trying to read between the lines. "I know that."

"I'll talk to your mom. I don't know, maybe we need to reassess things."

"It's not that bad," she said. "I guess I'm getting used to it."

I smiled. "I love you, sweetheart."

"I love you too, Dad."

"Be careful," I said as she gave my hand a squeeze and slipped out the door. I watched her run up the walk and ring the bell, and waited until she was safely inside the house before driving away.

Next stop: Andy's. He and Paul were already out by the end of the driveway, goofing around on skateboards, when my headlights swept around the corner and caught them. Paul grabbed his stuff out of the back seat and wasted as little time as possible on conversation. I think he was afraid I'd change my mind, tell him to get in the car and come home.

I was well over the limit heading back to our house, but I slowed the last half-block, looking for unfamiliar cars parked at the curb, people crouched in the bushes. I parked, locked the Civic, and scooted into the house, looking over my shoulder as I pushed the door in, expecting Rick to suddenly appear, leaping onto me like a wild beast.

But he wasn't there, and once I was inside I threw the deadbolt. And stopped, holding my breath, listening for sounds. Was he back in the house somehow? As someone who worked for Valley Forest Estates, did he have some sort of master key? Could he get into any house he wanted, any time he wanted?

All I could hear was the blood pounding in my temples. I shouted, "I know you're here, asshole! And that cop's back, right out front! So if you're smart, you'll get the hell out!"

Nothing.

Tentatively, I moved into the house, turning on every light switch I passed. The broadloom, with its upgraded underpadding, allowed me to roam about noiselessly. I peeked into the kitchen, the living and dining rooms, the family room where we watched TV. Then I eased the door of my study open, my crumbled Robot still on the carpet. So far, no guests.

I turned the knob on the door to the ground-floor laundry room where I had stashed Stefanie Knight's purse in the washing machine. I opened the lid, worked the purse out from around the agitator, and took it back into the study. There, just as Rick had done, I dumped its contents out onto the floor, just beyond the range of Robot debris. On my hands and knees, I started sorting.

I put the envelopes to one side. Ditto for makeup items, tampons, car keys, change, expired coupons.

And my eyes settled on the black plastic film canister. I gave it a shake to see that it wasn't empty. A roll rattled inside. I popped the gray plastic lid off and dumped the roll into the palm of my hand.

There was no strip of film extended from it, so it was clearly one that had pictures on it. It was high-quality, black-and-white film. Twenty-four exposures.

Time to go downstairs and develop some pictures.

19

❖ ❖ ❖

By the time I had the negatives developed and hanging up to dry, I had some sense that this film was, in fact, what Rick might have been looking for. These were not pictures from someone's trip to Disney World. The twenty-four images were not from an excursion to Mount Rushmore. While I couldn't yet see who, exactly, was in these images, I could tell that there were two people, and that one of them was a man, and the other was a woman. And that these were not taken out on the street, or looking down from the Eiffel Tower, or at a baseball stadium. These were definitely indoor shots.

I had a lot of time to think in the darkroom while the negatives developed. My eyes adjusted to the near-total absence of light and sound, and I thought back to the trip Sarah and I had taken to the grocery store only a few hours ago, and how much our lives had changed since then. So far, only I was aware just how much.

My guess was that Rick's version of the events

of the evening were not entirely as he'd related them. I believed he had gone to Stefanie's house. And it was obvious that he had been to Stefanie's mother's house. But I didn't believe that when he went to Stefanie's house, she hadn't been there. My guess was that he went there to get back this roll of film. That he had been waiting for her to get home. That would explain the second broken window. And when Stefanie finally showed up, probably on foot, and hadn't been able to produce the film because she'd lost her purse, he ended up whacking her in the side of the head with a shovel. But he didn't believe her story about a stolen purse, so he went looking places where he thought Stefanie might have been. Where she could have left that film. That led him to her mother's house, and the slip of paper I'd left behind had led him to me.

It was hard not to feel that I had, as they say, blood on my hands.

I exposed one neg after another and started dipping the photographic paper into the various trays. As the images became less soft, as graininess gave way to definition, I could see that these pictures were all of the same two people, coupling away on what appeared to be a king-size bed in a well-lit bedroom. The camera had been mounted overhead somehow, perhaps behind a two-way mirror, so the shots in which these two were engaged in the traditional missionary style of lovemaking afforded few clues as to the man's identity. I could see that he was overweight, and balding, but with enough hair on his back and butt that he should be considering some sort of transplant. (A comb-over was definitely out of the question.) It was not the kind of picture that would be useful in picking a guy out of a lineup.

But the woman's identity was a different matter. With her hair splayed out across the pillow, it was clear that she was Stefanie Knight.

As I suspected would be the case, subsequent prints made identification of the man much simpler. It was as though Stefanie knew there had to be some shots on the roll in which the man's face would be easy to see. "Let me get on top," she must have said to him. "Let me dangle these in your face." It would have been difficult for him to say no.

And it was a face that I recognized. It had accompanied the article in *The Suburban* about the death of Willow Creek's best friend, Samuel Spender.

It was Roger Carpington, Oakwood town councilman.

I felt — and I know this is going to sound awfully trite — dirty. Working alone here in the darkroom, no one else in the house, developing pornographic images. Not that I'm a prude about such things, but I think that if you're going to have your picture taken screwing somebody else's brains out, you should at least have the right to know there's a camera in the room.

Somehow I felt ol' Roger here didn't know. And I was betting that Mrs. Carpington didn't know, either.

I wanted several prints of the shots where he was most identifiable. I was sorry, for the first time, not to have a digital camera. I could have displayed all these images on a computer screen, selected the ones I wanted, and printed them off in a couple of minutes. Doing things the old-fashioned way was going to keep me down here a bit longer, which was frustrating because I was itching to move forward with a plan that was slowly taking shape in my head.

And then, upstairs, a noise.

It was the front door opening. The darkroom was right under the front hall where you stepped into the house.

I'd locked it. I was sure I'd locked it. I'd double-checked every door after coming in from delivering Angie and dropping off Paul's stuff. Maybe my worst fear was true. Rick did have master keys. He could get into any house in Valley Forest Estates.

The door closed. The sound of footsteps followed. But once they moved away from the front door and were no longer over the darkroom, I couldn't track them.

Maybe I could stay right where I was. Rick might stick to the main floor, go back into the study and look for the purse, never come down here.

Get real. He would have seen the car in the

driveway, suspect that I had to be in the house somewhere. He'd want to find me first, use his powers of persuasion to get me to hand over the film. Maybe arrange an encounter between me and Quincy in the trunk of his car.

Careful not to bump into anything, I shifted over to the corner of the darkroom, where a tripod was leaned up against the wall. It would make a good weapon, I figured, with its three metal legs, once I could get out of the confines of the darkroom and had enough room in which to swing it.

I thought I could hear the door to the basement open, someone coming down the steps. The element of surprise was everything. The darkroom door was only a couple of paces from the bottom of the stairs. I'd spring out, tripod in hand, maybe catch Rick on the side of the head this time.

I held my breath. Counted to myself. On the count of three.

One.

Size things up as fast as you can. Watch for a gun. If he's got a gun, try to swing for his arm.

Two.

If he's got someone with him, an accomplice, try to take out the bigger guy first. Go for heads. Go for their fucking heads. Okay, this is it, pal. It's showtime.

Three.

I burst out of the door, screamed something along the lines of "Ahhhh!" and, grasping the tripod legs down at the end, swung them back over my shoulder like a baseball bat, putting all my energy into the swing, getting ready to let loose with all the power I could muster.

"Dad!"

Paul sprang back, flinging himself into the stairs, raising his hands defensively. I put the brakes on halfway through the swing, which threw me completely off balance, and I staggered into the wall. The top of the tripod crashed into the drywall, creating a deep gash.

"Jesus! Dad! It's me!"

I stumbled onto the floor, threw my arms out to brace myself. "Paul!" I gasped. "What the hell are you doing here?"

"I live here!"

I was trying to catch my breath. "You're supposed to be at Andy's! I told you to stay there!"

"I forgot to ask you to bring some video games." He was as out of breath as I, still sprawled out across the stairs. "We needed some games. Andy's mom drove us over. They're out in the car, waiting for me."

Slowly, I got back on my feet. "Okay, go get your games."

"What were you doing in there? Were you hiding or something?"

"I was just developing some pictures, that's all."

"What pictures? Are you doing Angie's assignment for her?" Of all the things I'd done tonight, Paul would consider giving his sister an unfair advantage at school my worst crime. I decided to go with it.

"I was just doing up a couple of prints for her, that's all."

Paul was still breathing heavily. "I thought you were going to kill me."

"I was not going to kill you. You just startled me." I was rubbing my hand across my face. "Come here." Paul got to within a foot of me and I pulled him closer, threw my arms around him, patted his back a couple of times. "I wasn't going to kill you. Now get your games."

As I pushed him away, he looked at the hole in the wall. "Mom's going to love that."

"Yeah, no doubt."

Paul studied me for a moment and said, "Angie's right."

"What do you mean, Angie's right?"

"You're turning into some sort of crazy person." He went into the rec room, grabbed three game cartridges, and met me again at the base of the stairs. "I'll see you in the morning."

"Okay," I said. "I'll see you then." And he mounted the steps, two at a time. I heard him go out the front door, but I couldn't be sure he'd locked it, so I ran up, threw the deadbolt just as Andy's mother's car backed out of the drive and headed off.

Back in the darkroom, I dried half a dozen prints with Carpington's face fully visible. In the study I found a regular letter envelope for the negatives, and a larger one for the eight-by-ten glossies. I dug out the phone book and opened up the Oakwood pages to the C's, running my finger down the column until I encountered "Carpington R."

I glanced at the clock. It was nearly ten. I dialed.

After the third ring, a woman answered. "Hello?"

"Hi," I said. "Is this Mrs. Carpington?"

"Yes, it is."

"Sorry for calling so late, but I wondered if I could speak to Councilman Carpington." Make it sound like official business, I figured.

"I'm sorry, but he's not in. He's at a council meeting this evening, and they can run pretty late."

"A council meeting? That's going on now?"

"That's right. It started around six-thirty."

"At the municipal offices?"

"Yes. Of course. Would you like to leave a message? I'm sure Roger would be happy to get back to you, if not tonight, certainly by tomorrow."

"No," I said. "That's okay. Maybe I'll see if I can find him over at the meeting."

"Suit yourself," she said, and hung up.

I took the negatives and tucked them into the hull of my still-unassembled *Seaview* submarine model, then carefully glued the bottom in place, sealing them inside. And once again, I scooped everything back into Stefanie Knight's purse and took it with me, as well as the brown over-

281

sized envelope with the prints of Roger Carpington's rendezvous with Stefanie. From the front-hall table I grabbed my cell and slid it into my jacket pocket, double-checked that the front door was securely locked behind me, and went out to the car.

The municipal building, designed with as much style and imagination as the new developments in Oakwood, sat across from the mall where Angie had been picked up for passing counterfeit money. It was a redbrick-and-black-metal eyesore, sitting on the landscape like a big shoebox. There was a large parking lot around back, but it was mostly empty. Most of the town's employees were home and presumably getting ready for bed at this hour, but there were a handful of cars, belonging no doubt to the mayor and members of the town council and a few town administrators, plus a few taxpayers with some particular axe to grind or request to make.

I parked, took the brown envelope with me, and walked into the building, following the signs to the council chamber, a high-ceilinged room with light fixtures hanging from long wires, a slightly sloped floor, theaterlike, to allow spectators a chance to watch the council members in action, and two banks of slightly angled desks for the council members, with one in the middle for the mayor, forming a V at the front of the room.

There couldn't have been more than twenty

constituents watching the proceedings, plus a reporter from *The Suburban* taking notes, so my entrance was observed by nearly everyone who glanced up and watched me walk down the aisle and slip quietly into a seat.

There were six council members on either side of the mayor for a total of twelve, with nameplates in front of them. Roger Carpington, portly and balding, in a gray suit and tie, was seated at the far right end. With his index finger he pushed his glasses further up on his nose.

The mayor, a short woman with bluish hair in her late sixties, was speaking. "I think the next speaker on our list is Lucille Belfountain."

A woman in the front row got up and approached a microphone at the foot of the aisle.

"Uh, yes, hello?" she said. "Can you hear me? Is this mike working?"

"We can hear you fine," the mayor said patiently.

"Uh, Madam Mayor, members of the council, thank you for letting me speak to you tonight. I live at 43 Myers Road, and have lived there for the last twenty-seven years, and we have had, in the last few months, a severe problem with dogs running loose."

Not particularly interested in Lucille Belfountain's pack-of-dogs dilemma, my mind wandered. My eyes kept settling on Carpington at the end of the table. He was reviewing a stack of papers in front of him, making notes in the margins, looking up occasionally to hear what

Lucille had to say. If you only knew, I thought.

One of the other councilmen, who was apparently quite knowledgeable about animal control problems, promised Lucille Belfountain that he would make sure the town's animal control officers did extra patrols in her neighborhood and urged her to call him back in a couple of weeks if things did not improve. That business done, the mayor asked whether any members of the council had any other business to bring up before she adjourned the meeting.

Carpington leaned into his microphone. "Yes, Mayor, I had a matter I wanted to bring to the council's attention."

"Go ahead," she said.

"I just wanted to serve notice that at the next regular meeting of the council, I will be putting a motion on the table that we approve the final phase of development for Valley Forest Estates. I believe all the environmental concerns have been addressed and that it would be beneficial not only for the developers of this site but for the town as a whole to approve the development at this time. It broadens our tax base, means more jobs, and more families coming into the community of Oakwood and making contributions on so many levels."

I was thinking, You have a hairy butt. You have a hairy butt.

From the other end of the table, Councilman Ben Underwood spoke. "I can't believe what I'm hearing. Samuel Spender, who spoke to us so eloquently only a few weeks ago about the need to protect Willow Creek, died violently but a few days ago, and I think Councilman Carpington's motion is an insult to that man's memory and should be set aside at least until the police investigation into Mr. Spender's death has become fruitful."

"Now hold on," Carpington said. "I'm on record as saying that I had nothing but respect for Samuel Spender and the work he did throughout his life to protect the environment, and we should all be grateful to him for the concerns he raised about Willow Creek, and had he not done that, then Valley Forest Estates would not have had the benefit of his suggestions when it came to revising the plans for its final phase."

"Oh gee, Roger," Underwood sneered, "what did your friends do, cut back from 300 homes to 299?"

"That's a ridiculous comment to make," Carpington said. "You'd rather wipe out an entire neighborhood if it meant saving a salamander. Furthermore, I see no connection between police investigating the circumstances of Mr. Spender's death and the development plans for this property."

"Talk about ridiculous comments. You wouldn't —"

"I think we can hold this debate," the mayor interrupted, "when Councilman Carpington makes his motion. If there's no other new business, then I would like to make a motion to declare this meeting adjourned. Do we have a seconder?"

Carpington jammed his papers into a brief-case, shaking his head angrily. At the other end, Underwood grabbed his things and stormed out of the council chamber. This guy was clearly not a friend of Don Greenway's. Don't take any walks down by the creek, I thought.

Carpington was hotfooting it to the exit when I tried to head him off. "Mr. Carpington?" I said. "Excuse me?"

He glanced over at me, still bristling from his exchange with Underwood. "Yes?" he said, looking at me over the top of his glasses.

"Do you have a moment?"

"It's really late," he said. "Why don't you call my secretary tomorrow, or my home, and make an appointment?"

"I'm afraid it can't wait. It's rather urgent." I raised the brown envelope in front of me. There were other council members, within earshot, filing past us.

"I'm terribly sorry, but I have to insist. Another time."

I leaned in close to him, whispered. "It's about Stefanie Knight, Mr. Carpington."

It was like you'd turned on a tap and drained the blood out of him in a couple of seconds. He swallowed, glanced over at his colleagues, then whispered back to me, "My office."

He led me down a tiled hallway and into a small room that served as his municipal office.

It contained a small desk stacked with papers, a computer tucked in the corner, and several town surveys tacked to the walls. He quickly closed the door behind us and directed me into a chair. A cheap "World's Greatest Dad" statuette sat on his desk next to a family photo. He grinned at the camera, surrounded by his plain wife and generic-looking children — a girl and two boys, all under the age of ten.

"What's this about?" he said, slipping behind his desk. "I'm afraid I don't know anyone named, what was it? Stefanie White?"

"Knight," I said. "Nice try. I guess that was why you dragged me in here and closed the door, because you've never heard of her."

"I'm afraid I don't even know who you are."

"Zack Walker. I'm one of your constituents. I live in the Valley Forest Estates subdivision, on Greenway Lane."

"I see. Oh yes, Stefanie Knight. I believe she works in the Valley Forest Estates office. I think I've run into her there."

Fuck it, I thought. I opened the envelope, withdrew one of the prints, and flung it across the desk at him. It landed image down. He grabbed it by one corner, flipped it over.

I didn't believe he could lose any more color. He was the whitest, pastiest-looking weasel I'd ever had the pleasure of sitting across a desk from, and this included all the newspaper editors I'd ever worked for.

The hand holding the print began to shake.

Carpington ran his hand over his scalp, wiping away the droplets of sweat that were beginning to form.

"How much?" he asked. "How much do you want?"

20

❖ ❖ ❖

Right off the bat, Roger Carpington did not strike me as a guy skilled in the art of negotiating. Caving is not one of the standard tactics. One look at the picture of himself with Stefanie Knight and he was ready to cut me a check.

"You think I'm here to blackmail you?" I asked.

Carpington, still sweating, said, "What other purpose could you have in mind when you come to me with a picture like this? You're out to ruin me, that's obvious. But I'm guessing that you can be dissuaded from that if we can agree upon a price."

I leaned back in my chair. "I do think that the motive behind this picture, and the other ones I have in this envelope" — Carpington fixed his eyes upon it — "is definitely blackmail, Mr. Carpington, but I'm not your blackmailer. It's somebody else. Maybe it's Stefanie Knight. Has she been blackmailing you? Did she tell you she'd tell your wife about your affair if you didn't pay her off?"

Carpington was wide-eyed. "That's ridiculous. I'm not having an affair with Stefanie."

I furrowed my brow, slid another one of the prints from the envelope out halfway, and peered at it. "You're right. This one here, where she's got your dick in her mouth, that doesn't look like an affair. Maybe she's just a consultant helping you interpret the town's official plan."

"You're a disgusting man," Carpington said. "Get out of my office."

"Okay," I said, and stood out of my chair. "Ta-ta."

"Wait! Sit down. Sit down. Tell me what it is you want."

"I want you to tell me about Stefanie. Everything."

He shook his head slowly. "What do you care? And how do you happen to have these pictures? Do you know Stefanie? Are you working with her?"

"No, I don't know her," I said, "although I have seen her this evening." I watched for anything in Carpington's eyes, a glimmer. There was nothing. "How I happen to have these pictures is my business for now, but I can tell you that the negatives are safely stored away, and if something were to happen to me, there are people who'd know where to find them." I was surprisingly good at this.

"I see," Carpington said. He seemed to be abandoning any plans he might have had to leap

290

across the desk and rip the envelope out of my hands.

"How did you meet Stefanie?" I asked.

He squirmed in his seat. "I met her through a business acquaintance."

"Let me guess. Don Greenway."

"Yes, as a matter of fact. I've met with Mr. Greenway on several occasions, and Stefanie works in his office. I believe she's his secretary."

"You've been very supportive of Mr. Greenway's development proposals."

Carpington shrugged. "I think people like Mr. Greenway bring economic prosperity to a place like Oakwood. They bring jobs, and families, a broadened tax base, hope for the future of our community."

I needed some Maalox. "Not everyone agrees with you on that, though. Councilman Underwood, for example, and Sam Spender. Greenway's had to deal with formidable opposition to his subdivision, particularly the last phase near Willow Creek. He must really appreciate having someone like you, in a position of influence, on the council and all, on his side."

"Are you insinuating something?"

"You tell me. You're boffing his secretary. That seems like a pretty good inducement to vote in favor of his development. My guess is, keeping you entertained is part of Stefanie's job description. But just in case you start getting an attack of the guilts, or ever decide to vote against Valley Forest Estates, Greenway has a little something in reserve, these pictures, to make sure you do exactly what he wants you to do."

"Oh God," Carpington said, cupping his hands over nose and mouth. "Oh God oh God oh God."

"When's the last time you saw Stefanie?" I asked, ignoring his weeping.

"What? Uh, yesterday. At her house."

"Over on Rambling Rose?"

"Yes. It's not actually her house, it's one owned by Greenway's company, they built a lot of the homes in that area a few years ago, but she lives there."

"Is that where you'd have your . . . encounters?"

Carpington nodded.

"There's a mirror on the ceiling," I said. "In the bedroom."

Carpington looked as though he was getting jealous. "So you've been with her, too."

"No, can't say that I have, but I'm guessing that's how they got these pictures of the two of you. The camera was mounted behind two-way glass, looking straight down. I guess Greenway or one of his people was up in the attic while you two went at it, fired off the shots he needed, waited until you were gone, and came back down. Left the film with Stefanie to get developed."

Carpington fiddled vacantly with papers on his desk. "I'm finished. It's all over for me."

"Could be. But for the moment, as long as these prints and the negatives don't land in the wrong hands, you're still okay. So I've got a few more questions. You saw Stefanie yesterday, at her house. What did you talk about? How was she?"

"We didn't talk about that much. We just, you know. But she did seem, I don't know, different."

"How do you mean, different?"

"On edge, distracted. She had something on her mind."

"Did she say anything?"

"I don't know. Why does it matter? Why don't you just ask her yourself?"

"I'm asking you. What did she say?"

"She wanted to know how much it would cost to fly somewhere. The Bahamas, or Barbados, San Francisco. She was throwing out all these names of places. I asked her if she was going on a trip, and she said maybe. She said she might be going away."

"Alone, or with someone else?"

"She, she didn't say. It's almost like she was talking about running away. Like she was scared. But I may have read that wrong. Maybe she's just planning a vacation. Maybe she's going away with her boyfriend."

"Boyfriend? She has a boyfriend?"

"Well, I don't know for sure that she does, but I have this sense that there's someone else. Someone she's seeing. Or has been seeing."

"That must hurt," I said, "the idea that she might be unfaithful to you and all." I thought Carpington might shoot me a look, but he missed the irony and kept staring down at his desk.

"No, I know what we've got and what the limits are. I know she doesn't like me. I know why she's doing what she's doing. I'm not stupid. I mean, look at me. What are the chances a girl like Stefanie Knight would be interested in a guy like me?"

Well, he had me there, but I decided not to say anything. But what I was thinking was, Could this guy have any more motives for wanting Stefanie Knight dead? She was clearly part of some blackmail scheme against him. Maybe she'd been threatening to tell his wife about what they'd been up to. And there was the jealousy angle. Carpington figured she was seeing somebody else.

I was starting to feel better already. I was moving down from the number one spot on the list of possible suspects. "Sure, Detective," I could hear myself saying in an interrogation room, "I stole her purse, but you want an even better suspect? Check out *this* guy."

But all that aside, I didn't think he was the one who'd struck Stefanie in the head with a shovel. He just didn't seem to have it in him.

I said, "You think this boyfriend was Rick?"

"Rick?" Carpington, who I thought couldn't look any worse, moved toward bilious. "Don't even talk to me about him. He's a total psychopath. He's insane."

"We've met. To be honest with you, I don't care much for him, either. We didn't hit it off very well."

"Let me tell you what he did to me. He took me to this house they'd started building — this was back when he and Greenway and Mr. Benedetto first started talking to me about needing some help at the council level and at the planning committee — and all that was done was the basement, which they'd capped off with the beams and plywood for the first floor, and he took me down a ladder to show me — there were no stairs yet — how the first stages of construction are done. And I'm looking around, and I notice Rick's gone, and so's the ladder, and I'm trapped down there, in this wide-open basement with a layer of wood overtop, and then Rick drops this snake — and I'm not talking about some little snake or something — but this giant snake into the basement."

"Quincy."

"Yes! That was its name! And he starts slithering around, and I swear to God, I was never so scared in my life. I started screaming at Rick to let me up, to put the ladder back down, but he stood up there, looking down at me through this hole where the stairs would go, and he just laughed. I was running around the whole basement trying to stay ahead of this snake, and Rick's asking me whether they can count on my support at the council, and telling me that when I say yes, he'll put the ladder back and come down and deal with Quincy. He's the biggest snake I've ever seen."

"Who, Rick? Or Quincy?"

Carpington almost smiled. "Mr. Greenway apologized for him later. Said he wanted our relationship to be more cordial than that."

"The question was, do you think Stefanie is seeing Rick?"

"I suppose it's possible; they went out a long time ago. Rick still keeps in touch with her mother, that's who looks after the snake, I think. But I don't think Stef wants anything to do with him anymore. I think she's scared of him."

"What about Greenway? I mean, she's working with him every day in the office."

"Maybe." Carpington thought. "Or maybe Mr. Benedetto. He usually gets what he wants."

"Greenway's boss? Is that who you're talking about?"

"That's right. He's the one who bought the land for the development. But he turns things over to Greenway, to get the actual subdivision going." Carpington took another look at the photo, pressed his lips together. "I can't believe she'd be in on something like that. I thought she was better than the others, than the rest of that bunch at Valley Forest."

"Yeah, you must be very disappointed. You hang out with a woman whose coworkers resort to blackmail and drop you into basements with snakes, it must be a shock to learn she might be less than upstanding."

"I have to talk to her," Carpington said. "I have to find out why she'd do this to me." He grabbed the one print, folded it in half, and shoved it inside his suit jacket.

"That's okay," I said. "I have more. But I think you're wasting your time."

"What do you mean? Has she left? Did she actually go away? It was only yesterday that she was talking about this."

"No," I said. "Stefanie's dead."

He opened his mouth to say something, but there were no words. He got up suddenly, shoved his way past me to get to the hallway. By the time I was out of my chair and had my head out the door, I could see him running down the hall for the doors to the parking lot.

When I got to the door, I spotted Carpington getting into a dark blue or black Cadillac. I ran to my Civic, got in, and debated my next move. I'd rattled Carpington's cage, to be sure, and it seemed worth knowing what he'd do next. I'd set something in motion by letting him know I knew about his affair with Stefanie, and by telling him she was dead, and I wanted to see where it went.

He didn't immediately race out of the parking lot, as I'd expected. I could see him in the car, punching numbers into a cell phone, waiting for someone to answer, then talking rapidly, waving his one free arm around inside the car. He talked for two, maybe three minutes, then threw the phone down. The brake lights came on, the Cadillac was put into drive and squealed out of the lot.

The Caddy had a lot more pickup than the Civic, which wheezed in pursuit. There weren't many cars on the road this late at night, and I didn't want to follow so closely that he'd notice me, and that was exactly how it was working out. The Caddy's taillights receded into the distance as Carpington floored it.

He was heading in the direction of Valley Forest Estates. He approached the subdivision from the south side, down by the creek, and I watched as the red lights sped into an area where the homes were in the earlier stages of construction.

When I saw the red lights come to a stop, I hung back, pulled over to the side of the road and killed my lights. The Caddy sat there, idling, Carpington staying behind the wheel, evidently waiting for a meeting. I backed the Civic between a stack of lumber and an idle forklift, figured it was far enough off the street not to be noticed, and got out. I was a couple of hundred yards away from Carpington's car, and crept along carefully, behind the houses, making my way between wheelbarrows and stacks of bricks and two-by-fours. The sky was clear, the stars were out and the moon was nearly full, so I could see fairly well once my eyes adjusted. Still, at one point, my right leg dropped down into a shallow ditch and I went down, but I was still far enough away from the Caddy not to have attracted any attention. I got up, worried that I might have twisted my ankle, but everything seemed to be working properly. My jeans and shirt were scuffed with dirt.

I wanted to get as close to the Caddy as possible without being detected. It was parked, the motor still idling, directly in front of a two-story house still in the skeletal stage. Boards that would later be covered with insulation and drywall marked out the exterior and interior walls. I bypassed the door frames and slipped between two studs into the house, making my way to the front, where I got down on the floor, made myself as flat as possible, and settled in to watch the show.

Carpington constantly checked his mirror, made another call on his cell, fiddled with the radio, blotted his brow. The two of us waited nearly ten minutes before a set of headlights appeared at the far end of the street, followed closely by a second. The two cars approached slowly. The first, a four-door imported sedan, drove past the Caddy and angled in front of it, while the second car, a small Lincoln, pulled up tight behind it. Carpington was effectively boxed in.

The driver of the Lincoln killed the lights and engine and got out. In the moonlight, I could see that it was Don Greenway, still in his suit.

Carpington got out of the Cadillac, turning off the engine but leaving the headlights on. Rick, who got out of the import, shielded his eyes from the glare as he joined Greenway, who was standing in front of an already raving Carpington.

"She's dead!" he shouted. "This guy comes and sees me and tells me she's dead!"

"Roger, calm down," Greenway said, trying to maintain a normal tone of voice.

"How do you expect me to calm down? Stefanie's dead!"

"I only just heard about it myself," Greenway said. "The police were by the office."

"Look, I never signed on for anything like this! Spender was one thing, and I never wanted to go along with that, but this is too much!"

Rick said, "I think you should lower your voice, asshole. There's houses over that ridge people are living in, dickwad, and they might hear you."

"Maybe I don't care about that. Maybe it's too late to care about anything."

Greenway looked at Rick and nodded. Suddenly, Rick slapped Carpington across the face savagely, sending the councilman sprawling up against the side of his Caddy. Before he even had time to touch his cheek, Rick had him by the shirt and was dragging him across the mud-caked street in the direction of his car. Rick reached into his pocket, pulled out a set of remote keys, and popped the trunk on the sedan, which opened about an inch.

As Rick swung the trunk open a tiny light came on long enough for Carpington to see what was inside. There was barely time for him to scream "No!" before Rick had shoved him inside and slammed the trunk shut.

21

❖ ❖ ❖

Maybe, if I'd ever served my country in the military or something, I'd be more familiar with the sounds of a man screaming. Once, when called out around midnight to a particularly grisly highway accident as a young newspaper photographer, I listened while a man burned to death in a car, rescue crews unable to get close to him. The driver of a tanker truck had fallen asleep at the wheel and gone through a red light, virtually crushing a Chevette that was crossing its path. It was a wonder the man in the Chevette remained alive long enough for police and fire officials, and me, to arrive and hear him die. His final cries of anguish had stayed with me for a long time. Even now, some twenty years later, I can still hear him calling "Princess!" which I learned later was the nickname of the nine-year-old daughter he'd left behind.

And maybe those cries were worse than what I was hearing now. It's a tough one to call. But there was something about Carpington's screams that had nothing to do with pain. They were screams of outright terror and hysteria, and listening to them made my blood run cold. They were the screams — interspersed with cries of "Get me out!" and "Let me out!" — of a man finding himself locked in a trunk with his worst nightmare. The parked car bounced on its springs like it was being driven down a washboard road as Carpington rolled about and kicked and pounded at the trunk lid and walls.

It was hard to hear what Greenway and Rick were saying to each other, but they couldn't have looked more relaxed. At one point, Greenway pointed at the moon, and Rick looked up, nodded, as if to say "You're right, it is a beautiful moon tonight, isn't it?"

Finally, the screams not subsiding at all, Greenway nodded to Rick, who popped the trunk open and hauled Carpington out. I was surprised, frankly, to see him still alive. At the very least, I figured Quincy would already be in the process of squeezing the life out of him, which I'd have almost welcomed if it would have meant an end to the screaming. But aside from his clothes being all rumpled, and a cut on his face from bumping into something in the trunk, the councilman didn't look too bad.

Rick said, "Now, are you ready to calm down?"

"Yes, yes, thank you, thank you for getting me out of there."

"He's still pretty drowsy," Rick said. "Look at him, he's practically sleeping like a baby." He slapped Carpington in the face again. "I think you upset him."

"What, why isn't he moving more?" Carpington asked.

"He's on Prozac for Pythons. Merle and Jimmy gave him something, it's taking him a while to recover. But I think I can guarantee you that the *next* time we put you in there, if we have to put you in there, he's going to be right back to his old self."

"Okay," Carpington said. "Okay. That won't be necessary, I promise."

Greenway approached Carpington and slipped his arm around his shoulder like they were old friends. "Now, Roger, what's gotten you so upset tonight?"

"This man came to see me. He wanted to know about Stefanie, and he told me she was dead."

"Who was this man?" Greenway asked.

"I'm trying to remember his name. He said he lives in Valley Forest, on the street you named after yourself."

Rick cocked his head to one side. "Was his name Walker?"

"Yes, that was it."

"That fucker. He's turning up everywhere tonight. You know what he did?" He was asking Greenway.

"What did he do?"

"He fucking hit me right in the head with a robot."

Greenway appeared to be considering whether this was something he wanted to follow up on, then decided against it. But Rick wasn't through: "And I was really prepared to like the guy, you know? He wrote this book I got from the prison library, about these Earthlings who go to another planet, and they try to get everyone to stop believing in God, but when they do, there's all this shit." He paused. "I don't read all that many books, you know."

"Really," said Greenway.

"But I really liked that one. He told me he's writing a sequel, although I got a feeling he may not get a chance to finish it." He smiled to himself. "I'm gonna have to drop in on him again. He's got some of the coolest toys. Check this out." He pulled my Batmobile from his jacket pocket.

"That's very nice, Rick."

"You press this little button here on the hood, and this chain cutter pops out of the front bumper. It used to have an antenna, but I guess that snapped off."

That son of a bitch. Mint condition since I was seven years old, and now this.

Greenway waited a second to see whether Rick was done, concluded that he was, and said to Carpington, "Roger, why did this Walker guy come to see you?"

"Like I said, he wanted to know about Stefanie. What happened to her?"

"From what I understand," Greenway said,

"someone broke into her house and killed her. She'd been hit in the head."

"Oh my God."

"I know. It's been a terrible blow for all of us. She was a very special lady. I still can't believe it's happened." He said this all very evenly, as though he'd rehearsed it. Calmly, he asked, "It wasn't you, was it, Roger? Did you have a bit of a tiff with Stefanie?"

He recoiled in horror. "What? Of course not! It's not my style to go around hitting people in the head. Or leaving them dead in creeks, for that matter." Carpington was looking at Rick when he said this. "You said that was going to look like an accident."

Rick shrugged.

"You said it would look like he'd tripped and hit his head and drowned. But the police say he was murdered, that his head was bashed in before he hit the water. You're an amateur, you know that?"

Rick said, "Maybe you need a bit more time in the trunk."

Carpington thought about that. "No. That won't be necessary. All I'm saying is, it was supposed to be an accident."

"Water under the bridge, as they say," said Greenway. "We have to deal with things as they are now, not as we wish they were. The police have been to see me about Mr. Spender, but I can assure you that they don't think we have anything to do with this. We are businessmen.

We don't handle things that way."

Carpington swung his head back and forth briefly, as though trying to make the madness go away. He stopped, glared at Greenway accusingly. "Is it standard business practice to take pictures of people when they're making love?"

"I'm sorry, Roger, what's that?"

The councilman pulled the folded print out of his inside jacket pocket and thrust it before the developer. Greenway opened the Caddy door so the dome light would come on and examined the picture. Rick leaned in for a look.

"I always said Stef had nice tits," Rick said. "Do you have more of these?"

"Well, Roger, how did you happen to come into possession of this?" Greenway asked.

"Walker. He gave it to me. Said he's got the negatives. How would he have these? Is he working for you? Did you have these taken? Walker said there was a camera in the ceiling."

"That is interesting," Greenway said, thinking. To Rick: "Does any of this make any sense to you?"

"I haven't really had a chance to update you, Mr. Greenway. But you know how you sent me out earlier, to try to find Stefanie and see if she'd run off with the ledger —"

Ledger?

"— I went by her mom's house, and she said this guy had been by looking for her, said he had something of hers, which kind of sounded like bullshit, but I also thought it sounded kind of suspicious, so I tracked this guy down through his e-mail address, and it turned out to be this asshole who wanted his shower fixed? Remember you sent me out there to have a look at it?"

Greenway's head went up and down slowly. "The obnoxious man who came by the office, when Mr. Spender dropped by."

Obnoxious? I was the one who was obnoxious?

"Yeah, same guy, I guess. So I go see him, and he hands me Stefanie's purse."

"What was he doing with Stefanie's purse?"

Stretched out on the plywood floor, my head tucked low, I thought, Man, this is confusing.

"Said he'd found it, was trying to give it back. So I dumped it out, right, but there's no ledger there. It's too big to fit in it, I think. But you know what was in there?"

Greenway shook his head.

"Money. Two envelopes, stuffed with fifties. Tons of them. Looked like the stuff we make up on the photocopier sometimes, to pay off inspectors and stuff. But these bills, they didn't look like they'd been weathered at all like we usually do them. It's like she'd just made them."

Greenway took this in. "She must have been doing a lot of photocopying. It's like she was planning to make a run for it. Grab the ledger, print up some cash, head for the hills. Something spooked her."

"She was talking to me yesterday," Carpington offered, "about going away someplace. She was mentioning lots of different places, like she hadn't decided where to go, but she was going to go someplace."

"Did you notice anything else in the purse?" Greenway asked Rick.

He tried to think. "Now that you mention it, I think there was one of those little film things."

"Stefanie was supposed to have brought that in to me a couple of days ago," Greenway said. "Makes you wonder whether she was ever planning to do it."

"So she was in on it," Carpington said. "She let you take pictures of her with me."

"Roger, Roger, Roger, what am I going to do with you? Yes, I had those pictures taken. Just a little extra insurance for our relationship. It wouldn't be a good thing for you to suddenly get a conscience. That could be a very bad thing for all of us, but especially for you."

Carpington was quiet.

"You see, Roger, you don't work for the town of Oakwood. You don't represent all those people in your ward. You work for me. You represent me. You only have one constituent, Roger. I'm your constituent. I pay taxes, and I want to be represented well. You're my guy, and I want you to be doing your very best. You just might be mayor of Oakwood someday, once that blue-haired bitch decides to step down, and we might even have some ways of persuading her to do just that. We have things on you, Roger.

Things that could send you away for a very long time. We go down, you go down, but you go down a lot harder. Our lawyers have bigger dicks than yours, Roger. If things ever came crashing down, and I don't see any reason to think that they ever would, but if they did, you can be sure that the only person who's ever going to go away is you." Greenway paused. "If you were even lucky enough to make it to prison."

Carpington seemed to understand. Rick smiled at him and patted the trunk of his car loudly.

"It's very important to Mr. Benedetto that you keep doing the fine job you've been doing on the council. You've been speaking up for us at every opportunity, and we appreciate it. He and I were talking just the other day, and he said to me, 'Do you think Roger would like an addition built on his house?' "

"An addition?"

"A deck maybe. Or a family room? Someplace to put in a home theater? You've got kids. I'm sure they like to watch a lot of movies."

"It's true," Carpington said quietly. "They do like to watch movies. Especially those ones with that Adam Sandler guy."

"I like him, too," said Rick. "You know that one, where he's the water boy?"

"Yeah?" said Carpington.

"What's that one called?"

"*The Waterboy.*"

"I know, that's the one I mean. Where he plays the water boy."

"That's what it's called," said Carpington. "It's called *The Waterboy*."

"Oh yeah, I think you're right."

Greenway cut in. "I wish we had time to continue this conversation all night, gentlemen. But we have other matters to attend to. Roger, I'll talk to Mr. Benedetto about that tomorrow, see if we can't get something going on those home improvements for you."

"That would be very nice," Carpington said. "I'm sorry if I came on a bit strong tonight. I've been under a lot of stress lately."

"Of course. Haven't we all. The important thing, Roger, is that you remember whose side you're on. And don't you worry about this Walker fellow. We'll take care of him for you. You won't be bothered with him anymore."

"If you say so," Carpington said, much calmer now than he'd been when he first got out of the trunk. "But I have to know. What happened to Stefanie? If anyone ever sees those pictures of us together, they're going to think I had some reason to kill her."

"Yes, I suppose they would," Greenway said. "I guess we need to get those negatives back, don't we?"

"Leave that to me," Rick said.

That seemed to settle it. Then, suddenly, all three of them stopped talking and froze. They'd heard some kind of noise. They waited, no one breathing, to see whether they'd hear it again.

They did, and turned and looked in my direction.

The noise was coming from inside my jacket.

22

❖ ❖ ❖

I remember when I was shopping for a new cell phone, the salesman was very eager to sign me up for extra features. Call display, call forwarding, three-way calling, detailed billing, even video games I could play on the screen. Maybe, instead of a standard ring, I'd like to hear one of my favorite tunes when someone called me. And of course, there was the extended-warranty plan, for only seventy dollars. What the salesman seemed to be implying was, This is a great phone, the best on the market, but you better buy this added warranty, because, just between you and me, it's a piece of shit. And then, finally: "Would you like a phone that has the optional vibration feature, so that when you're in a theater you can tell someone's trying to phone you, but there's no ring to disturb everyone around you? It's a very good thing to have."

No, I said. I don't care about call display, call forwarding, three-way calling, detailed billing, or video games. I do not want to hear the theme from *Titanic* when someone calls me. I do not want an extended warranty. And I do not want a phone that vibrates. I turn my phone off when I go into a theater. I am not the guy who accompanies the President, who carries the briefcase with the codes. No one cares whether they can reach me immediately. I just want a phone that I can take with me. That's all.

But would it have killed the salesman to point out other possible scenarios where a vibrating phone might be an advantage? "What if, one night, you're hiding in a house under construction, eavesdropping on three guys as they discuss their murder plans and their wishes to kill you the next time they run into you, and your phone starts ringing, revealing to them your hiding spot? Wouldn't you want a vibrating phone then?"

And of course, I would have said yes.

It would have been very nice, at that moment, to have a phone that jiggled instead of ringing. But since I didn't, Don Greenway, Roger Carpington, and the psychopath I knew only as Rick were all looking in my direction.

"D'ya hear that?" Rick said.

"Sounds like a phone," Carpington said.

"No shit?" said Rick. "You think?"

By now it had rung three times. I was holding my breath, waiting for a fourth ring, but it never came. At the first ring, my mind was scrambling. My first impulse was to try to smother the gadget with my hands. If you could have seen me in the dark, you'd have thought I'd been shot in the chest, the way I was clutching it. I wanted to turn it off, but that would have meant taking it out of my jacket, at which point the ring would have become even louder. You had to press a button on the top and hold it hard for three seconds to shut it down, and it wouldn't take much more time than that for these three men to reach the building.

And then I had another idea. I slipped the phone out of my jacket and left it in plain view on the plywood floor, and scurried backward, crablike, into the darker recesses of the house. There was a stack of four-by-eight sheets of drywall, about two feet high, back around where the kitchen was going to be, and I slithered in behind it as the three men walked across the dirt toward the house. Now I could only hear what they had to say, not see them.

"It was right around here," Greenway said.

"Yeah, over this way," Rick said.

I heard feet stepping up into the house, then Carpington's voice. "Look, right here."

Then Greenway: "Must belong to one of the guys working on the site. Fell out of his pocket or something."

Yes, I thought. Keep thinking that way. It's just a cell phone. Not *my* cell phone.

"Prob'ly his mom calling to see why he isn't home yet," Rick cracked.

Greenway: "I'll take it back to the office, whoever belongs to it can claim it there. Maybe we should leave a note or something."

I heard the click of a ballpoint pen. "I'll leave a note right on this stud here," Rick said. " 'Lost a phone? Check at office.' That should do it."

"There's two 'f's in 'office,' " Greenway said.

Rick said nothing. I heard them step off the plywood, head back toward their cars. I felt it was safe enough to peek above the top of the drywall. They were huddled together by Carpington's Caddy, saying a few last words before they went their separate ways. And then, once again, the sound of a cell phone.

"I think it's mine," Greenway said. He reached into his jacket, opened a small flap, said, "Hello?"

But there was another ring.

"Not mine," said Greenway. Carpington reached into his own jacket, looked at his phone, shook his head.

Now Greenway reached down into his pants pocket, where evidently he had slipped my phone. As he pulled it out, the ringing became louder. He pressed a button.

"Yeah?"

I could hear my heart pounding in my chest.

"Who?"

The pounding got a little louder.

"No, I'm afraid this isn't Zack Walker. He's not available at the moment. Who's calling? Uh-huh. Well, I'm afraid you'll have to try again later." He ended the call, and as he slipped the phone back into his pants, all eyes were focused again on the house.

I ran.

I'd been out here so long, my eyes were well adjusted to the night light. I weaved my way through a couple of uncompleted walls and leapt out of the house on the back side. Somewhere behind me, I heard Rick shout, "I see him!"

As I'd learned on my way to my hiding spot, a construction site is not the ideal place to conduct a hundred-yard dash. The various stacks of building materials are bad enough, but the real problem is the ground surface. Sod is months away. I was dashing over mounds of dirt, rocks, and pebbles, a lunar landscape. It hadn't rained in a week or more, so the deep tracks left by trucks and digging equipment had hardened, creating a crisscross network of ruts of varying depths. Every time a foot landed, it hit the ground at a different angle, sending jolts of pain to my ankles and knees.

I ran between two houses, cut right, then down between another two, but given their skeletal nature, they didn't provide much cover. I didn't dare look back to see whether Rick was gaining on me, or whether he was there at all. Given the condition of the ground, and the limited light, taking my eyes off the path ahead of me for even a fraction of a second ran the risk of sending me flying.

But I couldn't hear him. The sound of my own panting, the hammering of my own heart in my chest, and my feet hitting the ground drowned out most other noises.

I'd cut back and forth between so many houses I'd lost my bearings. I wasn't sure which direction my car was in. So I leapt up into another house, aiming to cut through it on the diagonal, and once my feet were firmly planted on the plywood I took a moment to look back and could just make out a shadowy figure running across the site, about two houses back. He was slowing down, his head darting from side to side. Rick had momentarily lost me.

"Greenway!" he shouted. "I need some help out here!"

The house I'd slipped into was further along. Three of the outside walls had been packed with insulation, with clear plastic sheeting affixed over that. I crept from one room to another on the first floor, spotted a ladder up to the second, and scaled it as noiselessly as possible. The upstairs was still a see-through affair, at least between the rooms, and there was an opening in the ceiling where a skylight was planned. There was a plaster- and paint-stained stepladder up there, and I quietly moved it close to the opening, mounted the steps high enough that my shoulders were above the roofline, and hauled myself up.

Even in the night, it was dizzying up there. I moved a couple of feet away from the skylight opening and took a seat near the peak. The slope on the skylight side was gradual, but at the peak, the other half of the roof dropped away sharply, the slope so steep you couldn't walk on it. I looked out on the sea of roofs bathed in soft moonlight. When I was a kid and played hide-and-seek with my buddies, I always went up trees, scaling as far as I could. It was my experience that people weren't inclined to look up. They'd stand right under you, looking left and right, forward and backward, but they'd never bother to crane their necks skyward. I was hoping things hadn't changed that much since I was ten.

From the roof I had a chance to get my bearings. I could see the three cars to the north, which meant that my own car was over to the west, not that far from where I was now. And now that I wasn't on the run, I could listen more carefully for my hunters. Not that Rick was that hard to hear.

"That fucker! We're gonna find you, you fucker!"

Greenway and Carpington were navigating their way across the terrain with a lot more care. They were, after all, wearing expensive suits and didn't want to stumble. "Rick! Where are you?"

"Over here!" he shouted. He was in front of the house next to the one I was perched atop.

Greenway and Carpington caught up to him. The councilman said, "We should just get out of here. Even if you could find him, what are you gonna do? You can't deal with everyone the way you did with Spender."

319

Neither Rick nor Greenway answered. But after a moment, I did hear Rick say, "I lost him right around here. Let's check in here."

As they approached the house under me, they slipped from my range of vision. They were down on the first floor, shuffling about. They'd become very quiet, as though one of them had put his index finger to his lips. I peered into the skylight hole, but there wasn't enough light down there to make anything out. But I thought I could hear someone scaling the ladder to the second floor. If it was anyone, it would be Rick.

I moved away from the opening, trying to will myself to become weightless. The roof hadn't been shingled yet, so my knees and feet didn't make scuffing noises against the surface. Inside, it sounded as though Rick had made it to the second floor.

He would see the stepladder under the opening. Would he think it had been left that way by the workers? I didn't think he would.

I slipped one leg over the peak, down the steep side. I was straddled across it now, like I was riding a horse. Carefully, I pulled the other leg over, gripping the peak with my hands. Slowly I let my body slide down the steep slope, an inch at a time.

Inside, I heard Rick mount the stepladder. Once he was to the second step from the top, his head would be above the surface of the roofline. I hoped the moonlight wasn't bright enough for him to see my eight fingers that gripped the peak and kept me from plummeting down the other side, past the edge of the roof, and then two stories to the dirt below.

It didn't take any time at all for the pain to become excruciating. Not just in my fingers, but down the lengths of both arms. I squeezed my eyes shut, clamped my jaw tight, and breathed through the cracks between my teeth.

I was counting the seconds in my head. One thousand. Two thousand. Three thousand. Concentrating hard on the numbers so I wouldn't think about how my fingers couldn't hold on much longer. The side of my head was pressed hard against the roof, and the movements of the three people within the house gently reverberated through the lumber and to my ear. Eventually, I heard more footsteps, some muffled conversation, and then the sounds seemed to slip away.

Seconds later, they became much clearer. They were outside. Right below me. If I didn't hold on, I'd slide away and drop right on top of them. And I couldn't haul myself back over without scrabbling away at the roof with my legs, and that would make too much noise.

"I'm getting out of here," Carpington said.

"He was here!" Rick said. "I know he was here!"

"Let's go, Rick," Greenway said. "We'll never find him out here in the dark. He could be anywhere. He probably made a break for it while we were in the house. We'll get him. Don't worry about that. We'll find him at his house later."

"Fuck!" Rick said, and I could hear him kicking at something. My fingers were becoming numb. I thought I had another fifteen seconds, tops, before they let go.

"Come on," Greenway said, and I heard them moving away.

When the voices seemed a house or two distant, I drew on strength I never knew I had to get myself back over the peak, first to my waist, then one leg. I lay there for a moment, catching my breath, letting the feeling come back into my arms. From my perch, I saw the headlights of three cars come on. All three had to back up, turn around, and they left in a convoy, heading off in the direction of the sales office.

Even though I knew they were gone, I made my way back to the car moving along the edges of buildings, ducking behind front-end loaders. I wasn't taking any chances. I wanted to take a look through Stefanie's purse — it was probably too small to hold this ledger they'd been talking about, but it might offer some clues as to where I might find it. First, however, I had to get out of the neighborhood. I drove to a twenty-four-hour doughnut place on the outskirts of the subdivision and parked back by the Dumpster.

I decided the purse could wait two more minutes.

I went into the doughnut shop and swung open the door to the men's room. After taking a

322

whiz, I stood in front of the sink and as I washed my hands took a look at myself. I looked bad. The front of my jacket, shirt, and pants were scuffed with mud and grit, and my face was smeared with dirt. I took a moment to wash up, attempted to dry myself with the hot-air machine. (I still felt my book about the guy who goes back in time to keep the inventor of this infernal gadget from ever being born was my best.)

I lined up to buy a large coffee with triple cream and two double-chocolate doughnuts. It hit me that I was running on empty in every sense of the word. I took my order to a table in the corner and surveyed my fellow customers. A couple of teenagers on a date. An old man reading the paper by himself. Two cops, evidently bucking tradition, eating muffins. Upon seeing them I tried to draw into myself, to disappear. Even though I had no reason to think they were looking for me, specifically, I couldn't help but feel I looked like a suspect.

I wolfed the doughnuts, guzzled the coffee. I exited the shop through the door furthest away from the cops and got back into my Civic. I turned on the overhead light and grabbed Stefanie's purse from behind the passenger seat. I wanted her car key. It was a thick, black plastic thing, like a rounded oversized skipping stone emblazoned with a VW symbol, with buttons for opening the trunk and locking and unlocking the doors.

So Greenway and Rick wanted a ledger Stefanie'd run off with. It was too big for Stefanie's purse. But it would fit in a car. And I knew where she'd last parked.

I turned over the engine. It was time for me to return to the scene of my crime.

23

❖ ❖ ❖

Every time I saw headlights in my rear-view mirror, I held my breath. Maybe it was the police. Maybe they'd figured out I was involved in the Stefanie Knight matter, at least as some sort of witness, if not the actual perpetrator. Or maybe it was Rick. I guessed that he'd be cruising the neighborhood, looking for my car. He'd probably gone by the house, and when he hadn't seen it there, had trolled the neighborhood in the hopes of finding me.

The Mindy's Market parking lot was nearly empty, no more than half a dozen cars scattered about. Two of them, as it turned out, were Volkswagens. A Jetta and a Beetle. I seemed to remember Stefanie's mother saying that Stefanie drove a Beetle, a blue one, and the one in the lot here was a dark blue that reflected the lamps of the parking lot.

Not wanting to make my approach to the car too obvious, I parked the Civic across the street, in the lot of a darkened McDonald's. I locked up, the VW key held tightly in my fist. By the time I crossed the street I figured I was close enough to determine whether I had the right car. I aimed the key at the Beetle and tapped the unlock button. The taillights flashed.

I came around from the back and opened the driver's door. The floor was littered with candy wrappers, coffee cup lids, wadded tissues. I flipped the switch to unlock the trunk and walked around the back, lifting up the hatch that went all the way to the top of the rear window. The trunk was littered with debris as well, plus a couple of pairs of shoes, some Valley Forest Estates flyers and floor plans, an empty box of low-fat cookies. There was a strap at the front end of the trunk that lifted up the floor, revealing the spare. I peeked under there, but found nothing.

I looked under the front seats, in the glove compartment. I flipped the seats forward, ran my hand down the pouches behind each seat, came up empty. I lifted each of the four floor mats, found seventy-eight cents in change, which I left, and began to think that maybe this car had no secrets to share.

The car, as I'd noticed, was a hatchback, which meant you could fold the rear seats down to create a modest cargo area. It appeared that before you could fold the back of the seat down, you had to flip the base of the seat up.

I reached my hand into the crack where the two parts of the seats met and pulled, and as I'd suspected, the seat pulled away from the floor.

And there it was.

A pale green ledger book. I grabbed it, put the seat back in place, got out of the back and flopped into the front driver's seat, pulling the door shut. There was enough light from the parking lot lamps to see without turning on the inside light and attracting any more attention.

I opened the book up and saw dates and names and amounts. As I've mentioned, I can't balance a checkbook, so I wasn't sure what all this meant, but I had a pretty good idea. And I had an even better idea who'd be able to interpret what it all meant. I needed Trixie.

At that moment, I caught something out of the corner of my eye. A car slowing as it drove by on the street in front of Mindy's. A small foreign sedan. Just like Rick's.

The car's brake lights came on. The car stopped, backed up, idled in front of the McDonald's. Then moved forward, swung into the lot, parked alongside my car.

I slunk down into the seat of the Beetle, but not so low that I couldn't see what was happening across the street. Rick got out of the sedan, walked slowly around the Civic, confirming that it was in fact my car. He must have been cruising the neighborhood, hoping to find me, and when he spotted a car similar to mine, wanted to investigate. Chances are he wouldn't have taken notice of the plate number the other times he'd seen the car at my home.

He peered through the windows, looking first

in the back, then the front, and his eyes landed on the purse in the front seat. If he was anything like me, he couldn't tell one purse from another — this skill shortage had led me to hide in this Volkswagen in the middle of the night — but this purse looked close enough to Stefanie's that he figured he had the right car. He tried all four doors, found them all locked, and walked calmly back to his own vehicle, reaching for something from the back seat.

A baseball bat.

He swung it hard and took out the driver's-door window. Shards of glass flew across the interior. Inside the Beetle, with the windows up, I could barely hear it. He pulled up the door lock, opened the door, and took the purse, which he tossed into his own car. But he'd looked through this purse once before and knew it hadn't contained a ledger. Maybe, he thought, it was in my car somewhere.

So he began a search of it, not unlike mine moments earlier of the Beetle. He rooted through the trunk, looked under the seats, ripped up the back seat. Frustrated, he glared at the car, paced back and forth angrily, looking like Basil Fawlty getting ready to beat it to death with a tree branch. The bat, I suspected, would be more effective.

He took out the front window first. It took about ten swings of the bat to break out all the glass. Then the three remaining passenger windows, and finally, the back. But that wasn't enough to satisfy him. He smashed off the mirrors, then swung the bat into the middle of the hood. The fenders were next, followed by the headlights, taillights, and trunk lid.

Jeez, I thought, why don't you just set fire to it?

Rick went back to his car to hunt for something. He had a rag, possibly part of an old shirt. Then he opened the driver's door on my car, pulled the lever next to the seat that popped the tiny door on the back fender that covers the gas cap, unscrewed it, and stuffed the rag partway down the tube.

Then, with a lighter, he set it ablaze.

Now he had to move fast. He jumped back into his car, backed so far up the drive-through lane of the McDonald's that he was almost behind it but still able to watch his handiwork, and waited for the explosion.

It was a good one.

The back of my car was facing the front of the McDonald's, and when the car blew up, erupting into a huge ball of flame, the front windows of the restaurant shattered and fell, setting off alarms. Rick got out of his car, and even from where I was sitting, I could see the big grin on his face.

It must not have occurred to him until then to wonder why my car was parked there in the first place. He scanned around, looking to see where I might be, figuring that the noise of the explosion would draw me out. Finally, he looked across the street to the grocery store parking lot and saw the Beetle. I tried to slide even lower into the seat but still keep him in view. He knew Stefanie, and it was a pretty safe assumption that he knew the kind of car she drove.

He started coming across the street.

I slipped my hand down into the front pocket of my jeans and took the Beetle key out, then slid it into the ignition. Before I turned the engine over, I pressed the button to lock the two doors.

I had to slide up now to be able to see over the wheel, and when I did, Rick saw me and started to run. Perfect, I thought. I want you as far away from your car as possible before I pull out of this lot.

The engine caught as I turned the key. I threw my left foot down on the clutch, jammed the stick shift into first, and heard the rear tires squeal as Rick came up alongside, screaming obscenities, shaking his fist. He'd left his baseball bat in his car, and managed nothing more than a swat at the car as I peeled out of the parking lot.

Looking at him in the rear-view mirror, I gave him a friendly wave goodbye.

It was late to be calling on Trixie, but these were, as they say, desperate times. I drove quickly through the streets of our neighborhood. I sped down Chancery Park, approaching the corner of Greenway, and slowed only a little as I went past our house. No cars in the driveway, no unfamiliar lights in the house. I checked out all the nearby streets, including the block behind, to make sure Rick's car was no-where nearby. It wasn't safe to go back to the house — Greenway and Rick would be looking for me there — but I was curious about whether they were already waiting for me. It appeared not.

I couldn't leave the Beetle in our driveway, or Trixie's. I left it on Rustling Pine Lane, which was two streets over from Chancery, and hoofed it back, the ledger tucked under my arm. Even though our house appeared to be empty, I knew it was possible someone might be waiting inside, looking out the window, waiting for my return, so I got to Trixie's place by working my way through backyards, then coming up the side of her house that was the furthest away from ours. It was, as it turned out, a good thing Sarah had been called in to *The Metropolitan* to work an overtime shift. She wasn't going to be home until daybreak, and by then, I'd decided, I was going to go to the police with everything I knew. But before I did that, I wanted to be sure I had the deck well stacked against the friendly folks at Valley Forest Estates. And Roger Carpington, even though I was less than certain he'd killed Stefanie Knight. Not that the police wouldn't be able to find plenty of other things to charge him with.

I came around Trixie's garage, noticed her car

and one other in the drive, and rang the front doorbell. I figured one simple ring wouldn't be enough to wake her, so I leaned on the button, let it go for a full ten seconds before taking my finger off it.

The tiny speaker next to the door crackled almost right away. "Hello?" Trixie didn't sound as tired as I thought she would.

"Trixie, it's Zack. Let me in."

"Zack? It's one in the morning. What are you doing here?"

Down at the end of Chancery, a small car's headlights appeared.

"Trixie, listen, I don't have time to explain. Please let me in."

"I'll be over in a couple of minutes, I'm —"

"Trixie! I can't go home! You have to let me in! It's an emergency!"

"Hang on."

The headlights were getting closer, slowing as they approached the corner of Greenway. I pressed myself up against the wall, sliding down and behind a bush.

From inside, I heard a bolt being turned, and then the door opened a crack. I was grateful that Trixie did not turn on the front light and expose me to whoever was coming up the street.

I forced the door open and burst in, closing the door behind me and throwing the bolt even before Trixie had a chance to do it.

"Oh God, thank you," I said, turning to face her, holding the ledger out in front of me.

"You've got no idea the mess I've gotten —"

And then I stopped.

Trixie had not come to the door in her pajamas. Clearly, I had not roused her from a deep sleep.

She was decked out in a leather corset, wide garters that supported thigh-high black stockings, shiny high-heeled boots that came over the top of her knees, and in her right hand she held what appeared to be a whip.

"You picked kind of a bad time," she said, somewhat sternly.

From someplace else in the house — it sounded like the basement — came a very strange sound. Muffled sounds, of a man, it seemed to me. Groaning.

"Why don't you pour yourself a coffee," Trixie said, nodding her head in the direction of the kitchen. "I'm gonna have to go untie this guy and send him on his way. You've done me out of a thou, you know, and that's not counting the tip."

24

❖ ❖ ❖

"So you're not an accountant," I said when Trixie sat down across from me at the kitchen table. She had slipped on a robe, but every time she shifted in her chair, or leaned forward to get some cream for her coffee, or got up to put something in the fridge, I could hear the erotic creak of leather, the swish of nylon rubbing up against nylon.

"Yes, I'm an accountant," Trixie, slightly indignant, said. "I've got my degree and everything, worked for one of the big firms downtown. I was very good at it, still am. I can still do your taxes if you want. But I'm making a lot more now than then, and ever since Enron and Andersen and all that, I think I moved into a profession with more respect and dignity." She blew on her coffee and took a sip, leaving lipstick marks on the edge of the cup.

"I'm really sorry," I said. "About barging in."

"Whatever. It's just as well you showed up when you did."

As it turned out, she'd done up the chest strap on her client a little too tightly, and had asked me to come down to the basement to help her undo it.

It was not your typical rec room. The walls were painted black, and the red bulbs screwed into the sockets cast a sensuous, eerie glow. One wall was covered in pegboard, with hooks, the kind of thing you see in a well-organized workshop for hanging tools of every description. But these hooks were draped with ropes and straps and handcuffs and bungee-cord-type thingies with bright chrome buckles that looked like they would do a terrific job of strapping your luggage to a roof rack if you were taking a long vacation with the kids. But that, clearly, was not their intended use, as evidenced by George, the man strapped to a huge X made of timbers that was leaned up against the back wall. George, pasty, overweight, and extraordinarily white, was wearing nothing more than a black leather jockstrap arrangement, and a red ball in his mouth held in place with straps that went around the back of his head.

A broad leather strap around his chest helped secure him to the crossed timbers, and when Trixie had tried to release him, she couldn't pull far enough back on the buckle. That was when she called me down.

"Zack, this is George," Trixie said. "George, Zack." George, still gagged, nodded. "George, I did this thing a bit too tight, but let's not forget

335

who asked for it that way. Now, I don't quite have the strength to pull this back, and I could cut it, but I hate to do that, so I'm going to get Zack here to help me out."

I obliged, pulling the belt back far enough that it was cutting pretty deeply into his flabby bosoms. "There," I said.

Trixie went about untying his wrists and ankles, and removed the ball. "I'm really sorry about this, George. I know it's very unprofessional, sending you on your way early, but something's come up."

"That's okay," George said meekly. "Nice to meet you," he said, extending his hand to me. We shook.

George slipped into a downstairs bathroom, where he changed back into his regular clothes. Through the door, Trixie said to him, "No charge tonight, George."

"Are you sure?" he said from behind the door. "I still got half a session, so I'm not complaining."

"No, it wouldn't be right. I tell you what, we can just let this one go, or you can pay me, and next time it's on the house. I'll even do the thing with the cream cheese, no extra charge."

That sounded fair to George, who, once he'd emerged from the bathroom in a pair of dress pants, a crisp white shirt without a tie, and a sports jacket, discreetly slipped Trixie a wad of bills.

"Have you been coming to Trixie long?" George

asked me as we went up the stairs together.

"Uh, no," I said.

"Well, you won't be disappointed. She's the best. I can't recommend her too highly."

"Really."

Trixie saw him off at the door. "Say hi to Mildred for me," she said, giving George a peck on the cheek and sending him on his way. I watched through the glass as he got in his car and backed out of the driveway.

"Mildred?" I asked.

"His wife. She's not really into this. It's been a real load-off for her ever since she started sending George to me."

"She sends him?"

"She saw my ad. First time she sent him, it was for his birthday. Now it's a semi-regular thing, every month or so. Some people are very open-minded." She grabbed a silk robe hanging on a hook just inside the door to the basement, slipped it on, and went into the kitchen. "Did you get yourself some coffee?"

"I was about to, and you called me downstairs to help free George."

"That was so embarrassing. I could have cut him out of it, but that strap alone was three hundred bucks." She shook her head. "Now, what's got you so wound up you're busting in here in the middle of the night?" She smiled. "Did you see my ad, too?"

"No, I didn't," I said. "I'm in a bit of a mess, Trixie."

"Grab a chair."

It was after that that I asked whether she was really an accountant, and offered my apologies about busting in.

"What is it?" Trixie asked. "Another backpack incident?"

"Worse, although it started out in a similar way. But things have sort of spiraled out of control. There are men, at least one, trying to find me and, I think it's fair to say, kill me."

Trixie's eyebrows shot up a notch. "Why would there be men trying to kill you?"

"Well, for one thing, this." I slid the ledger book across the table at her.

"What's this?" she asked.

"Well, you're the accountant. Maybe you can tell me."

She opened the book. Her nails were long and bloodred, and I found that I felt just a bit feverish. Where her robe opened I could see the swell of her breasts, pushed up and out, courtesy of the spectacularly engineered corset.

"Let's have a look. List of payments, money coming in, some names here. Wow, I think I recognize this guy. He's a building inspector, comes here sometimes, likes to play doctor."

"Okay."

"So he's getting paid five hundred every, it looks like, every week or so. And here's another name I recognize. Carpington?"

"Roger. He's a client, too?"

"No, I just recognize the name. From the paper."

"He's a town councilman. How much is he getting?"

"Well, right here he's getting five thou." She thumbed the pages. "His name pops up a lot, but it's just one of dozens. Zack, where did you get this?"

"It's a long story."

"I've got time," she said, leaning back in her chair and crossing her booted legs.

"Sarah and I were shopping," I said, and went through the whole thing. Taking the wrong purse, trying to return it, finding Stefanie Knight's body, getting tracked down by Rick, the meeting with Carpington, the episode at the construction site. Trixie said barely a word, taking it all in, nodding slowly.

I finished with finding the ledger in Stefanie's car, and Rick's destruction of mine out front of McDonald's.

"You're in some kind of deep shit," Trixie said, running her tongue across her top teeth.

"Yes," I said. "That's a fairly good assessment of the situation. Thank you."

"Listen, don't get snippy with me. Did I tell you to take Sarah's purse to teach her a lesson?"

"No. Did I mention that, in addition to everything else that's happened tonight, she thinks I'm impotent?"

"No, I think you left that part out. Are you? I could check."

"She wanted to, you know, spend some time with me tonight, before she went to work, but it's a bit hard to concentrate when you think the police might be looking for you and charging you with murder. I think maybe it's time to go to the police."

Trixie thought about that. "How did you get here, if your car's blown up?"

"Stefanie's car. Her Beetle. I parked it one block over."

"So you not only stole her purse, but now you have her car? That'll look good to the police. You're not wearing her underwear, too, are you?"

I hadn't thought about the incriminating aspect of driving Stefanie's car all around town. I did not, it occurred to me, have the makings of a master criminal.

"But if I don't go to the police," I said, "how'm I going to protect myself from this Rick guy? He's a total nutjob. He killed that Spender guy down in the creek, probably killed Stefanie, and he's wandering around town with a python in his trunk."

Trixie blinked. "Does Sarah know anything about any of this?"

I shook my head. "She's noticed me acting kind of weird, but no. And she won't be coming home from work until morning, she's doing the night shift, and I farmed the kids out to friends' houses."

"You need some kind of backup," she said.

"You have a gun or anything?"

"Are you kidding? Do I look like someone who owns a gun? I don't even know anyone who owns a —" I stopped.

"What?" Trixie said.

"I do know one person. Who owns a gun. Someone who owes me a favor. Someone who might let me borrow it."

"Do you know what time it is?" Earl said when he opened his front door to me and Trixie. She'd changed out of her work clothes and into some jeans and a T-shirt, and had gone out of her house first, making sure there was no sign of Rick or anyone else at my house two doors down, then waved for me to join her. I ran across the street in a flash, ducked into some bushes as Trixie rang Earl's bell.

"Let us in," Trixie said. "Zack needs your help."

"Where's Zack?"

"He's the one here, in the bushes. Turn off your front light."

Earl was dressed in checkered boxers and a sweatshirt. He padded barefoot into the kitchen, where he found a pack of cigarettes and lit up.

"What the fuck's going on?" he said, running his hand over his shaved head. He looked nervous. "You told, didn't you?" he said, looking at me. "You told the cops about my business. How long before they get here?"

"I didn't do anything like that," I said.

"Did you tell that wife of yours? Did she call them?"

"That would be Sarah," I said. "And no. I didn't tell her. I'm here to ask a favor."

Earl squinted. "A favor?"

"I need a gun," I said. "I want to borrow your gun."

"Forget it."

"Earl, I wouldn't ask if it wasn't important. There are people looking for me tonight, and until I sort a few things out, I need some protection."

Earl glowered at me. "You ever owned a gun?"

"No."

"You ever fired a gun?"

"Not exactly, no."

"Zack, you ever even held a gun?"

I tried to think. Did toy guns count? And what about the G.I. Joe figures and accessories I'd had as a kid? Did that count for something?

"I guess, technically, no. All my shooting has been with a camera."

"And what the hell do you need a gun for anyway? How many enemies does a guy make writing space stories?"

"Come on, Earl. Don't you owe me one? Did I make a call to Detective Flint after I left here the other day?"

Earl shook his head. "Look, I appreciate that. But what you're asking, I don't know."

"Maybe you're going to have to explain," Trixie said.

And so I started in all over again, for the second time in the last hour and a half, although I gave him the *Reader's Digest* version. For example, I didn't tell him about trying to instruct Sarah in the fine points of purse safety. I said I'd found a purse.

"So I wanted to return it, and check the driver's license, and it was a woman named Stefanie Knight, who works over at Valley Forest Estates."

Earl turned away, shaking his head, and reached for a beer from the fridge.

"So I was trying to track her down, and left my name and e-mail address at her mother's place, and then this psycho named Rick comes looking for me, wanting what's in this purse, which at first I thought was all this money, but that turned out to be counterfeit, and then I figured it was this film —"

"Film?"

"A roll of film. Of Stefanie Knight and this councilman in the sack."

"What councilman?"

I told him. "But it turns out Rick and his boss, Greenway, wanted something more than just the film, they were after this ledger." I indicated it, on the table, as if I was pointing to Exhibit #1.

"So they're after you for this ledger?"

"Yeah, that, and I sort of pissed off Rick, hitting him in the head."

Earl sat down, alternating puffs of cigarette

and swigs of beer. "You hit him in the head."

"When he came to my house, and Angie came home. It was a kind of self-defense thing, although I think, under other circumstances, he might have liked me. He read my book and really liked it."

"That must have made you feel good. You never know when you're going to run into a fan. I've been meaning to read it someday myself."

"You kind of left out the most important part," Trixie said.

"Huh?"

"This Stefanie Knight chick, she's dead," said Trixie.

"I was getting to that," I said. "I'm having a hard time keeping it all straight. Maybe hanging off the roof of that house has made me forgetful." Earl took a long drag on his cigarette, blew the smoke over our heads, and I continued. "That's kind of why I've been on the run all night. She was murdered, and I've got her purse, well, I had her purse, and I've still got her car, and I think it's going to take a long time to explain all this to the authorities. But I'm thinking maybe it's time to go see them anyway."

Earl said nothing for a moment. He was thinking. Trixie looked at me and shrugged. Finally, Earl said, "You need more than a gun, my friend. You need muscle."

I smiled. "You have someone in mind?"

He returned the smile. "I might. Seems to me

you need to pay another visit to this Greenway guy and Carpington and find out just what happened. We might have ways of getting the information out of them that the police aren't really supposed to use. And if this Rick character shows up, we'll have to deal with him as well."

I felt a renewed sense of confidence.

"You know what might come in handy?" I said. "Some handcuffs."

Trixie brightened. "How many pairs you need?"

I held up three fingers.

"I'll get you two regular sets," Trixie said, "and one fur-lined. Don Greenway always liked the soft kind."

Earl and I looked at each other and then at Trixie.

"So he was a client." She shrugged. "But he was a lousy tipper. Fuck him."

25

❖ ❖ ❖

Earl said he had to get dressed and do a couple
of things before we headed out. First, I heard
him go into the garage, do something with his
truck, slam a tailgate, then he wandered past the
kitchen door on his way upstairs to put on some
clothes. In his absence, I gazed, tiredly, across
the table at Trixie and thought how fortunate I
was, in my time of trouble, to have a dominatrix
and a pot grower to bail me out.

"Thanks for not judging," Trixie said.

"What?"

"Back at my place. I was waiting for the lecture, the inquisition, why are you doing this,
what kind of girl, et cetera."

I shrugged. "I'm a bit past being able to point
a finger. People in glass houses, you know."

"Yeah, well, if having character flaws disquali-
fies people from throwing stones, how come
there's so much of it going on?"

"I guess people aren't very good at recog-
nizing their own faults. And I'm sure there's
much to recommend in your line of work. You

get to work from home, you can choose your own hours, and you get to meet a lot of interesting people."

"That's certainly true. And you get to learn a lot about what makes people tick."

"True." I paused. "Like cream cheese."

Trixie smiled. "You don't want to know."

"You're right."

"Things good between you and Sarah? Aside from her thinking you've got a problem with the hydraulics?"

"Yeah, they're good. But after all this comes out, I don't know. This has got nothing on The Backpack Incident, or when I hid her car down the street. I think I've been a bit of an asshole lately. A busybody."

"Well, you're an asshole, there's really no question about that," Trixie said. "But you're a reasonably nice asshole, and I think Sarah's a lucky girl." And then, for reasons I wasn't sure I understood, she looked away.

Earl appeared. He was wearing a Toronto Blue Jays sweatshirt, jeans, and heavy lace-up workboots that hadn't been tied at the top. "You ready?"

I nodded.

He went over to the kitchen drawers, opened the middle one, reached in toward the back, and brought out his gun. "Let's go see if we can solve a few of your problems," he said, tucking it into the top of his pants.

"Maybe you could go over some of this with

me again," Earl said, shoving in the cigarette lighter and waiting for it to pop. "This girl, the one who's dead, was on film boffing this guy?"

"Carpington."

"A councilman? For the town?"

"That's right."

"So, they just liked to record the moment or what?"

"My guess is Carpington was being black-mailed."

"So he finds out, he loses it and kills this girl?"

"It's a motive, but I don't know. He just didn't seem the type. I went to see him earlier tonight, at town hall, and he didn't seem to have it in him."

Earl nodded. The lighter popped and he lit his cigarette. "One thing I've learned, Zack, is that people are often not what they seem. They can surprise you."

I thought of Trixie. And, for that matter, Earl. Both of them ended up being in lines of work that had caught me off guard.

Earl slipped the gun out of his pants and slid it across the seat toward me. "Hold that and get a feel of it."

I took the gun in my right hand, startled, ini-tially, by how heavy it was.

"See that little thing there, the safety? Make sure it stays set that way so you don't shoot your nuts off. But if you think you're going to have to use it, you move it" — he reached over — "like that."

"Got it," I said. I put the safety back on, slid the gun back across the seat. "Maybe you should be the guy who uses this. And I'll ask the questions."

"Sounds good to me," said Earl, holding his cigarette between his lips as he turned the ignition. "Where we going?"

"Last time I saw Greenway and Company they were headed to the sales office. That was more than an hour ago, but they might still be there."

"Why don't we troll on by," he said, rolling the truck out of the garage and slipping back out momentarily to close the garage door. We turned left on Chancery and drove to the entrance to the Valley Forest Estates, where the sales office was set up.

"Drive by once," I said.

Earl slowed only slightly as we passed the office. Out front were Carpington's Cadillac and Greenway's Lincoln.

"Looks like Rick isn't there," I said with some sense of relief. "I don't see his car around. He may still be looking for me. I think he thinks I have the ledger."

Earl did a U-turn at the next intersection and came back slowly. "Whose car is whose?"

"The Caddy is Carpington's, and the Lincoln is Greenway's."

"Let's pay 'em a visit," Earl said, turning the pickup in to the sales office lot. The gravel crunched under the truck's tires. Suddenly, I felt overwhelmed. My breathing grew quicker and shallower.

"Earl, I don't know if I can do this," I said. "I gotta be honest with you. I'm scared. I'm out of my league. These clowns kill people to get what they want."

Earl gave me a gentle punch in the shoulder. "Don't worry, pardner. The ones who should be scared are these asswipes." He nodded toward the office. "We're gonna get the jump on them."

I swallowed, hard, took a deep breath, and opened the truck door. We strode toward the office, shoulder to shoulder, Earl holding his gun down at his right side. Three sets of handcuffs, which Trixie had run across the street to fetch before we left Earl's, jingled in my jacket pocket. Trixie had decided against giving me the fur-lined ones for Greenway, since it would be a dead giveaway where we'd gotten our restraining devices. She claimed not to have much use for him, but didn't see any advantage in advertising her disregard. I couldn't argue with that.

Earl, between puffs, suggested we circle the building once. Peeking through blinds, we saw Greenway behind his desk, lecturing a sheepish Carpington sitting across from him. All the other rooms were dark, indicating to us that we had only two people to deal with.

"But Rick might be coming back at any time," I whispered.

"We'll deal with that when the time comes," Earl whispered back.

We came back around the front of the building and I gripped the handle, squeezing gently and pushing to see whether it was locked. It was.

"Knock," Earl said.

I rapped on the door. There was some stirring inside, then Greenway's voice from behind the wood. "Who is it?"

My mind raced. "Rick!" I said. I forced my voice a little lower, trying to approximate Rick's tone.

"Where's your key?"

Would Rick have the patience to explain? I decided not. "Just open the fucking door!" I shouted.

I heard the bolt turn back, and once the door had cleared the latch, Earl put his boot to it. The door swung wide into the darkened outer office and Earl forced his way in ahead of me, gun slightly raised at two o'clock. Once we were both inside, I closed the door and locked it, and saw Greenway sprawled out on the floor and Carpington standing in the door of Greenway's office, looking more or less petrified.

"Both of you," Earl said, sounding very much in control, "in one place, please." He motioned, with his gun hand, for Greenway to get up and back into his office.

"Please don't shoot us," Carpington whined.

"Shut up," Earl said, shoving Greenway ahead of him into his office. He took his spot back behind his desk while Carpington retreated into the chair across from it.

"Cuff 'em, Zack," Earl said. And I thought, If only I had a nickel for every time someone has said that to me. By now, I'd have five cents.

Carpington was wide-eyed with horror, while Greenway tried harder to look composed, thinking maybe if he exuded confidence we'd be unnerved, that maybe he knew something we didn't. It might work. Even though we had the drop on them, I was definitely unnerved.

"Just tell me what you want," Carpington said to me. "You said you didn't want money before, but maybe you've changed your mind. I can get you some."

"Maybe you've saved up some of those weekly payments that are recorded in that ledger," I said, pulling two sets of handcuffs from my pocket. I grabbed his wrist and slapped one cuff on it while Earl held his gun up to discourage anyone from making any objections. With his left hand, he took his cigarette out of his mouth and tapped some ashes onto the floor.

I forced Carpington's hand behind his back, brought his other arm around, and cuffed his wrists together like I'd been doing this all my life. I felt a little rush.

"You're not doing that to me," Greenway said as I rounded the desk with the other pair.

"Maybe if you'd fixed my fucking shower I'd be feeling a little more kindly," I said. I reached for his wrist and he drew back.

"Keep away from me!" he said. "You have no

352

idea who you're dealing with."

"Neither do you," Earl said, and fired off a round into the site plan that hung on the wall behind Greenway.

The shot was deafening and caught me as much by surprise as it did our two prisoners. I felt the blast ring in my ears. Greenway jolted back into his chair and Carpington slunk down in his. With his hands cuffed, he couldn't stop his slide and went right to the floor.

"Jesus Christ, Earl!" I shouted. "What the hell you doing?"

"Getting their attention," he said calmly. "Mr. Greenway, would you be kind enough to let my associate here put some handcuffs on you?"

Greenway grudgingly obliged, then settled himself back into his leather business chair, trying to look as though having his hands trapped behind him didn't detract from his dignity in any way.

"Now," said Earl, "I need your car keys."

"Huh?" Greenway said.

"What?" Carpington said.

"Why?" I asked.

"I'm going to move their cars around back, and the truck. Best that no one thinks anyone's here, and that means it's less likely that Rick is going to be dropping by."

Anything that might keep Rick from showing up sounded like a good idea to me. Carpington and Greenway indicated which pockets held their keys, and I got them out. "Why don't I do that while you keep them covered?" I suggested.

Earl shook his head, handed the gun over to me in exchange for the keys. "You watch them."

The gun was warm. I didn't know whether that was from Earl holding it, or the fact that it had just been fired. My pulse raced as I wrapped my fingers around it.

"Uh, the safety?" I said to Earl. "Which way is the safety supposed to go?"

He rolled his eyes. I knew what he was thinking. This was not the way to inspire fear in your captives. First, I was scared shitless when he fired the gun, and now I needed a tutorial in its operation. "It's off now. That way, if one of them does something stupid, you can blow their fucking heads off."

"Sure," I said. I raised the gun up, moved it around, got the feel of it. Now Greenway and Carpington looked even more nervous, especially when the gun swung in their direction. They must have thought that their chances of being killed had risen exponentially now that the weapon had passed from Earl to me. It wasn't that I appeared more ruthless. On the contrary. But everything about me screamed incompetence. I made a special effort not to point the gun at either of them. I was as worried about my incompetence as they were.

Earl said he'd be back in a couple of minutes.

"Who's your friend?" Greenway asked once he heard the main door close.

"Just another happy resident of Valley Forest

Estates," I said, waving the gun about, trying to look casual with it. "So what brings you all out here tonight?"

"We're having a meeting," Greenway said. "And we're expecting someone. You might be smart to finish up your business and get out of here before he shows up."

"Who would that be? Rick?"

"I think he's out looking for you right now. He's very upset with you."

"You should see my car," I said, and Greenway just looked at me, not understanding. "He seems like a guy who could benefit from some anger management classes. But then, I guess if he were well behaved, he wouldn't have gotten the job of killing Sam Spender for you, or Stefanie."

"That's ridiculous. I don't know what you're talking about."

"I think you do, and that's why my friend and I decided to pay you a visit tonight, to find out what you do know. Because I have to tell you, it's very much in my interest to know as much as possible."

"I didn't have anything to do with those murders!" Carpington said, struggling to get back up off the floor and into his chair.

Headlight beams swept past the office window. Earl was moving the Caddy around back.

"So if it's not Rick coming by this evening, who is it?" I asked. "Let me guess. It's the famous Mr. Benedetto. He's heard about how much you guys have fucked things up out here and he's coming to assess the situation."

Their silence said everything.

Finally, Greenway said, "I have a question, if you don't mind."

"Shoot," I said, then regretted the choice of word as I caught my reflection in the window. I saw a man who looked remarkably like me, but holding a gun, trying to put some fear into a couple of slimeballs. I had no idea who this person was. And I could not believe that he was composing sentences in his head that contained words like "slimeballs."

"Just who the hell are you and what business of yours is any of this?"

It was a good question, no doubt about it. And one that would take, if you were to do it properly, too long to answer. I said, "I sort of stumbled into all this, but now that I'm in it, I need to know as much about it as I can before I get out. My questions will probably be easier to answer than Mr. Benedetto's. What's he going to think when he gets out here and finds the two of you handcuffed, the ledger missing, the negatives gone, plus a few thousand in cash —"

"That money meant nothing," Greenway said.

"I guess not," I said. "Since it was fake. Is that the machine" — I pointed to the one outside Greenway's office door — "you used to print the stuff?"

"Look," said Greenway, "it wasn't something

we did very often. Just when our cash flow was a bit down. Stefanie, I don't know what was up with her, sounds like she printed up a ton of the stuff before she decided to make a run for it."

Carpington said, "Fake? You were printing fake money?"

Greenway rolled his eyes. "No, Roger. We were printing real money. We got a franchise from the Mint."

"So you were paying me in counterfeit funds?" He was aghast. Imagine, buying a councilman's vote with bogus cash. Was that ethical?

"Not all of it, just the odd bill here and there. Look, you got to buy stuff, people accepted it, what are you worried about?"

"Why was Stefanie making a run for it?" I asked.

Greenway almost looked sad. "I don't know. I treated her well. Gave her one of our houses to live in."

"She needed a place to conduct your business. She fucks Carpington on your orders, he's happy and votes for your development. Plus, there's the added bonus of the hidden camera, so if he blabs, you've got something to show his wife and kids."

If Carpington had had his hands free, he'd have put them over his eyes and wept. I turned to him as another set of headlights swept past the window. Earl was hiding the second car.

"Isn't that about it, Roger? A little sex, a little cash, plus the occasional romp in the trunk with

Quincy, and you'd vote any way he wanted you to?"

He nodded, his eyes moistening.

"Plus, you knew about Spender, that Rick smashed his skull in down by the creek. And if Greenway could order Rick to do that, he could just as easily order him to do it to you."

Carpington swallowed hard. "I've been scared out of my mind for so long. I took the money, I, I slept with Stefanie. But I swear to God, I just wanted it all to end somehow, if I could just find a way that it wouldn't ruin me and my family, or hurt my chances of being elected mayor."

Where was this guy from? Neptune?

"You know, Roger," I said, "I think this is the sort of thing, that if it all came out in the open, might work against you in a mayoral campaign."

"Listen," said Greenway, thinking, looking for a way out. "What if we give you Rick?"

"Pardon?"

"We say it was Rick who did these things, killed Spender and Stefanie, but we didn't know anything about it."

"So you know he killed Stefanie, too?"

Greenway shrugged. "You've seen him in action. You know what a hothead he is. Who wouldn't believe it was him? But you leave us out of it. You let us go about our business. I could make it worth your while."

I said, "Would you fix my shower? And do something about the caulking around my bedroom window?"

"Of course. We'd make everything right. I'll send in a team. We'll fix your place up, give you some more upgrades you opted not to get when you purchased. What about a pool? We could put in a pool for you."

"Well," I said, appearing to consider his offer, "it's awfully tempting, but I'd really rather see the whole lot of you go to jail."

"No!" Carpington said. "Let me make a deal! I'll tell you everything! Just don't let them send me to jail! I wasn't the only one either! There are other politicians, from other towns."

"Roger!" Greenway bellowed. "Shut up!" And he rose up, a somewhat wobbly action since he didn't have his hands available to push himself out of the chair, and started coming around the desk toward Carpington. It looked as though he was going to try to kick him. "Shut up!"

"Sit down!" I shouted. I mean, *really* shouted. I thought, for a moment, that maybe Earl had returned, that it was him giving the order, but then realized the two words had come from me. I raised the gun, pointed it in Greenway's general direction, but not right at him, still not trusting myself.

Just as well, too. It went off.

My best guess is, when I shouted, every muscle in my body tensed, including the one in the finger that was on the trigger. I thought squeezing off a shot would require more pressure, more deliberation, but nope. One moment, things in the office were, relatively speaking, calm, and the next, there was a huge hole in Greenway's desk.

"Oh shit, I'm so sorry," I said.

Greenway jumped back, fell into the wall. Carpington screamed. The door burst open. Earl shouted, "What's happened?"

I stood there, gun in hand but pointed now at the floor, and said, "I shot the desk."

I felt I had not made sufficient apologies to Greenway. "Really, I'm very sorry, I'll pay for any damages. I really didn't mean for that to happen."

Earl took the gun from my hand. "Looks like I got back here just in time."

I surrendered the weapon without hesitation. Earl took the half-inch of cigarette from between his lips, exhaled, and said to Greenway and Carpington, "I think I just saved your lives."

"Thank you," Carpington said. "Thank you so much."

To me, Earl said, "Their cars are around back, and I was just about to hide my truck when I heard the shot. You about done here?"

"I think so," I said.

Outside, we heard the familiar sound of tires crunching on gravel. Earl slipped back into the main part of the office that was still in darkness and peered through the blinds.

"What kind of car does Rick drive?" he called out.

"A little sedan," I said. "Import, four-door."

"No, this ain't Rick then. It's a big Beemer. Seven series."

Greenway said, quietly, as though resigned to some terrible fate, "That would be Mr. Benedetto."

"The more the merrier," said Earl, who moved into position behind the door. When the first knock came, Earl swung the door in, held the barrel of the gun to Benedetto's nose, and said, "Won't you come in?"

He had a larger-than-life quality about him. Tall, broad, heavyset, immaculately dressed in a dark suit and expensive overcoat. Silver hair, wire-rimmed glasses, big bushy eyebrows. His mouth was wide and turned down at the ends. He didn't blink when Earl shoved the gun in his face, and he stepped into the Valley Forest Estates sales offices calmly.

Greenway called out from his office, "Mr. Benedetto! I can explain! We're just having a bit of a situation here."

I stepped out of his office. "Hi, Mr. Benedetto. I've heard a lot about you. And my friend and I would love to stay and chat, but we've pretty much finished conducting our business here."

While Earl kept the gun on him, I went back to Greenway. "Where's my phone?" I asked him.

For a moment, my question didn't seem to register. Then he recalled grabbing it at the construction site. "Desk drawer," he said. "Top right."

I looked inside and sure enough, there it was. I slipped it into my jacket pocket. "Good night, gentlemen," I said.

"Hey," said Carpington, trying to show me his cuffed wrists. "What about a key?"

I shrugged, smiled. "It'll just save the cops the trouble when they get here." And I walked out, past Benedetto, Earl following me. We ran to his truck and got inside, backing out of the lot and heading up the street.

"What about Benedetto?" asked Earl. "Should we have used our last set of cuffs on him?"

I shrugged. "I think we've got what we need, regardless of whether he's walking around free."

I took a couple of deep breaths, and then, out of nowhere, started making whooping noises.

"Whoa! Jesus! Did you see us in there? Were we bad?"

"We were bad," Earl said.

"We were baaad!"

"Sure," he said, lighting up. "We were bad."

"We were some bad motherfuckers, weren't we?" I slapped the dashboard. I felt like we'd just walked out of a scene in *Pulp Fiction*. "I can't believe we went in there, pushed them around, got some information. We kicked ass, didn't we?"

Earl nearly smiled. "Yeah, kicked ass. Nearly killed them, too, you dumb fuck."

We drove along in silence for a moment. I re-alized we were heading out of the neighborhood, nowhere in particular, it seemed.

"Where we going?" I asked.

"Hey, you're the navigator. I just wanted to get us away from there. I thought maybe we needed a drink or something."

"No," I said. "No. I gotta finish dealing with this. I think I'm ready to go to the cops. I've got what I need."

Earl nodded thoughtfully. "There's a couple of things," he said.

"Okay."

"First, I'd appreciate it if you could keep me out of this. I was happy to help you out tonight, but maybe you can find a way to keep from mentioning my presence to the authorities. I don't want them coming by and asking a lot of questions. I've got a business to run."

"Sure," I said. "I'll do what I can. I guess it depends on how much Greenway and Carpington say. They'll probably have enough to worry about without filing any sort of charges about our busting into their offices."

"I expect. And there's something else, that can't come from me, since I'd like to keep a low profile."

"What?"

"When you call the cops, you might want to suggest to them that they check those clowns' cars. I noticed, when I was moving them, there's a lot of shit in those cars, books and files and stuff. Might be just the thing they're looking for."

I nodded. "Sure, I'll be happy to pass that along."

"You want me to drop you at the police station?" he asked.

I thought. "No. There's a street behind ours, where I parked Stefanie Knight's Beetle. I'll pick it up, drive it over to the police station, get them to give me a ride home later."

"Sounds good."

He turned around, headed back to our neighborhood, and pulled up alongside the Volkswagen. As I opened the door, I said, "Thanks, Earl. You didn't have to do this."

"S'okay. Just remember to do what I told you."

I nodded, slammed the truck door shut, and, as Earl drove off into the night, reached into my jeans for the VW keys. I got into the car, fired it up, and decided to check that my cell phone was on.

I dug it out of my pocket and saw that Greenway had turned it off, not keen to have to take my messages, I guess. I watched the tiny screen as the phone became activated, searched for a signal. And then: "You have 4 new messages."

I could guess who they were from. Before I went to the police station, I thought I'd better give Sarah a call at work. It was time to come clean. She was going to be pissed, I knew that, but there was going to be no way to keep all this from her once the police were involved.

Without bothering to check the messages, I called her extension at work.

A male voice answered. Not Dan. Thank God. "City."

"Sarah Walker, please."

"Not here. Can I take a message?"

"It's her husband. She go home in the middle of her shift?"

"Some emergency. Had to go home."

And I thought, What if that was her who phoned when I was hiding out in the construction site? And when a strange voice answered — Greenway's — and said I was unavailable? What would she have thought? Especially when she was unable to raise me, or the kids, at home?

Shit.

"Thanks," I said, and then, as soon as I'd ended the call, I realized the gravity of what Sarah's colleague had just said to me. Sarah had gone home. To the one place where I'd felt, all night, it was unsafe to return.

I started to key in our home number when the phone rang shrilly. I nearly dropped it. I pressed the green button and put the phone to my ear.

"Hello?"

"Zack?" Sarah.

"Yes, yes, it's me!"

"Didn't you get any of my messages? God, I've been trying to get you all night."

"I just got my phone back and hadn't had a second to check them yet. I'm so sorry, it's been quite a night."

"I phoned you, and this other man answered, and I tried to call back, and I called home, and you haven't been here, I couldn't get the kids. So I left work and —"

"Sarah."

"— I've never been so worried in my entire life, especially when —"

"Sarah."

"— only a few blocks from here, they found this woman with her head smashed in, I think I told you about that —"

"Sarah."

"— drove home as fast as I could and —"

"Sarah!"

"What?"

I tried to stay calm. "Get out of the house."

"What?"

"Just get out of the house. Walk out the door, get in the car, and, and just drive to the doughnut shop. I'll find you there."

"What do you mean, get out of the house?"

"Sarah, I'll explain later, but right now it's important that you —"

"Hang on," she said.

"What?"

"Just hang on. There's someone at the door."

"Sarah, don't answer the —"

And I heard her put the phone down. She must have been using the one in the kitchen, not a cordless, otherwise she would have kept talking as she went to the door.

"Sarah."

Nothing.

"Sarah?"

Still nothing.

"Sarah!"

And then, a minute later, the sound of the receiver being picked up.

"Sarah?"

"Hey," said a voice I recognized. "I'll bet this is Zack."

"Rick," I said.

"Gotcha. Why don't you come home, bring along that ledger I think you got, before I kill your wife."

26

❖ ❖ ❖

I was barely two minutes from home, but it was the longest drive of my life. I stomped hard on the gas pedal of the Beetle, screeched around two corners and through two stop signs, and drove right up onto our front lawn, jumping out of the car without turning it off or bothering to close the door. Sarah's Camry was in the drive, blocked in by Rick, who had parked his car behind it.

The front door was locked, so I fumbled in my pocket for my own set of keys, got the right one into the lock after a couple of tries, my hands were shaking so badly, and burst into the house.

"Sarah!"

The house was eerily quiet. I paused, just for a moment, wondering where Rick and Sarah were. Blood pounded in my temples.

"Hey, Zack!" Rick called out casually. "We're in the kitchen!" Like he was saying "Come in for a beer."

I moved through the house slowly, wondering

how I should be handling this. The truth was, I had no idea how to handle this. I was already thinking I'd made a terrible mistake, that before I got here I should have dialed 911, or grabbed Earl again, or banged on Trixie's door and gotten the ledger, but I wasn't thinking all that straight. Sarah was in trouble, and all I could think to do was get to her as quickly as possible.

And now I was here, and there she was, sitting in one of the kitchen chairs, duct tape wound about her waist several times to secure her. Her hands were bound behind her, and there was more tape around each of her ankles, securing her legs to the chair. Rick stood by the sink, wielding the switchblade I'd seen him use to pick out loose pieces of caulking in our shower.

"Hi, honey," I said weakly.

She looked too frightened to speak. Tears had streaked her mascara, and there were a couple of dark trails leading down across her cheeks. But she managed to say one word, a question.

"Kids?"

I nodded. "They're fine. They went to stay with friends overnight."

"Isn't that keen," said Rick, looking at me. "I used to love sleepovers when I was a kid. This could have been such a great night for the two of you, kids out of the house, chance to get it on, right?"

I said nothing. Rick waved the knife about, swung it into the corner of the countertop, chipping it. He whacked at it again, taking out a chink. He was going to whittle away our kitchen.

"So, Zack, good to finally catch up with you," Rick said. "I feel like I've been running around all night looking for you."

"It's all over," I said. "Your boss Greenway, and Carpington, the police are going to be on to them in no time. Just get out of here and make a run for it. It's not going to take any time for them to figure out you killed Spender, and Stefanie."

"Whoa, you got that all wrong, fella."

"Just go. Don't hurt us. We won't call the cops for an hour. That'll give you time to get away."

Rick looked hurt. "But Sarah here and I were hoping to get to know one another. I feel that you and I have had a chance to get acquainted, but Sarah and me, we don't hardly know a thing about each other." To her, he said, "You know I didn't even realize, until the second time I was here, that your husband wrote one of my favorite books."

"Really," Sarah whispered.

"That's a fact. And I'm not a big reader, so you can imagine my surprise when I found out."

"Of course," Sarah said.

Could I rush him? There was the matter of the knife. At least it wasn't a gun. He couldn't get me from where I was standing. Suppose I ran? Just bolted, went for help? Outran the son of a bitch? And while it seemed like at least a possibility, I had some trouble with the optics of it all, of fleeing the house, leaving Sarah behind with this guy. At least now, if he went after her with the knife, I could try to do something about it. Try to be some kind of hero.

"In fact, I was wondering if you've got a copy of that book," he said to me, "and if you could autograph it for me."

"Of course," I said, my eyes moving back and forth between the knife and Sarah. "I'd be happy to do that for you. And anything else you want, I'll give it to you, if you'll go, and leave us alone."

Rick considered my request. "Well, when I was here last time, I was really only looking for one thing. This big book, with payments and everything listed inside. It was very important to Mr. Greenway that I get that back. And I still want that, no question about it. And maybe those negatives that asshole Carpington says you've got, although I don't really give a fuck about them one way or another."

Sarah, in addition to looking frightened beyond her worst nightmare, had this look of total bewilderment. Big book? Negatives?

"But what I was wondering was, you said you'd nearly finished the sequel to that book."

"Yes."

"Is it, like, printed out on pages and everything?"

"Uh, yes, it is."

"Terrific. I want that, too."

"The manuscript."

"The what?"

"The manuscript. That's what the book is called."

"Manuscript," he said, as though he was picturing the word in the air. "That's the title? Like, not *Missionary Part Two*?"

I shook my head. "No, a manuscript is what you call the printed-out pages of the book."

Rick eyed me suspiciously, as though I was trying to make him look stupid. "You fucking with me?"

"No, listen, sorry. Yes, you can have it."

"The problem is, didn't you say you hadn't quite finished it?"

"That's right. There's a chapter left."

Rick nodded, thought. "Well, let's deal with the most important matter first. I want that ledger."

"I don't have it," I said. "Not anymore."

"Where is it?"

I couldn't put Trixie at risk. I couldn't send him next door. So I said, "I dropped it off on the doorstep at the police station. They'll find it, and start figuring out what it all means."

Rick shook his head slowly. "I think you're shittin' me there, Zack. I don't believe you did anything like that at all. But I think I'll be able to get the truth out of you eventually. Sit down in that chair."

He indicated the one across from Sarah. When I didn't move right away, he took a step forward, waved the knife. "Chair! Now!"

I sat down. Rick tossed a roll of duct tape that

he'd left sitting by the phone in my direction. "Gimme your cell phone. Wrap that around yourself so you're tied into the chair," he said.

"I'm telling you the truth," I said, handing the phone over. "The ledger is with the police and —"

Rick suddenly waved his knife around Sarah. She tried to pull back into herself as he sliced through the air near her neck.

"Start taping yourself up," he said to me.

I found the end of the roll, gave a tug, heard the familiar rip of duct tape separating from itself. I slapped one end onto my shirt, then pulled the roll around me, handing it off from one hand to the other behind my back, then again in front of me. I went around a couple of times and stopped.

"No, a little more," Rick said.

"There's no way I can get out," I protested.

"Just do it."

I did one more loop around myself, tore off the tape from the roll, and set the roll on the kitchen table.

"Now your ankles," Rick said.

"I can't do my ankles. I can't bend over because I've got all this tape around my stomach."

"Shit," Rick said. Talk about a master plan falling apart. He set the knife down on the counter and approached me from behind.

Now or never, I figured.

I stood up and rushed backward. Sarah screamed. The chair came up at a forty-five-degree angle, my butt still attached to it, my body hunched over. The legs of the chair tangled with Rick's, and the weight of my coming after him propelled him into the vertical blinds that hung over the sliding glass doors to the deck. Rick's arms flailed, grabbing slats, ripping them from their moorings as I squeezed him against the door.

I took a step away, bound to the chair but my arms still free, and spun around. I threw myself into him, punching randomly. Except for Rick, a few hours earlier, I'd never hit anyone in my adult life. And the last time I'd hit him, I'd used a robot. This time, I was connecting with my hands, and the pain traveled straight up my arms and into my shoulders, which still hurt from dangling from that roof peak.

"You fucker!" Rick screamed, and shoved back. It was only reasonable to expect that a guy who'd spent several years working in construction, when he wasn't in jail probably lifting weights, was going to have stronger arms than a guy who daydreams at a computer all day. When he shoved, his arms were like pistons, driving me back across the kitchen and into a set of floor-to-ceiling cupboards. The chair hit them first, and inside I could hear stacked cans rattle and fall over.

Sarah kept screaming.

Rick ducked down, rushed me, grabbed me around my taped waist, and dragged me and the chair down to the floor. Then the pummeling began. This was very serious pummeling. I felt his fist connect with my chin, then my right cheek, bounce off my forehead, crush my lip. Blood filled my mouth where my tooth had gone through it. Some time around then, I started blacking out.

This was not good. This was not good at all.

I was vaguely aware of the sound of more duct tape being ripped from the roll, and of Sarah's voice.

"Zack? Can you hear me? Zack? Zack, say something."

It was like coming out of a deep sleep, except this time, while snoozing, someone had rearranged my body parts. My head, hanging down on my chest, was throbbing, and I could hardly see anything out of my left eye, or focus very well with the other.

"Zack, you there? He's in the other room. Zack, what's happening?"

I went to stretch, like I normally do when coming out of a deep sleep, but very little of me moved. My legs were held in place, and my left hand was trapped at my left side. Only my right arm was free.

My right eye was starting to focus, and I saw that I was pushed up to the kitchen table. I found the strength to lift my head up slightly, and confirmed that all that had happened before wasn't some bad dream. I was still in my kitchen, Sarah was still tied up in a chair across from me. And I was tied into a chair, too.

I was in a great deal of pain.

I looked over at Sarah and tried to smile, but using those muscles made me wince.

"Zack," she said. "Zack, can you understand me? Can you hear me?"

I nodded. God, it hurt.

"Who is that man? Why does he want to kill us? What's this ledger he's talking about? What on earth is going on?"

"Fucked up," I mumbled. "Big time."

"What? What did you do?"

"The purse. I took that woman's purse, at the grocery store. I thought it was yours." I paused. "Big mistake."

Sarah took it in. "My God," she said. "But I was wearing my fanny pack. You were trying to teach me a lesson and . . ."

"If it had been anybody else's purse," I whispered. "Any purse but that one . . ."

"Zack, stay awake. We've got to get out of here. This guy's crazy. I think he's going to kill us, even if you give him this ledger he's asking about. Do the police really have it? Because if they don't, just give it to him. Give him whatever he wants."

I nodded weakly. "I've got some more bad news," I said.

"What?" she said, holding her breath.

"I don't have anything for your birthday. I know you thought I was up to something, you know, about a gift. But I haven't gotten to it yet."

Sarah's eyes glistened, and she sighed. "That's okay," she said. "It's not actually until tomorrow."

I attempted another nod. "We'll pick something out later today. Something nice."

"Sure," she said, fighting to keep it together.

"And maybe after that, we'll go out for dinner, come home and celebrate. I'm okay, you know."

"You're not okay. You need to get to a doctor."

"No no, I mean, you know. My plumbing. It's perfectly operational. I just had a lot on my mind, earlier."

"Hey," said Rick, strolling back into the kitchen. "This it?" he asked, and dumped a stack of white paper, several hundred pages' worth, on the kitchen table. I struggled to look at it.

"Is this what?" I asked.

"The book. I was looking around in there, found this, it's lots of typed pages, so I figured that was it."

I knew that was it. "Yeah," I said. "It's yours. Go somewhere and read it."

"Naw, I'll just take it with me. But just tell me, since the last chapter's missing, how does it end?"

I blinked to get some blood out of my eye. "It turns out there is no God after all," I said.

Rick nodded. "Fuck, is that supposed to be some sort of surprise ending? I could have told you that."

27

❖ ❖ ❖

"I hope you don't mind but I'm also going to take some of your toys with me," Rick said, motioning in the direction of my study. "You've got some of the neatest stuff in there. I love that Klingon warship, and you've got some terrific little *Star Wars* spaceships." He came over, looked at me. "Can I ask you a question?"

Still taped into the chair, I raised my head feebly. "Go ahead."

"Which do you think is better? *Star Trek* or *Star Wars*?"

"I don't know," I said, looking at Sarah, tied up in her chair across from me on the other side of the kitchen table, who'd already seen too much to be surprised by this line of questioning. "Which do you think is better?"

"I think *Star Trek*."

"Me, too."

"Really? You know why I like it better? More chicks in little short outfits. At least in the original one. The *Next Generation*, they toned it down a bit. Until that *Voyager* show, and the

Borg chick, with the really tight costume. Man."

Suddenly, as if he'd forgotten something, he went back into the study. A moment later he returned to the kitchen holding a model of the saucerlike spacecraft from *Lost in Space*, the *Jupiter 2*. Actually, he was flying it more than holding it, carrying it a couple of inches away from his eyes. One was closed, the other squinting, like he was picturing the craft zooming through the galaxy.

"Okay, I'm taking this, too, but there's a part that's broken off it."

"It's the door," I said. "It needs to be glued back on. It's on the shelf right where the model was."

And then he was gone, looking for it. He returned with the model ship, the door, and a small container of liquid plastic cement he'd found on my modeling table.

"I want you to fix it," he said. "I was never very good at this sort of thing. I always put on too much glue and ruin it."

"I'm kind of tied up at the moment."

"Okay," he said. "I'm going to let you use your right hand." He began to unwind the duct tape that held my right wrist to my chair.

"I'm gonna need both hands," I said. "If I'm going to glue it and then hold the door in place."

"I look stupid to you? You can do it with one hand. I'll help you, and then we're going to talk about finding that ledger for Mr. Greenway."

He unscrewed the cap on the liquid cement. With my free hand I set the door on its back side so I could apply cement to the parts that would come in contact with the ship.

"How about this," I said to Rick as I dabbed a bit of glue onto the door. "I'll tell you more about that ledger, but you have to let me tell you about another story I'm working on first."

"What? Like another science fiction book?"

"No, this one's a bit different. It's sort of a mystery, about a double-cross."

"Oh yeah? I always like those. Like you think the guy is your friend, but then you find out he's your enemy."

"This one's about a guy who does all the dirty work for his boss, takes all the risks, but gets shafted in the end."

Rick eyed me warily. "Go on."

"He even kills for his boss, that way the boss is protected, you know? There's some distance between him and the crime, so that if he has to, he can deny knowing anything about it."

Rick frowned. "Doesn't sound like something that would interest me."

"No? It should. I'm basing it on you. Here, press the door into place, now hold it for a few seconds till it sets. In this story, you're the central character. You're the one getting double-crossed."

"Sure I am."

"You know what your boss Greenway said to me — I don't even know how long ago, I got no idea what time it is now. But earlier tonight, he said something very interesting to me."

"What he say?"

"He said, 'What if we gave you Rick?' "

Rick ran his tongue around the inside of his mouth. "Whaddya mean, what if he gave you Rick?"

"He said, 'What if we give you Rick for the murders of Spender and Stefanie? We get him to take the fall for that, and then we give you whatever you want.' "

"That's bullshit."

"It didn't sound like bullshit a little while ago. You see, I may not look like I'm in a good bargaining position right now, but a couple of hours ago, I kind of had the jump on your boss and his friend Carpington, and they were ready to say anything to put themselves in the clear. Greenway said you're a hothead, that you killed those people, and he's prepared to give you up to save himself. He's in some pretty deep shit now. This whole thing's falling apart around him, and if he can keep his ass out of jail by giving you to the cops, I think that's what he's going to do. And you know Roger will go along. That guy cries for long-distance commercials."

"You're lying."

"And it seemed like a good idea to Mr. Benedetto, too. He just showed up at the office, I think they're going over the final details now of how to hang you out to dry for all this. And if you kill us, thinking you're doing it in

Greenway's interests, well, I wouldn't be looking for him to back you up."

"That's fucking shit!" Rick said, making a fist and bringing it down hard on the model, shattering it into a hundred pieces. Sarah, even tied in the chair, jumped, the chair legs squeaking as they moved an inch across the floor.

Then Rick was very quiet, thinking about it, not sure whether to believe me or not. But it was probably the kind of thing he'd always suspected. Slowly, the rage was boiling up in him. Pretty soon he'd have to get out his baseball bat and smash another car. "Those fuckers," he said. "They can't do that."

"You think they wouldn't? You really think they —"

There was a loud banging on the front door. We all turned our heads in the direction of the noise. Rick sidled over to the counter and took the knife into his hand.

Sarah and I exchanged glances. It couldn't be Angie or Paul. They had keys. And even if they'd forgotten them, they'd never bang the door that way.

The police, we thought. Maybe, finally, the police had figured out I was somehow involved in this mess. Maybe they'd checked the last few calls made to Stefanie Knight's phone, recorded the numbers. Discovered that one of them was my cell, and now they wanted to know what I knew about her murder.

Lots! Ask me anything! I'm ready to talk!

"You stay here," Rick said to both of us, and I thought: Duh. And: "Don't make a sound."

I guess, realizing he might not be able to count on us in this regard, he put the knife back down and ripped off two broad pieces of duct tape. One piece got slapped across my mouth and the other across Sarah's.

There was another loud knock on the door.

Rick grabbed the knife and ran out of the kitchen. I reached up with my one free hand and pulled the tape back off my mouth. Sarah rolled her eyes, as if to say, "Can this guy not get anything right?"

I heard him reach the front hall, and imagined that he had probably peeked through the glass beside the door to see who'd come calling.

I heard him throw the bolt. Whoever it was, it was someone he was willing to admit into the house. I started clawing at the tape that was wound around my body.

"Mr. Benedetto," Rick said. There was no warmth in his voice.

"Rick," Mr. Benedetto said. I heard the door close again. "Mr. Greenway had a feeling you might be over here, tending to a few things."

"Yeah."

There were so many layers of tape, I was having a hard time tearing through them. So I tried reaching around, to free my left hand.

"We've got a bit of a problem, and you being quite the handyman, we thought you might be able to assist us. If you take a look out there, you'll see Mr. Greenway and that Mr. Carpington out by the car there, and they're both in handcuffs."

"What?" said Rick. In his mind, handcuffs meant cops. Clearly, there had been developments he was not aware of. "So it's true."

"What, Rick? What's true?"

"The cops have already picked them up. And they're going to cut a deal. What did the cops say to you? That if you came in here and got me, they'd cut you a deal, too?"

I peeled one layer of tape from around my left wrist. There felt like only one layer left. As I picked at it, I wriggled my left wrist around, trying to stretch the tape enough to slip my hand out.

"I'm afraid I don't know what you're talking about, Rick. But maybe you could tell me what's going on here. Is Mr. Walker here? Did you recover the ledger?"

"Walker told me what's going on. That you guys are going to turn me over for the Spender thing. And for Stefanie. You know I didn't have nothin' to do with that."

"I still don't know what you're talking about, Rick. Maybe you could come out and give us a hand."

My left hand broke free of the tape. But I was still wrapped into the chair, and my ankles were anchored to the legs.

"A hand?" Rick's voice suddenly became more calm. "Sure. I've got some tools out in my trunk. Why don't you come with me, I can show you. I got all kinds of stuff in there."

And the door opened again, and closed. And there were no more voices in the house.

I looked at Sarah. I said, "He's out of the house." She nodded furiously, her eyes wide with hope above the band of tape. "If I can get to the door, I can lock it."

I tipped forward, the chair moving with my body, tried to balance on my tiptoes. I put my hands on the table, balanced on one and leaned across to pull the tape off Sarah's mouth.

"Hurry," she whispered.

I tried to hop, but fell. But with my arms free I was able to drag myself, and the chair, forward. I scrambled across the kitchen's linoleum floor, reached the broadloom with upgraded underpadding in the hall. There wasn't time to try to force myself back into a sitting position, regain my equilibrium, and take another run at hopping. I just kept dragging myself, trying to push with my toes. The rug burned against my elbows as I neared the front door, and if my knees could have screamed they would have. I could see the deadbolt, set in the unlocked position. Only a few more feet. Just a few more.

I reached the door, and, lying on my side with the chair still attached to my body, I reached up and turned the bolt.

"It's locked!" I screamed to Sarah.

"Good!" she screamed back.

"Can you get to the phone?"

"I'll try!" There was the sound of her chair

sliding across the floor in short bursts.

I shifted my head over toward the edge of the door, trying to catch a glimpse of what was happening outdoors through the narrow floor-to-ceiling pane of glass. The sun had crested the horizon, and I could see clearly what was happening.

Stefanie's Beetle still sat in the middle of the yard. Benedetto's BMW was parked at the curb, Greenway and Carpington, their hands still cuffed behind them, leaning up against it. From my vantage point, I couldn't quite see Sarah's Camry, or Rick's car behind it. Greenway and Carpington were watching something take place in the vicinity of Rick's car, and it scared Carpington enough that he turned and began running down Chancery Park, toward Lilac. Greenway was shouting, shaking his head no, ordering Rick to do something. It looked like he was yelling "Let him out!"

I was guessing that, by now, Quincy was wide awake.

Now Rick came into view, still waving around his switchblade. He grabbed Greenway by the shoulder and started hustling him in the direction of the front door. He grabbed the handle and pushed as though he expected it would open. When it didn't, he shouted, "Open this fucking door!" He slapped it with the palm of his hand.

"I'm almost there!" Sarah called. "But I can't get my hands free!"

"Open it! Walker! Open this door!"

He kicked at it twice, but it didn't budge. Then he kicked at the glass, but it only cracked slightly. "You're dead!" he screamed. "When I get in there you're dead!"

And he disappeared.

He was running around the house, looking for other ways in. I heard him try the garage doors, but they were locked as well. A few seconds went by and then Sarah screamed, "He's here!" She would have meant the sliding glass doors, but I knew they were locked, too. Would he try to smash them in?

Even from my position at the front of the house, I could hear Rick screaming at the top of his lungs and banging the knife against the glass. "I'm going to cut out your fucking hearts!"

"Oh God!" Sarah said.

"What?"

"The ladder! He's going up the ladder!"

Oh no. The ladder I'd left leaned up against the back of the house so that I could regularly caulk around our bedroom window. And I was betting that our bedroom window was open. We usually left it that way, to allow fresh air in at night while we slept. With that knife, he'd be through the screen in seconds.

"Zack! He's at our window! He's going in!"

I tried to shift around the floor, the chair legs digging sideways into the carpet. I thought about how Sarah would hear him kill me before her. From where I lay, I could see the stairs to the second floor, and of course he'd spot me first on the way down. Sarah would have to listen to me scream as he cut me open. I wondered if there was a way I could face the end with anything resembling dignity. If I could keep from screaming, would it make Sarah's last few moments any less terrifying? At that moment, that was all I could think to give to her, to let her die knowing that I had not suffered that severely. That while not painless, it had not gone on long. It wasn't much of a birthday present, but it was all I had to give.

"He's in! He's in!"

She didn't have to tell me. Rick's entrance into our bedroom had been announced with a crash. Our dresser is under the window, and in coming through it, Rick had sent a lamp to the floor.

I heard him cackle. "Your hearts!" he screamed. "I'm gonna fucking eat them!"

And I thought about Paul and Angie, about how sorry I was to have done this to them, to have allowed their parents to be taken away from them, much too soon, and in such an ugly fashion. Would my dad take them in, or maybe Sarah's parents? Or would Angie turn into an adult overnight, look after Paul herself, tell her grandparents that she could handle this on her own? It would be like her to try, I thought. She was tough, and proud, and she'd feel honor bound to look after her little brother all by herself.

Rick was out of the bedroom and running down the hall. I saw his shadow fall across the top of the stairs.

This was it.

"Sarah," I said. Not a scream. I just wanted to say her name. And to make one final apology: "I'm sorry."

Rick came flying down the stairs. I don't mean he was running quickly, taking the steps two or three at a time. He was airborne.

His head was thrust out well ahead of his body. His arms were outstretched, the knife forging out ahead of him in his right hand. His feet were off the ground. If he'd worn a cape, it would have been flowing and rippling in the breeze behind him.

His mouth was open in astonishment. This, evidently, was not how he'd planned to come down this flight of stairs. Now his arms were waving, his legs kicking, trying to make some sort of purchase, to regain his footing.

As he pitched forward, his right arm hit one of the lower steps first, his elbow cracked, and his forearm snapped back, angling the knife toward himself. And then his neck connected with the upturned blade, and the weight of his body drove it deep into him, and his mouth opened even wider, but no sound came out.

He came to rest two steps from the bottom, his arms and legs twisted at unnatural angles. From his neck, the blood spilled forth as if from an open tap. The gathering pool spread from the second step and down to the first.

And tumbling after him, like an afterthought, like a second punch line to a joke you thought was over, came Paul's backpack. It bounced a couple of times, then settled next to Rick's head in the blood.

28

The man who delivers papers to our neighborhood showed up not long after that. He didn't even get close to our door. Who could blame him? Here's what he found:

A man in handcuffs sitting out on our front step.

An abandoned Beetle parked on the front lawn, door open, engine still running.

From inside the house, a woman's screams, a man's cries for help.

From the trunk of a small car parked at the end of our driveway, even louder screams. They sounded like a man's.

The paper man (there are almost no boys anymore; papers must be picked up in the middle of the night and delivered before six, and this was a sight you wouldn't have wanted a young lad to see) went back to his car, where he kept a cell phone, and called for help.

What a production.

Two police cars and an ambulance converged on the scene within five minutes. When the am-

391

bulance attendants, who, I'm told, looked upon our house with a certain familiarity, arrived, they were directed first to the trunk of the car by the paper guy. But the handcuffed man sitting on our front step, Don Greenway, advised them not to think, even for a moment, of opening that trunk. You might, he suggested, want to call someone from the zoo.

I was able to reach up and unlock the door to let everyone in. The police came in first, putting some muscle behind the door so as to move me out of the way, duct-taped to the overturned chair as I was. Their eyes had barely landed on me when they saw Rick at the bottom of the stairs, a much more convincing dead person than I ever was in that same spot, a very long time ago.

They must have thought, at that moment, that whoever'd done that to Rick had been the same person who'd put me in the chair, but gradually, the truth began to emerge. I told them to please check on my wife, in the kitchen, and one officer ran ahead to do just that while another stayed with me, wanting to know who else was in the house, how many hurt.

"There's one guy out there in the trunk," I said as the officer cut me out of the chair, "but it may be too late for him. And there's another one, not hurt, but running around the neighborhood someplace with his hands cuffed behind his back."

"There's already a guy here in handcuffs."

"There's a second one. It's a long story."

Once I was free, I was on my feet and running to the kitchen where Sarah was now standing, and we threw our arms around each other and started to cry. I held on to her for a very long time.

"Mom? Dad?"

It was Paul, calling from out front. The police wouldn't let him inside. We both ran out to see him and embraced him, so happy that we were all alive, except that Paul had no reason to think that all of us being alive was in any way an extraordinary thing.

"What's going on?" he asked. "What the hell happened to your face?"

"You're a hero," I said, hugging him again. "And you don't even know it."

"Huh?"

It was my first time outside of the house since the police had arrived, and it was wild. At least half a dozen police cars, three ambulances, a fire truck, just in case. A couple of SUVs with TV station logos splashed across the sides. And nearly everyone on the street was outside, standing in their yards, gawking. It was the first time I'd ever seen the housecoat lady outside without a hose in her hand.

Trixie approached me tentatively as I stood out there with Paul.

"Oh God," she whispered. "All hell broke loose."

"Kinda," I said. "I need you to get me that ledger."

She nodded and slipped away. I saw Earl across the street, standing by the back of his pickup. Our eyes met, and he nodded, as if to say "I'm glad you're okay, man, but if you don't mind, I'm going to stay on this side of the street while the cops are around." That was just fine with me.

Sarah grabbed one of the ambulance attendants as he walked past, and said, "My husband's been hurt."

I recognized him as the male attendant who'd come to our house during The Backpack Incident. While he might have remembered coming to this address, he made no suggestion that we had met before. My face was too badly bruised and bloodied to be recognizable.

They ended up taking both of us to the hospital. Even though Sarah showed no obvious signs of injury, they wanted to check her out just the same. I told Paul to get in touch with Angie, let her know that we were okay.

"Does she think you're *not* okay?" he asked.

And tell her not to worry about going to school today, I said. Get one of the officers to bring you to the hospital to meet us once she shows up, I said.

Turns out all Sarah had were some tape burns on her wrists. Hospital officials would later tell the press that she was "in good condition," but I knew better. Nobody came out of something like this in good condition. I figured the nightmares would begin that night, and would be with her for a very long time.

The doctors and nurses had a fair bit of work to do on me. I needed stitches in three places on my face, my left eye was puffed up the size of an egg but the color of a prune, and I had an assortment of bruises all over my body from my tangles with Rick and crawling across the floor while still secured to a chair.

The police interviewed us separately. Needless to say, I had a lot more to get off my chest than Sarah, who was still pretty much in the dark, and was kept busy with detectives, including my friend Detective Flint, for a lot longer.

Hours and hours longer.

I started from the beginning. I'd considered, briefly, telling them I'd grabbed Stefanie Knight's purse by mistake, but knew I'd get caught in a lie somewhere down the road once they turned on the hot lights and brought out the rubber hoses.

I spelled out for them the whole Valley Forest Estates thing. The blackmailing of Carpington, the murder of Spender, how Stefanie was offered up for sexual favors. They'd found Carpington, by the way, sitting down by the edge of Willow Creek, listening to the sound of the water as it flowed by, and when two officers approached him, he turned to them and smiled and said, "It's beautiful down here, don't you think? They should never build homes around here."

The police wanted to know: Did I kill Stefanie Knight?

No, I said.

Did I know who had killed Stefanie Knight?

Not for certain, I said. But my money was on Rick. He certainly had an unlimited capacity for violence.

They told me that his full name was Richard Douglas Knell, that he was thirty-eight, and that while he'd spent much of his life working in construction, he'd also spent some time "inside" (where he did his reading), having kicked in a man's head outside a bar six years earlier. There was evidence that he'd acted, in some small way, in self-defense, otherwise the sentence would have been longer. He'd come back to work for Don Greenway, who'd been his employer years ago, and Greenway found a way to exploit Rick's special talents of persuasion.

"He liked snakes," I said.

My interrogators concurred. But Quincy, alas, was no longer with us. When they popped the trunk of Rick's car, they found he'd already squeezed the life out of Mr. Benedetto, and was in the process of digesting him. He'd only gotten to his knees, and when the panicked officers saw what they were dealing with, they unloaded several rounds into the snake, trying not to disgrace the body of Mr. Benedetto in the process, although they did nick his shoes. They'd remarked later, privately, that since Mr. Benedetto was already dead, it would have been interesting had they opened the trunk much later. They wondered just how much of the guy the snake would have managed to get down its throat. It would have been something to see, no doubt about it.

Anyone else on my list of suspects? they asked.

Well, there was Greenway, of course. Stefanie had decided, it appeared, to get out of Dodge, and she was leaving with her homemade supply of cash, plus a ledger for possible future blackmail purposes, and the roll of film. It wasn't clear whether she had the film because she was tired of being used for such seedy purposes, or simply hadn't gotten around to turning it in to Greenway for developing. I wondered where he normally had his film processed. Mindy's would do it for you in an hour, $6.99 for twenty-four exposures, another set of prints for two bucks.

I promised to hand over the negatives, still hidden in my *Seaview* model, and the ledger.

Earl's name never came up. As far as the police knew, I'd busted into the Valley Forest Estates office alone. I didn't have to bring Trixie into it, either. The police were left with the impression that I had something of a handcuff fetish. Later, when we compared notes about what we'd been asked, Sarah said to me, "When did you switch from sci-fi modeling to handcuff collecting?"

When the police finally decided to let me go home, with the proviso that they would be wanting to talk to me again, probably several times, I said to them, almost as an afterthought:

"You might also want to take a look in Carpington's and Greenway's cars. I don't think there's any snakes in them. They're out behind the Valley Forest Estates offices. You never know, you might find some interesting things in there."

"Already have," said Detective Flint.

I wondered whether they would charge me with something. There had to be lots of offenses to choose from. Not reporting Stefanie's death to them immediately, hindering prosecution, who knew? They take their time with these things, and I knew that if they wanted to lay charges, they might take months to get around to it.

But they didn't waste any time charging others. Greenway, who hadn't bothered to make a run for it that morning, who knew the game was over and simply waited for the cops to arrive, was arrested, as was Roger Carpington.

A couple of days later, with some fanfare, they announced that they were charging Carpington with the murder of Stefanie Knight.

They had found, in the trunk of his car, a bloody shovel. They'd run DNA tests on the blood, and it turned out to be, without a doubt, Stefanie Knight's.

And I thought: I'll be damned.

Life took some time to get back to normal.

Sarah's bosses told her to take off as much time as she wanted, which meant she probably had about a week. In seven days or so, her editors would be calling to say "You okay? You think, you know, coming back to work and editing stories about murder and mayhem would help take your mind off things?"

There were insurance matters to deal with. We'd lost a car. There was a big hole in the basement wall, from my doing batting practice with the tripod. And there was the grisly matter of the blood-soaked carpet where Rick had fallen on his sword.

And there was some other damage that the insurance adjusters weren't equipped to handle. Sarah didn't want to talk to me.

She was there for me, of course, while I recovered from my injuries. She'd make me tea, bring me an ice pack, get me a glass of water to help me wash down my Advils. But she didn't have much else to say, and I couldn't blame her. I'd nearly gotten us both killed by being a busybody. I'd nearly turned our kids into orphans.

They weren't that pleased with me, either, but they were more upset that their mother and I weren't speaking. Or that their mother wasn't speaking to me.

"I'll talk to her," Angie said to me.

"Thanks, honey," I said. "But I just think it's going to take some time."

"How much time?"

When I crawled into bed next to Sarah, she

flicked off her light, turned her back to me, and pulled the covers up around her neck. I stared at the ceiling for an hour or more before finally falling asleep.

It was during this time, while still awake, that I started thinking about things that I had no business worrying about. For me, this should all be over, and yet . . .

Roger Carpington. They'd charged Roger Carpington with murder. They'd found the shovel in the trunk of his car.

I'd seen that shovel. It had been there, on the floor, next to Stefanie Knight's body. How had it traveled from there into the trunk of Roger Carpington's car?

Maybe, after I'd left, he'd come back. Maybe he was concerned that he'd left his fingerprints on it, so he came back, snuck inside, grabbed the shovel and threw it in his trunk.

I suppose.

Except by the time I'd left Stefanie Knight's house, there was an Oakwood Town Council meeting under way. Carpington's wife had told me, when I'd phoned his house looking for him, that the meeting had started at 6:30 p.m. The councilman would have had to excuse himself in the middle of a council meeting, drive across town, retrieve the shovel, drive back across town, take his seat again in the council chambers.

And he couldn't have grabbed the shovel after the council meeting, after I'd seen him, because by then the police were already at the scene. Sarah had phoned when I was at the interview with Paul's science teacher — Ms. Winslow or Wilton or whatever — and told me she'd sent a reporter to cover it.

The next morning, after a nearly sleepless night, I phoned the town clerk.

"Did Roger Carpington leave during the council meeting for a long time?" I asked.

"I'm not sure I should be answering your questions, Mr. Walker. This is a police matter."

"I'm only asking the one question. Was he there for the whole meeting, or did he skip out for a while?"

The clerk sighed. "He was there the whole time."

"Thank you."

I called my good friend Detective Flint and told him what I had uncovered. He was not impressed. "Mr. Walker, really, you've done more than enough. We can look after this investigation on our own, thanks very much."

"But what about that shovel? I saw it with my own eyes. I was there, in the garage, and saw it."

"You must have the times screwed up, then. Maybe you were in her house earlier than you think. Listen, Mr. Walker, once again, we thank you for your help and all, but we've got our guy."

So I let it go.

Maybe I was wrong about the time. Or maybe, just like there could have been a second shooter on the grassy knoll, there was a second shovel.

Did it really matter?

Carpington was a weasel. Did it make any difference, if they were already going to send him away for five years for municipal corruption, if they left him there for another five for murder? What was it to me?

I mentioned to Sarah, in the kitchen, that we should go away. Leave the kids with her parents, go someplace for a week or two. Maybe rent a cottage, or spend some time in New York. She could use her contacts in the entertainment department to wangle some tickets to a couple of shows. Or maybe even Europe. Spend a week in London, or better, a week in Paris. How did that sound? Tom Darling thought the *Missionary* sequel was going to do better than expected, what with — I hate to say it — all the media exposure I'd gotten in the last week. So there was bound to be a little extra money coming in.

Sarah said she didn't know, and went outside.

I wanted to throw a little party. Okay, "party" is too strong a word. But I wanted to do something for Trixie and Earl. Have them over for a drink. I mentioned this to Sarah.

"So we're going to throw a bash for a pot grower and a hooker," she said.

"Well," I said, "to the best of my knowledge, she just ties them up and spanks them, but she doesn't fuck them."

"Oh, my mistake. I'll get out the good china."

But she was actually pretty decent about it. At some level, Sarah seemed to understand that once I was in this mess I'd created for myself, I had to find a way out of it, and that Trixie and Earl were the unlikely pair who'd been there when I needed help. So we invited them over for a Wednesday evening, early. Trixie explained that she had a nine o'clock, and there was a lot of prep work. Costuming and all. Sarah made a lasagna and we uncorked a few bottles of wine.

Earl had said no, at first. He was glad to have helped out, but he wasn't sure he felt comfortable coming over. He knew Sarah was pissed. But I leaned on him a bit, reminded him that, up to now, I'd managed to avoid mentioning his role to the police, and I was pretty sure they weren't going to hear about him from Greenway or Carpington, who'd both hired high-priced lawyers and weren't saying a word to anyone.

Trixie, too, had concerns about coming over. "Sarah knows what I do?"

"Yeah."

"And the kids?"

"I'm less sure. I haven't told them directly. But they're not stupid. I don't want you to take this the wrong way, but as long as you're not going to be their guidance counselor, I think it's okay."

And so they came. We even invited over some of the other neighbors, the ones who'd stood out on the sidewalk the morning everything happened. We thought they might like to get to know what we were like when there weren't so many emergency vehicles around. We finally met the people directly next door, in the house between ours and Trixie's — the Petersons — a couple who worked as control room technicians for a Christian television network. I so wanted to tell them what their other neighbor did for a living, but held my tongue.

We didn't all sit around the same table. It was informal. You grabbed a drink, scooped out a heap of lasagna and some salad on a plate, and ate it wherever you wanted. In the kitchen, in front of the TV, whatever.

"You're back to work?" I heard Trixie ask Sarah from across the kitchen.

She nodded. "I took a week, went back. But Zack and I, we're thinking maybe of taking a vacation."

I stopped chewing so I could hear more.

"Maybe a cottage, maybe even a week in Paris."

"That would be fabulous," Trixie said. It sure would, I thought.

Earl came up to me, kept me from hearing anything else. There was a bit of tomato sauce on the cigarette he had between his lips. "So you're sure you kept me out of it?"

"So far," I said. "What if I have to tell at some point?"

Earl shrugged. "Thing is, I'm thinking of moving on. Let the Asians get somebody else to run the house. I don't own it. I can walk away. Chances are, by the time you have to tell all, I won't be around."

I smiled. All I could think to say was "Yeah."

Angie strolled by, rubbed her hand on my shoulder. I'd noticed both the kids were more physical lately. A hug here, a pat on the back there. I touched her hair as she passed me.

Paul, his plate heaped with lasagna and two rolls, came around the corner.

"Man of the hour," Earl said.

Paul grinned. "For once, I didn't get reamed out about leaving my backpack at the top of the stairs."

Earl blew out some smoke, shoved a piece of bread into his mouth.

"You still going to help me with the yard?" Paul asked. "I want to put in some rosebushes, maybe."

"I don't know, sport," Earl said. "I don't think I'm the kind of guy your dad wants you to associate with." I had, once the dust settled, told the kids how Earl made his living.

"Jeez, Dad, they're going to legalize the stuff any day now."

I felt awkward. "I think Earl's thinking of moving on, anyway. Maybe I'll have to learn a little about yard work myself. Or you can teach me, and I'll just push the wheelbarrow around."

"You know, Dad," Paul said. "There's something I've been wanting to talk to you about."

I eyed him warily. "What?"

"The way I see it, if it hadn't been for me, you and Mom, like, you probably wouldn't be here now. So I was thinking some kind of reward was in order."

I ran my tongue around inside my cheek. "Like what?"

"I think you should let me get a tattoo."

"No way."

"Come on! Look, if that guy had —" and he paused here "— killed you and Mom, I'd have been able to go ahead and do it anyway."

"Too bad things worked out the way they did."

Now he was frustrated. He hadn't meant anything like that, and I was instantly sorry that I'd made the crack. But Earl seemed to find the exchange amusing.

Paul said, "You're screwing up my words. I guess I'm saying, I mean, couldn't I just get one? Remember I told you how people you know have them, and they're not bad people? Like my math teacher, Mr. Drennan?"

"I don't know."

"And what about Earl here? He's got one. Do you think he's a bad person?"

Earl's smile vanished. "Hey, Paul, don't go dragging me into this. This is strictly between you and your parents, okay?"

"But the thing is, you've got one, and here you are, talking to my dad and all, and I don't think he thinks any less of you because you've got one."

"Of course I don't," I said to Paul. "But Earl's an adult, and you're not."

"Just show it to him," Paul coaxed Earl.

"I don't think so, really."

To me, Paul said, "It's so cool, although I've only seen it once. Remember, Earl, we were putting in those shrubs, and you took off your shirt that one day, it was so friggin' hot?"

Now I was curious. "What is it, Earl? A naked lady, I'm guessing."

"No," said Paul. "It's way more cool than that. It's a watch."

Earl took a very long drag on his cigarette.

I said, "You might as well show me, Earl. Paul's going to hound you until you do."

Earl put his plate of lasagna down on the counter and slowly rolled up the right sleeve of his black T-shirt. He got it up above his shoulder and took his hand away.

It was a watch. But not a normal watch. It looked like a pocket watch, no strap, and it was melting, just like in that Salvador Dali painting.

He gave us a second to look at it, then rolled the sleeve back down.

"That's quite something," I said, and Earl's eyes caught mine.

29

❖ ❖ ❖

"You coming to bed?" Sarah said. There was nothing in her voice that said she wanted me there for any other purpose than company. These days, Sarah definitely didn't want to sleep alone.

It was after midnight; our guests had left several hours ago. Trixie, as I mentioned, had to work, and Earl left much earlier than planned. I had retired to my study, and was sitting at my desk when Sarah appeared in the door, leaning, one hand propped up against the frame. She was in a long nightshirt featuring a big picture of Snoopy in karate garb.

"Soon," I said. I had a folder in front of me, stuffed with newspaper clippings.

"Okay," she said, and turned to go.

"I heard you tell Trixie," I said, and she stopped, "that we might be going away. For a trip."

Sarah said nothing for a moment. "I guess I did."

"Were you just saying it, or would you like to go?"

She pressed her lips together, ran her hand through her hair. "I don't know. I think, sometimes, that I would. I let myself stop being mad at you for a while, and I like the idea. And then I get mad again, and stop thinking about it."

I nodded. I sat there, and she stood in the doorway, and about a minute went by.

"What if I could get our house back?" I said.

"What?"

"What if I could get our old house back? Move back into the city."

"I don't know what you're talking about."

"I'm talking about moving. Back into our old neighborhood. It might, it might not be the same house. Not the exact same one. But something in that neighborhood, on Crandall, or maybe a street over. We could shop at Angelo's again, and you could get cannolis, and the kids could go back to their old school. It would be like we never lived out here at all."

Sarah bit her lip and looked away for a moment. She took a finger and wiped at the corner of one eye.

"I could call somebody, get this place assessed, put this place on the market, see what we could get for it. I mean, we'd probably have a mortgage again, it's going to cost us more to buy down there, but I could go work for a paper again. Cover city hall, take pictures, whatever."

Sarah sniffed, took a tentative step into the room, then a couple more. When she was a foot away, I leaned forward in my chair and slipped

409

my arms around her thighs, pressed my face into her stomach. We remained that way for a while, and then I said, "I'm not sure this house is a place anymore from which to make good memories. And I know we have lots more to make."

She nodded, sniffed again, looked at the folder of newspaper clippings on my desk.

"What are you doing?" she asked.

"Just some stuff," I said. "Why don't you go to bed, and I'll be up in a bit. And in the morning, we can talk some more about what we should do."

When she left, I closed the door and returned to my desk and opened the folder. Back when I had first collected these clippings, with the idea of possibly doing a book on the case someday, I had arranged them in chronological order.

The first story, dated October 9, carried this headline: "Police Comb Neighborhood for Girl, 5."

My recollection was that this story hadn't made the front page. It had been splashed across the top of page three, six columns, with a picture of Jesse Shuttleworth. It was a blurry photo, no doubt blown up from a cheap snapshot, and the larger it got, the poorer the definition. She had curly red hair, brown eyes, a smile to melt your heart. The story rated about fifteen inches. The editors probably hadn't wanted to go crazy with it. Not yet. She would only have been missing a few hours by the time the first edition closed. She could be at a friend's, she might be lost. You didn't want to go and put it on page one, then, just as the paper hit the streets, have people hear on their car radios that she'd been found at a sleepover. So you hedged your bet, you put it on three.

The story, by Renata Sears, one of the paper's tireless police reporters, read:

The city was holding its breath last night as police combed the Dailey Gardens neighborhood in their hunt for little Jesse Shuttleworth, a 5-year-old kindergarten student who vanished from the park sometime yesterday afternoon.

Jesse's mother, Carrie Shuttleworth, 32, of Langley Ave., told police Jesse had been playing across the street from their home, in the Dailey mini-park, around 4:15 p.m. when she went missing.

The teary-eyed mother, at a hastily called news conference on her front porch last night, said Jesse had been playing on the swings, and was always good about coming straight home.

"I just want her to be okay," she said. "I'm just praying that she gets home safely."

Police refused to speculate about the nature of Jesse's disappearance, but they have set up a command post at the park, and asked neighbors with any possible information to please drop by. "At the moment, this is a missing-child case, as simple as that," said Sgt. Dominic Marchi. "We're hoping that she'll turn up any time now."

Police would not discuss a rumor of a scraggly-haired man who was seen near the park earlier in the day.

The second day, however, the Jesse Shuttleworth disappearance was the only story in the city. It took up three-quarters of the front page, with a simple two-word headline in a font size normally reserved to announce the end of the world: "Where's Jesse?" Sears was still on the story.

Her dolls are lined up along the top of her pillows, as though waiting for Jesse to come home.

Renata knew how to lay it on.

It has been more than 30 hours since little Jesse Shuttleworth went missing from a park in Dailey Gardens, and despite one of the most intensive police searches in the city's history, there's so far no sign of her.

A mother sits in anguish at the kitchen table, waiting for a call, any news, good or bad, about Jesse's whereabouts. Carrie Shuttleworth, a single mom who works by day in a laundry and at a coffee shop at night to support herself and her only daughter, says Jesse is a wonderful child, who loves Robert Munsch stories and, perhaps most wonderful of all, shuns Barney the purple dinosaur.

Neighbors have joined in the search, examining their own backyards and pools and garages. Perhaps, police say, Jesse wandered off and injured herself and no one has heard her cries for help. That's why, they say, it's so important to find her quickly.

Today, police are asking for volunteers to meet them at Dailey Park at 9 a.m. From there, they intend to have teams of people walk shoulder to shoulder through the nearby ravine looking not only for Jesse herself, but any possible clues to her disappearance.

Randy Flaherty, a father of two who lives next door to the Shuttleworths, is among those who plan to be at the park this morning to help.

"We can't imagine what might have happened. This is such a nice neighborhood, the families know each other, we all look out for each other, and we're all thinking the same thing."

Police still refuse to say whether they think Jesse's disappearance is an abduction. They've already ruled out family abduction — Jesse's father, who lives in Ohio, flew in yesterday to console his ex-wife and help in the search.

As for whether it could be an abduction by a stranger, Sgt. Dominic Marchi would only say, "We have to accept that that is a possibility. While we don't know that it is at this time, it is one of the avenues we have to explore."

The third-day story focused on the search and Carrie Shuttleworth's continued anguish. And they kept finding new pictures of Jesse, at a community pool, on a nursery school trip to a petting zoo. It was for faces like hers that cameras had been invented. I knew. I had seen her at Angelo's Fruit Market.

The ravine search turned up nothing. No Jesse. No scraps of clothing. No discarded shoe.

On the fourth day, the story went in the direction everyone feared most.

A woman about ten houses up from Jesse's, who rented out rooms, had gone looking for some overdue rent from one of her boarders, a man named Devlin Smythe. She hadn't seen him around for a couple of days, not since the news broke about that poor girl down the street. She had wondered if maybe he'd volunteered for the search, and that had made her hold off for a day on demanding the money she was owed. How would that look? she thought. A guy's trying to help find some little girl and you throw him out on the street.

But she hadn't seen Smythe around, not even at night, and she began to wonder whether he'd skipped out on her for good.

She went upstairs and banged on the door of his room, but there was no answer. So she used her passkey to go inside.

It was as she'd feared. There were no shoes or boots by the door, no clothes in his closet. He'd packed up and gone, but not without leaving her a mess. There were dirty dishes in the sink, cereal bowls filled with ashes from his smoking. The place reeked of cigarette smoke. It was going to take a few days to clean up before she could rent to anyone else.

How bad, she must have wondered, had he left the fridge?

Sears wrote:

She had been jammed in with a container of sour cream that had turned green, some wilted celery, and an open can of chicken noodle soup. It was a final resting place of such monstrous indignity that even hardened officers found themselves turning away.

Jesse Shuttleworth had been suffocated.

Subsequent stories yielded further details. The landlady was interviewed at length and put together with a police sketch artist. The man known to police as Devlin Smythe had a shaggy head of dirty blond hair, a moustache, strong chin. He was described as stocky and stood an inch or two under six feet.

They reproduced the sketch in the paper. I

tried to imagine him without the hair and the moustache. How he might look with a shaved head.

He was a chain-smoker. "You never saw him without a cigarette," the landlady said.

He did odd jobs. He was, according to one man, a talented electrician. He had rewired a house for someone in the neighborhood. "He was good at it, and quick, too. He liked to get paid under the table."

He possessed the skills, I thought, to bypass an electric meter.

Another man came forward to tell police Devlin Smythe had done some landscaping work for him. It was from this man that police learned Smythe had a tattoo.

It was on his right shoulder. Small, police said. Of a melted watch, in the style of Salvador Dali.

I put the clipping down, went into the kitchen, and ran myself a glass of water from the tap. In the cupboard I found a bottle of Tylenol, shook out two caplets, and downed them. Standing there in the kitchen, where so much horror had transpired only a few days earlier, it occurred to me that maybe it wasn't over yet.

Sleep never came to me that night. I kept running things through my mind, bits and pieces of conversation.

How Earl claimed never to have lived down-town, that he'd come from the East Coast, or the West, I was trying to remember. But there was that night, when I'd blundered into his house and discovered his growing operation, and I'd happened to mention that this sort of thing had never happened when we'd lived in the city, on Crandall.

Earl had said something along the lines of "You lived on Crandall? Nice area. There was that little fruit market down at the end of the street."

The inconsistency hadn't meant anything to me then. But it meant a lot now. Especially knowing that Carrie Shuttleworth used to take her daughter to that fruit market.

It didn't have to mean anything, I told myself. There had to be at least a few guys in the world with tattoos of melted watches on their shoulders. Dali had pretty much made the melted watch an iconic symbol.

And the chain-smoking. Millions of people chain-smoked.

And the business about being skilled at electrical work. And the landscaping. That could all be coincidence, too.

You wouldn't hang a guy based on evidence this flimsy.

So why couldn't I sleep? Why did I have this terrible feeling in the pit of my stomach?

"Why don't we do something on the barbecue tonight?" Sarah said. I was walking her out to her car.

"That sounds good," I said. It was also good to have my wife speaking to me again, even if it was only about menus.

"When did you come to bed last night?" she asked.

"It was late, sometime after midnight."

"You working on something new?"

"Sort of. I was looking through some old clippings I'd kept, on the Jesse Shuttleworth case."

Sarah frowned, shook her head sadly. "With all we've been through, I can't even think about something like that right now. Why were you looking at those?"

Across the street, Earl was throwing some gardening tools in the back of his pickup.

"I don't know," I said. "I guess I'm just trying to find some sort of focus."

Sarah got in the car, did up her seat belt. She powered down the window. "Why don't you pick up some burgers, stuff like that? For around six? And then, after, we can talk about that other thing you mentioned last night."

I nodded. I leaned down, kissed her through the open window, a little peck on her cheek, up close to her eye. She backed out and drove off, but didn't wave.

Earl did, though. And started walking across the street. Earl never came across the street to initiate a conversation. I was usually the one who drifted over there.

"Hey, Zack," he said.

"Earl," I said, smiling.

"I see things are getting back to normal, little bit more every day." He put a cigarette between his lips, lit up.

"For sure. Got to go shopping for another car. Insurance company's going to give us what the Civic was worth, but that doesn't amount to much. It was pretty old."

Earl stood three feet away from me, gazed up and down the street.

"So," he said.

"Yeah," I said.

There was a slight breeze, and his smoke blew into my face.

"Sorry," he said.

"No problem," I said.

We watched two cars drive by, then a minivan. "Paul," Earl said. "You decide to let him get that tattoo?"

I shook my head. "No. He's too young."

Earl nodded. "I think you're right. That's too young. Got to be at least old enough to get drunk. That's how most people get their tattoos."

We shared a laugh over that one.

"Well," Earl said, "I got work to do."

"Same here," I said.

I turned back to the house and Earl walked back across the street to his. I glanced back once and saw that he was watching me over his shoulder.

Shit.

Now I was rethinking everything. Not just

whether Earl was, in fact, Devlin Smythe. I'd pretty much made up my mind on that one. Now I was rethinking motives.

Why had Earl agreed to help me that night?

A man with a marijuana-growing operation in his basement had a lot to lose by getting mixed up in somebody else's business, especially if that business was likely to involve the police.

Why hadn't he turned down my request for help? Or at the very least, just given me his gun to use? Why come along?

I'd thought it was because, deep down, Earl had some sense of honor. I hadn't turned him in, and he owed me one. But now I had a feeling there was more to it than that. That maybe Earl had acted out of self-interest. That helping me out of a jam that night had provided him some sort of an opportunity. And it seemed to me that he had made this decision around the time that Trixie and I told him about the murder of Stefanie Knight, and the roll of film that showed her in bed with Roger Carpington.

Why would Earl care about any of that? Who were these people to him?

Later, in the afternoon, I put in a call to Dominic Marchi. I was transferred a couple of times before we connected.

I introduced myself, said I was looking into the Jesse Shuttleworth case with the idea of doing a freelance article on it for *The Metropolitan*.

"I know that name," Marchi said, referring to

mine. "You're the guy, was in the house with his wife, the crooked development thing, nearly got killed."

"Yes."

"Used to cover city hall a few years ago, too, am I right?" I admitted it. "I remember names," he said. "Faces too. Anyway, I'm not your guy."

"What do you mean?"

"I'm going to put you through to one of the detectives who's still working that case. Lorenzo Penner. Hang on, I'll try to transfer you. But if the line goes dead, call back the main switchboard and ask for extension 3120."

He conducted the transfer successfully. The extension rang twice, then picked up. "Penner."

I identified myself again, and for a second time admitted that yes, I was the guy in the house with the wife and the killer, et cetera. I told him I had questions about the Shuttleworth murder.

"File's still open. We're still workin' it. What can I tell you. It's been nearly two years, but we check out every lead we get."

"There was something on the radio a couple of weeks ago, that Devlin Smythe had been spotted out near Seattle and Vancouver."

"Yeah, we had some tips, but they didn't pan out. We don't have any reason to believe he's out there any more than any other place."

"Do you think he could still be in the area?"

"I suppose it's possible. But he would have had to change his appearance. The sketch we put out was pretty good, we think."

"Did you ever do up any other sketches, of how he might have looked if he'd done that? Changed his look? Like if he'd grown a beard, say?"

Penner said, "Yeah, we did. But we didn't release them to the media because really, even your first sketch is still just that, a sketch. Once you start drawing different variations of what's already an artist's impression of someone's recollection, well, you see the problem."

"Sure, I guess. Did you ever do one as if he'd shaved his head, lost the moustache, anything like that?"

"I think we did."

"How would you feel about faxing it to me?"

Penner hesitated. "Mr. Walker, do you know something about this?"

"I'm interested," I said. "I've followed it from the beginning, and I've been thinking about maybe doing a book on the case."

"I thought you just wrote science fiction. That's what it said in the paper."

"Up to now, yeah."

"So, you think maybe this Smythe guy, he was an alien?"

You see what I mean about respect and sci-fi writers? I didn't take the bait, and said instead, "Will you fax it to me, or not?"

"Give me your number. Five minutes." And he hung up.

I sat in my study, staring at the fax machine

for a good half hour before it rang, started doing its little hum.

And then the sketch started sliding, scalp first, out of the machine. Then it beeped, disconnected. I took the single sheet out of the tray, turned it around, and looked at it.

Howdy, neighbor.

I kept coming back to the shovel.

Walking over to Mindy's Market — it was only about a twenty-minute stroll — to pick up some ground beef and buns and some fixings for salad, I tried to work things out in my head.

Let's say Roger Carpington had killed Stefanie Knight. Waited for her inside her house. That would explain the broken glass at the back door. Maybe he already knew he was being blackmailed. Or Stefanie had threatened to expose him. To tell his wife. To ruin his political career. She had the ledger by this point. Maybe she was going to rip the lid off the whole Valley Forest Estates thing. He takes her into the garage, grabs the shovel from its hanging place on the wall, strikes her in the head with it. Runs.

Okay, possible.

I show up, find Stefanie. See the bloody shovel. And then I hightail it out of there.

Carpington thinks, Hey. My fingerprints are on that shovel. I have to go back and get it before the police arrive.

It would make sense. Except by this time,

Carpington's at the town council meeting. And according to at least one witness, never left the meeting.

So someone else grabbed that shovel. It was either (a) someone helping cover Carpington's tracks, or (b) a different killer, coming back to grab the shovel for the same reason Carpington would have: fingerprints.

If it was someone helping Carpington cover his tracks, to keep him from being connected to the crime, then why did the shovel show up in the trunk of his car?

But if the killer was someone else, and had that shovel, placing it in Carpington's trunk was a stroke of genius. Its presence there was guaranteed to incriminate.

But this killer would have to know that Carpington was a logical suspect already. This killer would have to know that a bloody shovel in the trunk would be just one more part of the puzzle.

"That's $14.56."

"Huh?"

It was the cashier at Mindy's. She'd rung through my groceries and informed me of my total. I handed her a twenty and held my hand out for the change.

I was in another world.

On the way back, I thought about the conversation Earl and I had had on the way to the Valley Forest Estates sales office. How he'd wanted to confirm that Carpington had been caught on film with Stefanie, how he'd even suggested that the councilman had a pretty strong motive to kill her.

How, when we pulled into the parking lot, Earl asked whose car was whose.

And how, once we'd gotten the jump on Greenway and Carpington, Earl insisted that I stay and keep them covered while he left with their keys and moved their cars behind the office.

That would have been when he took the shovel from his pickup and put it in the trunk of Carpington's car.

The only thing I hadn't worked out a theory for was why Earl killed Stefanie Knight. But I had enough.

I started running, the grocery bag flopping at my side. I jogged all the way up Chancery Park, was struggling to catch my breath as I inserted my key into the door. I dumped the groceries on the kitchen counter and grabbed the phone.

I got the main police switchboard, then keyed in Lorenzo Penner's extension. It rang three times before the voicemail cut in.

"This is Detective Lorenzo Penner. Leave a message at the tone."

"Hi, it's Zack Walker. Call me back as soon as you get this message." And I left my number.

I glanced at the clock. After five. Sarah would be home soon. Where were Paul and Angie?

I'd grabbed the receiver off the phone so quickly when I'd come in that I'd failed to see the flashing message light. There were two, one from Paul and one from Angie.

Paul said, "I'm at Hakim's, hanging out, should be home by six."

Angie said, "I'm working in the school darkroom. I'm getting a lift, see you around five-thirty."

Ever since that night, we'd all been very good about letting each other know where we were going to be, and if we were going to be late.

I unpacked the groceries, tore the wrapper off the ground beef and began forming patties. It looked as though Paul and Angie were going to join us for dinner, although with teenagers, you never knew until the last second who was actually hungry or not.

So I made half a dozen. Paul, if he had any appetite at all, could be counted on to eat at least two. I rinsed lettuce leaves, cut up some tomatoes, glancing every few seconds at the phone, willing Penner to call.

"Come on," I said out loud. "I'm solving your goddamn case for you, asshole."

Maybe my message hadn't been detailed enough. Maybe he'd think I wanted him to call back because I had more questions. I should leave another message. Tell him I'd found Devlin Smythe. That Jesse Shuttleworth's killer was living right across the street from us. And that he'd killed someone else, too. A woman out here in Oakwood, whose murder at the moment was being pinned on somebody else.

But first, I'd fire up the barbecue. While it was heating up, I'd try Penner again, maybe get the switchboard to try to find him.

The phone rang. I had the receiver off the hook before the end of the first ring. "That was fast," Sarah said.

"Oh, hey," I said.

"Sorry, expecting someone else?"

"Actually, yeah. I'm waiting on a call."

"Something going on?"

"Sort of, but let me tell you all about it when you get home. How close are you?"

"Another fifteen minutes, I'll be there."

"Great, I was just about to get the barbecue going."

I opened the sliding glass doors, stepped out onto the deck with a plate of patties. I set the plate on the counter to the left of the barbecue, opened the lid, and turned the valve on the gas tank. I heard the familiar hiss of gas escaping from the jets in the bottom of the barbecue.

I pressed the red ignition button. Click. Nothing.

I pressed it a second time, faster and harder, figuring this would force a spark. Again, nothing.

We were going to have to use the old drop-the-lit-match-in-the-bottom trick again, I figured, and —

"Zack."

I whirled around, startled. Earl was standing at the step that led up from the backyard to the deck. He was in a pair of dirt-caked jeans, his Blue Jays sweatshirt, and there was the familiar cigarette tucked between his lips. In his right hand, he held his gun. The same one we'd taken with us the other night.

"Earl, Jesus, you scared the shit out of me there," I said. "You shouldn't sneak up on people like that."

Earl took a step toward me, and I backed up, away from the barbecue, toward the door into the kitchen. "Earl, what's with the gun?"

"You know who I am," he said. "When you saw the tattoo, you knew."

"I don't know what you're talking about, Earl." As I took another step back, Earl moved forward. He was standing almost in front of the barbecue now.

"I know you. And I know Sarah works for the paper. You mentioned one time she worked on the Shuttleworth thing. I know you guys follow the news, and that a melted-clock tattoo would mean something to you. Besides, I could see it in your face the moment you saw it."

I said nothing. I was listening to the almost noiseless hiss of unignited propane.

"I gotta move on," Earl said. "But not before I take care of a few unfinished matters."

I swallowed, hard. I took my eyes off the gun and looked into Earl's. "How could you do it, Earl? Or should I call you Devlin from now on?"

"Do what?"

"How could you murder a five-year-old girl?"

"She saw me."

"Saw you what?"

"I was breaking into someone's house, forced the back door open, and there she was in the yard, standing there. Says to me, you're not supposed to do that. Says she's going to tell. I tried talking to her, but she started to cry, and I had to stop her from doing that." Earl shook his head. "Women are always ratting me out. Young, old, doesn't matter."

"So you killed her."

"I had to hold my hand over her face to make her stop making noise. I told her to stop crying but she wouldn't pay any attention."

"And Stefanie," I said. "Why did you kill her?"

Earl's eyebrows shot up. I guess he didn't realize that I'd figured that part out as well.

"That didn't work out with her. We went out a couple times, nobody knew. But I don't know, I just can't figure out what it is about women. They don't connect well with me. I don't think many women have the capacity to understand, do you know what I mean?"

I said nothing.

"And then I found her looking through some of my stuff, she found these other IDs I had, for Daniel Smithers and Danny Simpson, and she asked about them, said she'd heard those names on the news, that they were other names some guy the cops were looking for had used.

Stefanie, she was in no position to judge me. She fucked guys so they could be blackmailed. She was of very low moral character."

The smell of gas was reaching me, and I was further away from the barbecue than Earl. Couldn't he smell that?

"But I guess even Stefanie couldn't abide a child-killer," I said. "That's why she was on the run. She was scared of what she'd found out about you. She was scared of what you might do. So she printed herself up some cash, grabbed the ledger with the idea of maybe selling it back to Greenway, and decided to get as far away as possible."

Smythe reached up with his left hand, took out his cigarette for a moment, exhaled. The tip glowed red as he put it back in his mouth and drew in. And I thought, No, he can't smell it. He couldn't smell that rotting food in his refrigerator. He had no sense of smell.

"I broke into her house, waited for her. A long time. She didn't have her car. And I took her into the garage to try to talk some sense into her."

"You decided to go back for the shovel."

Smythe nodded. "I just wasn't sure I'd wiped down the handle. They got me on file, my prints were all over my room in the city. I hadn't gotten rid of it yet, when you came over in the middle of the night with Trixie."

"And that gave you the perfect place to put it. In the back of Carpington's car."

"And it worked. You did good. You told them to look inside, just like I said, didn't you?"

It had to be only a moment away. The gas was everywhere.

"Yeah, I did just what you said."

"I'm sorry, Zack. You seem like a good guy. You could have ratted me out before, but you didn't. I think it's 'cause you're a guy, and guys understand each other. I think you have good moral character, and I respect that. Which makes me feel bad about having to do this."

And he raised the gun in his right hand, pointed it directly at my chest.

The fireball erupted right in front of his mouth, at the tip of his cigarette. The burst of flame enveloped his shaved head, then spread back through the air to the barbecue. I turned and dove for the open glass door, but I could feel the heat at my back, and the force of the explosion, which sounded like a thunderclap. I threw myself on the floor, face down, closed my eyes, and covered my head with my hands.

The glass doors blew in, throwing shards across the kitchen and me.

Somewhere behind me came a man's screams of torment. And then, after a few seconds, there was nothing left to hear.

30

❖ ❖ ❖

With any luck, the For Sale sign on the front lawn won't be there that much longer. We had an open house last weekend, and quite a few people came through. Needless to say, we had a fair bit of repair work to do before putting the place on the market. There was several thousand dollars' worth of damage out back. Loads of glass to replace. The eaves were bent out of shape, the deck was pretty much destroyed, and several rows of bricks were badly chipped. The contractors — not from Valley Forest Estates — did a respectable job. If you didn't know what had happened at our address, you'd never notice a thing. Of course, some people toured through because they did know what happened here. There's a certain notoriety factor. It wasn't clear when we listed the house whether this would work in our favor, or against.

A few things:

The barbecue was a write-off. We haven't bothered to get a new one yet. I've read even more stories about the transformation food undergoes when you barbecue it, the cancer risks, health issues. I don't think you can afford to ignore that kind of thing. I was eating too much red meat, anyway. I've taken a lot more interest lately in eating healthily.

Our insurance company is making noises about dropping us.

Sarah's editors asked me to write them an exclusive about finding the killer of Jesse Shuttleworth. Plus, they had an opening for a feature writer, and I jumped at it. Like I'd told Sarah, if we were back into a mortgage, we'd need two steady incomes. They also offered me a chance to write a monthly column in the book pages on new SF releases; I said I'd like to review all sorts of books, and they weren't too excited about that, given my nonliterary background.

We learned, upon house-hunting in our old neighborhood, that Mrs. Hayden, who'd lived just down from us on Crandall, and who liked to point out the paper's misdeeds to Sarah whenever they ran into each other, had recently passed away. We felt badly that we hadn't been informed. She was a sweet old lady, and we would like to have paid our respects at her funeral.

As it turned out, her children put the house up for sale. We had always admired it. A porch out front, beautifully carved railings, separate garage tucked around back. No gaping door out front big enough to accommodate a Winnebago.

We put in an offer.

Our real estate agent suggested going in with something $15,000 under what they were asking, and Sarah and I conferred quietly, and came back and said we wanted to offer $10,000 more. The agent wrote it up.

And there's the business of Earl, or Devlin Smythe, as I always think of him now. He didn't make it to Emerg alive. His head, police told us, was a burnt marshmallow.

I took one of my walks down by Willow Creek the other day. It's the most beautiful part of the neighborhood, still untouched as it is by development. It's up in the air whether houses will ever be built along its banks, but there's a greater chance now than ever before that they won't be. The Oakwood Town Council has decided to reopen all deals it had made with Valley Forest Estates, now that corruption charges had been laid against one of its own and Don Greenway was being charged with murder. Greenway was the one who'd ordered Rick to kill Spender, after all, and even though Rick was no longer around to cut a deal and testify against him, Carpington seemed prepared to say anything in a bid to reduce his sentence. There are new environmental hearings scheduled, and a raft of lawsuits between Valley Forest Estates and the town are under way.

The Suburban has been running stories with all the details, but I don't read that many of them. I just want to get out of town, put all this behind me. One thing that has allowed me to move forward is the knowledge that my stealing Stefanie Knight's purse wasn't what led to her death. Smythe was already in that house, waiting for her to come home, before I'd blundered my way into this mess at the grocery store. It was even possible, although this was not a point I went out of my way to make, that her killer, and Jesse Shuttleworth's, might never have been uncovered but for my foolishness.

I walked back up our street, smiled at the housecoat lady as she watered her driveway, and saw that Sarah was home from work. Her Camry sat in the driveway. We haven't bothered to replace the Civic, figuring we won't need but one car when we move back downtown. We're putting the insurance money toward the new house. I wandered up onto the lawn, ran my hand along the top of the For Sale sign, then rounded Sarah's car as I headed for the front door.

As I came up alongside the Camry on the passenger side, I happened to notice, glancing through the window, that the keys were still in the ignition. It could have been Sarah's set or, possibly, Angie's. One or the other of them had forgotten to remove them, and the Camry sat there, a statistic just waiting to be added to the stolen-car lists.

I stared at the keys, wondering what, if anything, I should do about them, when Sarah came out the front door, smiling.

"Hey," she said. "They accepted."

"Great," I said. She was referring to the Hayden family. The house on Crandall was ours.

"And some agent's coming by with an offer on this place at seven," she said, coming up to the driver's door of her car, facing me across the roof.

I opened the passenger door, leaned in, took out the keys, walked around the car, and handed them to her. "Here," I said. No lecture, no smartass comment, no rolling of the eyes, no shaking of the head.

"Thanks," Sarah said, pocketing the keys, and smiling with amusement at my restraint. "You keep acting this way, people will start wondering whether you're such a big asshole after all."

And she reached her hand out to mine and led me inside.

Acknowledgments

I want to thank my agent, Helen Heller, who helped bring this book into focus before she found it a home, and pretends you're not high maintenance even if you really are.

To all the folks at Bantam, and in particular Bill Massey and Andie Nicolay, my thanks for their confidence, attention to detail, and making the process so much fun.

Special credit goes to my wife, Neetha, whose practice of leaving her purse unwatched in grocery store shopping carts sparked the idea for this story. Why she sticks with a guy who's more like Zack than I'd like to admit is beyond me.

About the Author

Linwood Barclay is a staff columnist for the *Toronto Star*, where he has worked for more than twenty years. He's the author of four books published in Canada, including his memoir, *Last Resort: Coming of Age in Cottage Country*, which was shortlisted for the 2001 Stephen Leacock Medal for Humour. *Bad Move* is his first novel. He lives in Burlington, Ontario, with his wife and two children, where he is at work on the sequel to *Bad Move*.